10/22/97

TO MIKE,

FOR CHINA.

FROM,
USIA

*Judge Dee*

(born A.D. 630, died A.D. 700)

After an old Chinese woodcut. The top inscription, in archaic script, reads: "Portrait of Dee, Duke of Liang."

# CELEBRATED CASES
# OF JUDGE DEE
## (Dee Goong An)

An Authentic Eighteenth-Century
Chinese Detective Novel

TRANSLATED AND WITH AN
INTRODUCTION AND NOTES BY
ROBERT VAN GULIK

DOVER PUBLICATIONS, INC.
NEW YORK

This Dover edition, first published in 1976, is an unabridged, slightly corrected version of the work first published privately in Tokyo in 1949 under the title *Dee Goong An: Three Murder Cases Solved by Judge Dee.*

The work is illustrated with three reproductions of original Chinese pictures, and six plates drawn by van Gulik after ancient Chinese models.

*International Standard Book Number: 0-486-23337-5*
*Library of Congress Catalog Card Number: 76-5059*

Manufactured in the United States of America
Dover Publications, Inc.
180 Varick Street
New York, N.Y. 10014

This translation is chiefly a product of the Pacific War years, 1941-1945, when constant travel on various war duties made other more complicated Sinological research impossible. Preface, postscript and notes were added later, during my stay in Washington D.C.

I wish to express my gratitude to my friend Karl H. Bachmeyer, whose serious turn of mind did not prevent him from reading and correcting the manuscript and who offered many useful suggestions.

R.H.v.G.

# LIST OF ILLUSTRATIONS

# CONTENTS

# TRANSLATOR'S PREFACE

## I

For many years, Western writers of detective novels have time and again introduced the "Chinese element" in their books. The mysteries of China itself or of the Chinatowns in some foreign cities, were often chosen as a means of lending a weird and exotic atmosphere to the plot. Super-criminals like Sax Rohmer's Dr. Fu Manchu, or super-detectives like Earl D. Biggers' Charlie Chan, have become nearly as familiar to our readers as the great Lord Lister, or the immortal Sherlock Holmes himself.

As the Chinese have been so often represented—and too often misrepresented!—in our popular crime literature, it seems only just that they themselves be allowed to have their own say for once in this field. All the more so because this branch of literature was fully developed in China several centuries before Edgar Allan Poe or Sir Arthur Conan Doyle were born.

Short stories about mysterious crimes and their solution have existed in China for over a thousand years, and master-detectives have been celebrated in the tales of the public story teller and in theatrical plays for many centuries. The longer Chinese detective novel started later, about 1600, and reached its greatest development in the 18th and 19th centuries. The longer crime and mystery stories were and still are very popular in China. Even to-day the names of the great detectives of olden times are household words all over the country, familiar to old and young alike.

As far as I know, none of these Chinese detective stories has ever been published in a complete English translation. Occasionally extracts or translations of fragments have appeared in sinological journals, and a few years ago Vincent Starrett published a brief but well-written survey of a few of the better-known of these novels (in his "Bookman's Holiday," New York 1942). It cannot be denied, therefore, that Western students have treated the Chinese detective novel in a very stepmotherly way; all the less since most of the famous Chinese historical novels and "romans de moeurs" are available in excellent complete translations.

The reason for this state of affairs must be that most of these Chinese crime novels, although as a rule well written and quite interesting to the student of "things Chinese," are not very palatable to the Western public in general. During its long history the Chinese detective novel has developed a character of its own. These novels are, of course, completely satisfactory to the Chinese. But the Chinese conception of the requirements a crime story should answer differs so much from our own, that such novels cannot be of interest to those of us who read detective novels for their relaxation values.

Chinese detective stories have five main characteristics that are foreign to us.

In the first place, the criminal is, as a rule, introduced formally to the reader at the very beginning of the book, with his full name, an account of his past history, and the motive that led him to commit the crime. The Chinese want to derive from the reading of a detective novel the same purely intellectual enjoyment as from watching a game of chess; with all the factors known, the excitement lies in following every move of the detective and the counter measures taken by the criminal, until the game ends in the unavoidable check-mate of the latter. We, on the other hand like to be kept guessing, the identity of the criminal remaining shrouded in mystery till the last page of the book. Thus in most Chinese crime novels the element of suspense is missing. The reader knows the answer to what to us is the basic question of "Who done it?" after the first few pages.

Second, the Chinese have an innate love for the supernatural. Ghosts and goblins roam about freely in most Chinese detective stories; animals and kitchen utensils deliver testimony in court, and the detective indulges occasionally in little escapades to the Nether World, to compare notes with the judges of the Chinese Inferno. This clashes with our principle that a detective novel should be as realistic as possible.

Third, the Chinese are a leisurely people, with a passionate interest for detail. Hence all their novels, including detective stories, are written in a broadly narrative vein, interlarded with lengthy poems, philosophical digressions, and what not, while all official documents relating to the case are quoted in full. Therefore, most Chinese detective novels are bulky affairs of a hundred and more chapters, and each of them would, when translated, fill several printed volumes.

Fourth, the Chinese have a prodigious memory for names and a sixth sense for family relationships. An educated Chinese can reel off without the slightest effort some seventy or eighty relatives, each with his name, surname and title, and the exact grade of relationship, for which, by the way, the Chinese language possesses an amazingly rich special vocabulary. The Chinese reader likes his novels well-populated, so that the list of dramatis personæ of one single novel usually runs into two hundred or more characters. Our contemporary crime novels have mostly only a dozen or so main characters, and yet editors have found it necessary of late to add a list of these at the beginning of the book, for the reader's convenience.

Fifth, the Chinese have quite different ideas as to what should be described in a detective novel, and what may well be left to the reader's imagination. Although we insist on knowing in minute detail how the crime was committed, we are not interested in the details of the punishment finally meted out to the criminal. If he does not crash his plane into the sea, or hurtle his car over a cliff, or is not removed from the scene in some other tidy way, we leave him at the end of the book, with some dark hints, to the hangman or the electric chair. The Chinese, however, expect a faithful account of how the criminal was executed, with every gruesome detail. Often also the Chinese author throws in as an "extra" a full description of the punishment the unfortunate criminal received, after his execution, in the Chinese Inferno. Such an ending is necessary to satisfy the Chinese sense of justice, but it offends the Western reader, since it reminds him too much of beating a man who is already down.*

If, in addition to the above, it is remembered that the Chinese author as a matter of course takes it for granted that his reader is thoroughly familiar with the working of the law in China, and Chinese manners and customs, it will be clear that translating a Chinese detective novel for the general Western public implies re-

---

* Modern Chinese writers realize that there may come a time when a demand for detective stories of another type will develop among the general Chinese reading public. Some modern authors have tried their hand at re-writing Chinese detective novels of former centuries in a form that is closer to our Western pattern. The best known example of such an attempt is the Djiu-ming-chi-yuan 九命奇寃, "The Strange Feud of the Nine Murders," written by the famous novelist Woo Wo-yao (吳沃堯, 1867-1910). He took as his basis an 18th century crime story, entitled Djing-foo-hsin-shoo 警富新書, which describes a notorious nine-fold murder that actually occurred in Canton in about 1725. Woo Wo-yao's attempt is rather interesting and its literary qualities are highly praised by so eminent a modern critic as Dr. Hoo Shih 胡適. Thereafter, however, a number of entirely original modern Chinese detective stories were published in China, which presented plots that were much more interesting than that worked out by Woo Wo-yao. It cannot be denied that the writers, just as Woo Wo-yao, were strongly influenced by Western detective stories; they were eager students of the adventures of Sherlock Holmes and Arsène Lupin, which have appeared in more than one Chinese translation. Yet their efforts deserve more attention than they have hitherto received. Although it may take many years before the detectives celebrated in these new stories will replace Judge Bao 包公, Judge Dee 狄公, Judge Peng 彭公 and the other ancient heroes of detection in the affection of the Chinese people at large, these young writers are paving the way for a new genre of purely Chinese literature.

writing it from beginning to end, and even then the pages of such a translation would be bristling with footnotes. It is true that an occasional footnote lends an air of dignity and veracity to a detective story, as in Van Dine's novels describing Philo Vance's exploits, but one can hardly expect the reader to like a lengthy footnote on every other page.

Thus, in setting out to present to the Western lover of crime literature a complete translation of a Chinese detective novel, my main problem was to find one that combines a maximum of un-diluted detection and of general human interest, with a minimum of the peculiarly Chinese features discussed earlier.

I think I have found these requirements in the *Dee Goong An,* a Chinese detective novel written in the 18th century by an anony-mous author.

This novel conforms to our accustomed standards in that it does not reveal the criminal at the very beginning, lacks the more fantastic supernatural element, has a limited number of dramatis personæ, contains no material that is not germane to the plot, and is relatively short. At the same time the plot is quite ingenious, and the novel is well written, with all our familiar tricks to keep the reader in suspense, and with a judicious mixture of tragedy and comedy. It is even up to modern Western standards in so far that, next to being treated to the detective's mental "tours de force," we also follow him when actually engaged in some dangerous exploits. And in one respect this novel introduces a new literary device that, as far as I know, has not yet been utilized in our popular crime literature, *viz.* that the detective is engaged simul-taneously on three different cases, entirely independent of each other, each with its own background and dramatis personæ.

Further, the author of the *Dee Goong An* exercises remarkable restraint as regards moralizing lectures. As a matter of fact, there occurs only one such digression, and that at the very beginning, in the author's introductory remarks. And it would have been an unforgivable offense against an age-old Chinese literary tradition if some moralistic reflections had been missing in that particular place.

Its weakest point, to our taste, is still the supernatural element. This, however, is only introduced twice in this particular novel, and both instances are not entirely unacceptable as they concern phenomena of a kind that is frequently discussed in Western parapsychological literature. Moreover neither of them is a decisive factor in the solution of the crime, because they merely confirm the detective's previous deductions, and stimulate his attempts at analysing the cases. The first instance concerns a manifestation of the spirit of a murdered man near his grave. Even in Western countries a wide-spread belief exists that the soul of a person done violently to death remains near its dead body, and may, in some way or other, make its presence known. The second instance is a dream which visits the detective at the time when he is most perplexed and worried over two cases. The dream confirms his suspicions, and enables him to see several known factors in their proper relation. This passage, occurring in Chapter XI, will be of some interest to our students of dream psychology.

In this novel we find some rather gruesome descriptions of torture inflicted on prisoners during sessions of the tribunal. The reader will have to take these as they are. The scene on the execution ground, in the last chapter, on the other hand, is more brief and more matter-of-fact than in many other Chinese detective novels.

Special attention must be drawn to the brief interlude, that occurs halfway in the novel, between Chapter XV and XVI; at first sight, this interlude has absolutely nothing to do with the story. This is a very interesting feature, common to most of the shorter Chinese novels. Such an interlude is always written in the form of one scene of a Chinese theatrical play: a few actors appear, and engage in a dialogue, interspersed with songs, as is usual on the Chinese stage. These actors are indicated only by the technical stage terms for their role, such as "young man," "père noble," etc. It is left to the reader's ingeniousness to find out which characters of the novel they represent. The interesting point is that in such an interlude we are given an insight directly into the subconscious mind of the main characters. They have cast off all their inhibitions and restraint. Thus these Chinese interludes are, in a way, the counterpart of the psychological character sketches of our modern novels. Ancient Chinese novels never indulge in a psychological analysis of the characters they describe, but grant the reader glimpses of the innermost thoughts and emotions of the characters either through such theatrical interludes, or through dreams. This device of "a dream in a dream," or "a play in a play" also was utilized by our ancient Western writers, for instance, such a famous example as Act II, scene 2, in "Hamlet."

Although some peculiar Chinese features are less pronounced in this novel than in other Chinese stories, the *Dee Goong An* is still thoroughly Chinese. In addition to giving a faithful description of the working methods of ancient Chinese detectives, and of the problems they are confronted with when trying to solve a crime, and of the ways and byways of the Chinese underworld, this story at the same time gives the reader a good idea of the administration of justice in ancient China, acquaints him with the main provisions of the Chinese Penal Code, and, finally, with the Chinese way of life in general.

As to its content, this novel describes three criminal cases.

The first might be called "The Double Murder At Dawn." This is a crude murder, committed for gain. This case introduces us to the hazardous life of the traveling silk merchants. They buy raw silk cheaply during the season in Kiangsu Province, and then sell it for a profit along the highways of the northern provinces. These itinerant merchants are tough customers, shrewd businessmen and good fighters, familiar with all the dangers and pitfalls of the Chinese highways. This case takes the reader up and down the famous silk roads of Shantung Province, and acquaints him with wily managers of silk depots, inn keepers, robber gangs, and all the other types of people that make their living from the road.

The scene of the second case, "The Strange Corpse," is laid among the population of a small village. It is a crime of passion, which proves uncommonly hard to solve. Here a most realistic portrait is drawn of the woman who is suspected of having committed the murder. Although she is but the wife of a small shopkeeper, her iron will and great force of character remind one of the formidable Empress Dowager of the last years of the Empire, and of other Chinese women who have played a predominant role in Chinese history. We also learn about the duties and the worries of the village warden; we enter the public bathhouse, which serves as a club for the local people, and we assist at a full-fledged exhumation and the subsequent autopsy.

The third case, "The Poisoned Bride," concerns the local gentry. The lovely young girl that meets with a horrible death on her wedding night is the daughter of a Bachelor of Arts, and the bridegroom the son of an old prefect, who lives retired in a spacious mansion, with countless courtyards and galleries. To complete this dignified picture, the suspect is a Candidate of Literature.

Thus this novel presents, as it were, a cross-section of Chinese society. But all three cases have one factor in common, and that is that they occur in one and the same district, and are solved by the same detective.

This novel *Dee Goong An* is offered here in a complete translation. Possibly it would have had a wider appeal if it had been entirely re-written in a form more familiar to our readers. Then, however, much of the genuine Chinese atmosphere of the original would have disappeared, and in the end both the Chinese author, and the Western reader would have been the losers. Some parts may be less interesting to the Western reader than others, but I am confident that also in this literal translation the novel will be found more satisfactory than the palpable nonsense that is foisted on the long-suffering public by some writers of faked "Chinese" stories, which describe a China and a Chinese people that exist nowhere except in their fertile imaginations.

The central figure, the master-detective of this novel is, as in all Chinese detective stories, a district magistrate. From early times until the establishment of the Chinese Republic in 1911, this government official united in his person the functions of judge, jury, prosecutor and detective.

The territory under his jurisdiction, a district, was the smallest administrative unit in the complicated Chinese government machine; it usually comprised one fairly large walled city, and all the countryside around it, say for sixty or seventy miles. The district magistrate was the highest civil authority in this unit, he was in charge of the town and land administration, the tribunal, the bureau for the collection of taxes, the register-office, while he was also generally responsible for the maintenance of public order in the entire district. Thus he had practically full authority over all phases of the life of the people in his district, who called him, therefore, the "father-and-mother official." He was responsible only to the higher authorities, *viz.* the prefect or the governor of the province.

It was in his function of judge that the district magistrate displayed his talents as a detective. In Chinese crime literature, therefore, we find the master-minds that solve baffling crimes never referred to as "detectives," but always as "judges." The hero of our present story, who bears the surname *Dee*, is always called *Dee Goong*, "Judge Dee." In Chinese a criminal case is called *an*, thus the original title of this novel, *Dee Goong An*, in literal translation means "Criminal Cases Solved by Judge Dee."

This is the stereotype title of all Chinese detective novels. We have the *Bao Goong An* "Criminal Cases Solved by Judge Bao," the *Peng Goong An* "Criminal Cases Solved by Judge Peng," and so on.

The anonymous author of the *Dee Goong An* evidently at some time or other in his career himself occupied the function of district magistrate. This need not astonish us, since most writers of novels were retired officials, who wrote them for their own amusement, and preferred to remain anonymous because formerly all novels were considered as inferior literature in China. The Chinese word for "novel" is *hsiao-shwo*, "small talk," and novels should never be mentioned together with works on history, philosophy, poetry and other instructive subjects. As it is, this novel shows that the author was thoroughly familiar with judicial procedure, and with the Chinese Penal Code. I have checked the conduct of the cases as described here with the provisions of the code, and found it correct in all details; those interested are referred to the "Translator's Postscript" at the end of this book, where the pertinent laws are quoted.

This novel clearly shows the comprehensive duties of the magistrate in his quality as presiding judge of the district tribunal. Crimes are reported directly to him, it is he who is expected to collect and sift all evidence, find the criminal, arrest him, make him confess, sentence him, and finally administer to him the punishment for his crime.

To assist him in this onerous task he receives but little help from the permanent personnel of the tribunal. The constables, the scribes, the guards, the executioner, the warden of the jail, the coroner and his assistants, all these minions of the law perform only their routine tasks. The judge is not supposed to require their help in the gentle art of detection.

Every judge, therefore, has attached to his person three or four trusted lieutenants, whom he carefully selects at the beginning of his career, and keeps with him while he is being transferred from one post to another, till he ends his days as a prefect or a provincial governor. These lieutenants derive their rank and position (which is higher than that of any of the other members of the tribunal), from the personal authority of the judge. It is upon them that the judge relies for assistance in the detection and solving of crimes.

In every Chinese detective story these lieutenants are described as fearless strong-arm men, experts in Chinese boxing and wrestling. And in every Chinese detective story the judge recruits these men from the "brothers of the green woods," that is to say highway robbers of the Robin Hood type. They usually became robbers because having been falsely accused, having killed a cruel official, beaten up a crooked politician, or for other similar reasons, they were forced to live by their wits. The judge induces them to reform, and thereafter they become his loyal helpers, faithful servants of justice.

Judge Dee, the hero of the present novel, has four such lieutenants. Two, Ma Joong and Chiao Tai, are former "brothers of the green woods"; the third, Tao Gan, is a reformed itinerant confidence man, while the fourth, Hoong Liang, is an elderly retainer of the judge's family. Judge Dee made the latter sergeant over all the constables, and we therefore refer to him in our story as Sergeant Hoong. This sergeant also serves Judge Dee as a kind of Watson; for having seen the judge grow up, he can, as an old and trusted servant, give his master advice, and Judge Dee can freely discuss with him his problems without losing "face," or jeopardizing the dignity of his office.

These lieutenants are the judge's legmen. He sends them out to make discreet inquiries; he tells them to interview witnesses, trail suspects, find out the hiding place of a criminal and arrest him. It is very important for them to be experts in wrestling and boxing, for the Chinese detective has the same noble tradition as his later colleagues of Bow Street, he carries no arms, and catches his man with his bare hands.

Except for Sergeant Hoong, however, they have more brawn than brains. It is the judge who tells them where to go and what to do, and it is he who sifts and coordinates the information they bring him, and then solves the crime by sheer mental power.

This does not imply that the judge does not move at all, and, like Rex Stout's ponderous Nero Wolfe, refuses to budge from his quarters. The code of conduct for the Chinese high official prescribes that whenever the judge leaves the tribunal on official business, he shall do so with all the pomp and circumstance incident to his office. But the judge can go about incognito, and often does. Having disguised himself, he leaves the tribunal in secret, and sets out on private tours of investigation.

Still it is true that the main scene of the judge's activity is the court hall of the tribunal. There, enthroned on the dais behind the high bench, he confuses wily suspects by his clever questioning, bullies hardened criminals into a confession, wheedles the truth out of timorous witnesses, and dazzles everybody alike with his brilliant wit.

As to the methods followed by the judge to solve a crime, he is naturally handicapped by the lack of all the aids developed by modern science: for him there is no fingerprint system, there are no chemical tests, no photographic experiments. On the other hand his work is facilitated by the extraordinarily wide powers granted him under the provisions of the Penal Code. He can have anyone arrested, he can put the question to suspects under torture, have recalcitrant witnesses beaten up on the spot, use hearsay evidence, bully a defendant to tell a lie, and then trip him up with relish, in short he can openly and officially use all kinds of third and fourth degrees which would make our judges shiver in their gowns.

It must be added, however, that it is not by the use of torture or other violent means, the judge achieves his successes but rather by his wide knowledge of his fellow men, his logical thinking, and, above all, by his deep psychological insight. It is mainly due to these assets that he succeeds in solving many a case that would have been a hard nut to crack for our modern detectives.

Chinese magistrates like Judge Dee were men of great moral strength and intellectual power, and at the same time refined literati, thoroughly conversant with Chinese arts and letters. In short a kind of man, whom one would like to know better.

It is unfortunate, therefore, that the Chinese detective novel cannot afford to devote much space to detailed character sketches any more than ours. This is all the more to be regretted in the case of the present novel, since Judge Dee was a real person, one of the famous statesmen of the Tang dynasty (618-907). He was born in 630, the son of a distinguished scholar-official, and died in 700, as a Minister of State.* During the latter half of his career, when he was serving at the Imperial Court, he played an important role in the national and international affairs of the Empire. Chinese historical records give a detailed account of his brilliant official career. But such biographies are of a strictly factual character. They are silent upon Judge Dee's private life.

The present novel takes this same aloof attitude. When our story begins, we meet Judge Dee "sitting in his private office, attending to some routine business," and at the end of the book we leave him in that same office "putting the files in order for his successor." Not one word about his home, his children, his hobbies.

---

* It is a curious fact that "Judge Dee" already was introduced to Western readers more than 150 years ago. The fifth volume of the monumental work *Mémoires concernant l'histoire, les sciences, les arts etc. des Chinois,* published in Paris in 1780, and one of the first Western source books with reliable information on China, gives in the section "Portraits des célèbres Chinois" a brief biography of our "Judge Dee," which bears the title "Ty-Jin-Kie, Ministre."

Literary sources say that Judge Dee left "collected works," but these seem to have become lost; only nine of his memorials to the Throne are preserved. Although Judge Dee lived in the age of the great poets, he himself does not seem to have indulged much in this elegant pastime of the Chinese scholar-official. The *Chuan-tang-shih,* a collection of Tang poetry in no less than 120 volumes, gives only one poem of eight lines written by Judge Dee. And that is a complimentary poem addressed to the Throne, which so bristles with difficult literary allusions that a later editor had to add two pages of closely printed explanations. Thus this last chance of catching a glimpse of Judge Dee's personal feelings is lost.

This scarcity of literary information makes the few images of the judge that have been preserved all the more precious. The frontispiece of this book shows Judge Dee in full ceremonial dress. This is a Chinese woodcut, which evidently was struck off from an old block, that had been re-cut a number of times. Yet one can easily imagine that the original painting which served as a model was no mean work of art. Judge Dee is represented in a delightfully informal pose. His right hand plays with his side whiskers, his left is stuck carelessly between the folds of his robe. Doubtless Judge Dee is ruminating over a particularly puzzling case. His face must have worn an expression of immense scepticism, which is still faintly noticeable in this blockprint.

Despite its worn condition, I prefer this print to some conventionalized "portraits," preserved in several collections of "Famous men of succeeding dynasties." In my opinion, there can be no doubt that the original painting was a very old one; it turns up in most later works that figure Judge Dee, and can be recognized even in a small illustration in the most recent edition of the *Dee Goong An,* published in Shanghai in 1947.

Leafing through old Chinese illustrated books, we may obtain at least some hints as to how Judge Dee spent his few hours of

Judge Dee reading in his library.

(After an old Chinese woodcut)

leisure. The accompanying plate shows the library in the house of a high official, and gives a general idea of how that Chinese 7th century 221B Baker Street looked like. Let us hope that Judge Dee at least occasionally thus relaxed, late at night, after he had at last left the tribunal.

Stretched out on a pantherskin, reclining comfortably against a backrest, an informal cap on his head, our judge is immersed in his book. On the table by his side other books lie ready. Probably these are not volumes on jurisprudence, and certainly not love stories. Judge Dee was married, and had the usual number of concubines a man of his official rank was entitled to, and it must be feared that he took love in a rather casual way. No, it is practically certain that these books are the works of some Taoist philosopher like Chuang Tzu, where the deepest wisdom is expressed in humorous little parables, or some minor histories, written in a light vein, and describing the complicated intrigues in the official world of bygone times. A graceful coral tree in a craquelé vase gives rest to the eye, and fragrant smoke curls up from the incense burner.

Finally, his reading finished, and the deep silence of night reigning outside, Judge Dee may well have played, just before retiring, a few melodies on the Chinese lute, the seven-stringed psaltery that is lying on the table, still half in its brocade cover. And then he will have done better than Sherlock Holmes on his violin, for playing this instrument was one of the accomplishments of every refined scholar-official.

# II

It is hoped that the foregoing will suffice as a general introduction to this Chinese detective novel. Details about the Chinese original, longer notes to the translation, references to the Chinese Penal Code, and other information of a more or less technical

character, will be found at the back, in the "Translator's Postscript."
It was my sinological conscience that prompted me to add this
postscript. The general reader can ignore it without any incon-
venience, since a knowledge of the details given there is not necessary for following the story.

There are, however, a few elementary facts regarding the
administration of justice in ancient China, a knowledge of which
will help the reader to better understand the situations described
in the present story, and will enable him to read much of what is
written between the lines. I take the liberty, therefore, to impose
still further on the reader's patience, inviting him to glance
through the following very brief summary.

The tribunal, which plays such a prominent role in every
Chinese detective story, is a part of the offices of the district magistrate, the town hall, as we would call it. These offices consist of
a large number of one-storied buildings, separated from each other
by courtyards and galleries. This compound is surrounded by a
high wall. On entering through the main gate, an ornamental
archway flanked by the quarters of the guards, one finds the court
hall at the back of the first courtyard. In front of the door a large
bronze gong is suspended on a wooden frame. Every citizen has
the right to beat this gong, at any time, to make it known that he
wishes to bring a case before the magistrate.

The court is a spacious hall with a high ceiling, completely
bare except for a few inscriptions on the wall, quotations from the
Classics that extoll the majesty of the law. At the back of the
hall there is a dais, raised one foot or so above the stone flagged
floor. On this dais stands the bench, a huge desk, covered with
a piece of scarlet brocade that entirely hides its frontside. On the
table one sees a vase filled with thin bamboo tallies, an inkstone
for rubbing black and red ink, a three-cornered brushholder with
two writing brushes, and the seals of office, wrapped up in a piece
of brocade. Behind the bench stands a large armchair, occupied

by the magistrate when the court is in session.  Over the dais one sees a canopy with heavy curtains, which are drawn when the session is over (see the plate facing page 62).

Behind the bench, a doorway gives entrance to the private office of the magistrate, the judge's chambers, as we would say. This doorway is covered by a screen bearing a large image of the unicorn, the ancient Chinese symbol of perspicacity.  In his private office the magistrate conducts all routine business when the court is not in session.  There are three of these sessions every day, one in the morning, one at noon, and one in the afternoon.

This private office looks out on a second courtyard, around which one finds a number of smaller offices, where the clerks, the archivists, the copyists, and the other personnel of the tribunal and the district administration do their work.  Having passed these, one enters another, larger courtyard with miniature lotus and gold-fish ponds, flower beds or artificial rocks; at the back of this court-yard stands the large reception hall, used for various public occasions, and for receiving important visitors.

Behind this reception hall lies still another courtyard, at which we have to stop, for now we have arrived at the living quarters of the magistrate and his family.  These form a small compound in themselves.

Before every session, the constables gather in the court hall, and range themselves in two rows on left and right, in front of the bench.  They carry bamboo sticks, whips, handcuffs, screws and other paraphernalia of their function.  Behind them stand a few runners, carrying on poles large signboards with "Silence!," "Clear the Court!," and such like inscriptions.

When everybody is in his appointed place, the curtains are drawn up, and the magistrate appears on the dais, clad in his official dark green robe, and with the black judge's cap on his head.  While he seats himself behind the bench, his lieutenants and the senior scribe take up their positions, standing by the side of the judge's chair.

The judge calls the roll, and the session is open.

The judge has the defendant brought in, and he has to kneel down on the bare floor in front of the bench, and remain this way for the duration of his case. Everything is calculated to impress the defendant with his own insignificance, particularly in contrast to the majesty of the law. Kneeling there far down below the judge, on a floor probably still showing the blood stains of people beaten or tortured there on a previous occasion, the constables standing over him on both sides, ready to curse or beat him at the slightest provocation, the defendant's position can hardly be described as a favorable one. The kneeling on the stone floor is already quite unpleasant in itself, and becomes acute agony when a thoughtful constable first lays a few thin chains under the defendant's knees, as is done in the case of recalcitrant criminals.

Since complainants, irrespective of rank or age, are placed in exactly the same position, one need not wonder that the Chinese on the whole bring a suit before the tribunal only when all attempts at effecting a settlement out of court have failed.

The law permits the judge to put the question to the defendant under torture, provided there is sufficient proof of his guilt. *It is one of the fundamental principles of the Chinese Penal Code that no one can be sentenced unless he has confessed to his crime.* In order to prevent hardened criminals from escaping punishment by refusing to confess, even when confronted with irrefutable proof of their guilt, various methods of severe torture, although officially forbidden by the law, have received legal acquiescence. If, however, a person should die under this "great torture," as the Chinese call it, and it should be proved later that he was innocent, the judge and all the court personnel concerned will receive the death penalty.

Legitimate means of torture are flogging on the back with a light whip, beating on the back of the thighs with bamboo sticks, applying screws to hands and ankles, and slapping the face with leather flaps. Every bamboo tally in the vase on the bench stands for a number of strokes with the bamboo. When the judge orders a constable to beat the defendant, he throws a number of tallies on the floor, and the headman of the constables therewith checks that the correct number of blows is given.

When the accused has confessed, the judge sentences him according to the provisions of the Penal Code. This code, the history of which goes back to 650 A.D., was in force until a few decennia ago. It is a monumental work of absorbing interest, and all together an admirable example of law-making. Its merits and defects have been aptly summed up by the eminent authority on Chinese criminal law, Sir Chaloner Alabaster, in his statement: "As regards then the criminal law of the Chinese, although the allowance of torture in the examination of prisoners is a blot which cannot be overlooked, although the punishment for treason and parricide is monstrous, and the punishment of the wooden collar or portable pillory is not to be defended, yet the Code—when its procedure is understood—is infinitely more exact and satisfactory than our own system, and very far from being the barbarous cruel abomination it is generally supposed to be" ("Notes and Commentaries on Chinese Criminal Law," London 1899).

On the whole much latitude is given to the judge's discretion while applying the provisions of the code. He is not as strictly bound by precedent in interpretation as our judges. Furthermore the judge can have all punishments executed on his own authority, except the capital one, which must be ratified by the Throne.

As has already been remarked, a complainant's position is as unfavorable in court as that of the defendant. Neither complainant nor defendant is allowed legal counsel; neither may they have witnesses called. The summoning of witnesses is a privilege of the court.

The only persons that in some way could be compared with our lawyers are the professional petition-writers. This is a class that is not regarded very highly in Chinese society. Usually they are students who failed in the literary examinations, and to whom the entrance to official life being thus barred, eke out a meagre existence by drawing up written complaints and defenses for a small remuneration. Some among them have quite an extensive knowledge of the law and legal procedure, and by cleverly formulating a case they often assist their client in an indirect way. But they get little credit for their labors, the tribunal ignores them, and there is no Chinese detective novel that celebrates a figure like Erle S. Gardner's famous Perry Mason.

At first glance the above summary would give the impression that the Chinese system is a travesty of justice. As a matter of fact, however, it has on the whole worked admirably during many centuries. Although the author of our novel lived in the 18th century, and described the judicial system as he knew it in his own day, it was substantially the same system as that in operation during the Tang dynasty (618-907), the period in which the scene of the present novel is laid. During the ten centuries that intervened, even the court procedure hardly changed, which is shown by the accompanying plate, a copy of an original Tang scroll picture; the judge is seated behind the high bench, flanked by his assistants, while complainant and defendant are standing in front, below.

Literary evidence shows that the same applies to the following remarks as to how the system worked. The social structure of the 18th century does not differ in substance from that prevailing during the Tang dynasty.

The Chinese judicial system can be understood properly only if one views it against the peculiar background of the ancient Chinese government system, and the structure of Chinese society in general.

Abuse of judicial authority was checked by several controlling factors. In the first place, the district magistrate was but a small

## One of the Ten Judges of Hell.

According to a very ancient Chinese conception, the souls of the dead must appear before a tribunal in the Nether World, which is an exact replica of the tribunals on earth. In front of the bench, on the left is the accused. On right is the registrar of the Infernal Tribunal, carrying a roll on which the sins of the accused are recorded. For some reason this registrar and the two attendants by the side of the judge are represented as females.

Drawing after an illustrated scroll dating from the Tang dynasty, and entitled *Foo-shwo-shih-wang-djing*.

cog in the colossal administrative machinery of the Empire. He had to report his every action to his immediate superiors, accompanied by all pertaining original documents. Since every official was held completely responsible for the actions of his subordinates, these data were carefully checked, and if there was any doubt, a retrial was ordered. Furthermore anyone had the right to appeal to a higher judicial instance, going up as high as the Throne. Finally, there were the dreaded Imperial Censors, who traveled strictly incognito all over the country, vested with absolute powers, and responsible only to the Throne; they were empowered to have any official summarily arrested, and conveyed to the capital for an investigation.

A second control lay in the practice of denunciation. Every official had the right to denounce his superior to higher authorities. He was even compelled to do so for his own safety, for he would have been held responsible for a judicial error to the same degree as his superior; "acting under orders" was not accepted as a valid excuse by Chinese law. If, for instance, an innocent prisoner died under torture, the judge who ordered the torture, the constable who executed the order, and the headman who supervised it, might all have been decapitated.

It does credit to the democratic spirit that has always characterized the Chinese people, despite the autocratic form of their ancient government, that the most powerful check on abuse of judicial power was public opinion. All sessions of the tribunal were open to the public, and the entire town was aware of and discussed the tribunal proceedings. A cruel or arbitrary judge would soon have found the population against him. The teeming masses of the Chinese people were highly organized among themselves. Next to such closely-knit units as the family and the clan, there were the broader organizations of the professional guilds, the trade associations, and the secret brotherhoods. If the populace were to choose to sabotage the administration of a magistrate, taxes would not

have been paid on time, the registration would have become hope-
lessly tangled, highways would not have been repaired; and after
a few months a censor would have appeared on the scene, for the
purpose of investigation.

The present novel describes vividly how careful a judge must
be to show to the people at large that he conducts his cases in the
right way.

The greatest defect of the system as a whole was that in this
pyramidal structure too much depended on the top. When the
standard of the metropolitan officials deteriorated, the decay
quickly spread downward. It might have been held in check for
some time by an upright provincial governor, but if the central
authority remained weak for too long, the district magistrates were
also affected. This general deterioration of the administration of
justice became conspicuous during the last century of Manchu rule
in China. One need not wonder, therefore, that foreigners who
observed affairs in China during the 19th century, did not have
much favorable comment on the Chinese judicial system.

A second defect of the system was that it assigned far too many
duties to the district magistrate. He was a permanently over-
worked official. If he did not devote practically all his waking
hours to his work, he was forced to leave a considerable part of
his task to his subordinates. Men like Judge Dee of our present
novel could cope with this heavy task, but it can be imagined that
lesser men would soon have become wholly dependent on the
permanent officials of their tribunal, such as the senior scribes, the
headman of the constables, etc. These small people were particularly liable and most prone to abuse their power. If not strictly
supervised they would engage in various kinds of petty extortion,
impartially squeezing everyone connected with a criminal case.
These "small fry" are wittily described in our present novel. More
especially the constables of the tribunal are a lazy lot, most reluctant to do some extra work, and always keen on squeezing a few

coppers here and there; yet at times surprisingly kind and human, and not without a certain wry sense of humor.

It may be added that the function of district magistrate was the stepping stone to higher office. Since promotion was based solely on actual performance, and since the term of office rarely exceeded three years or so, even lazy or mediocre persons did their utmost to be satisfactory "father-and-mother officials," hoping in due course to be promoted to an easier post.

All in all, the system worked well. The most flagrant violations of the principles of justice recorded in Chinese history concerned cases of political and religious persecution—a respect regarding which our own record is not too clean either! Finally, the following statement by Sir George Staunton, the capable translator of the Chinese Penal Code, may be quoted here as a tribute to the ancient Chinese judicial system, all the more so since those words were written at the end of the 18th century, when the central authority, the dynasty of Manchu conquerors, was already disintegrating, and when consequently many abuses of judicial power had set in. "There are very substantial grounds for believing," this cautious observer says, "that neither flagrant, nor repeated acts of injustice, do, in point of fact, often, in any rank or station, ultimately escape with impunity."

R.H.v.G.

# CELEBRATED CASES
# OF JUDGE DEE
## (Dee Goong An)

THE CASE OF THE DOUBLE
MURDER AT DAWN

THE CASE OF THE STRANGE
CORPSE

THE CASE OF THE POISONED
BRIDE

# DRAMATIS PERSONAE

This list has been drawn up by the translator for the reader's convenience. It should be noted that in Chinese the surname (here printed in capitals) precedes the personal name.

### Main characters:

DEE Jen-djieh, referred to as "Judge Dee," or "the judge." Magistrate of Chang-ping, a town district in the Province of Shantung. The three criminal cases solved by Judge Dee occurred in the town itself, and the villages surrounding it.

HOONG Liang, sergeant over the constables of the tribunal of Chang-ping, and Judge Dee's trusted adviser. Referred to as "Sergeant Hoong," or "the sergeant."

MA Joong, first lieutenant of Judge Dee.

TAO Gan }
CHIAO Tai } second and third lieutenants of Judge Dee.

### Persons connected with
### "The Double Murder at Dawn":

PANG Deh, warden of Six Mile Village, where the murders were committed. Referred to as "Warden Pang."

DJAO San, his assistant.

KOONG Wan-deh, owner of the hostel in Six Mile Village, where the two victims stayed.

LIU Guang-chi }
SHAO Lee-huai } traveling silk merchants from Kiangsu Province.
DJAO Wan-chuan }

WANG, a carter.

MRS. WANG, his widow.

DJANG, owner of a hostel in Divine Village.

DJIANG Djung, warden of Divine Village.

LOO Chang-po, manager of a silk shop in Divine Village. Referred to as "Manager Loo."

*Persons connected with*
*"The Strange Corpse"*:

HO Kai, warden of Huang-hua Village, where the murder was committed. Referred to as "Warden Ho."
BEE Hsun, a shopkeeper in Huang-hua Village, the victim.
MRS. BEE, his old mother.
MRS. BEE, née DJOU, his widow. Referred to as "Mrs. Djou."
TANG Deh-djung, a Doctor of Literature. Referred to as "Dr. Tang."
DOO
HSU Deh-tai } students of Dr. Tang.

*Persons connected with*
*"The Poisoned Bride"*:

HUA Guo-hsiang, a former Prefect, living retired in Chang-ping. Referred to as "Mr. Hua."
HUA Wen-djun, a Candidate of Literature, Mr. Hua's son, and groom of the unfortunate bride. Referred to as "Wen-djun."
MRS. LEE, mother of the bride.
MISS LEE, the bride.
HOO Dso-bin, a Candidate of Literature, class-mate of Wen-djun. Referred to as "Candidate Hoo."
MRS. HOO, his mother.
CHEN, an old maid servant in the Hua mansion.

*Occurs in Chapters 29 and 30 only*:

YEN Lee-ben, an Imperial Censor.

# First Chapter

JUDGE DEE IS APPOINTED MAGISTRATE OF CHANG-PING;
THE PEOPLE CROWD HIS TRIBUNAL TO REPORT GRIEVANCES.

*Although all people hanker after a magistrate's office,*
*Few realize all that is involved in solving criminal cases:*
*Tempering severity by lenience, as laid down by our law makers,*
*And avoiding the extremes advocated by crafty philosophers.*

*One upright magistrate means the happiness of a thousand families,*
*The one word "justice" means the peace of the entire population.*
*The exemplary conduct of Judge Dee, magistrate of Chang-ping,*
*Is placed here on record, for the edification of the reading public.*

In the end, as a general rule, no criminal escapes the laws of
the land. But it is up to the judge to decide who is guilty and
who is innocent. If, therefore, a judge is honest, then the people
in his district will be at peace; and if the people are at peace, their
manners and morals will be good. All vagabonds and idlers,
all spreaders of false rumors and all trouble makers will disappear,
and all of the common people will cheerfully go about their own
affairs. And if some wicked people from outside should happen
to settle down in such a district, they will better their lives and
reform of their own accord; for they see with their own eyes, and
hear with their own ears, how strictly the laws are enforced, and
how sternly justice is meted out. Therefore it can be said that the
amelioration of the common people depends on the honesty of the
magistrate; never yet has a dishonest official improved the people
under him.

The honesty of a magistrate does not only consist of negative qualities like not accepting bribes and not doing harm to the
people; it also implies positive qualities such as, in serving the
State, doing what others cannot or dare not do, and, in

ruling the people, rectifying wrongs that others cannot or dare not rectify. The subtle clues to be found among the populace, and the complicated intrigues in the official world, all such things a judge should investigate impartially. His motto should be: "To demonstrate clearly the just retribution meted out by Heaven, never failing in its hair-fine accuracy." Judges answering these high qualifications, have been duly honored by our August Rulers, since the days of remote antiquity.

There are, however, also magistrates who let their conduct of a case be influenced by bribes, or who, fearing lest they lose their position if they do not dispose quickly of a great number of cases, pronounce hasty verdicts on the basis of confessions obtained by torture, or from some shreds of evidence. Such officials have failed to cultivate themselves, and therefore should never be appointed as rulers over others. For how could such men make their subordinates honest, and bring peace to the common people!

In moments of leisure, leafing through books old and new, and searching through all kinds of minor historical records, I have come across many a weird story concerning criminal cases solved by famous judges of former times. Few of these, however, can match what is placed on record here.

The present book describes complicated criminal investigations, baffling crimes, astounding feats of detection, and marvelous solutions of difficult cases. It tells about people who commit murder to be able to live to the end of their days in an odor of sanctity; who commit crimes in order to amass riches; people who become involved in crimes through adulterous relationships; people who meet sudden death by drinking poison not destined for them; people who through words spoken in jest lay themselves open to grave suspicion, and who, although innocent, barely escape heavy punishment. All these things could never have been set aright if there had not been an able and diligent magistrate who, on occasion altering his voice and dress, went about in disguise to make secret investigations himself, or who sometimes even assumed the role of a ghost from the Nether World, just to find the solution of a case, to redress a wrong, and to apprehend a criminal, thus successfully bringing to an end the most strange and most amazing trials.

Now, while the vernal breeze encourages idleness, and I find myself with time hanging heavily on my hands, I am putting this story on record, to be offered to the reading public. While I would not make bold to assert that the narrative of these strange happenings will caution the people and thus improve their morals, I yet venture to hope that its perusal will serve to beguile some idle hours.

\*　　　　　\*

\*

A poem says:
> *While placing on record these strange and baffling cases,*
> *One cannot but admire this judge of days gone by:*
> *Unselfish and perspicacious, he was a man of supreme rectitude,*
> *He shall always be remembered as redresser of grievous wrongs.*

The present book describes some exploits of a magistrate who lived during our glorious Tang dynasty, in the first half of the seventh century A.D.

This magistrate was a native of the town Tai-yuan, the capital of Shansi Province. His family name was Dee, his personal name Jen-djieh, while he had adopted the literary appelation of Hwai-ying. Being a man of exemplary honesty and penetrating wisdom, he was in due time appointed to a high position at the Imperial Court, and by his frank and courageous memorials to the Throne helped tide over many a crisis in state affairs. In recognition of his loyal service, he was later appointed a governor, and finally ennobled as duke Liang.

His illustrious deeds are duly entered in the official "History of the Tang Dynasty", and this material is thus easily accessible to all interested persons.

A number of facts, however, relating to the early career of Dee Jen-djieh, who at that time was famous as "Judge Dee", have either been omitted or only treated cursorily in the official records. One must search for them in minor historical writings, in the local records of the towns where he served as magistrate, and suchlike sources. Yet these lesser-known facts are of no mean interest. They serve to heighten our respect for Judge Dee. These facts show that, next to being a loyal servant of the Throne, Dee Jen-djieh was also a wise magistrate, a great gentleman who combined remarkable acumen with a benevolent and justice-loving disposition and who, as a district magistrate, succeeded in solving an amazing number of strange and puzzling criminal cases.

The present story, therefore, is concerned only with the early phase of Judge Dee's career, going back to the time when he was appointed district magistrate of Chang-ping.

Having assumed his office there, Judge Dee immediately devoted all his energy to the weeding out of unruly elements, the protection of the law-abiding citizens, and to the disposition of pending litigations.

Judge Dee was ably assisted by four trusted followers in accomplishing these burdensome tasks.

His chief assistant was a man called Hoong Liang, an old servant in the Dee paternal mansion, who had seen Judge Dee grow up from a small boy. Although well advanced in age, Hoong Liang was nevertheless a courageous person, who promptly executed any dangerous or delicate job that Judge Dee assigned him, showing considerable tact and a natural gift for detection. Judge Dee appointed him sergeant over the constables of his tribunal, and treated him as his confidential adviser.

Two others, Ma Joong and Chiao Tai, Judge Dee used for all

especially dangerous jobs connected with the apprehension of criminals. Originally these two had been "brothers of the green woods", or, in plain language, highway robbers. Once, when Judge Dee was traveling to the capital on some official business, these two men attacked him and his party on the road intending to rob them. Judge Dee at once saw that Ma Joong and Chiao Tai, far from being common thieves, were men of a heroic disposition, while the passes they made at him showed him convincingly that they were well versed in the arts of fencing and boxing. It seemed to Judge Dee that he might well try to reform these men, and engage their service later to assist him in executing the King's business; in such a way their talents might be used to good purpose. Thus Judge Dee, not deigning to draw his sword, just ordered them sternly to desist. Thereupon he gave them a good talking to which greatly moved Ma Joong and Chiao Tai. The former said respectfully:

"The two of us have resorted to this despicable occupation only because we found the Empire in turmoil, and wicked ministers in charge at Court. We, having nothing in this world but our able bodies and our knowledge of the martial arts, and finding no one who would employ us, thus had no other course open to us than to become highwaymen. But since Your Honor has now so kindly spoken to us, our only desire is to be allowed henceforward to follow your whip and hold your stirrup, in order thus to show our gratitude for Your Honor's favor".

So Judge Dee accepted these two braves as his lieutenants.

His fourth lieutenant was a reformed itinerant swindler, named Tao Gan. This man had long before mended his ways, and he had become a runner for a certain magistrate's tribunal. But since there were many people who harbored grudges against him, he was continually harassed and bothered by these old enemies, and finally sought refuge with Judge Dee. He was a man of many parts and great cunning, so Judge Dee retained him as his assistant. This Tao Gan became a close friend of Sergeant Hoong, Ma Joong and Chiao Tai.

Since his assumption of office in Chang-ping, these four men proved very useful to Judge Dee. They were kept busy on secret investigations for the Judge, and the information they gathered helped him to solve not a few difficult criminal cases.

*     *

*

One day Judge Dee was sitting in his private office at the back of the court hall, attending to some routine business, when he suddenly heard the sound of the gong at the entrance of the tribunal. Thus apprised that a case was being brought in, he hurriedly donned his official robe and cap, and having entered the court hall, seated himself behind his high bench. Below, in front of the bench, the clerks, constables and other minions of the law had already lined up themselves in two rows, to the left and right. Looking towards the entrance of the hall, Judge Dee there saw a man of the common people, of about forty years old. He seemed in a state of great agitation, his face was all covered with perspiration. He stood there incessantly crying that a great wrong was being done him.

Judge Dee ordered two constables to bring the man in. As he knelt down before the bench, Judge Dee thus addressed him:

"Who are you, and what grievous wrong did you suffer, that you beat the gong before the hour on which this tribunal convenes?"

"This insignificant person", the man said respectfully, "is called Koong Wan-deh. I live in the Six Mile Village, outside the southern gate of this city. Since my house is fairly large, and I have only a small family, I use the greater part of it as a hostel. For more than ten years I have been peacefully engaged in this business. Yesterday, towards twilight, there arrived two traveling silk merchants. They said they had come from Kiangsu Province, and were only passing through, doing business along the road. As it was getting dark, they wanted to stay overnight at my hostel. I, seeing that they were much-traveled men, accordingly gave them a room. They had their dinner, drank wine, laughed and talked, as can be attested by several witnesses. This morning, just before daybreak, these two merchants departed.

"Then, unexpectedly this morning the village warden Pang Deh at nine o'clock, came to see me, saying that two dead men had been found lying by the roadside, before the gate of the market-place nearby. 'These two men', he said, 'stayed as guests in your hostel, and you murdered them to rob them of their money. Then you dragged their dead bodies to the market gate'. Having thus addressed me, before I could say one word in my defense, he had the two corpses dragged to my hostel, and threw them down right in front of my door. Thereupon he started to shout, and threaten me, demanding five hundred pieces of silver for hushing up this crime. 'These two men came from your hostel', he roared, 'it is therefore evident that you murdered them there, and then dragged their bodies to the market, to cover up the traces of your crime'. I immediately rushed here in great anguish, praying Your Honor to redress this wrong."

Having heard this statement, Judge Dee looked at the man kneeling in front of the bench, and thought that he certainly did not look like a dangerous criminal. On the other hand this was apparently an important murder case, and of course he could not decide its merits on the statement of this man alone. Hence he said:

"You claim to be a law-abiding citizen of this locality. Why then did Warden Pang immediately pounce on you as the criminal? I find it hard to believe that you are really the innocent citizen you profess to be. I will have to hear Warden Pang, in order to check your statement."

Thereupon he ordered a constable to fetch the warden, and soon a man of about thirty years was brought in. His face was covered with wrinkles, and he wore a blue robe. Kneeling down before the bench, he said:

"I, Pang Deh, warden of Six Mile Village, respectfully greet Your Honor. This murder falls under my jurisdiction. This morning I saw the bodies of two men lying by the roadside, in front of the market gate. At first I did not know where these two men had come from, but on questioning the people living in the neighborhood, I found that they all said that these men had stayed as guests in the hostel of this man Koong last night. Therefore I questioned Koong, pointing out that it was evidently he who had dragged these two corpses to the market, having murdered them in his hostel for the purpose of robbing them. For according to Koong these two men left his hostel before daybreak. Now at that time there were already a number of people on that road, and none of them reported having seen any suspicious characters about. Furthermore, on questioning the people living near the market, it appeared that none of them had heard any cries for help. These facts prove to my satisfaction that the victims were killed during the night in Koong's hostel, and that afterwards Koong dragged their bodies to the market gate, in order thus to divert suspicion from him. Since the culprit is already here, I beg Your Honor to proceed against him."

Judge Dee thought to himself that Warden Pang's argument seemed not without reason. On the other hand, giving Koong another good look, he still felt that that man could hardly be a brutal criminal, murdering people in cold blood in order to rob them. After some reflection, he said:

"You two have made conflicting statements. Without having held an inquest, I cannot proceed with this case. The investigation shall be continued after inspection of the scene of the crime".

He had Koong Wan-deh and Warden Pang led away by the constables, and ordered the necessary preparations for proceeding to the scene of the crime with the tribunal.

WARDEN PANG'S SLANDER BRINGS HARM ON HIS OWN HEAD;
SERGEANT HOONG OBTAINS A CLUE BY A CLEVER SURMISE.

After returning to his private office, Judge Dee ordered a constable to summon the coroner. After three beats on the gong, he
donned his official robe and cap, and proceeded to Six Mile Village
in his palanquin, surrounded by the constables and other servants
of his tribunal. The people living along the road had heard
about the double murder. Knowing Judge Dee's reputation as a
great detector of crimes, a vast crowd gathered and followed the
procession, in order to see what was going to happen.

Before noon they arrived at the market of Six Mile Village.
Warden Pang, his assistant Djao San, and the village-headman
had already arranged a temporary tribunal, and came forward to
bid Judge Dee welcome.

After the customary exchange of amenities, Judge Dee descended from his palanquin, and said:

"I shall first go to Koong's hostel for a personal investigation,
and then open the tribunal and proceed with the inquest".

He ordered them to lead him to Koong's hostel, where he found
the dead bodies of the two men, showing several wounds apparently
inflicted with a knife, lying on the ground in front of the door.
Judge Dee asked Warden Pang:

"Where were these two corpses originally found?"

Warden Pang answered hurriedly:

"By Your Honor's leave, these men were killed by Koong Wan-
deh for gain; thereafter he removed the bodies to the market gate,
so as to be able to repudiate his crime later. Since I would not
have innocent people become involved in this affair, I had the
bodies moved to this place in front of Koong's hostel. I beg Your
Honor to verify this".

He had hardly finished speaking, when Judge Dee roared at him:

"You dogs-head, I am not asking to be advised by you as to the identity of the criminal. What I demand to know is, how can you, charged with an official function, and supposed to know the rules and regulations, thus offend against the law? You ought to know what the punishment is for wilfully moving dead bodies, and thus tampering with important evidence. Quite apart from the question whether or not Koong is guilty of murder, you had no right to remove the two bodies from the place where they were originally found, before having duly reported to me, explaining your reasons, or before I held the inquest and drew up and sealed the official report. Why, I ask you, did you thus dare to offend against the laws of the land, and were you so bold as to tamper with the bodies without authorization? Evidently you yourself are trying to cover up some nefarious scheme. Probably you planned this crime together with Koong, and having quarreled with him over the division of the loot, now try to shift all the blame on to him. Now I shall first have you beaten with the heavy bamboo, and then I shall question you under torture."

Judge Dee ordered the constables to let Warden Pang have hundred strokes with the heavy bamboo, then and there. Warden Pang's wails rose to heaven, and soon blood began to trickle from his bursting skin. By now all the onlookers were convinced that Koong had been wrongly accused, and they admired Judge Dee for his shrewdness.

After Pang had received the full hundred strokes, he still persisted that he was innocent. Judge Dee decided for the time being not to press him further, but entered Koong's hostel with his retinue. First he asked Koong:

"Your hostel has a great number of rooms. Give me a clear account of where the two murdered men stayed".

"The three rooms at the back of the house are the living quar-

ters of myself and my wife, and our small daughter. The two
rooms on the east side are used as kitchen. Thus these five rooms
are never used by the guests: for them I have reserved the rooms in
the first and the second courtyard. Since the two guests that
arrived yesterday night were silk merchants, I knew that they
would not grudge expense, and so offered them the best room of
the second courtyard, this being more comfortable than the first,
by reason of its being further removed from the noise and dust
of the street".

Koong then led Judge Dee and his assistants to the second
courtyard, and showed him there the room that had been occupied by the two murdered merchants.

Judge Dee and his lieutenants carefully scrutinized this room.
They saw that the remainder of yesterday's dinner was still on the
table, and that in front of the couch two night utensils were still
standing about. There was not the slightest evidence of a struggle,
let alone of a murder having been committed there. Judge Dee,
thinking that Koong might still be holding back something, asked
him:

"Since you have been keeping this hostel for more than ten
years, surely there is much coming and going of guests. I presume that yesterday you had also other guests staying here, next
to the two silk merchants?"

"Aside from them there were three others. One was a leather
merchant on his way to Shansi, and the two others were a gentleman with his man servant, from Honan Province. Since the
gentleman became ill, he and his servant are even now resting
in their room in the first courtyard."

Judge Dee had the leather merchant and the man-servant of
the sick traveler brought before him. He first questioned the
leather merchant.

"I am a leather merchant from Shansi", the man said, "and I
have been engaged in this trade for a number of years. When

passing through here I always stay in this hostel. I actually saw the two silk merchants leave here just before daybreak, and I can also attest that during the night I heard no cries, nor any commotion. Of course, I am completely ignorant as to how and where the two men met their death".

Judge Dee then turned to the man-servant. This man confirmed what the leather-merchant had said, adding that, owing to his master's illness, he had hardly slept during the night. If anything out of the ordinary had happened in the hostel, he would certainly have noticed it.

On hearing this evidence, Judge Dee thought that it tended to confirm his doubts of Koong Wan-deh's guilt. To be doubly sure, however, he ordered his men to go over every single room of the hostel inch by inch. This they did, but they failed to discover any trace of a crime having been committed there.

Judge Dee was now convinced that the murder had been committed somewhere outside, after the merchants had left the hostel. For even if one assumed that all three witnesses were in the plot together with Koong, how could they have obliterated all the traces of the crime?

Deep in thought he took his retinue back to the market place, and closely scrutinized the spot where the two bodies had been discovered. There, ample evidence sprang to the eye that the murder had been committed right on the spot: the ground showed that much blood had been shed.

There were no houses in the immediate vicinity, but some stood a little farther away, on the market place itself. Judge Dee had the people living there brought before him, and questioned them. But this produced no results. The first thing they knew about were the shouts of some early passers-by that woke them calling out that a murder had been committed. Thereupon they had immediately reported to the warden, and during his investigation it had become known that the victims had been staying at Koong's hostel.

This information made Judge Dee incline to believe that Warden Pang might after all turn out to be the culprit. But since night was falling, it was too late to start holding the inquest. He decided to send his assistants out to do some private sleuthing that same night, and see what information they could gather. The inquest could be held early the next morning. He said to the village headman:

"When I started investigating this case, one problem arose after the other, and each made the case more complicated. Therefore I came here today directly after the case had been reported, for the purpose of making a personal investigation. In a case like this it is of the utmost importance that an inquest is held as soon as possible; thus I shall stay right here over night, so that we can open the inquest tomorrow morning".

He ordered a close watch to be kept over the two bodies, and went to the official quarters set up for him. After having chatted there for some time with the village head, he finally allowed everybody to retire. But he retained Sergeant Hoong, and, after all the others had gone, he said to him:

"This crime certainly was not committed by Koong. I rather suspect Warden Pang. He immediately accused some one, in order to prevent us from suspecting him. You had better go out tonight, and try to gather some information. As soon as you have found something worth while let me know immediately".

Sergeant Hoong took his leave, and first went to see Warden Pang's assistant Djao San, taking three constables on duty with him.

Djao San was with the people standing guard over the two bodies. Sergeant Hoong walked up to him, and addressed him in a conversational tone.

"I have come together with His Excellency Judge Dee to take part in the conduct of this case. Until now I have not bothered your superior. The only conclusion I have come to is that old man

Koong must be innocent. And although I and my companions here are government servants, we never bother innocent people. All in all we had, however, rather a trying day, and we have a rather empty feeling inside. Would it be too much to assume that your boss, Warden Pang, has a bit of food and a jar of wine lying around somewhere? It is not that we are out to get a gratis meal, everybody knows how honest our master is. To-morrow he shall certainly give me and my colleagues some money for our trouble, and out of that we shall pay you for the meal. So, in the meantime, don't let us go hungry!"

Djao San hurriedly paid his respects to the sergeant, and said: "Please don't be angry, Sergeant. Our warden is so occupied with this case right now, that he completely forgot to give the necessary instructions for the entertaining of His Excellency's staff. But since you and your colleagues are hungry, allow me the honor of being your host. Let us go and have a snack and a drink in the market inn".

He then ordered a few men to take over the guard of the bodies, and took the sergeant and the constables to the inn. The servants there, seeing that this party consisted of official persons engaged in the investigation of the murder, stormed them with questions about this and that, and immediately brought a profusion of delicacies and plenty wine. Sergeant Hoong told them: "We are not like ordinary constables, who, as soon as they go somewhere to work on a case, immediately start gorging themselves with wine and food at their master's expense, and on top of that demand a few pieces of silver from the inn to cover their traveling expenses. You bring only two dishes of plain food, and give each of us two cups of wine, that is all. We shall settle the bill later."

After Sergeant Hoong had made this nice gesture, they all sat down.

Now Sergeant Hoong, of course, knew perfectly well that

Warden Pang, after having received his punishment, was being detained in Koong's hostel, guarded by Chiao Tai and Ma Joong; but the rules of propriety had prevented his mentioning this painful fact right at the start of his conversation with Pang's subordinate Djao San. Now, however, he thus spoke to him:

"Your boss is, frankly speaking, too careless about his duties. Why, yesterday he was out all night. Coming home early in the morning, upon learning about the murder, he suddenly remembered that old Koong was a wealthy man, who could afford some squeeze, and then hit on this wicked plan to remove the corpses to Koong's hostel. Is that not overdoing it a bit? And where, now we come to it, did your boss go last night? The place where the bodies were found is on the open road. How is it that neither he nor you, who are supposed to make the nightrounds together, noticed them during your last watch? Today His Excellency the Judge let Pang have a hundred strokes with the heavy bamboo, and tomorrow he will certainly press the warden again to produce the criminal. Now say for yourself, is this not wilfully getting oneself into trouble?"

"Sergeant", answered Djao San, "you don't know the inside of this affair. Since all of us are gathered now together around this table as old friends, there is no harm in telling you. You must know that our warden has an old grudge against Koong. Every New Year this man Koong presents our warden with only a niggardly few coppers, and everytime the warden thinks he can squeeze a nice gratuity out of Koong, that old skinflint persistently refuses.

"Now last night Warden Pang happened to be engaged in a small gambling party at Lee's place and lost heavily. He went on gambling till dawn, until he heard people shouting that a murder had been committed. As soon as he heard that the victims had come from Koong's hostel, he immediately thought that this was a splendid opportunity to get even with old Koong, and squeeze some badly needed funds out of him. So you see that Warden Pang has nothing to do with the murder itself. He only tried to cheat old Koong, and got a sound thrashing as his reward! Rather than harming others, he has harmed himself!

"Now as to this murder, this surely is a most baffling affair. It is perfectly clear that the deed was done at daybreak. It must have occurred after I had returned from that place after I had made the last round of the night, and then everything was still quiet. It is true that old man Koong is a skinflint, but as far as I can see, he certainly is not the murderer".

Sergeant Hoong, on hearing this story, mumbled some noncommittal remarks, thinking by himself that thus neither was Warden Pang the criminal. He had only tried to swindle old Koong out of some pieces of silver, and had already received his just punishment in the form of the hundred strokes with the bamboo. So we are still faced with our original problem: who did commit the crime? Having thus ruminated, Sergeant Hoong set upon the meal with gusto, and made short work of it.

Having eaten the last morsel, and drunk the last drop of wine, the sergeant had the bill drawn up, and, to keep up appearances, told the innkeeper to come to the tribunal the next day to receive payment. Then he left his friends, and went along to call on Judge Dee.

After he had reported what he had just heard, Judge Dee said:

"This is indeed a difficult case. If Koong did not commit the murder, then the two victims must have let it become known somewhere else that their pockets were well-lined; some criminal must have heard this, and followed them all the way here, till this morning, when they had left the hostel, he saw his chance to kill them. This is the only explanation for the two bodies found near the market gate. Now I, as district magistrate am considered as the father and mother of the people here. I cannot but see to it that this murder is avenged. Only then can I face our Sovereign on high, and the common people below. However, there is nothing more that we can do to-day. Let us see to-morrow morning, after the inquest".

He then allowed Sergeant Hoong to retire.

KOONG AVERS THERE IS SOME MISTAKE ABOUT THE BODIES;
JUDGE DEE GOES TO SELL DRUGS IN A PHYSICIAN'S DISGUISE.

The next morning Judge Dee rose early, and after having attended to his toilet and eaten some breakfast, he ordered his men to stand by at the place where the corpses were lying. There, in front of Koong's hostel, a large group of constables and other minions of the law had gathered. Judge Dee left his quarters, arrived at Koong's hostel, and seated himself behind the high bench of the temporary tribunal erected there. First he ordered Koong to be brought before him, and thus addressed him:

"Although you claim to be innocent of this murder, yet it is a fact that its roots lie in your hostel. You cannot, therefore, act as if this case did not concern you at all. We shall start by asking you the names of the victims, so that the inquest can proceed in the proper manner".

"When these two men", answered Koong, "came to my hostel last night, I asked them for their names. One said his surname was Liu, the other Shao. Since at the time they were unpacking their luggage, I did not have an opportunity for asking their personal names."

Judge Dee nodded and taking his vermillion brush, he wrote on a slip of paper: "One male person, of the surname Liu". Then he ordered the coroner to look over the corpse. The coroner, carrying the slip with Judge Dee's inscription respectfully with both hands in front of him, entered the court, and with the assistance of Djao San and the constables on duty, dragged the corpse lying on the left side to the center, in front of the bench. Then the coroner said:

"I beg that Koong Wan-deh be ordered to come forward, and identify this corpse as that of the man called Liu."

Judge Dee ordered Koong to do as required.

Koong, although he thought this a gruesome affair, could not but come forward, and approach the body all covered with blood. Trembling all over, with a great effort he collected himself, and gave it a good look. Then he said: "This indeed is the man Liu who stayed at my hostel last night."

The coroner thereupon spread a reed mat on the ground, and had the corpse placed on top of it. He washed it clean with hot water, and then looked over the body inch by inch. He thus reported to Judge Dee:

"One male corpse, one knife wound at the back of the shoulder, 2½ inches long, ½ inch broad. On the left side a wound caused by a kick, ½ inch deep, 5 inches in diameter. One knife wound in the throat, 3 inches long, ½ inch broad, a deep cut right through the windpipe".

This report was duly entered in the records by the coroner's assistants, and the document was placed on the desk of the judge.

After Judge Dee had pondered over this report for a few moments, he descended from his chair, and himself carefully looked over the corpse. Having verified the coroner's report as correct, he affixed his red seal to this document, and gave orders to place the corpse in a temporary coffin, and to put up an official notice to the public, asking all who knew the murdered man to present themselves at the tribunal.

Having resumed his seat behind the bench, he again wrote with his vermilion brush on a separate slip of paper: "One person, of the surname Shao". Then the coroner proceeded as before, and asked Koong to identify the body.

Koong approached with bowed head, and dared to look up only when he was right in front of the corpse. Then he suddenly started violently, his eyes bulged, and uttering some incoherent sounds, he swooned.

Judge Dee, knowing that some unexpected development was

about to occur, ordered Sergeant Hoong to assist Koong to regain his spirits, so that the inquest could be continued after he had given a full explanation.

A deep silence reigned, all spectators looking intently at Koong.

The sergeant made Koong sit up on the ground, and ordered his wife to bring a bowl of sweet tea quickly.

The crowd of spectators, who first had been fretting at this delay in the inquest, and had been thinking of returning home, now stayed where they were, eager to see further developments.

After a while Koong came to. He tried to speak, but only could bring out: "This....is all wrong, this....is a mistake!"

"Old man", Sergeant Hoong said to him, "His Excellency is waiting for your report. Now speak up, who has made a mistake?"

Then Koong said:

"This is the wrong corpse. The Mr. Shao of last night was a youngster, while this body is that of an elderly man with whiskers. How could he be the second guest? Evidently there is some mistake here. I pray Your Honor to clear this up".

Both the coroner and Sergeant Hoong were quite disturbed by this new development. They looked to Judge Dee for clarification. Judge Dee said:

"How can this be? These two corpses have been lying here all day, why did Koong not discover earlier that one was a stranger? Now at the inquest, at the very last moment, he changes his mind. This proves clearly that he is trying to cheat us".

He had Koong brought before him and angrily shouted at him to tell the truth.

Koong, in great trepidation, knocked his head on the ground several times, and said in a wailing voice:

"When Warden Pang tried to involve me in this affair, and threw the two corpses in front of my door, I was completely confused, and immediately rushed to the city to report. How could

I be expected first to look over those two corpses carefully? Moreover this second corpse was partly covered by that of Liu, and
having recognized that at first glance, I took it for granted that
the other body was that of Shao. How could I have foreseen this
development? I truly am innocent, and place my fate in Your
Honor's hands".

Judge Dee recalled that when he saw the corpses the day before,
one had actually been lying half over the other. Therefore he
thought it quite probable that Koong's mistake was unintentional.
On the other hand this did not tend to simplify the case. He ordered
Warden Pang to be brought in court, and Pang duly made his appearance, guarded by Chiao Tai and Ma Joong. Judge Dee said:

"You dogshead, you tamper with corpses and slander innocent
people. You said that Koong murdered these men, and yesterday you therefore moved their bodies from the market to here.
Thus you must have had ample opportunity for observing them.
Now speak up quickly, what did they look like?"

Warden Pang, who had already heard the news that there
had been some mistake about the corpses, now, being thus addressed by Judge Dee, greatly feared that he himself might be
accused of the crime. He hastened to come forward with the
truth, saying:

"I said that Koong was the murderer, only because the victims
had been staying in his hostel, and because the murder happened
to have been committed near there. One victim certainly was a
youngster, and the other an elderly person with whiskers. But
since Koong Wan-deh, displeased about my placing the corpses
in front of his door, immediately rushed to the city, I had no
opportunity to check with him whether he recognized both corpses.
Whether or not there is a mistake about the identity, I therefore
could not say, since I did not meet the two merchants when they
arrived at Koong's hostel the evening before".

Judge Dee ordered the constables to give Pang a second beating with the bamboo, pronouncing that Warden Pang had been guilty of entering a false accusation, and of trying to involve an innocent person.

Then he had the other three guests who were staying at Koong's hostel brought before him, and again questioned them. All the three of them confirmed that both merchants had been young men, and that the elderly victim had not stayed at the hostel; they could not identify him, and did not know how he met his death.

Then Judge Dee said:

"This being so, it is clear to me where we shall find the criminal".

He ordered the coroner to proceed with the inquest on the corpse of the unknown man. The coroner reported:

"One corpse of an unidentified male person, on the left arm a bruise mark, measuring 3 inches, and in the small of the back a wound caused by a kick, measuring 3 by 5 inches. Under the ribs a knife wound, 1¼ inches broad, 5½ inches long, and 2¼ inches deep. And one knife wound in the back, 2¾ inches long."

These details were duly noted down by the coroner's assistants.

When the formalities had been completed, Judge Dee said:

"Since this man was probably from this district the corpse is to be left here, in a temporary coffin. His relations and his friends may not be living far from here. I shall now affix my seal, and have a notice put up, calling upon those who knew the man to report to me. In due time, as soon as the criminal is arrested, the trial shall proceed!

"Koong Wan-deh is released on bail, but must present himself again at the tribunal when this case is tried, to testify as a witness. For the time being, Warden Pang Deh will be kept under detention".

Having issued these orders, Judge Dee then ascended his palanquin, and surrounded by the personnel of the tribunal, left Six Mile

Village and returned to the city.

There he first proceeded to the temple of the tutelary deity of the town, and he burned some incense.

Then he proceeded to the tribunal, and seated himself behind the bench. He called the roll of the court personnel, and finding everything in order, retired to his private office at the back of the court hall.

Taking up his writing brush, he first drew up a dispatch to the authorities of Kiangsu Province, giving a full description of the murdered man Liu, and asking them to try to locate his family and relations. Then he drafted a circular letter to the magistrates of the districts neighboring his own, with the request to have their men watch out for a man answering the description of Shao, the merchant who had disappeared.

He handed the drafts to his clerks to be written out and dispatched, and then called Chiao Tai and Ma Joong.

"This case has now become clear", he told them. "There can hardly be any doubt that that man Shao is the murderer. If this man is caught, then we can try him and close the case. So I now order you two to make a search for him, arrest him and bring him here without delay."

When Chiao Tai and Ma Joong had departed, Judge Dee called Sergeant Hoong. To him he spoke as follows:

"This unknown murdered man is probably an inhabitant of this district. You must make inquiries all over the countryside, and try to locate somebody who knows him. Further, I don't think that the murderer will have fled to some remote locality; probably he finds it safer first to remain in hiding somewhere in the country around here, delaying his escape till the hue and cry has died down. Thus at the same time you might make discreet inquiries about this man Shao".

Several days elapsed while Judge Dee waited for his detectives to return. But they neither appeared nor were they heard from.

At last Judge Dee became alarmed, and thought: "Since I assumed my office in this district, I have solved not a few intricate cases. How can it be that that which is apparently the last phase of this investigation, is so slow in materializing? It is best that I myself set out on a secret investigation to see whether I cannot trace this murderer".

So the next morning Judge Dee rose early, and disguised himself as an itinerant physician. Like all literati, he had a good knowledge of drugs and the arts of healing, so that he did not risk exposure through ignorance of the medical science. Moreover he knew that people in general will tell a doctor more than others. He also reasoned that it was probable that the murderer during the scuffle would have suffered some injuries himself, and, being in hiding, would rather invoke the help of an itinerant doctor, than of a local physician.

Shouldering a portable medicine chest well stocked with herbs, pills and powders, Judge Dee set out on his investigation.

Leaving the city by the South Gate, he strolled along the road leading to Six Mile Village. For a considerable time he loitered about in the marketplaces along this highroad, but nobody approached him.

"Perhaps", he thought, "I will have more success when I look for the portal of a large shop, and there display my drugs, in order to attract the people."

At last he arrived at a marketplace that, although not as bustling with people as the shopping centers in the town itself, yet was doing a fairly brisk business. For it was situated at the crossing of two highroads, where there was a constant coming and going of officials, tradesmen, and peddlers. In the northeast corner stood a large memorial archway, with the three words "Huang Hua Chen", "Imperial Glory Market" inscribed over it. Passing below this arch, he saw a three-storied building, with "Pawnshop" written in large characters on its signboard. Judge

Dee thought that the large portal of this shop was an excellent place for setting up his temporary consultation room. He unpacked his medicine chest, and spreading out a piece of cloth on the stoneflags, thereupon displayed his collection of drugs and herbs. Then he made a bow, and recited the following verses in a powerful voice:

> *Passers by from north and south, pause here for a little while.*
> *When you are in good health, you are apt to forget about illness.*
> *But skilled doctors are not easily found in this world,*
> *And when an ailment strikes you, it will find you unprepared.*

Then he continued:

"I humbly announce my surname as Jen, and my personal name as Djieh, and I am from Shansi Province. Since my youth I have been engrossed in the study of rare books on medicine, and fully mastered the secrets of the art of healing. Although I would not dare to rank myself with the celebrated physicians of remote antiquity, I yet dare to say that I know the tradition of later famous doctors. I feel the pulse of men and women, I know both internal medicine and surgery, and also am expert in diagnosing strange maladies. Please consult me, and you will find out for yourself. You will see me issue the right prescription, which will cure light maladies right here and now, while I guarantee that serious illness will be cured within three days. To-day I happen to be here on the request of an old patient who especially sent for me. And, my duty being to help all who are in need of my service, I now pray everyone among you who might be suffering from some disease, to come forward to be treated".

During the recital of this harangue, a large crowd of idlers had been gathering around him, and Judge Dee had been examining them carefully out of the corner of his eye. He noted that all of them seemed people of that neighborhood, happily chatting amongst each other. He particularly noticed an elderly woman, with bent back, who, wedged in between the other spectators, seemed eager to come forward. When he had finished his speech, this woman actually addressed him, saying:

"Since you, Master, are so well versed in the arts of healing, you must be able to cure this inveterate disease of mine."

"Certainly", Judge Dee said, "If I did not possess this skill, how would I dare to travel hither and thither, indulging in vain boasts? Just give me a clear description of your symptoms, and I shall cure you".

The woman said:

"The roots of my disease have embedded themselves here right in my heart. Could you cure this ailment?"

"What is impossible for me?", Judge Dee replied. "You have an ailment of the heart, and I have medicine for the heart. Turn your face to the light, and let me have a good look".

When she had turned her face to Judge Dee, he gave it but a casual look. For although he engaged in this business in the interests of justice, he still remained a high official, and she a woman unrelated to him, so that it was against the rules of propriety that he should allow her to come too close to him. He said:

"I know what is troubling you. Your skin is parched and sallow, and blue veins are standing out. This is a sure sign that your liver is inflamed, and your nervous system weakened. Sometime in the past you must have been in great mental anguish. Brooding over this, your liver became irritated, and your digestion became impaired. You have this ache in your heart region all the time, have not you?"

The woman hastened to answer:

"Master, you indeed are a physician of uncanny skill! I have been suffering from this malady now for a considerable time, but never yet has any doctor so accurately determined its cause. Since you have made now your diagnosis, do you think there is a medicine that can cure me?"

# Fourth Chapter

When Judge Dee saw that the woman believed in his medical skill, he thought he might as well find out something more about her case. Thus he asked her:

"You have been suffering from this ailment already for a long time. I take it that you have a husband and children, who could have called in a doctor for you? Why did they allow your disease to develop into a chronic malady?"

With a sigh the woman answered:

"It is sad to tell, but my husband died already many years ago. He left me one son, who now would have been twenty-eight years old. Formerly he had in this market a small shop of woollen and cotton goods. Eight years ago he married. Then, last year May, on the day of the Dragon Boat Festival, he stayed at home till noon, and thereafter took me, his wife and their small daughter for an outing, to see the Dragon Boat races on the river. That evening my son was still as cheerful as usual. But after dinner he suddenly complained of a violent pain in his stomach. I thought that he probably had caught a touch of the sun that afternoon on the river, and told his wife to bring him to bed. During the third nightwatch, I suddenly heard him cry out loudly, and then his wife rushed into my room crying that my son had died.

"This terrible calamity struck both myself and his wife as if the vault of Heaven had fallen down on us. Our family line had been broken off.

"Although we had this small shop, there was hardly any capital, so it was only with great difficulty that, by borrowing here and there, we could at last scrape together enough money for his burial.

When the corpse was going to be dressed, I noticed that the eyes were bulging from their sockets. This sorry sight increased my grief, nights and days I passed crying over my son. That is the way how I got this ailment of my heart".

Upon hearing this story, Judge Dee's trained mind forthwith spotted some suspicious features. "It may have been", he thought, "that this young man died from sunstroke. But how then to explain his crying out suddenly before he died, and why his eyes have been bulging from their sockets? There must be more there than meets the eye. I came here to-day for investigating further the double murder case, but perhaps it will turn out that instead of getting the murderer Shao, the only thing I get is a new case!"

To the woman he said:

"Now I have heard your story, I realize that your disease is even more serious than I had surmised. If only caused by melancholy, this illness, although still a major one, yet can be cured comparatively easily. But when a deep grief has started to gnaw at the heart and the bones, that is an illness that cannot be cured in a few moments. Now I have a drug here that will help you, but it is absolutely necessary that I boil it myself, to add the right quantity of water. Then only will this drug have its powerful effect. How could I perform this difficult task right here in the street? I do not know how serious you are to have this illness cured. Should you really want to get rid of the very roots of this malady, then the only way is that I go together with you to your house, and there prepare this potion for you."

The woman hesitated for quite some time, before she answered:

"If you, Master, kindly consent to go back with me, then I certainly want to be delivered from this ailment. But there is one problem which I should first discuss with you. After the death of my son, his wife has strictly preserved a chaste widowhood. She even refuses to see anybody who is not a near relative. After noon each day she locks herself within her room, and should strangers as much as enter the house, from within her room she scolds me no end, crying 'Mother, why do you let these people in this house where there is a young woman?'. Thus our male relatives, knowing my daughter's firm resolution never to remarry, do not visit our house, and recently also our female relations have stopped coming. Thus nowadays my daughter and I are always alone in the house. In the morning we work together at our household tasks, but after noon each of us stays in her own room. If you should consent to come, you will, therefore, have to prepare the medicine in the courtyard, and I shall have to ask you to leave immediately after. Else my daughter will start quarreling with me again".

This information made Judge Dee all the more suspicious that there was some strange secret here. He thought "It is true that fortunately there are not a few constant widows in our Empire; but this young widow is overdoing it. That she won't allow men to come to the house and talk to her, this of course is the proper behavior. But that she refuses to see other women, and moreover locks herself in her room every afternoon, that is highly suspicious. I shall go with this woman to that house, and have a look what this daughter-in-law of hers is really up to." Then he said to the woman:

"That your daughter is such a constant widow is indeed worthy of the greatest praise and admiration. I shall stay at your place just long enough to prepare your medicine, and leave immediately after, without even drinking a cup of tea, or insisting on the other amenities".

The woman, seeing that Judge Dee consented, was overjoyed, and said:

"I shall first go home alone, and explain to my daughter, and then come back here".

Judge Dee, fearing lest her daughter would not allow her to

come back, said quickly:

"That would not do. After having prepared your medicine, I must hurry on to the city, to attend to my business there. You make a lot of conditions, despite the fact that, as I presume, you have not enough money to give me a suitable fee for my trouble. Yet I am willing to go with you, taking as my sole reward the enhancing of my reputation as a skilful physician. But then we must start right now".

Then he gathered up his drugs and herbs, and, having with a deep bow taken leave of the crowd of spectators, he departed together with the woman.

They passed through some narrow alleys, and then came to a small modest dwelling in a backstreet. A girl about seven years old, who had been standing in front of the door, came running to meet them with evident joy, as soon as she saw them approaching from afar. With one hand she took the woman by her sleeve, and with the other she gesticulated wildly; but the only utterance she made were some incoherent sounds.

Judge Dee, seeing that this young girl was dumb, said:

"Who is this girl that has lost the power of speech? Was she born this way?"

But the woman had already opened the front door, and hurried inside, apparently to apprise her daughter in advance of their arrival. Judge Dee feared that the daughter-in-law would disappear before he would be able to catch a glimpse of her, so he quickly followed the woman inside. At the back of the courtyard he saw a one-storied dwelling of three rooms next to each other. The door of the room on right opened, the occupant evidently having heard the sound of the frontdoor; she looked through the half open door, right into the face of Judge Dee.

He thus saw this daughter-in-law. She was a woman of about thirty, wearing a simple house dress, and not yet made up; but this did not hamper her voluptuous beauty. Judge Dee could well imagine that one glance of her would be enough to make men dizzy. Her forehead was snow-white and beautifully shaped, and her cheeks were a rosy color.

On seeing a stranger entering the courtyard, she hastily withdrew into her room with a cry of annoyance, and immediately locked the door. From within Judge Dee heard her scolding her mother-in-law, crying:

"You wicked old woman, now you bring even a miserable quack to our house. After a few days of quiet, I shall again have to quarrel with you the whole evening. Why do I deserve this bad luck?"

Hearing this language, Judge Dee thought that he could make a good guess at what was really going on there. "This young woman must be a bad person", he thought, "and up to nothing good. Now that I have gone as far as this, I shall not leave here before I know something more, no matter how I am cursed and reviled."

He sat down on a seat in the courtyard, and said politely:

"This humble person is now visiting your mansion for the first time, and has not yet even inquired your honorable name. And that young girl who came to meet us is, I presume, your worthy granddaughter".

"Our surname", the woman answered, "is Bee. My late husband was called Bee Chang-shan, and my son was called Bee Hsun. Alas, after his demise he only left me this small granddaughter of seven years old".

Thus speaking she drew the young girl close to her, and started crying. Judge Dee said:

"Madam, it is already quite late now, please bring me a portable tea stove, so that I can boil the medicine. But, by the way, as a doctor I am interested in this case of your granddaughter. How did it come about that she lost her power of speech?"

Mrs. Bee said: "This is all part of the terrible fate that befell our house. This girl, when still a baby, showed promise of great talents. She was very clever, and when she was four she was talking all the time. But two months after her father's death, one morning on waking she was found stricken with dumbness. Since that day, although she understands everything well enough, she has not been able to utter one single intelligible word. That such a nice and promising child should change overnight into such a useless creature, is that not a great misfortune?"

Judge Dee inquired:

"In whose room was she sleeping at the time she became dumb? Could somebody have robbed her of her power of speech by administering some drug to her? You should investigate this properly, for if it should turn out that some evil person really made her dumb with a drug, I have means of curing her".

Before Mrs. Bee could answer, her daughter was heard calling from her room:

"In broad daylight, this fellow is trying to swindle good people out of their money, just by talking some palpable nonsense. Who could possibly have drugged my daughter, who never leaves my eyes? Since olden times till the present, there have been doctors of all descriptions, but I have never yet heard of a doctor who could cure dumbness. You old woman, you only dragged this quack here to be entertained by his attempts at doctoring you, without even having inquired previously as to what kind of man this fellow is. This is indeed a poor way of showing sympathy with my grief over the loss of my husband".

Mrs. Bee, thus reviled, did not dare to say one word in return.

Judge Dee thought: "That daughter of hers is certainly engaged in some nefarious scheme. Her mother-in-law does not know this, simply because she is a stupid woman; she thinks that her daughter is really intent only on preserving her chaste widowhood. But I, on the other hand, suspect that she killed her husband. For really chaste widows are also loyal daughters-in-law; honoring their husband, they also show proper concern over the health of their husband's mother. So why did this young woman do nothing to have her mother-in-law's disease cured? And also, why did she do nothing about the dumbness of her own small daughter? Moreover, on hearing that someone can cure her, instead of being filled with joy, she not only does not show the slightest interest, but even starts cursing and scolding. These two inconsistencies constitute a valuable clue. I had better not press the matter further now, however, lest I rouse the woman's suspicions. After having returned to the tribunal, I shall start making careful inquiries."

Rising from his chair, he said aloud:

"Although I am but a travelling doctor, I still expect that people show me due respect, else I must refuse to treat them. Now this daughter-in-law of yours without any reason insults me, who am not asking one copper for my services. I therefore don't see why I should thus help you. You had better look for some other doctor".

He then took his leave. Mrs. Bee did not dare to beg him to reconsider his decision, she silently conducted him to the door.

When Judge Dee had returned to the market, the sun was setting. Since it was too late to return to the city, he decided to stay there over night. He would return to Chang-ping the next morning, meanwhile trying to gather some more information in that locality.

He found a large hostel right opposite the market, and entered there. A waiter came forward, and inquired whether he would like to rent a bed, or have a room all to himself. Judge Dee saw that the courtyard of the hostel was crowded with sedan-chairs and carts. As he did not like to be packed in one room with a number of other people, he said:

"I am alone, but since I am planning to engage in my trade in this place for a couple of days to get together some travelling funds, I would like to rent one single room".

The waiter, learning that the doctor was going to see patients and sell drugs, which would give him many opportunities for earning a commission, quickly answered with a polite "Yes, Sir", and led Judge Dee inside, to a guestroom on the second courtyard.

The waiter tidied up the room for Judge Dee, and as he had no bedroll with him, the waiter went and rented bedding for him in the hostel's office. When he had made the bed, he asked whether Judge Dee had already had his dinner. Judge Dee ordered two dishes of simple but good food, and a pot of wine.

The waiter first brought a cup of hot tea, and then went to fetch the food. When Judge Dee had finished his dinner, he reflected that since there were so many guests staying in the hostel, there was just a chance that he might learn there something about the murderer of Six Mile Village. He strolled out into the courtyard, and saw that although the paper lanterns were being lighted, there still was a constant coming and going of guests.

Scrutinizing this bustling crowd, he noticed a man who, as soon as he had seen Judge Dee, stood still and made as if he would greet him.

Judge Dee had instantly recognized this person, and before the other could say anything, Judge Dee quickly called out:

"Honorable Mr. Hoong, whence have you come? It is fortunate indeed that I should thus happen to meet you here. Please come inside with me, Sir, so that we can have a chat".

## Fifth Chapter

A CONVERSATION IN A BATHHOUSE REVEALS NEW FACTS;
IN A GRAVEYARD A PRAYER CALLS UP A LOST SOUL.

Now the man whom Judge Dee addressed was nobody other
than Sergeant Hoong. Ordered by Judge Dee to search in the
vicinity of the town for the murderer of Six Mile Village, he had
been looking around for several days, without, however, finding
any clue. That day he had been making inquiries in the market
place, and then, the hour being late, had decided to stay over night
in that very same hostel. Fearing lest he betray Judge Dee's identity, he followed his cue, and addressing him like an old friend, said:

"I never thought that I would meet you here. I shall be glad
to chat with you for a while inside".

Judge Dee took him to his room on the second courtyard, and
bade him enter. Sergeant Hoong first carefully locked the door,
and then inquired respectfully:

"When did Your Honor arrive here?"

Judge Dee said quickly:

"We are in a hostel, and the walls have ears. So don't address
me thus again. Now, tell me how matters stand".

Sergeant Hoong sadly shook his head, and said in a low voice:

"Following your instructions, I have been searching diligently
for several days, but could not discover anything. I fear that this
man Shao has already left the neighborhood. Perhaps Ma Joong
and Chiao Tai have had better luck".

Judge Dee said:

"While this double murder is not yet solved, today I discovered
something in this locality that may well turn out to be a new
case. Tonight we must gather some more information about it,
so that tomorrow I can start an investigation".

Then he told Hoong Liang about his encounter with Mrs. Bee,

and related what had happened. Sergeant Hoong observed:

"Although this affair certainly looks very suspicious, nobody has filed an accusation, while there is no evidence of a crime having been committed. How then can we open this case?"

"That", Judge Dee answered, "is precisely the reason why we need some more information. Later this evening, you might go to the street where Mrs. Bee lives, and see whether you can discover anything about what is going on there. Furthermore you should gather some more details in that neighborhood about the death of Bee Hsun, and where he has been buried."

He then had some food brought in for the sergeant, and when he had finished his dinner, they waited till the first nightwatch. Then Sergeant Hoong called the waiter and told him to bring a pot of hot tea and help Judge Dee with his evening toilet. "I myself", he added in a familiar tone, "am now going out to see a friend, but I shall be back presently".

The waiter, hearing him speak thus, had not the slightest idea that these two were the district magistrate and one of his subordinates. He did as he was told, and Sergeant Hoong left the hostel.

Following Judge Dee's directions, he found his way through various narrow and winding alleys without difficulty, and finally came to the street where Mrs. Bee lived. He walked up and down that street several times, but everything was as silent as the grave, and there were no passers by. He thought that it was probably too early in the evening, and went back to the market; after having had a look around there, he would return to the house of Mrs. Bee.

The market shops had not yet closed their doors for the night, and the streets were brightly illuminated by countless paper lanterns. Since the market was situated on the crossing of two highways, the place was still full of people.

Loitering about there, Sergeant Hoong came to a large public bathhouse. He thought: "What about entering here and taking a bath? Such a place is always full of idle people, and therefore most suitable for picking up some information". He went in.

The bathhouse was indeed overcrowded, both pools being occupied by a number of bathers, who sat in the hot water. But he succeeded in finding an empty place on top of the large stone oven-bench by the side of the pools, and there squatted down. He said to the bath-attendant:

"How far is this market from the city of Chang-ping, and how many bath houses have you got around here?"

The attendant, seeing that this man was a newcomer to this locality, answered:

"It is about five miles to the city. Are you planning to go there tonight?"

"I have a relative there whom I wanted to visit. I suppose that this village here comes under the jurisdiction of the magistrate of Chang-ping. Who is the present magistrate, and has there been happening anything of interest here of late?"

The attendant was glad to find somebody who had not yet heard the great news, and said: "Our magistrate is the famous Judge Dee, one of the best in the empire. As to the news, it is just too bad that you did not come here a few days earlier. Then you could have seen something!" Thereupon he related with great relish the double murder of Six Mile Village, and what had happened during the inquest.

Sergeant Hoong showed suitable interest, and then took off his clothes, and enjoyed a good soaking in the hot water. Drying himself on the oven, he resumed his conversation with the attendant:

"I have heard", he said, "that the Dragon Boat races are especially good in this locality. But I was told also that last year there was a dangerous epidemic here right during the festival, and that not a few people who went to see the races caught it and died miserably".

The attendant laughed, and said:

"You are telling jokes, stranger! I have been born and bred in this place, and I have never even heard about such an occurrence. Who tried to fool you thus?"

"When I first heard it", the sergeant said, "I doubted it myself. But then the fellow came with proof, and said that a certain Mr. Bee of this place had died directly after he had come back from the races. Now what about that?"

Before the bath attendant could answer, a young man of about eighteen years old who was sitting nearby said:

"Yes, that is actually true. But that man did not die because he went to see the races. According to what I heard, he died during the night from a stomach-attack".

Then a third guest said to the attendant:

"That certainly was a rather strange affair. How could it be that a strong fellow like young Bee, who that very day was still in perfect health, suddenly cries out once in the middle of the night, and then dies immediately? And remember, when his corpse was dressed, the eyes were bulging from their sockets in a perfectly gruesome manner. There are also people who say that strange apparitions are often seen near his grave. No wonder that people here have their doubts about his death. Have you seen that widow of his?"

The attendant said: "Now, now, you must not talk nonsense. That she, still such an attractive person, remains so true to her dead husband, and does not even once leave her house, that proves that she is faithful. How else could she endure all this? And as to the weird apparitions in the graveyard, out there at Gao-djia-wa are any number of tombs. How do you know that these ghosts have anything to do with young Bee?"

The other said: "I was just indulging in some random talk. We in this world are like floating clouds passing before the eye.

Today we are here, and tomorrow we may be dead. And then, after Bee Hsun had died his young daughter was stricken with dumbness. What a sad story".

So saying he put on his clothes, and left the bathhouse.

Sergeant Hoong concluded that this young man knew much about the Bee affair, and asked the attendant:

"Who is this gentleman? He seems a pleasant and honest fellow".

"He is a shopkeeper of this market", the attendant answered, "and formerly Bee Hsun had a small shop of woollen and cotton goods right next to his. His name is Wang, and since all of us have known him since he was born, we call him Little Wang. He is not too clever and loves to blurt out everything that comes to his mind, but he does not mean any harm".

Sergeant Hoong made some appropriate reply and, after having given the attendant a generous tip, he left the bathhouse.

He first returned to Mrs. Bee's house. On the way he reflected that although the features of the case had become outlined somewhat more clearly, there still was not yet a shred of proof; so how would the judge be able to go on with this case?

He again loitered about for half an hour or so in the narrow street where Mrs. Bee lived, but everything was perfectly quiet, and he could find no indication that anything was going on there. He went back to the hostel, and reported in detail to Judge Dee what he had heard in the bathhouse. Judge Dee said:

"Our best course evidently is to go to the graveyard of Gao-djia-wa tomorrow, and have a look there".

The next morning Judge Dee and Sergeant Hoong rose early, and having breakfasted together, they paid the waiter a few pieces of silver and left the hostel, Judge Dee shouldering his portable medicine chest.

They asked an old man on the road for the way, and after a brisk walk they arrived at a barren plot of land, overgrown with weeds. Bleached bones were lying about everywhere, and all around were the earthen mounds of tombs.

Sergeant Hoong looked disconsolately around, and said:

"Now that Your Honor has arrived here, how are we to find Bee Hsun's tomb among all these grave mounds?"

Judge Dee said gravely:

"I, the magistrate, have come here with the express purpose of avenging his death. Now although the living and the dead are living in worlds apart, I still believe that if my intention is earnest and true, the dead man will succeed in giving us some sign. If Bee Hsun died a natural death, we shall probably not find his grave. But if he was dastardly murdered, his soul must still be hovering about near his dead body, and will manifest itself in some way or other".

Then, standing there among the graves, Judge Dee sank in an earnest silent prayer.

By this time it was just noon. Suddenly the light of the sun darkened, and a violent gust of wind blew over the graveyard, making sand and stones whirl in the air for more than a fathom. Then there appeared a dark shape of indistinct outline, floating towards them in midair.

Seeing this weird phenomenon, Sergeant Hoong's face turned ashen, his hairs stood on end as he tried to hide himself behind the judge.

Judge Dee, however, remained unmoved, and said in a solemn voice:

"I, Judge Dee, know that you have suffered a grievous wrong. But I cannot proceed to redress it without knowing your grave. I ask you to show us the way".

Then a new gust of wind blew the shape about among the gravemounds, and Judge Dee and the sergeant followed it, till it stopped near a lonely mound, standing somewhat apart from the others. Then suddenly it disappeared, the wind ceased and everything was normal again.

Judge Dee and the sergeant examined the mound, and saw that it seemed fairly recent.

Judge Dee said:

"A communication from the dead has directed us here. Now you had better go and find the undertaker or someone else around here, to make sure that we have not been fooled by some evil ghost, and that Bee Hsun really was buried under this mound. I shall wait for you here".

Sergeant Hoong was still feeling far from well, and he set out alone rather reluctantly. After half an hour or so he returned together with an old fellow with a grey beard. That man immediately thus addressed Judge Dee:

"You drug-peddler, you must be a very dumb fellow. Finding on the market nobody who would buy your pills, are you now trying to do business on this lonely graveyard? I was peacefully working on my field, when this man of yours came and dragged me along, saying that you wanted to ask me something. Now speak up, what does all this mean?"

Judge Dee, disguised as an itinerant physician, asks the old undertaker about Bee Hsun's grave. Sergeant Hoong is standing by on left.

## Sixth Chapter

AN OLD MAN INDULGES IN DISRESPECTFUL LANGUAGE;
JUDGE DEE INITIATES THE OFFICIAL INVESTIGATION.

Judge Dee said:

"Keep a civil tongue. Although I am but a traveling doctor without any reputation, I yet am not as stupid as all that. My coming here has a definite reason. In my opinion this graveyard is situated very favorably from a geomantic point of view. If a man is buried here, within ten years after his death his sons and grandsons shall greatly flourish.* Therefore I want to ask you whether you know who the owner of this plot of land is and whether he would be willing to sell".

When the greybeard heard this, he just sneered, turned round and wanted to walk away. But Sergeant Hoong ran after

---

* *Translator's note.* According to a very old Chinese belief, the entire universe is maintained and regulated by the unceasing interaction of two primordial forces, one negative, and the other positive. Localities where these two forces are deemed to meet in a harmonious manner, are favorable for human beings to dwell, and when a dead body is buried in such a place, the soul of the deceased shall enjoy great bliss in the Hereafter. In a country like China, where filial piety and ancestor-worship play such a paramount role, the latter fact especially is of supreme importance. Moreover, if the dead are buried in an auspicious place, they will use their influence in the Nether World to benefit their descendants. Geomancy, therefore, is a science in itself, which boasts of an extensive special literature. If a grave is disturbed, this harmonious interaction of the two primordial forces loses its balance, and the peace of the dead is menaced. The ancient Chinese Penal Code therefore mentions the desecration of a grave as a heinous crime, punishable by death. Hence Chinese magistrates are extremely reluctant to order an exhumation. For should it turn out to have been unnecessary, the official who issued the exhumation order risks dismissal from his post, or even heavier punishment. The reader will have to bear these facts in mind while following the further developments of this case.

him, gripped him by his jacket, and shouted angrily at him:

"Don't think that your advanced age gives you the liberty to pick a quarrel with anybody you choose! If you were twenty years younger, I would give you a sound thrashing right here and now, and see whether you then still dare to insult people. You are not dumb, are you? Now answer a civil question, and quickly!"

The greybeard, in the firm clutch of the sergeant, could not but obey.

"It is not", he said, "that I do not want to speak with your master, but he must at least talk reasonably. Now he says that this is a very auspicious graveyard; but how then do you explain that all the families that were buried here died out long ago? Don't you see the neglected condition these tombs are in? Since last year's burial, neither I nor the other undertakers have seen one single person who came to visit that last grave. And the daughter of the man buried there was stricken with dumbness shortly after her father's death! How can you possibly say that this graveyard is auspicious from the geomantic point of view? Is that not pure nonsense?"

Sergeant Hoong said:

"You must be wrong. Although we don't belong to the local people, we come here very often. That family where the young daughter turned dumb was that of Bee Hsun. Now do you mean to say that the man buried under this mound is that selfsame Bee?"

"Fortunately you seem to know that at least," the old man said sourly. "If he is not called Bee, then you must have altered his surname for him. Now this old man has some work to do on his field, I have no time for idle talk. If you don't believe me, you had better go to the village and ask the people there".

Then he wrenched himself loose, and quickly walked away.

Judge Dee, having waited till the old man was out of earshot, said:

"There can be no doubt any longer that this Bee was done to death in dastardly manner, as is clearly proved by the manifestation of his ghost which we witnessed a while ago. Let us return to the city".

They walked back to the market, and ate a hasty luncheon together in a small inn. Then they set out on the highway and reached the city just before nightfall. Having entered the tribunal by the backdoor, Judge Dee sat down in his private office.

In the meantime the constables of the court, and the other members of Judge Dee's retinue, had become anxious when the judge did not appear in court for two successive days. They were just busily discussing whether it was possible that the judge had left on a private investigation in connection with the double murder, in the court hall, when Judge Dee suddenly emerged on the dais, and seated himself behind the bench.

After having called the roll, he first inquired whether Ma Joong and Chiao Tai had returned. The constables reported that they had come back the night before, but on hearing that the judge was away, they had again set out to continue their search. As yet there had been no report.

Judge Dee nodded, and told them to bring in the runner on day-duty. When he had come before the bench, Judge Dee said:

"I have here an official summons. Early to-morrow you take this to Huang-hua Village, and bring the local warden here. While there, you also go to a place nearby, called Gao-djia-wa, and tell the undertaker in charge of the graveyard there to accompany you here together with the warden. I shall question them during the morning session of the tribunal".

The runner went to the guardhouse and said to the guards who were sitting about there:

"The last two days have been nice and quiet, we have not heard about one single new case. And now suddenly there is this job to do. What can our judge have heard that he thus rushes

me to Huang-hua Village? Who is the warden there anyway?"
One of the guards said:

"Have you forgotten that man Ho Kai? Last year, when he received the appointment of warden of Huang-hua Village, he entertained all of us at a fine dinner party. Have you forgotten all this? Go to-morrow to Huang-hua Village and you are sure to find him. And you had better hurry. You know our boss".

The runner went home to have a good rest, and early the next morning hastened to Huang-hua Village. He first went to the house of Warden Ho Kai, and had him send an assistant to Gao-djia-wa, to fetch the undertaker there. In the meantime he had a good luncheon with the warden at the latter's expense. They had just finished their meal when the old undertaker was brought in. Then the constable took both the old man and the warden back to the city.

The noon session of the tribunal had opened and Judge Dee was sitting behind the bench. He first addressed Warden Ho Kai:

"Has nothing occurred in your village since you were appointed warden? Why are you so negligent about your duties, that you have failed to report?"

Warden Ho knew now that Judge Dee thought he had discovered some crime committed in his village, and hastened to reply:

"This insignificant person was appointed in March last year, and early in April assumed his post. Since then I have diligently executed my duties. But since Your Honor has assumed this office, the lower functionaries are honest and the people at peace, so that in my village there was nothing to report. How would I dare to neglect my duties since I was deemed worthy of being honored by receiving this appointment? I beg Your Honor's favorable consideration".

Judge Dee said:

"Since you say that you assumed your duties in April, why then

are you ignorant of the fact that in the following May a murder
was committed in your village?"

Warden Ho Kai, on hearing this, felt as if a tub of cold water
had suddenly been poured over his head. In great confusion
he said:

"I make my rounds regularly every day and night, but never
knew of such a case. If such a heinous crime had actually
occurred, how would I have dared to keep it secret and not have
reported it to Your Honor?"

Judge Dee said:

"For the time being I shall not press you further. But how did
Bee Hsun of your village meet his death? You are the warden,
you must know something about this. Tell me the truth quickly!"

Warden Ho Kai answered:

"I always thought that in my function there were on the one
hand things that should be reported, and on the other routine
matters that I need not report. Now several hundred families
live in my village. There is not a single day that I don't get
a notice of a marriage, a burial, or the birth of a child. I could
see nothing out of the ordinary in Bee Hsun's death; his relatives
did not report that there was anything suspicious about his demise,
neither did the neighbors file any complaint or accusation. I
know only that he died last year on the day of the Dragon Boat
Festival. This is the complete truth."

Judge Dee shouted angrily:

"You dogshead, be more careful about your duties! I know
the truth, and you keep quibbling. This is sufficient to give me
a very good general idea of your conception of your duty".

Having thus scolded Warden Ho Kai, Judge Dee had the old
undertaker brought before him.

That greybeard trembled in abject fright. Kneeling in front
of the bench he said:

"I old man am the undertaker of Gao-djia-wa, and respectfully greet Your Honor".

Judge Dee, seeing him so submissive, could hardly conceal a smile remembering his rude behavior on the day before. He asked:

"What is your name, and how long have you been undertaker there?"

"I old man am called Tao..." started the greybeard, but the constables standing by his side immediately shouted at him: "You old dog, you insolent yokel. How dare you use the expression 'I old man' when reporting to His Excellency? Don't you know you have to say 'the insignificant person' when standing before your magistrate? Here, we shall let you have a few with the bamboo, whether you are old or not".

Thus barked at by the constables, the greybeard in great consternation hastily said:

"This insignificant person deserves to die. I have been an undertaker now for the last thirty years. How can I serve Your Excellency?"

Judge Dee said:

"Look up at me, and see whether you recognize your magistrate".

The undertaker looked up timidly, and seeing Judge Dee thought that his soul was going to leave his body. He knocked his head on the floor several times and wailed:

"This insignificant person deserves to die! I did not know that yesterday I was addressing Your Honor. But believe me, henceforward I shall never again be rude to anybody who comes to that accursed graveyard!"

Hearing these words, the constables and other court attendants knew for the first time that Judge Dee had been out there himself on a secret investigation. Thereupon Judge Dee said:

"Now tell me exactly the circumstances of Bee Hsun's burial; tell me who brought the coffin, and all you know about this affair".

"Everytime a family comes to the graveyard to have somebody buried", the old undertaker said, "they give me two hundred coppers for digging the grave, and making the mound over it. Last year, three days after the Dragon Boat Festival, a coffin was brought to the graveyard, accompanied by two women. They said that the dead man was Bee Hsun from the village, and that one lady was his old mother, and the other his widow. I first planned to bury that coffin right among the other tombs. But when I had dug the hole, and was going to shove the coffin into it, I heard a sound inside. That gave me quite a fright, and I asked the women whether they were sure he was really dead, and what had been his malady. Before the mother could say a word, the widow started scolding me, shouting that things had come to a bad pass if decent people were not allowed to bury their dead in peace any more. Then the old woman also went for me. Now I found it awkward to quarrel with two women, but on the other hand I was not going to let myself become involved in trouble, if later it should turn out that this man had not died a natural death, and if an exhumation were to be ordered. Thus I selected an easily recognizable spot, somewhat apart from the other tombs, and there buried the coffin. Thereafter, however, every night I heard ghostly cries near that spot, which never let me sleep in peace. That I was so rude to Your Honor yesterday, was simply because I have a deadly fear of that particular spot, and did not wish to tarry there. That is what I have actually seen and heard. But as to the manner of Bee Hsun's death, I am completely ignorant. I beg Your Honor's favorable consideration."

Judge Dee said:

"This being so, you may return home. But see to it that in due time you stand by in the graveyard."

Then Judge Dee wrote out a Court order, and told Sergeant Hoong to go to Huang-hua Village that same night and summon Mrs. Bee and her daughter to appear for questioning at the noon session of the tribunal that very same day. After having given this order, Judge Dee retired to his private office.

The constables shook their heads, and said: "We have been visiting Huang-hua Village at least six or seven times every month, but we have never heard about this case! Certainly our judge has long ears! But he is really overdoing it, the double murder of Six Mile Village is not yet solved, and already he is working on a new case! What a hard life we have! And tell me, is there, among those concerned with all these cases, one person from whom we can squeeze a few coppers?"

Thus muttering amongst each other, they prepared to accompany Sergeant Hoong to Huang-hua Village.

MRS. BEE DENIES THAT HER SON HAS BEEN MURDERED; JUDGE DEE'S FIRST INTERROGATION OF BEE HSUN'S WIDOW.

Early the following morning Sergeant Hoong and two constables, having stayed at Huang-hua Village overnight, went to Mrs. Bee's house and knocked loudly on the door. From within Mrs. Bee called out:

"Who is knocking on the door at such an early hour?"

She came to open the door, and seeing three tall fellows standing outside she quickly placed herself in the doorway to prevent them from entering, saying:

"You surely must know that there is no man in this household, but only two poor widows. Who are you, who come to disturb us this early in the morning?"

One of the constables said: "We have come here on orders, and certainly not for our own pleasure! Imagine that at this very hour we could be sleeping nicely at home! Why do you think we rush out to this dismal place? For exercise? We have a Court Order from His Excellency the Judge, instructing the sergeant here to take you and your daughter to the tribunal at Chang-ping immediately, for questioning during the noon session. So don't stand there in our way!"

Thus speaking he pushed Mrs. Bee back and they entered the courtyard. Seeing the door of the middle room open, they went in and there seated themselves. The door of the room on right remained firmly closed.

Sergeant Hoong then produced the Court order, and said:

"This is official business, which brooks no delay. Where is your daughter-in-law? Tell her to show up, and accompany us to the tribunal. Talking won't help you."

Mrs. Bee, hearing that they came on behalf of the district magistrate, started trembling all over, and wailed:

"We never have done anything we should not, and now you want us to go before the judge! Probably some of our creditors have filed a suit against us because we have not yet returned their money? Please gentlemen, have pity on this poor house. Since my son died, it is only with great difficulty that we scrape together just enough for our daily needs. How can we repay the debts we incurred to meet the costs of the funeral immediately? Although we are but small people, we never before suffered the disgrace of being taken by the officers of the law. Please gentlemen, show some human kindness, and first return to the tribunal without us. You can report to the judge that we shall quickly sell our furniture and clothes, and then pay off our debts. Please show some consideration, and don't drag us off to the tribunal!"

Having thus spoken, Mrs. Bee burst out crying bitterly. Sergeant Hoong, seeing that she was an honest woman, said not unkindly:

"You need not worry, it is not your creditors who have filed a suit against you. Our judge only wishes to see your daughter-in-law, to ask her a few questions. You just produce her, then we shall leave you in peace, and only take her to the tribunal".

But even before he had quite finished, Mrs. Bee cried out:

"I don't believe you fellows are really constables! First you say both of us must go with you, then you say that only my daughter need go. You must be kidnapers who, knowing that there are no men here in this house to protect us, plan to abduct my daughter. I know your sort, you first rape her and then sell her to a brothel. But in order to get my daughter, you will have to kill me first!"

And she went for the sergeant. The patience of the constables was exhausted, and they dragged her roughly away, and planted her on a chair, saying:

"You old woman, are you so stupid that you don't see that it is only his kindness that makes the sergeant here say that you need not go? And have you not seen this summons, written out by His Excellency himself? Would you say that this is false too? You are so stupid that one need not wonder that this daughter-in-law of yours completely fools you. If His Excellency in his wisdom had not discovered this, your own life would probably have been in danger soon!"

With all this excitement none of them had noticed that during the altercation the sidedoor had opened, and that young Mrs. Bee had been standing there for some time, hearing every word that was said.

"Mother", she said now, "leave them alone, and let me ask them some questions. First, is it not that you have only a summons, and no warrant for arresting us? And second, is it not true that nobody has filed an accusation against us? Well then, neither my mother nor I have ever offended against the law. Have the ancients not said so well: 'Although the steel sword is sharp, it shall not cut off the head of the innocent?' Now although the judge admittedly is the magistrate of this district, he should not indulge in making unreasonable demands. When the Imperial Court hears about a widow who died remaining true to her husband, the government often erects a memorial temple in her honor and the high officials sacrifice there every spring and autumn. There is not the slightest reason to send constables to arrest us, two bereft widows. If the judge wants to ask us something, he has only to say so. We have committed no crime, and we are not afraid to appear in court and state so publicly. But we are not going to let ourselves be dragged away like this. And if you force us to go, then we shall refuse to leave the court again before this affair has been fully cleared up, and then the judge won't be able to say that we didn't obey his orders".

On hearing this eloquent speech, every word of which hit the mark, the two constables were dumbfounded, and looked to Sergeant Hoong for dealing with this affair. The sergeant said smiling:

"Well, well, young lady, for a person so young you certainly know how to talk. I now understand how you could perpetrate such amazing crimes. As to what is the real charge against you, I, young lady, am not the magistrate of Chang-ping. The only thing I know is how to execute a warrant for an arrest. If you want to know anything more, you can ask your questions in court. You can never intimidate us with your clever tongue."

Thus speaking he gave a sign to the constables, who took young Mrs. Bee by her arms, and dragged her out of the room, without letting her say another word. Old Mrs. Bee, unable to resist the constables, threw herself on the floor in despair. But without giving her as much as one look, the sergeant and the constables took her daughter away.

A crowd of villagers had assembled in the street, curious to know what was happening. The sergeant called out to them:

"We are taking this woman to the tribunal for questioning, on the orders of His Excellency, the magistrate of Chang-ping. If you people hinder us in the execution of our duty, you will certainly get involved in this case. And let me tell you that it is not a small case either!"

Thus admonished the crowd dispersed quickly, since no one wanted to become involved in a court case.

The sergeant and his party hastened on to Chang-ping, and arrived at the tribunal at noon.

When their arrival was reported to Judge Dee, he ordered them to wait in the court hall. Then he donned his official robe and cap, the curtain of the dais was drawn, and the judge appeared seated behind the bench. Looking at the scribes and the constables lined up below, Judge Dee ordered in a loud voice: "Bring in the criminal!" The constables shouted: "We obey!" and bringing forward the young Mrs. Bee, made her kneel in front of the bench.

But this impressive court ceremonial did not overawe Mrs. Bee. Before Judge Dee could address her, she spoke:

"This insignificant woman, Mrs. Bee *née* Djou, respectfully knocks her head down to greet Your Honor. I was brought here on a warrant issued by Your Honor, and beg to be apprised of my crime. I am a young, bereft widow and cannot remain kneeling on this stone floor for long."

Judge Dee, incensed at such insolence, said angrily:

"You, woman, dare to use the words 'bereft widow'? You can fool your stupid old mother, but not me, a judge. Look up, and see who I am!" Mrs. Djou—as we shall now call her—looked up and got a bad fright. "That," she thought, "is that doctor who came to our place the other day. Now I understand why I distrusted him that very first time, and why I kept wondering all these days what had been wrong about that doctor." But although in her heart she was quite alarmed, she showed nothing of her consternation on her face, and said in a firm voice:

"The other day I did not know that Your Honor was that doctor and spoke some impolite words. I offended you unintentionally and you should not hold this against me. Your Honor enjoys the fame of being a just magistrate. How could such a small thing like this anger you?"

Judge Dee shouted:

"You lewd woman, you don't know me yet! While your husband was still young, you should have lived happily with him, and so have grown old together. Why did you form an illicit relationship, and thereafter murder your own husband? But know that he, your husband, finding no rest in his grave, has accused you before me. Don't you know that for a woman to murder her husband is one of the most heinous crimes known to the law? Now confess how you killed your husband, and who your lover is."

Mrs. Djou, hearing that she was being accused of having killed

Bee Hsun, felt as if she had received a heavy blow that pene-
trated into her very heart. But she mastered her emotion and
answered coolly:

"Your Honor is the father and mother of us, the common
people. The other day I really offended you unintentionally.
How can you slander me for such a flimsy reason, and think up
such a crime against me? And the crime you falsely accuse me
of, Your Honor, is one punishable by death. You should not
make light of such serious matters."

Judge Dee then knew that Mrs. Djou, relying on her beauty,
was manœuvring him into an awkward position, insinuating that
he had visited her with an ulterior motive, and, being rebuked,
thus tried to take his revenge. He said:

"I know you are clever, but your sharp tongue shall be of no
avail to you. I shall show you proof and see whether you won't
confess then. Your dead husband told me clearly that you murdered him. And also that you, fearing that your small daughter
might tell somebody about your adulterous affairs, gave her a
drug that made her dumb. The other day I saw her myself.
How dare you still deny your crime? If you don't confess now,
I shall question you under torture."

Mrs. Djou, however, was not to be intimidated. She replied:

"How could I confess, when there is nothing to confess? You
can torture me to death but you can never make me confess to a
crime which I never committed!"

Judge Dee shouted:

"You, woman, dare to defy me right here in this court? Now
I shall risk this black cap of mine and chance getting the name
of being a cruel magistrate. We shall see whether or not you
will confess under torture. Give her first forty lashes with the
whip!"

The constables tore her robes down and bared her back, and
gave her forty lashes with the whip.

# Eighth Chapter

ACCUSED OF MURDER, MRS. DJOU SPEAKS CLEVER WORDS;
HER MOTHER'S STUPIDITY EXCITES EVERYONE'S PITY.

This torture failed to make Mrs. Djou confess. Instead she said:
"Your Honor is the father and the mother of the entire population of this district. How can you harm good people like this without a shred of proof? Is that your conception of being a magistrate? But if you think that torture can make me confess, you must be dreaming. You maintain that I murdered my husband on no more evidence than the testimony supplied by a ghost. But how can you prove that? Can you show me a written accusation, produced by that ghost? Let me tell you that although you are a district magistrate, you are not omnipotent. If you, because of a private grudge, persist in slandering and torturing me, well, they say that the doors of the higher authorities are always open for the persecuted and the oppressed. And even if your superiors should refuse to take action against you, I shall, after you have tortured me to death, bring the case before the judges of the Nether World. And remember, when a magistrate has been proved to have falsely accused an innocent person, the law will mete out to the accuser the punishment he wanted to give to the accused. I may be but a young and defenseless widow, but I shall do my utmost to have that judge's cap removed from your head."

Judge Dee then ordered the constables to put the screws on her. They did so, and vigorously turned them tighter and tighter. But Mrs. Djou only cried louder and louder that she was being falsely accused.

Then Judge Dee said:

"I know you are a brazen person but your skin and flesh are not cast in iron. If necessary, I shall go on with this the whole day." And again he ordered the constables to turn the screws tighter.

The constables, seeing that Mrs. Djou still protested her innocence under this severe torture, began to doubt whether she was really guilty. Giving each other a secret sign, they made great ado about turning the screws, all the while shouting to Mrs. Djou that she must confess, but in fact they loosened up the screws a bit. And their headman, seeing Sergeant Hoong standing by the side of the dais, gave him a sign to step back to where the judge could not see him. Then he walked over to him, and whispered:

"Sergeant, when the other day you went with His Excellency to investigate, what proof did you find exactly? The judge has just ordered us to turn the screws tighter, but what if she dies, and later is proved to have been innocent? That will cost His Excellency his name and position, and us our life. That talk about the ghost of her husband accusing her was evidently but a ruse to frighten her into confession, but it failed. It seems to me, Sergeant, that our judge, who usually is shrewd enough, is not at his best today. If he really has proof that she murdered her husband, why then does he not first have the corpse exhumed, and then, when the proof is there for everybody to see and she still won't confess, start torturing her? I beg you to use your influence with the judge, Sergeant, and make him stop the questioning at least for to-day. We can always see to-morrow."

The sergeant thought that there was much in what the headman said. After all this affair was nearly a year old, no accusation had been filed, and all direct proof was lacking; one could hardly bring a disembodied ghost to court to testify. So Sergeant Hoong ascended the dais, and standing behind Judge Dee's chair, whispered in his ear whether it would not be better to stop for the day.

Judge Dee said angrily:

"What I have found out myself convinces me that we are right.

Judge Dee questions Mrs. Djou under torture. Sergeant Hoong counsels the judge to desist. The sign on left reads: "Awe and silence!"

How can I ever justify in my own conscience letting this murder go unavenged? If the men are afraid to go on with the torture, I shall order an exhumation to-morrow. Then if the corpse fails to show clear proof of the murder, I shall gladly take the punishment that was to be meted out to that woman. I am not going to let this case rest here."

Then he said to Mrs. Djou:

"You, woman, persist in protesting your innocence, but I tell you that next time I question you, I shall confront you with proof which you won't be able to refute."

Then he ordered the constables to take off the screws, and take her back to the jail, to be held for further questioning. He ordered the constable on outside duty to go to Huang-hua Village, and bring Mrs. Bee to the tribunal. Finally he told other constables to go to Gao-djia-wa, and prepare in the graveyard there everything necessary for an exhumation, which was to take place on the following day.

After the court had closed, all the constables and the guards of the tribunal discussed this case amongst each other in great detail. They were full of doubts, and feared that Judge Dee had overreached himself this time. "This is no child's play," they reasoned, "for although there is ground for suspicion, our judge runs a grave risk. If the autopsy should show no traces of a murder having been committed, he is done for."

Now the constable who had gone to fetch Mrs. Bee arrived at her house when night was falling. The latest news about the happenings at the tribunal had already reached there and on the corner of the street a crowd of neighbors and idlers were busily debating the matter of Mrs. Djou's guilt. The constable, seeing that this crowd was blocking the street, shouted:

"Make way, I have come here on official business. Make way, here is nothing to see. If you want to see something, you must come to-morrow to Gao-djia-wa!"

Then he knocked on the door, and Mrs. Bee let him in, her face wet with tears. She wailed:

"Is this not a calamity like heaven falling down upon us? The other day he said he was a doctor and he certainly looked like one, and then my daughter said a few hasty words. But that is hardly a crime, is it not, so why is he now raising all this trouble? To-morrow I, an aged woman, shall go to the tribunal myself, to tell him what I think of him!"

"You stupid woman," the constable said, "don't you see that His Excellency only tries to avenge the death of your son for you? But as to your wanting to go to the tribunal, that is fine. I was just ordered to bring you there, so that your daughter would not feel lonely in jail." Then the constable started to drag her to the door. But the old woman, beside herself with grief and rage, shouted:

"You dog of a constable, you only know how to file false accusations. Here, I don't want this house of mine any more. I don't want a single piece of furniture any longer." She wrenched herself loose, and started throwing pieces of furniture into the street.

"Now there you are!", the constable said indignantly to Warden Ho Kai, who had just come in, "I came all the way out here, just for her sake, and now she acts like this! How difficult to handle are even these small people. This furniture of hers is not worth much, but anyway let a couple of your assistants stand watch here overnight. For if someone stole her things, it is we who would get into trouble."

Ho Kai agreed and the constable set out with Mrs. Bee in the moonlit night. It was late at night when they knocked at the city gates. Fortunately the soldiers of the guard knew the constable, and opened the heavy gates for him.

Once arrived at the tribunal, the constable arranged for Mrs. Bee to sleep in a room in the guard house.

The next day, Judge Dee had Mrs. Bee brought in during the

morning session of the tribunal. He said kindly to her:

"Now madam, your husband's name was Bee, but what is your maiden name? Then I want to explain to you that the other day when I went to your house, it was solely because of your dead son. He died under highly suspicious circumstances, and it is my opinion that he was killed by his wife. Since I as magistrate have the duty to avenge the wrongs suffered by the people in my district, the ghost of your dead son requested me to punish his murderer. I have had you brought before me to-day only because your daughter-in-law stubbornly refuses to confess, and moreover accuses me of wantonly slandering her. If the corpse is not exhumed and an autopsy performed, this case can never be brought to an end. I felt it my duty to tell this to you, who are his mother."

Mrs. Bee, however, was not mollified by this kind address. She said:

"My son has now been dead for almost one year. What could be the use of examining his corpse? That very evening on which he died, many people saw it. Your Honor says that he wishes to redress the wrong that my son suffered, but in fact my son did not suffer any wrong. Why did you subject my poor daughter to torture without having a shred of proof? You are the father and mother of the common people, how can you harm us like this on such flimsy pretexts? Now my maiden name is Tang. I belong to a family that has been living in this locality for generations. We are decent people, as everyone around here knows. I tell you frankly that I shall not leave this tribunal before you have set my daughter free, if it should be my death! Neither am I going to listen to any more speeches from you, who, not content with having harmed the living, now are out to disturb the peace of the dead!"

Having thus spoken, she burst into tears.

Judge Dee, seeing that she was as stupid as she was honest, and believed implicitly all that her daughter-in-law chose to tell her, said impatiently:

"You stupid woman, the death of your son failed to cause you even the slightest misgivings. And when I explain everything to you, you refuse to understand. But let me tell you that if your daughter should prove to be innocent, I, the magistrate, am willing to undergo the punishment that was destined for her myself. I am fully prepared to do this, for the sake of your dead son. But you, his mother, even refuse to have his corpse exhumed, so that his wrong will never be redressed. Now I am the magistrate here, and I cannot allow this murder to remain unsolved. I am going to risk my black cap in order to find the truth. I therefore decide that this exhumation shall take place, whether you consent or not!"

He ordered her to be led away, and fixed the exhumation for the following day. He would leave the tribunal at eight o'clock, and the exhumation would be started at two o'clock. Then, returned to his private office, he drew up a detailed report to the higher authorities.

The constables outside now saw their worst fears come true. Amongst each other they criticised the judge, but nobody dared to ask him to stop the exhumation. Thus they reluctantly set to work to collect the necessary implements.

Early the following day the constables assembled in the court-hall, the gong was sounded three times, and Judge Dee seated himself behind the bench. He first addressed himself to the coroner:

"This is quite an extraordinary case. If no wounds or other signs of a violent death are found, then my name and my position are lost. That is my least concern, but more important is that in such an event also you, and the constables who assist in the exhumation, will get into trouble. Therefore I enjoin you to perform the autopsy with the greatest care, so that this case can be disposed of, and the dead avenged."

Then he had Mrs. Bee and Mrs. Djou brought before him, and thus addressed the latter:

"The other day you preferred torture to confessing your crime. Perhaps you have thereby succeeded in deceiving others, but I shall not let myself be caught by your wiles. Today you and your mother shall be present at the autopsy and we shall see what you will say then."

Mrs. Djou fully realized that the judge was in dead earnest about the exhumation, but she could not imagine that he would discover any trace of a crime when the autopsy took place. Therefore she thought that at least she should show him that she was not to be trifled with. She said:

"That I have been tortured and grievously slandered, that at least leaves the dead in peace. But that you now, after one year, are going to disturb the corpse of my poor husband, that is outrageous. But go ahead, if the corpse shows one single trace of his having been murdered, I shall gladly say that it was I who killed him. But if such proof should be lacking, I assure you that although you are a ranking official, the law provides for stern punishment for you! The laws of the land shall not be considered as child's play, they don't allow that innocent people are falsely accused!"

Judge Dee, however, only had a cold smile.

## Ninth Chapter

THE UNDERTAKER SHOWS THE LOCATION OF THE GRAVE;
JUDGE DEE HAS THE COFFIN EXHUMED FOR AN AUTOPSY.

The constables made Mrs. Bee and Mrs. Djou enter a separate
sedan chair and set out for Gao-djia-wa.

Thereafter Judge Dee, having ascended his official palanquin,
also left the tribunal, accompanied by his entire retinue, including
the coroner and his assistants.

The people living along the road, on hearing that the corpse
of Bee Hsun would be exhumed, were unanimously of the opinion
that this was a very serious matter. When the judge and his
retinue passed along the highway to Huang-hua Village, young
and old followed the procession, to see what would happen.

Shortly after noon they reached Huang-hua Village, where
Warden Ho Kai and the old undertaker came to greet the judge.
They reported that out on the graveyard in Gao-djia-wa every-
thing had been put in readiness.

Before proceeding there, however, Judge Dee called Sergeant
Hoong to the side of his palanquin, and said to him in a low
voice:

"The other day the attendant in the bathhouse here told you
about a young man who used to be Bee Hsun's neighbor. You
had better go there now, and see what you can find out from him.
Furthermore, since this will be a long day, I shall not return
to the city tonight, but stay here in the same hostel where we had
a room a couple of days ago." Then he went on to Gao-djia-wa.

In the graveyard, near Bee Hsun's tomb, a large shed of
reedmatting had been erected, and therein a temporary tribunal
had been set up. A group of constables had already assembled
there and laid out the implements necessary for the exhumation.

Judge Dee descended from his palanquin, and first went to

have another look at Bee Hsun's grave. Seeing that nothing had been disturbed since his last visit, he seated himself behind the bench, and had the old undertaker and Mrs. Djou led before him. He first spoke to the undertaker.

"The other day you told me that this grave is that of Bee Hsun. It is my duty to warn you that, if after the exhumation this should prove to be the wrong grave, you will be guilty of a heinous crime. And then all remorse will be too late."

"How would I dare," the undertaker said, "to lie about this, seeing that both the dead man's mother and widow are present here?"

"It is not," Judge Dee said, "that I am an incredulous man. But Mrs. Djou here has tried to deceive me in every possible way, and even threatened me with the punishment for those guilty of making false accusations. If this should turn out not to be Bee Hsun's grave, not only would the investigation be obstructed, but I should be guilty of having wantonly desecrated the grave of an innocent person. Therefore I want you now to impress your thumbmark on this document, testifying that this is indeed Bee Hsun's grave. Should there be a mistake, then you will have to bear the consequences."

Then, turning to Mrs. Djou, he said: "Listen well to this. I am having this exhumation executed in the interests of justice, and not to prove that I am always right. This exhumation, however, is cruel to the remains of your husband. You are his wedded wife, and irrespective of whether or not you killed him, it is your duty now, before the work starts, to offer a prayer to his soul."

He ordered the undertaker to lead her in front of the grave. Old Mrs. Bee, knowing that now the body of her son was really going to be exhumed, was beside herself with grief, and crying bitterly she said to her daughter, clutching her sleeve:

"My daughter, terrible indeed is our lot. That my son died

when he was still in the prime of life that was apparently not enough. Now, his bones are going to be disturbed and we must face this cruel official."

Mrs. Djou, however, was quite calm. She said in a loud voice to her:

"There is no need for crying now. At home you never leave me in peace. You brought all kinds of people to our house and thus caused this affair. To cry now won't do you any good. But wait till after the exhumation, when it has been proved that Bee Hsun was not murdered. Then I shall not be afraid of this magistrate. The laws established by our august Emperor enjoin him to rule the people, not to harm them. He himself shall have to undergo the punishment he wanted to mete out to me. If he orders me to offer a prayer to my husband, I shall do it, to get over with this affair!"

She pushed her mother back, went to stand in front of the grave, and there bowed three times. She did not only not show any grief, but on the contrary seemed full of defiance. She even reviled the old undertaker, calling him an old dogshead, and promised to get even with him after the exhumation. "What are you waiting for?" she added. "The lady has done, get to work!"

The old undertaker was highly indignant on being thus reviled, but he did not like to start a quarrel with a woman right there. He went before the judge to ask whether he could start.

Judge Dee had closely observed what was happening. He had ordered Mrs. Djou to pray before the grave, only because he wanted to see her reactions. Now he had seen that she did not show the least grief, but even spoke in this heartless way, he was all the more convinced that she had murdered her husband. He ordered the undertaker to start the exhumation.

The old man and his assistants took their tools, and started digging. After half an hour, the front part of the mound had been shoveled away, and the coffin became visible. They slowly dragged it out, and wiped it clean of the earth and mud that were covering it.

Judge Dee ordered them to bring the coffin to the matshed, and there had it placed on two trestles by the side of the bench.

Mrs. Bee, seeing the coffin of her son right in front of her, promptly fell in a swoon. Two constables helped her up and made her sit down.

Judge Dee then ordered Warden Ho Kai and his assistants to open the coffin.

When the heavy sliding lid was pushed off, the crowd of on-lookers who, in their eagerness to miss nothing, had come nearer and nearer, drew back hastily.

The corpse was slowly lifted out of the coffin, together with the thick mat on which it had rested inside, and placed on the reed mats that had been spread out for that purpose in front of the bench. The hermetically sealed coffin of heavy wood and the dry air had preserved the corpse in fair state, but in some parts decomposition had set in. All in all it still was a gruesome sight, especially since the eyes were still open, and showed the shrunken, ash-colored eyeballs. Several people in the crowd of villagers commented on this fact, and said to each other that this was a sure sign that Bee Hsun had met a violent death.

Judge Dee left his seat behind the temporary bench, and went to the corpse. He looked for a long time at its sightless eyes. Then he said gravely:

"Bee Hsun, Bee Hsun, today I, the magistrate, have come here to redress your wrong. Should you have met with a violent death, and your soul still be there, I ask you to show your presence by closing your eyes."

Then, to the horror and amazement of all present, the dried out lids of the corpse started to flutter, and closed over the eye-balls.

When the excitement over this ghostly phenomenon had abated, Judge Dee ordered the coroner to do the autopsy.

The coroner, having looked over the corpse, said:

"Your Honor, this corpse has been interred for a considerable time. It cannot be examined in its present condition. I beg to be allowed to cleanse it first."

Judge Dee having given him permission, the coroner and his assistants first tried to remove the shroud. On most places the cloth came off easily, but there where decomposition had set in, it proved difficult to peel it off without damaging the skin underneath. The coroner then told the undertaker to heat water in a large iron pan. When the water was hot, he soaked the corpse several times with it, and then the shroud was removed.

The coroner took two gallons of undiluted wine, and therewith carefully washed the corpse from head to feet. When this was done, he reported to the judge that he would now begin with the examination.

Although there were more than several hundred people assembled there, not one sound was heard. They all craned their necks to see, following the coroner's every movement.

The coroner first closely observed face and throat, and then went on downwards, examining the corpse inch by inch. The crowd watched his progress in tense silence. When he had finished with the belly, and still not reported to the judge, the people became restive, and some began to whisper to each other. When the coroner had finished with the legs, he told his assistants to turn the corpse over. Then he examined the back, giving special attention to the back of the skull and the neck. But still there was no report.

Judge Dee now became worried. He left his seat, and standing near the coroner, anxiously followed his examination. At last the coroner had finished, and turned to the judge to report:

"Having now completed the examination of the outside of the body, I report that there are no marks whatsoever that could point to this man having been done to death. I now, therefore, ask

Your Honor's permission for employing the usual means for an inside examination, to see whether poison has been administered."

Before Judge Dee could answer, Mrs. Djou had started already to protest vehemently. She cried that even if her husband had been poisoned, there would have been outside signs of it. She would not allow the corpse to suffer further indignities.

MRS. DJOU REFUSES TO LET HER HUSBAND BE BURIED; JUDGE DEE VISITS THE TEMPLE FOR SPIRITUAL GUIDANCE.

"Since the outside of the corpse shows no traces, its inside must be probed," Judge Dee said firmly. "This is the fixed rule for an autopsy."

He did not allow Mrs. Djou to say another word, and ordered the coroner to proceed.

The coroner poured hot water into the mouth of the corpse, and by exercising pressure with the palms of his hands on its breast and belly, made the water first enter, and then come out again. Then he took a thin lamella of polished silver, of about eight inches long, and slowly pushed it down till it had entered deep down in the throat. He left it there, and turning to the judge, asked him to witness the withdrawal of the lamella.

Judge Dee left his seat and stood next to the corpse while the coroner drew the lamella out again. Its surface did not show the slightest discoloration.

The coroner was perplexed, and said:

"This, Your Honor, is passing strange. I cannot but state that I did not find one single trace of this man having met with a violent death. I beg to advise, however, that an older coroner of established reputation be ordered to perform a second autopsy, to see whether he confirms my findings."

Judge Dee now was in great consternation. He slowly resumed his seat, and said to Mrs. Djou:

"Since no trace of a crime having been committed was revealed by this autopsy, I shall so report to the higher authorities, and take full responsibility for the consequences. In the meantime we cannot leave this corpse lying exposed here. We shall replace it in its coffin, so that it can be interred again."

Before he had quite finished, however, Mrs. Djou had already kicked away one of the trestles from under the empty coffin; it fell down with a crash, and broke to pieces. She cried:

"I maintained that he died of an illness, but you, dog-official, insisted upon an autopsy. And now, having failed to discover any trace of a crime, you want to bury it again as if nothing had happened. What kind of a magistrate are you? Although I am but a poor woman of the common people, you have no right to beat and torture me when I am innocent. Yesterday you tried to compel me to make a false confession, to-day you are desecrating a grave. Since you have had the corpse exhumed, it shall not be interred again. Although we are but common people, we need not let ourselves be trod upon in this way. This corpse shall not be interred again until the day this case is solved, and you have lost your black cap!"

She went on reviling Judge Dee, and her mother soon joined in the chorus. Judge Dee could answer nothing in return.

The crowd of onlookers, however, seeing that the judge, whom they knew as an honest official, was thus being insulted in public, were all of the opinion that this was a disgraceful situation. A few elders closed in on Mrs. Djou and her mother, and reprimanded them, saying that since the corpse had already been subjected to the disgrace of the autopsy, it was outrageous to let it lie there exposed in broad daylight. Others added that the judge was an honest official who, although he had erred in this case, had done so in good faith, and after all only for her dead husband's sake. Others again declared that they would not stand for a woman of their village to shout at and curse an official in public. Would not the people from the neighboring hamlets deride us of Huang-hua Village, and say that we did not know the rules of propriety? She had better follow the instructions of the judge, and consent to the corpse being buried again.

Mrs. Djou, seeing that this was the general opinion of the

crowd did not think it expedient to insist further. She thought by herself that by her threats and recriminations she had at least achieved that no other coroner would be asked to perform a second autopsy. The main thing was to have the corpse placed again in a coffin, and buried safely underground.

Judge Dee, seeing that the old coffin could not be used anymore, sent a few constables to the village, to buy a temporary coffin. When this had arrived, the corpse was hurriedly dressed, and the coffin closed. For the time being it was to be left there on its bier.

Judge Dee had the necessary documents relating to the exhumation filled out, and then returned to Huang-hua Village, followed by the crowd.

Since it was growing dark already, he decided to stay there for the night in the same hostel. He ordered that Mrs. Bee would be allowed to go home, but that Mrs. Djou be returned to the jail of the tribunal, to be kept there until further notice.

Having issued these orders Judge Dee retired to his room in the hostel, and there sat down, alone with his troubled thoughts.

Then Sergeant Hoong came in, and after having greeted the judge, reported the following:

"Obeying Your Honor's instructions, I have made inquiries with that young man who used to be Bee Hsun's neighbor. I found that he had been quite friendly with Bee Hsun and regrets very much that death separated them. But he could add little to what we know already about the crime itself. He mentioned, though, that when Bee Hsun was still alive, his wife loved to show herself in the streets, joking and laughing in public and altogether did not behave as a self-respecting housewife should. Bee Hsun often scolded her for this, but that always resulted only in some violent quarrels. When, after his death, his wife locked up herself in her house, and refused to see anybody except her mother, it caused no little surprise among the neighbors.

"Now that the autopsy has produced no results", the sergeant added, "how shall we proceed with this case? Although we are firmly convinced that Bee Hsun was murdered, as long as there is no proof, we can hardly again question Mrs. Djou under torture. Moreover, the double murder of Six Mile Village has not been solved either. More than two weeks have elapsed, but still there is no news about Ma Joong and Chiao Tai having traced the murderer. It is true that Your Honor is indifferent with regard to his own reputation, but both cases are heinous crimes which cry for justice. Cannot Your Honor devise some way..."

While the sergeant was saying this, he was interrupted by the sounds of loud crying, outside in the courtyard. Fearing that Mrs. Bee had turned up again to annoy Judge Dee, he wanted to go outside to intercept her. But then he heard the constable standing guard outside saying:

"So you are asking for His Excellency the Judge? Well, you may be the wife of that man, but that is no reason to get in such a state. His Excellency is doing what he can. You first rest here a while and explain to me, then I shall report it to the Judge. Now how do you know that that man was your husband?"

Sergeant Hoong went hastily outside and heard that the wife of the unidentified victim of the crime at Six Mile Village had arrived to file her case with the judge. When he had reported this to his master, Judge Dee ordered the woman to be brought in.

She was a woman of about forty, her hair was disheveled, and tears were streaming down her face. Kneeling down in front of the judge, she started wailing loudly, imploring him to avenge her husband's death.

When asked to explain, she told the following:

"My poor husband was called Wang, he was a carter by profession. We live in Liu-shui-kow, about twenty miles from Six Mile Village. On the eve of the murder, the wife of our neighbor became very ill, and begged my husband to go to Six Mile Village at once and fetch her husband, who happened to be staying there for transacting some business. Now my husband was going there anyway with his pushcart to fetch some goods, so he set out that same night expecting to be back early the next morning. But I waited for him the whole next day in vain. First I did not worry, thinking that he might have found some carting to do there. When, however, after three days, our neighbor came back and told me that he had not seen my husband at all, I became very much worried. I waited another few days, and then asked some of our relatives to go out and make inquiries along the road, and in Six Mile Village. They came upon a coffin placed on its bier near the guard house and read the official notice put up by its side. From the description given there, they immediately knew that the unidentified victim was my husband, dastardly done to death by some unknown person. I beg Your Honor to avenge his death!"

Judge Dee was moved by her grief, and said some comforting words, assuring her that everything was being done to apprehend the murderer. He then gave her some silver, and told her to use this sum for having her husband properly buried.

After the widow Wang had left, Judge Dee remained sitting there, sunk in melancholy thoughts. He reflected that since he had sadly failed in his duties as a magistrate, how could he still remain in office, having proved incapable of serving the State and the people?

The waiter brought his dinner in, but Judge Dee felt no appetite and he had to force himself to eat a few morsels. With the dejected sergeant standing by, the meal was finished in dismal silence. Judge Dee went to bed shortly afterwards.

The next morning Judge Dee left the hostel early, and, accompanied by his retinue, went back to the city. He made, however, a detour via Six Mile Village, where he personally ordered the headman to give Mrs. Wang all assistance for having the coffin with her husband's corpse transported to her own village.

As soon as he was seated in his private office, Judge Dee moistened his writing brush, and drew up a report for the higher authorities. He described in full detail how he had committed the crime of desecrating a grave, and recommended himself for appropriate punishment. When he had acquitted himself of this melancholy task, he ordered the servants to prepare a bath, and told them that he would not require any food, as he was going to fast that day.

When he had bathed, and put on clean clothes, he ordered Sergeant Hoong to go to the city temple, and inform the superior that he intended to stay there that night; the main hall of the temple was to be closed to the public after nightfall, and all persons except the priests were to be told to leave.

When night was falling, Judge Dee proceeded to the temple. Arrived before the gate, he sent his escort back, and ascended the main hall alone.

There Sergeant Hoong had already prepared a couch for him in a corner, and a cushion for meditation was placed in front of the altar.

The sergeant added new incense in the burner and then took his leave. He spread his bedding out below on one of the broad steps leading up to the main hall, and there lay down.

Then Judge Dee knelt down on the bare floor in front of the altar, and prayed fervently. He supplicated the Powers on High that they, knowing his earnest desire that justice be done, would deign to show him the right way.

He sat down on the cushion, with crossed legs and his body erect. Closing his eyes, he tried to achieve a tranquil state of mind.

A HINT IN A BOOK PROVES APPLICABLE TO THE CASE;
A DREAM SUPPLIES HIDDEN CLUES TO PAST EVENTS.

Judge Dee, however, found he could not concentrate his thoughts. The vexations over Bee Hsun's case, the suspense over the exhumation and the autopsy, together with the threats of Mrs. Djou, and the lamentations of Mrs. Wang, all those things kept going round and round in his head. He remained seated on the prayer cushion for a long time, but although he kept his eyes closed, trying to achieve a tranquil state of mind, all his doubts and suspicions continued to vex him.

When the first nightwatch had nearly passed, Judge Dee started to fret. He had come to this temple with the express purpose of obtaining some help in a dream, but if sleep refused to come then all would have been in vain.

Rising he walked down the steps, and there saw Sergeant Hoong, who was already sound asleep. He did not wish to disturb him, so he went again to the main hall, and there started walking up and down.

On passing for perhaps the twentieth time in front of the large altar table, he noticed a book lying there. "They say that reading will attract the spirit of sleep. Let me read a while, perhaps this book will help me to pass the time, or else bore me to such an extent that I shall fall asleep." Thus he picked up the book, and opened it at random.

This book, however, was only the collection of answers, used when consulting the divination slips.* Judge Dee thought:

---

\* (Translator's note) There exist various forms of divination in China. The one here alluded to is a very popular one, practised in most temples. About fifty numbered bamboo slips of about 1½ foot long, are placed in a vase of about one foot high. The person who wishes

"Since I have come here to receive instruction from the powers on high, I might as well consult fate through these divination slips. Who knows whether the spirits have not chosen these particular means for manifesting themselves?"

He reverently replaced the book on the altar, lighted the candles, and put new incense in the incense burner. Then he made a profound obeisance in front of the altar and silently prayed for some time. Rising again he took the vase in both hands, and shook it well, until one bamboo slip dropped out. He quickly picked it up, and saw that it bore the number 24. He again opened the book, and leafed it through till he found the entry under No. 24. The item was headed by the two words "Middle" and "Even", and underneath there was written a name, "Lady Lee".

Judge Dee remembered that this Lady Lee was a well-known historical person, of more than a thousand years ago. Being the concubine of an ancient king, she instigated him to kill the crownprince; shortly afterwards that kingdom was defeated, and the king had to flee for his life. Judge Dee reflected that this could point to Mrs. Djou, who, through murdering her husband, was bringing calamity to her house.

Finally the entry gave a brief poem, that said:

*Dawn never is heralded by the hen instead of the cock.*
*Why did the king take Lady Lee in his favor?*
*In women's hearts many an evil scheme is born.*
*And many are the intimacies on the shared couch.*

---

to consult fate, first burns incense, and then in a silent prayer states the question he seeks an answer for. Thereafter he takes the vase with the bamboo slips, and raising it before the altar in both hands, he shakes it till one of the slips drops out of the vase. Then the entry indicated by the number of the slip is looked up in the book with answers, and this entry, usually some cryptic verse, is studied to find some indication of the answer to the question which the consultant had in his mind. As in most Chinese poems of four lines, also in oracle verses the last line usually contains the climax.

Judge Dee mused that although these lines could be made to apply to the murder of Bee Hsun, they did not help to clarify the issue. The first line could well refer to Mrs. Djou's insolent behavior, taking on the role of the man in the house, and reviling her mother and the judge alike. The second line referred to the fact that Bee Hsun, in taking Mrs. Djou as wife, had himself brought on his misfortune, and the third line implied that it was Mrs. Djou who had planned the killing of her husband. But the fourth line, that should have contained the clue, did not seem to make any sense. Bee Hsun and his wife were a wedded couple, what was more natural than that they should have the normal marital relations?

In the uncertain light of the candles, Judge Dee thought over this line for a considerable time, without arriving at a plausible explanation.

When the second night watch was sounded outside, he felt much calmer, and very tired. Thus he drew his robes closer about him, and lay down on the couch to sleep.

Then, just as he was nodding off, he saw an old gentleman with a flowing white beard entering the hall. This new arrival greeted the judge as an equal and said:

"Your Honor has had a trying day, why should you remain here in this lonely place? Come with me to the teahouse, and let us, sipping the fragrant brew, listen for a while to the talk of the people there."

Judge Dee thought that the old gentleman looked exceedingly familiar, but for the moment he could not place him. Finding it awkward to show that he had forgotten who the other was, he hurriedly rose and accompanied him into the street.

Outside a teeming crowd was still filling the streets. They walked through a number of thoroughfares, and finally arrived at a large teahouse, that Judge Dee could not recall ever to have seen before. The old gentleman bade him enter.

Inside he found a spacious courtyard, with in a corner a hex-
agonal pavilion.  There, seated around small tables, a large number
of guests were talking and drinking tea.  They went up the steps
of the pavilion, and sat down at an empty table.  Looking around,
Judge Dee noticed that this pavilion was appointed in quite elegant
taste.  Its walls consisted of intricate lattice work, and roofbeams
and pillars were decorated with boards of black lacquer, engraved
with quotations from the Classics and lines of poetry in golden
letters.  His attention was drawn especially by two lines of poetry
displayed there, which greatly puzzled him.  Somehow or other
this verse seemed familiar to him, but he could not remember in
what book he had read it.  The verse read:

> *Seeking the lost traces of the Child, one descends the couch,*
> *And finds the answer to all past riddles.*
> *Asking Yao Foo about the secrets of divination,*
> *It proves hard to discover the man in Szuchuan Province.*

These lines intrigued the judge, and he asked the old gentleman:
"One would expect to find on the walls of a tea house some
well-worn lines by famous poets about the delights of drinking
tea.  Why did they put up this verse here?  It mentions historical
persons who must be unfamiliar to most of the guests that fre-
quent this place, and moreover the verse does not scan well."

"Your remarks", the old gentleman answered with a smile,
"are very much to the point.  But then, who knows whether they
did not put up this verse not for the common guests, but especially
for such a learned gentleman like you?  Some day you may make
some sense out of it".

Judge Dee did not quite get his meaning and he was just debating with himself whether it would be impolite to press the old
gentleman for a further explanation, when suddenly he heard a
terrific clanging of gongs and the strident sounds of music that
nearly deafened his ears.  Looking up he found that the tea pavilion
had disappeared altogether and that he was standing in a theater,

right among the noisy crowd of spectators.

On the scene an acrobatic act was in progress, there were spear-dancers, sword swallowers, jugglers, and what not. Among these acrobats he especially noticed a woman of about thirty years of age, who was lying on her back on a high tabouret. On her raised legs she balanced a huge earthenware jar, making it spin round on her footsoles like a wheel. Then a good looking young man approached the tabouret and smiled at the woman. She seemed overjoyed at seeing him, and giving the jar a kick, she sent it up flying in the air. Then she jumped up with amazing swiftness, and caught the jar in her arms when it came down. Having performed this feat, she said with a smile to the young man:

"So you have come again, my husband!"

Then a tiny girl climbed out of the jar's mouth, and crawling to the young man, clutched at his robe.

Just when those three were laughing together, the crowd of spectators suddenly melted away, the stage was empty, and Judge Dee found himself standing there all alone. Before he could start wondering, however, suddenly the old gentleman with the white beard again appeared at his side, and said to him:

"You have now seen the first act, but not yet the second! Come along with me quickly!"

Without giving the judge time to ask a question, he took him along over what seemed a lonely plot of land, overgrown with weeds. There was a thick mist all around, through which weird birds could be seen fluttering about. Every now and then they came upon a corpse, lying among the weeds.

Suddenly Judge Dee came upon a naked corpse, of a greenish color. A bright red adder came out of one of its nostrils and started crawling towards the judge.

Judge Dee was terribly frightened, perspiration broke out all over him, and he woke up.

He found himself again on his couch in the temple hall and

heard the third night watch being sounded outside.

He sat upright and remained thus for some time, trying to collect his thoughts. His mouth was parched, so he called out to Sergeant Hoong. The sergeant brought the portable teastove, and poured him a cup of hot tea. After the judge had thus refreshed himself, the sergeant asked:

"Your Honor has been here now for the greater part of the night. Did you sleep at all?"

"Yes, I did sleep for a while", Judge Dee answered, "but I still feel very confused. What did you dream when you were asleep there below?"

"To tell Your Honor the truth", the sergeant answered, "these last days I have been so busy running hither and thither on this case, and so worried over the trouble you got into over Bee Hsun's murder, that I slept like a log. And if I had any dreams, I don't recall a single one of them! But perhaps Your Honor was more lucky".

Judge Dee then told him all, from his consulting the divination slips to the strange dream he had had. Again taking up the divination book, he read out aloud to the sergeant the verse he had found there. The sergeant said:

"Usually the explanations given in these books are very obscure. Yet although I am but an unlettered man, the meaning of this particular entry seems obvious to me. I don't look for an explanation in the old story the poem refers to, but take the words as they stand. Now, as for the first line, this refers plainly to the last hour of darkness, before daybreak. That is the quietest time of the night, and that is the usual time for secret lovers to sneak out of the house of their lady love. The intimacies mentioned in the fourth line don't refer to wedded love, but to the illicit relations of Mrs. Djou and her paramour. You assumed from the very beginning that there must be such a person. Now this poem advises us that he was present when the crime was

committed, and probably an accessory. This would fit in with
the time schedule. We know that Mrs. Bee, her son and his wife,
after they had come back from the races, had an elaborate dinner.
Then they drank wine, and talked some. When Bee Hsun complained of his stomach ache, it must have been quite late in the
night. Then Mrs. Bee told his wife to bring her son to bed. She
tidied up, made her toilet, and it was thus very late in the night
when she was awakened by her son's cry. Now is it not probable
that Mrs. Djou's lover came during the third night watch, was
surprised by Bee Hsun, and that Mrs. Djou thereupon killed him,
in a manner as yet unknown to us? That must have been the
way it went."

Judge Dee nodded and said:

"There is much in what you say. I assumed that there was a
third person involved, because else Mrs. Djou would have had
nothing to gain and everything to lose by killing her husband.
But I was sure that she would confess, and then we could know
who her lover was, and what part he took in the murder. Thus
I made no attempt to locate this man. This was a bad mistake.
Now, however, it is even more important to find him, for now
it is he who must tell us how the crime was committed. But how
do we find him?"

"That", Sergeant Hoong said, "cannot be difficult. When you
have returned to the tribunal, set Mrs. Bee and Mrs. Djou
free. Then we secretly send some of our best men to Mrs. Bee's
house and watch it closely, especially during the night, the last
hours before daybreak. This lover is certainly somewhere about,
and when he hears that Mrs. Bee has been released, he will try to
contact her sooner or later. And then we catch him."

Judge Dee was very pleased with this plan, and complimented
the sergeant on his clever reasoning. Then he asked him what
he thought about the dream.

"When you meditated here", asked Sergeant Hoong, "did you

think only about Bee Hsun's murder, or also about the double murder of Six Mile Village?"

"As a matter of fact", Judge Dee answered, "before I went to sleep I had been going over in my mind again all features of both of them. But I fail to see what bearing my dream can have on either case".

The Sergeant said:

"I must confess that this dream is completely obscure to me also. Would Your Honor perhaps kindly again recite for me the verse that you saw in the tea pavilion? There was something about a child, and about a couch".

# Twelfth Chapter

A VERSE IN A DREAM DIRECTS SUSPICION TO A MR. HSU;
MA JOONG OBTAINS IMPORTANT CLUES IN A VILLAGE INN.

Judge Dee, seeing that the sergeant was not familiar with the literary allusion contained in that verse, said with a smile:

"The word 'child' here is a name. In olden times there lived a wise man, whose surname was Hsu, while his sobriquet was 'The Child'. In the same locality where this sage lived, there was a certain gentleman who had a great admiration for him, and everytime he had some decision to make, he invited this sage to his house for consultation. He had placed a large couch in his main hall, especially for Mr. Hsu and nobody else was ever allowed to sit on it. Now this story of Mr. Hsu and the couch is often quoted as an illustration of how the ancients used to honor wise men. But I fail to see how it could have any bearing on either of the two murder cases".

The sergeant quickly interposed: "Your Honor, it seems to me that there is little doubt about the meaning. The verse in the book pointed out that we should search for Mrs. Djou's lover. Now there exists a direct link between that verse, and the first line of this: it is clearly meant to convey to us that this lover bears the surname Hsu. Now could Your Honor instruct me further as to Yao Foo, mentioned in the second line?"

"The second half," Judge Dee answered, "is fairly clear. Yao Foo also refers to an historical person, it was the sobriquet of Shao Yoong, the great authority on divination. So this is in perfect accord with our surmise that the murderer of Six Mile Village is that missing merchant Shao, and that either now he is being hidden by natives of Szuchuan, or that he has fled to that province. In any case it will be useful if you and your men be on your guard, as soon as you meet some one during your investigations who speaks the Szuchuan dialect."

"This", Sergeant Hoong said, "is certainly the right explanation. Now we have only the woman acrobat balancing the
jar, and the field with the corpses remaining. These things can be
explained in so many different ways, that I am at a loss where
to begin. Perhaps we shall understand their meaning during a
later phase of our investigation".

While Judge Dee and the sergeant were engrossed in these
speculations, the red glow of dawn was already beginning to show
on the paper windows, and, soon after, daylight filled the hall.
Judge Dee did not feel like sleeping any more, so he rose from the
couch and ordered his robes.

When the superior, who had already been waiting for some
time outside in the corridor, heard that the judge had risen, he
hastily entered the hall, and wished the judge a good morning.
Having prayed before the altar, he told a young priest to heat the
water for Judge Dee's morning toilet, and bring a cup of hot tea.
When the young priest returned, Judge Dee washed his face,
rinsed his mouth, and combed his hair. In the meantime Sergeant
Hoong had packed their luggage, and given the bundle to the
superior, to be kept in the temple until the judge could send
someone to fetch it. Furthermore he gave the superior strict orders
that not one word about their stay in the temple should be allowed
to leak out. Then he left the temple together with Judge Dee.

Upon his return to the tribunal, Judge Dee found Tao Gan waiting in his private office. Tao Gan eagerly asked Sergeant Hoong
whether the stay in the temple had produced any results, and the
sergeant gave him a brief account of what had happened. Then
he told Tao Gan to go to the kitchen, and order Judge Dee's
breakfast.

Since it was a fine morning, Judge Dee had his breakfast outside, in the small courtyard in front of his private office, the sergeant
and Tao Gan waiting on him.

After breakfast Judge Dee ordered Sergeant Hoong to go with the runner on day duty to Huang-hua Village, and bring Warden Ho Kai. Then he had the scribes bring in the business of that day.

In the afternoon the sergeant came back with Warden Ho Kai. Judge Dee this time preferred not to see him officially in the court hall, but had him brought in his private office.

The warden respectfully greeted the judge, and then remained standing in front of his desk.

"If", Judge Dee opened the interview, "we cannot discover how Bee Hsun was killed, this affair will end in disgrace, not only for me, but also for you, the local warden. I assume, therefore, that you have been very busy these last days trying to discover some new clues. Speak up, what have you been doing and why did I have to send for you? Why did you not come here on your own accord to report to me?"

Warden Ho Kai, thus reprimanded, hastily knelt down and knocked his head on the floor several times, saying:

"This worthless person has been busy investigating day and night, without allowing myself one moment of rest. But up till now I have not found one single new clue, and I still do not see how this case could be solved".

"For the time being," the judge said, "we shall not discuss the solution of this case, and I shall not go any further into your slackness. But I do want to know more about the situation in your village. How many families are living there, and how many of those bear the surname Hsu?"

"In my village there are about three hundred families, and among them there are about ten by the surname of Hsu. About which family Hsu does Your Honor want more information? I shall immediately go back, and make the necessary inquiries."

"You blockhead", said Judge Dee, "if I knew that, I would have had that man here for questioning a long time ago.

The fact is that I know only that a man of the surname Hsu is involved in this case, and probably even was an accessory to Mrs. Djou's crime. If we can locate that man, the case is solved. Therefore I now ask you whether any of those people called Hsu in your village had any connection with Bee Hsun or his household".

The warden thought hard for sometime, and then said:

"I must confess that I don't know much about the friends and acquaintances of Bee Hsun. But fortunately there are not many people by the surname of Hsu in my village. If Your Honor will allow me to go back, I shall make careful inquiries."

"Now," Judge Dee said, "you think that that is an excellent idea. But let me tell you that your plan is the best method to ensure that our suspicions leak out, and to drive our man into hiding. So don't you go running about, making inquiries openly. You first ask, in a roundabout way, those people living in Bee Hsun's neighborhood. And as soon as you get the slightest clue, you hurry back here to report. Then I shall look after the rest."

Then he dismissed the warden and when he had gone, he ordered Sergeant Hoong and Tao Gan to leave that same evening for Huang-hua Village, after dark. He told them to follow the warden secretly, and to see how he would go about making the inquiries. Thereafter they were to find a hiding place in the neighborhood of Mrs. Bee's house and keep watch the whole night.

Judge Dee had a low opinion of Warden Ho Kai's mental powers and he was none too happy to be obliged to use him for discreet inquiries. But since the inquest the villagers of Huang-hua Village had become familiar with Sergeant Hoong's and Tao Gan's faces. He feared that the suspect, on learning that Judge Dee's assistants were making inquiries about a man called Hsu, would take to his heels. Moreover, to make inquiries of this kind was part of the routine business of a warden, so even if Warden Ho Kai went about it in a clumsy way, there still was little chance that the suspect would connect such questions with the investigation of the crime. But Judge Dee still thought it necessary that the sergeant and Tao Gan kept an eye on the warden's activities, to step in in case of emergency. Further he wanted to verify at the same time whether Ho Kai was indeed neglecting his duties, or was just stupid.

When he had dealt with the routine matters of that day, night was already falling. Judge Dee had candles brought in, and, alone in his private office, started to dispose of some matters that had accumulated during the last few days. Thereafter he had his dinner brought in and was just dozing off into an after-dinner nap, when he was startled by sounds outside the window. Before he had quite opened his eyes, Ma Joong and Chiao Tai were standing in the room.

After they had greeted the judge, Ma Joong said:

"We have found a clue, but as yet it is hard to assess its real value. As verifying this clue would be liable to get us into trouble, we decided to come back first in order to report to you, and to receive further instructions."

"Tell me what you have found, my braves", Judge Dee said, "so that we can consider the problem together".

"After having received your instructions," Ma Joong said, "I roamed over the countryside in the eastern part of the district, making discreet inquiries everywhere. A few days ago, when night was falling, I arrived at a small bridge, and decided to stay overnight in one of the small hostels that cluster about there. Engaging in a desultory conversation with the other guests, one said a few words about the murder of Six Mile Village, and his two friends smiled and nodded knowingly. I immediately started to sound them out further, but they shut up like clams. Now I knew from the waiter that these men were leather-merchants, so I offered them a round of wine, and said that I myself was a leather merchant. I added that I was naturally curious about the murder, since another member of our guild had been staying in that hostel in Six Mile Village. Then they loosened up, and said that since I was a brother in trade, they need not fear that their story would go further. Then, over a few cups of wine, they told the following.

"The day after the murder they were travelling along the high-road with a big cart, on their way to Six Mile Village. They met a tall fellow about thirty years old, pushing a smaller cart loaded with bales, going in the opposite direction. That fellow seemed in a great hurry, and he wanted to pass them without a few words such as are exchanged as courtesy on the road. But while passing their cart struck his, his left wheel got detached from the axle, and the bales fell into the mud. They expected some fisticuffs, or at least a stream of invectives. But no, the fellow did not say a word, but hastily adjusted the wheel and started to gather up his two bales. One had got loose and we noticed that it was packed with raw silk. He hastily stuffed it back in the bale, and mumbled a few words of excuse, whereby we noticed that he spoke the Kiangsu dialect. Then he hurried along. Now, when we heard about the double murder of Six Mile Village later, we were sure that this fellow was the criminal.

"I asked them why they had not reported this occurrence to the proper authorities; they might have rewarded them for this information with a few good silver pieces. But the merchants laughed and asked me whether I thought they were fools. The murderer by then would have fled to some distant place already, and did I think they were going to get themselves mixed up in a criminal case? They were busy merchants and gladly left the apprehension of criminals to those who were paid to do so.

"Having sought out Chiao Tai, we stayed together one more day at the inn, without, however, learning more than we already knew. So we set out together along the road taken by that tall fellow, taking many short cuts over mountain paths, where a man with a cart could not pass.

"When we had crossed the boundary into the neighboring district, we found the highway blocked by a number of local farmers, who were crowded around a cart that had gone off the road, and were shouting and cursing at the top of their voices. We joined a group of spectators standing a little apart and saw the following. On the cart stood a tall young fellow, who was not at all afraid of the threatening crowd, but lustily reviled them for a bunch of clayhoppers. He shouted that he had traversed the Empire from north to south, had had any number of adventures and feared nobody under heaven. 'If I have done damage to your field,' he wound up, 'at best this miserable land is not worth more than a few coppers. But if you had let me pass, and talked over the matter nicely with me, I would have given you some raw silk, to make up for the damage. But since you are out for a fight, allright, you shall have it!' Then he sprang from the cart right among them, and with his bare fists started a real onslaught. Then a group of farmers, armed with hoes and sickles, came to help their friends. But the tall fellow rushed to meet them, wrenched a hoe out of the hands of one of the attackers, and let them have it.

"When he had dispersed them, with one powerful push he brought his cart on the road again and went on. We followed him at some distance, till he had reached a fairly large trade center, called Divine Village. There he rented a room in one of the local hostels. We found out from the waiter that he planned to stay there at least for one week, to dispose of his wares. Since we were outside our district, we thought that if we tried to arrest him there, we might get into trouble with the local authorities, especially since we were lacking direct proof that that fellow was indeed the criminal we were looking for. As he was going to stay there for at least a week, we hurried back here to report to Your Honor, and receive further instructions".

# Thirteenth Chapter

JUDGE DEE HIMSELF SETS OUT FOR DIVINE VILLAGE;
THE SILK MERCHANT STARTS PRELIMINARY NEGOTIATIONS.

Judge Dee was very pleased to hear this report. After having thought a few moments he said:

"In my mind there is little doubt that the fellow you traced is our elusive friend Shao, the young silk merchant who stayed at Koong's hostel. His strange behavior when he met with the leather merchants near the scene of the crime, the fact that he was carrying bales of raw silk, and that he was a man from Kiangsu Province, all these facts tally. His violent behavior with the farmers shows moreover that he is a dangerous ruffian, who might well have murdered his fellow traveller, and the unfortunate villager Wang, who happened to witness the crime".

Ma Joong, however, was not so sure that they had at last located the murderer. He observed that after all most silk merchants were from Kiangsu, and that a number of them were continually travelling along the highroads of the district. It might well be a coincidence, and the fellow might turn out to be a honorable merchant, though a bit short tempered.

But Judge Dee shook his head, and said:

"I have proof that this is no mere coincidence". Then he told Ma Joong and Chiao Tai about his dream in the temple. He quoted the verse he had seen in the tea pavilion of his dream, and pointed out to them that the name "Divine Village", next to the obvious meaning of "Godly Village", could also be connected with "divination". "This" he said, "clearly implies that we shall find our criminal in Divine Village."

Ma Joong and Chiao Tai were overjoyed on hearing this, and asked the judge how they should proceed further.

"The problem is", Judge Dee said, "how to arrest this man

outside my own district. I can, of course, apply to my colleague of the neighboring district for help, but I greatly fear that before all formalities are concluded, either that fellow will have left the village on his own accord, or that the affair will have leaked out and made him flee to some outlying district where we shall never find him again."

Knitting his eyebrows, Judge Dee remained for some time in deep thought. Then he said:

"The only solution I can see is the following. Tomorrow morning we shall set out together for Divine Village. There we will rent a room in the largest hostel and find out who is the most important silk merchant in that locality. You then go to visit him and tell him that I am the representative of a wealthy silk firm in Peking who is on his way to Kiangsu Province to buy a large quantity of raw silk, to be used by my firm for producing Peking brocade. You tell him that unfortunately I fell ill underway and had to break my journey for a couple of weeks. You add that now I am in great fear that I will not be able to reach Kiangsu in time before the silk season is over, and that I would prefer to call off the journey out there, provided that I can here purchase the silk at a reasonable price. That will be an attractive proposition for him and he will certainly start to collect all the raw silk he can lay hands on locally. The rest you leave to me".

After he had thus outlined his plan, Judge Dee returned to his official work. Since he knew that he would probably be absent for a number of days, he disposed of all pending business and moreover drew up a detailed report to the higher authorities. Then he summoned the warden of the jail and placed the seals of his office in his hands, charging him to deal on his behalf with all routine matters during his absence, and apprising him in a few words of the planned journey to Divine Village. He added that he expected to be back in two weeks at most, and finally enjoined him not to breathe a word to anybody.

With all this it had become very late, so Judge Dee went to sleep on the couch in his private office.

Next morning he rose before daybreak and put on ordinary clothes. He sat down at his desk and drew up a document addressed to the magistrate of the neighboring district. This he concealed on his body together with a sum of silver. When he left the tribunal with Ma Joong and Chiao Tai it was still dark and nobody saw them.

There is no need to describe their journey which was uneventful. After three days they reached Divine Village in hired sedan chairs and halted at the outskirts of the village.

During his previous visit to this village, Ma Joong had learned that the largest hostel there belonged to a certain Mr. Djang. Thus Judge Dee first sent Ma Joong and Chiao Tai ahead to see whether they could rent a room there.

When he arrived at the gate of Djang's hostel, Ma Joong called out:

"Is there anybody inside? We are travellers from Peking, where my master is a great silk merchant. Have you room for us?"

The waiter, hearing that important guests had arrived, hastened to open the gate and bade them enter. He assured them that they themselves could choose the room they liked. When he asked about their luggage, Ma Joong told him that their sedan-chairs and their luggage were waiting outside the village. He told Chiao Tai to go out there with the waiter and conduct Judge Dee to the hostel, while he himself went inside. The manager of the hostel came out into the courtyard to greet Ma Joong and personally showed him the guestrooms. Ma Joong selected two clean rooms and supervised the waiters in putting everything in order. Then he went out again to the front gate where Judge Dee had just arrived in his sedan chair. While Chiao Tai and the waiter unloaded the luggage, Ma Joong paid the chair bearers off, and then conducted Judge Dee to his room. He ordered hot tea for the judge. When they had refreshed themselves, the manager came in to pay a courtesy call. He said politely:

"I come to inquire the honorable guest's name. I hear that the gentleman is from Peking and intends to do some business here. I act as a broker for all kinds of business and am always honored with the patronage of the merchants who pass through here. Moreover the kitchen here can supply any kind of food or wine you might desire!"

"My surname", Judge Dee answered, "is Liang and my personal name Dee-goong. I am the representative of a large silk firm in Peking. We left there about one month ago, intending to proceed via this place to Kiangsu Province where we were to purchase a large quantity of raw silk for our firm. But unfortunately I fell ill en route and we arrived here only today. Now I fear that I won't be able to reach Kiangsu before the silk season is over. Since the great silk routes from North and South meet here, I hoped to be able to purchase the silk here. How is the market for raw silk at present?"

"This place", the manager said, "is quite some distance from Kiangsu but still we are kept informed regularly about market conditions there. People say that the spring was unusually mild, so that there is an abundance of raw silk. One hundred catties sell there for only 35 silver pieces. The local market price is about 39 silver pieces for a hundred catties. When you consider that it takes several weeks to travel here from Kiangsu and you reckon the transportation costs, then, as I see it, the local price of 39 silver pieces is really cheaper than in Kiangsu".

Judge Dee pretended to hesitate and began asking all kinds of questions about the quality of the raw silk sold locally. When Manager Djang had answered these, Judge Dee added that this was the first time that he was acting as a travelling representative for his firm. "The old representative", he said, "died recently, and the boss chose me to succeed him. It is very awkward that I fell ill. I am still eager to do some good business for my firm. Since the silk price here seems not to be excessive I might as well ask you to introduce me to some one who is willing to sell, and then see whether we can do business. If I can purchase all I need here, it will save me the journey to Kiangsu".

Manager Djang was overjoyed on hearing this, for not only could he make a good commission by acting as broker in this transaction, but he would also have this wealthy merchant and his servants as guests for a couple of days, thus making a tidy bit of profit on the rooms and the food. He gladly promised to do all he could to bring "Mr. Liang" into contact with a dependable silk dealer. He took his leave after ordering the waiter to bring some refreshments and to tell the cooks to prepare a good repast.

When they had finished their meal, Judge Dee told Chiao Tai to stay in the room to guard their luggage. He went with Ma Joong to the manager's office and asked him whether it would be convenient for him to go out with them.

Manager Djang came hastily out from behind his counter, saying that he would be glad to act as guide. He took them through some winding streets to a busy shopping center. Large shops occupied both sides of the street. The place had a very prosperous look.

While he stood still in front of an impressive establishment the clerk came out to greet him, saying:

"Mr. Djang, please enter with your friends. My master is out just now but he will be back soon".

Judge Dee thought that it was fortunate that the superior was out, for now he could try to get some information out of the clerk. Thus he said to Manager Djang:

"We have no other pressing business, so let us sit down here a while and wait for the manager's return".

Upon entering, Judge Dee saw a spacious room, without a counter or the other usual appointments of a shop. At one side all kinds of merchandise were piled up high against the wall. On the other side there was a beautiful tea table of carved wood and a set of chairs. The white-washed wall bore the name of the firm in large red characters, while the additional information imparted that transit business was done here in all goods from north and south.

They sat down. The clerk served them tea. During the exchange of the usual amenities, it transpired that the name of the manager was Loo Chang-po, and that his family had lived there for generations. The clerk asked more closely about Judge Dee's business and what firm in Peking he represented. Fortunately Judge Dee remembered that when he was in Peking in his student days, he used to pass through the Yao-djia Street, where there was a large silk firm called Way-yee or something like that. Thus he told the clerk that his firm was called Way-yee.

The clerk immediately smiled broadly and said:

"That is a famous firm! Excuse me. I should have treated you with more respect! When our former manager was still alive he did much business with your firm. Thereafter, when business in Peking flourished more and more, your firm sent its representatives directly to Kiangsu and did not come here any more. Why is it that you are now coming here again to buy raw silk?"

Judge Dee recited the same tale he had foisted on Manager Djang. He was still at it when a man about forty entered the room. Manager Djang hastily rose from his chair, saying: "Manager Loo has returned."

After the introductions were over and Manager Loo had heard about Judge Dee's plan, he said:

"You have timed your visit here nicely. Only a few days ago a silk merchant by the name of Djao arrived from Kiangsu.

He is an old client of my firm and gave me his bales of raw silk to sell for him. If you like you can have a look at them".

He took Judge Dee to the other side of the room, and showed him a large pile of bales of raw silk.

Judge Dee looked them over. He saw that most bore the name of a well known Kiangsu firm stamped in large letters. But there were two that were so covered with dry mud that the name of the firm could not be deciphered. Seeing these two bales was enough. He called out to Ma Joong:

"You have long experience in appraising raw silk. Come over here and have a look. It seems to me that the gloss is not all it should be".

Ma Joong knew that the judge had discovered something. He walked over to the bales, but he first opened a few others and then turned to the two muddy ones.

"The silk", he said, "is all right. But it has been exposed to moisture on the road. That is why the gloss has gone. Now the contents of these two bales, although they are a bit dirty, still have the right kind of gloss. If the owner is still here, we might try to make a deal with him".

Judge Dee expressed his approval, and added that if the price was reasonable he might buy the entire lot. Then he inquired whether the merchant Djao was still in town. Manager Loo, eager to do business, said to the clerk:

"Mr. Djao is gambling in the warden's house now. You go over there and tell him to come here immediately, since there is a party who wants to buy the entire lot of raw silk".

The clerk went out, and Manager Djang took his leave shortly after, remarking that night was falling and that his presence was required at the hostel to receive new guests.

They all had some more tea. Then the clerk came back with a tall fellow. Ma Joong immediately recognised him as the ruffian he had followed the other day.

# Fourteenth Chapter

MA JOONG AND DJAO ENGAGE IN A BOUT OF WRESTLING;
A MEETING OF TWO BROTHERS OF THE GREEN WOODS.

Ma Joong gave a secret sign to Judge Dee indicating that this indeed was their man.

Judge Dee eyed him carefully. He was over six feet tall. His face had a dark color, with small, glittering eyes under bushy eyebrows. He was clad in a short jacket with narrow sleeves, and wore his blue robe tucked up between his legs, so that his trousers were visible. Furthermore he wore thin-soled sandals on his feet, altogether presenting the appearance of a "brother of the green woods" rather than of an honest merchant.

As soon as Manager Loo had seen the new arrival, he stood up to greet him and said with a smile:

"It is said that if you are eager to sell a chicken, it is hard to find a man who wants one. But you are lucky. Only a few days ago you commissioned me to sell your silk, and here I have a buyer for you already".

Then he told merchant Djao Judge Dee's story.

Merchant Djao had seated himself in the mean time. While Manager Loo was talking he had given Judge Dee a good look. Then he said with a wry smile:

"It is quite true that I want to sell my goods. But I fear that this gentleman here has no real intention of buying".

Manager Loo was quite taken aback by this unexpected answer, and said hurriedly:

"Mr. Djao, you are joking; you should know better than to say that I would deceive you. This gentleman is a representative of the Way-yee firm of Peking, a house of excellent standing, as everyone in our trade knows."

The tall fellow's remark, however, had startled Judge Dee

Judge Dee's first meeting with Djao Wan-chuan.  Manager
Loo bids Djao welcome to his shop.  Judge Dee, disguised as
a silk merchant, is standing on right, behind the manager.

The vertical signboard hanging from the eaves bears the
name of Loo's shop.

even more. He thought that this man, who had at a first meeting found out that he was not the merchant he pretended to be, must be an uncommonly shrewd observer. The only thing he could do was to try to convince merchant Djao that he was wrong. So he rose from his chair and said with a deep bow:

"Greetings to you, Mr. Djao".

The tall fellow immediately answered him with a still deeper bow and said respectfully:

"Your Excellency, please remain seated. This insignificant person has delayed too long in paying you a courtesy visit, for which I implore your pardon".

This speech amazed the judge still more, for apparently this man Djao knew exactly who he was.

"Elder brother", Judge Dee said, "what makes you address me like this? Are we not all businessmen who are wont to talk as equals? What is your honorable name?"

"My surname", the other answered, "is Djao, and my name Wan-chuan. I am a much-travelled man. I have traversed the Empire from north to south and moreover am conversant with the art of physiognomy. Now what might be Your Excellency's business here? May I respectfully ask your honorable name and inquire what your official position is at present? Would I be far wrong if I took it that you are now the magistrate of some district or other?"

On hearing this Judge Dee felt greatly ashamed, for evidently he had played his role as merchant very badly. However it was too late to go on pretending, so he said sharply:

"If you know exactly who I am, you cannot be ignorant of the case that brought me here!" Then he gave Ma Joong a secret sign.

Ma Joong jumped forward shouting:

"You dog of a robber, did you think you could escape by fleeing to this place? Now our judge has come here himself to arrest you. We shall drag you to the tribunal in chains!"

Then he placed himself in front of the door to prevent Djao from escaping and crouched in the wrestler's stance to hurl himself on the tall fellow.

Manager Loo, seeing these sudden developments, thought he was having a bad dream. He cried: "Gentlemen, gentlemen, this is a decent shop. We cannot have fisticuffs here!"

He had hardly finished speaking when Djao Wan-chuan had rolled up his sleeves, and cursing Judge Dee and Ma Joong for a corrupt official and his running-dog, he sprang towards Ma Joong swift as an arrow, aiming a long blow at his heart region, using the stance called "a tiger clawing at a sheep". But Ma Joong dodged the blow by withdrawing one step to the left, a trick called "enticing the tiger out his forest"; at the same time he hit Djao's outstretched arm a sharp blow with two fingers exactly on the vein inside the elbow. Djao's right arm was temporarily lamed, his attack was stemmed, and he was trying to regain his stance when Ma Joong followed up his success with a sharp blow below Djao's ribs. Now Djao was fully aware that he had an expert opponent and went on strictly according to rules. Using his lamed arm to protect his body, he quickly caught Ma Joong's right wrist with his left arm. But before Djao could twist his arm and place a kick, Ma Joong quickly countered with the trick called: "The Phoenix bird spreading its wings"; he sprang two feet in the air, thus loosening Djao's grip, at the same time aiming a left kick at his face. Djao, however, had expected this move; he quickly ducked between Ma Joong's legs before he had come down and threw him on the floor with a crash.*

---

* (Translator's note) Chinese boxing is a very ancient art dating from the beginning of our era. In the 4th century when Northern Buddhism entered China, Chinese boxers borrowed much from the corporal and mental discipline of the Indian Yoga school, also making use of Taoist mysticism. It was developed into a highly efficient art

Judge Dee, seeing his lieutenant floored, thought that all was lost and that Djao would now make his getaway. Just while he was debating what to do, a man of about thirty burst into the room, with shoulders broad as a bear, and a waist as slim as that of a tiger. He gave Ma Joong and Djao Wan-chuan one look, shouting:

"Stop it, brother Djao! This is a friend of mine!" And to Ma Joong he said: "Brother Ma, how did you come here? Why are you fighting with one of our brothers?"

As he spoke he helped Ma Joong up. Ma Joong smiled all over when he saw the newcomer, and said:

"Elder brother, so we meet again! But before we say one other word, let us first make sure that this ruffian here does not escape. He is being sought for murder!"

The newcomer told Djao to stay right where he was. He ordered the crowd of onlookers that had assembled at the door to make themselves scarce and then said to Ma Joong:

"This Djao Wan-chuan is an old friend of mine. Why are you fighting with him. What is this talk about a murder?"

"That", Ma Joong said, "is a long story. But first I must tell you that this is my master, the district magistrate of Chang-ping,

---

of attack and self-defense without weapons, which reached its greatest perfection towards the end of the Ming period in the 17th century. When the Manchus conquered China, most of the martial arts languished. A few Ming refugees, however, had fled to Japan, and taught this art to the Japanese, who used it as the basis of what is now widely known as *judo* or *jiujutsu*, viz. Japanese wrestling. In order to prevent this art being practised by unworthy persons, its finer points were always kept as a deep secret that was only transmitted orally by the teacher to his favorite pupils. For the same reason the few books that were published on the subject are written in a special technical language, ununderstandable to the outsider; the names of the tricks and stances quoted here are an example of this jargon. In recent years interest in this art has revived in China, and nowadays it finds many eager students among the younger generation.

His Excellency Judge Dee".

The newcomer hastily knelt down before the Judge, saying:

"Your Honor is the famous magistrate of the neighboring district. Please forgive my remissness in not recognizing you earlier".

Judge Dee made him rise, and said:

"You are not under my jurisdiction, my man, and you need not be so ceremonial. Please sit down and tell me who you are, and in what way you are connected with my lieutenant Ma Joong and this fellow Djao?"

"My humble surname", the newcomer said, "is Djiang and my name Djung. Formerly I was a brother of the green woods, and together with Ma Joong here studied under the same master the arts of boxing and fencing. Soon, however, I found that wild life not to my taste. I thought I could use my strength for a more worthy cause. I settled down in this village and soon was elected as the local warden.

"As to this Djao Wan-chuan, he is a man of Kiangsu province. He used to study under my father who taught him medicine, boxing, and the art of physiognomy. He led a roving existence for a time, but then inherited some money from an aunt and set up in the silk business. He did very well, travelling all over the Empire as a representative of a large firm. He often comes here on business. He always stays at my place. Today we were just having a small gambling game together, when Djao was called away by the clerk here. When he stayed away so long, I came here to see what had happened to him.

"I can personally guarantee that Djao is an honest man, although he may be quick-tempered. If he had killed sombody in a fight, he would have given himself up. He certainly would not have fled here and stayed with me, without saying a word about this affair."

## Fifteenth Chapter

DJAO GIVES A CLEAR ACCOUNT OF THE REAL MURDERER; JUDGE DEE ALLOWS MRS. DJOU TO RETURN TO HER HOME.

This story impressed Judge Dee, but it failed to convince him. He thought that this man Djao had all the marks of a hardened criminal. Djiang Djung, after all, was a former highway robber. He would not put it beyond them to have invented this story just to avert suspicion.

Ma Joong guessed the judge's train of thought, and said:

"Your Honor, there is no reason to doubt. Since brother Djiang has guaranteed that this man Djao is an honest merchant, it is certain that he is not implicated in this case. Perhaps he himself can give an adequate explanation of how he happened to have the bales of the murdered man".

"Brother Djao", Warden Djiang said, "report to His Excellency here exactly what happened. In our brotherhood everything must be clear and honest. Moreover I am the warden of this village, on the border of the Chang-ping district and so I am also partly responsible for seeing that the real murderer is brought to justice".

"This", Djao began, "is a most vexing story. The murder was committed by a man called Shao, who, not content with having done this foul deed, also managed to drag me into it. The full name of the fellow is Shao Lee-huai, a native of Kiangsu Province. Just as I, he is a travelling silk merchant, who buys the raw silk cheaply in Kiangsu during the season and then peddles it along the highways here in Shantung. I often met him on the road.

"Last month, when I was buying raw silk in Kiangsu, he left there earlier, together with a young colleague of ours, called Liu. Now the other day I met Shao alone on the road near Chang-ping, pushing a cart loaded with bales of silk. I asked him

where young Liu had gone and why he was travelling alone.
That is not a wise thing to do if you carry valuable merchandise.
He sighed and told me a long tale of woe. Liu had succumbed
from a sudden and violent illness on the road; by dint of much
trouble he had purchased a coffin for him and had it temporarily put up in some temple, spending the last copper of his
travelling funds on a fee for the priests. Then it proved that,
through this delay, he had missed the right time for selling his
silk at a good profit. If it were not for his efforts to help a dead
colleague, and have his body decently encoffined, he would have
been back home again by now with a sizable profit in his pocket.
I believed this story and asked him where he was going. He said
that for the time being he did not intend to go back south since
he feared that Liu's family would hold him responsible for his
death. He borrowed 300 pieces of silver from me and gave me
the cart with the silk as a security. I could sell Liu's half of it,
and return the proceeds to his family, while his own half would
more or less correspond to the 300 silver pieces he had borrowed
from me. That is how that crook managed to involve me in
this affair. He himself ran away with my good money".

Judge Dee asked quickly:

"Do you know where this man Shao went, after he had given
you the cart and the silk?"

"He did not tell me", answered Djao, "but I can make a good
guess. I knew the teacher of this fellow Shao many years
ago. He thought that young Shao was a promising fellow and
gave him his daughter in marriage. But this Shao, instead of
showing his gratitude for this mark of his teacher's affection,
maltreated his wife. She died of a broken heart. Thereafter
I heard that he had started an affair with an abandoned woman,
who lived in a place in this province called Turn-up Pass or
something like that. I think it is most probable that Shao went
there, to spend the money he robbed from Liu with his paramour.

I am perfectly prepared to go to Turn-up Pass myself and get that fellow for you, just to get even with him".

By now Judge Dee was fully convinced that Djao was speaking the truth. He marveled again at the accuracy of his dream in the temple; the verse had suggested that the criminal's name was Shao; only the reference to Szuchuan Province remained un-explained. He could not remember having ever heard of a place called Turn-up Pass and asked Manager Loo. The manager, who by now had gradually understood what was going on, started on a long apology to the judge, saying that he had not known that such a famous and high official had honored him with a visit and so on. But Judge Dee cut him short, remarking that he had come in the role of a merchant and that Manager Loo had treated him with all the courtesy he was entitled to. Manager Loo then started to think hard about a Turn-up Pass, but he could not remember ever having heard of such a locality.

In the meantime the paper lanterns were being lighted. Judge Dee decided to go back to the hostel. He rose from his chair and said a few appropriate words to Manager Loo about having caused him all this trouble. Then he invited Warden Djiang and Djao Wan-chuan to go back with them for the evening meal. They gladly accepted and the four of them strolled back to the hostel.

Chiao Tai had become worried over their long absence and was most eager to hear the news. Ma Joong introduced Warden Djiang and Djao Wan-chuan and told him the new developments, while Judge Dee retired for a rest. After a while Manager Djang came in. Ma Joong told him briefly who Judge Dee was and the real purpose of their visit to Divine Village. Manager Djang was overjoyed to have such a distinguished guest and went im-mediately to the kitchen to order a magnificent repast.

When the steaming dishes and a jar of wine were being brought in Judge Dee invited all present to sit down and have an informal meal and a frank discussion without regard for rank or age.

Djao Wan-chuan proved to be an engaging fellow who could tell many a story about his adventures on the road. Warden Djiang went into some detail about his exploits together with Ma Joong when both of them were still "brothers of the green woods". Then Djao Wan-chuan said to Judge Dee:

"In our guild of travelling silk merchants, news travels fast. I fear that if we don't make haste to apprehend that fellow Shao in Turn-up Pass he may hear about his having been traced there and escape to some of the outlying provinces".

Ma Joong thought that this was excellent advice, adding:

"Your Honor, in Chang-ping the case of Bee Hsun still awaits its solution. I propose that you leave the arresting of Shao Lee-huai entirely to Djao Wan-chuan and myself, and that we return to-morrow to Chang-ping. For although we have good reason to think that Shao Lee-huai is hiding in Turn-up Pass, we have yet to locate that place. In Chang-ping in order to obtain this infor-mation we can have the records of the tribunal searched and ask some of the old inhabitants".

Judge Dee agreed, and after a few more rounds of wine, War-den Djiang and Djao Wan-chuan took their leave and all went to rest.

The next morning Judge Dee ordered light horse carts in order to reach Chang-ping as quickly as possible.

Ma Joong paid Manager Djang their bill. The grooms shouted, whips crackled, and Judge Dee left the hostel, his party augmented by Djao Wan-chuan. Warden Djiang and Manager Djang bowed their farewell in front of the gate.

They reached Chang-ping before noon. Judge Dee first went to the tribunal where he had the seals of office returned to him. Then he called in the head of the archives and told him to search through the records for a locality called Turn-up Pass. Thereafter he had the official correspondence brought in, disposing of the most urgent despatches.

Only after he had dealt with these matters did he go to his living quarters and there had a bath, and late luncheon. Returned to his private office, he asked the clerk whether there had been any news from Sergeant Hoong and Tao Gan. The clerk reported that they had been back twice during the judge's absence. The first time Sergeant Hoong had said that Warden Ho Kai went about his business with commendable zeal, but that the men called Hsu investigated thus far proved to be law-abiding citizens, who moreover had hardly known Bee Hsun. The second time Tao Gan had come alone and left a message requesting that Mrs. Djou be released from prison as soon as possible. He and the sergeant kept Mrs. Bee's house under constant observation, but nothing had happened beyond Mrs. Bee coming out and telling the neighbours every day several times how badly Judge Dee treated them. He saw no hope for anything developing there unless Mrs. Djou be released to act as a decoy.

Judge Dee nodded, and gave orders to have the court hall arranged for the opening of the session.

When it was reported to him that the scribes and the constables had assembled in the hall, Judge Dee donned his official robe and cap and left his private office. The curtains over the dais were drawn. Judge Dee appeared, seated behind the bench.

First he had a few documents relating to official routine brought in. Having unrolled the first one, he took in its contents with one glance and issued the necessary orders to the scribes while he was already unrolling the second one. Thus in half an hour all the routine business that had accumulated during his absence was speedily and accurately dealt with.

Then he filled out a slip for the warden of the jail and handed it to a constable with the instruction to bring Mrs. Djou in.

As soon as the constables had made her kneel before the bench, she began reviling Judge Dee. But he cut her short peremptorily, and said:

"Hold your insolent tongue. In due time the criminal shall be revealed. Meanwhile, I think it is not right that your old mother suffers for you, and has to run her house all alone. I therefore shall now release you on bail, so that you can serve your mother, as is proper".

Mrs. Djou, however, cried:

"You dog official, first you drag me here and torture me, an innocent woman, and then you talk about my poor mother alone at home! It is you who caused all her grief, by cruelly throwing her daughter in jail, and then maltreating her poor son's corpse! Do you expect me to go home now quietly, so that you can hush up this outrageous affair? I tell you for all to hear, that I stand by my word. I am not going to leave this tribunal until the high authorities have punished you, and have removed your judge's cap. Then, my wrong avenged, I shall leave this place, and not one day earlier".

At this moment Ma Joong interrupted her, and said:

"Woman, come to your senses! It is a special favor that we allow you to do your duty towards your mother-in-law. But if you refuse, well, everybody will know what to think".

Mrs. Djou in her heart was very keen to go home but she did not dare to say so right away for fear that thus she would excite further suspicions. Ma Joong's words gave here a welcome cue, and she said:

"I gladly sacrifice my personal grievance to the duties of filial piety. I shall go now, and as regards bond, you can send one of your men with me. He can have my mother sign a guarantee that I shall not try to escape".

Judge Dee ordered the constables to take the chains off and told Ma Joong to bring her back to Huang-hua Village in a small sedan chair.

# INTERLUDE

Three actors enter. The stage is supposed to represent a
scene on a river bank. It is late in the season, but the prune
trees are still in bloom.

The first actor plays the role of the "young maiden," the
second plays the role of the "young lover," and the third the
role of the "elderly man."

MAIDEN, *speaks:*

"I have come here many times, but never, it seems to me, were
the blossoms as beautiful as to-day."

*sings:*

"Only sing of beauty, only sing of love,
Never think of duty, when you think of love!"

MAN, *speaks:*

"How is it an attractive young maiden like you has come out
here all alone? At home there must be someone who loves you
dearly?"

MAIDEN, *acts coy, speaks:*

"That may be so. But on a day like this who thinks of the
people at home?"

YOUNG MAN, *speaks:*

"The other day passing along here, I admired this same view."

MAIDEN, *acts eager, speaks:*

"Did you walk along the bank and see the green willow trees?"

YOUNG MAN, *acts happy, sings:*

"Wherever I went were flowers, were flowers all the way,
"I took from fragrant bowers, of blossoms a tender spray"

*speaks:*

"It is late in the afternoon, I shall have to leave now."

MAIDEN, *speaks:*

"I don't want to go home. At home there is a cruel, cruel man,
who asks, always asks me questions. He presses me so I sometimes want to drown myself in a well!"

MAN, *speaks:*

"Let you and I go together and look at the blossoming trees. I would like to help you."

MAIDEN, *acts laughing, sings:*

"Last year, last month, yesterday,
I knew no love, and I knew no pain;
This year, this month, and to-day,
I have both love and I have pain"

MAN, *speaks:*

"Let us go there then all three together. It would be sad if we were to forego this feast."

YOUNG MAN, *speaks:*

"The season is already nearly over; who thinks this year of last year's bloom?"

MAN, *acts sad, speaks:*

"A flowering sprig, well tended, will last long."

MAIDEN, *sings:*

"I dream of the candles, the candles red and bright,
"Who thinks of tomorrow, on her wedding night?"

YOUNG MAN, *speaks:*

"It is said that on the festival of the flowers there shall be no difference of rank or position. Let the three of us go together, without inquiring name or surname. For after to-day we shall never meet again."

MAIDEN, *speaks:*

"Yes, how sad it is that nothing is so brief as a day-dream late in spring!"

YOUNG MAN, *acts happy, sings:*

"When you seek for beauty, when you seek for love,
"Never think of duty, only think of love!"

Exeunt

# Sixteenth Chapter

A DEAF CONSTABLE REVEALS THE KEY TO THE PROBLEM;
JUDGE DEE SENDS OUT HIS MEN FOR APPREHENDING SHAO.

Judge Dee left the court hall and, having seated himself in his private office, had the head of the archives brought in.

He reported that a search in the old records of the district administration had failed to produce any results; there was no mention of a place called Turn-up Pass in the Province of Shantung. He respectfully suggested that Judge Dee circulate his colleagues in the other districts, asking whether they could perhaps supply the required information.

Judge Dee gave a non-committal answer and sent him away. He knew that there was no time to write a circular to the other district magistrates; by the time their answers came in, Shao Lee-huai would have received news about what was afoot and he would never be arrested. After some thought, Judge Dee ordered the clerk to select the oldest men among the constables, and bring them in.

When three greybeards had come in and respectfully greeted the judge, he asked them whether in their long careers they had ever been in a locality called Turn-up Pass. Two of them said immediately that they had never in their lifetime even heard about a place of that name.

Now the third was an old man of about seventy, who was half deaf. He had heard only vaguely what Judge Dee asked, and had stood there mumbling by himself, pulling at his beard. When the two others had answered the judge, he cackled:

"Turnips! Now, there Your Honor is saying something! The right season has not yet arrived, but if Your Honor wants some, I have in my garden quite a few, imported from another locality. They ripen earlier, and they are real juicy turnips. If Your Honor wants some, I shall be glad to oblige..."

The other constables, fearing that Judge Dee would be angry, hastened to say that the old man was deaf, but that he knew all the tricks of the trade and often gave excellent advice; moreover, he still was quite useful for light guard duty. Judge Dee, however, smiled a little and told the old man that for the moment he did not require the turnips, but that he would like to try them some other day.

The old constable, thinking that Judge Dee had misgivings about taking these special turnips from him, insisted:

"Please, Your Honor, allow me to go home and get some nice ones for you. I have more than enough of them, and moreover having come all the way from Szuchuan Pass, they are a rare treat".

The mention of the name "Szuchuan Pass" startled Judge Dee to no small degree. He remembered how accurately the first part of the verse that he had seen in his dream tallied with the name Shao, and with Divine Village; could it be that the reference to Szuchuan in the second part did not refer to that distant province at all, but to a place that happened to bear that name, right here in the province of Shantung? Would this greybeard have the key to the final solution of the double murder of Six Mile Village?

Thereupon he turned to the other constables and the clerks, and said:

"I have to ask this man a few questions in private. Your presence is no longer required".

The others thought for themselves that this was going to be a queer conversation, with one of the parties half deaf; but they hastened to obey the judge.

When they were alone, the judge first asked the old constable some routine questions, such as his name and surname, where he came from and how long he had been serving in the tribunal. When he noticed that the greybeard was completely at ease and had become accustomed to his voice, Judge Dee said:

"Now these turnips from Szuchuan Pass, that is a subject I would like to know more about, because I am very fond of eating turnips. Where is that place where they grow, and how far is it from here?"

"None of those young whippersnappers over here", the old constable said, "know about that place. Yes, I may be old and deaf, but I still know a thing or two that those young constables have never even heard of. Now I don't say that they don't treat me as they should a man of my age, and fortunately Your Honor is such a kind master, that.. "

"I was asking you", Judge Dee hastily interrupted before the old man could stray from his subject again, "how many miles that place where the turnips grow is from here".

"Yes, yes", the old man said, "I was just coming to that. This Szuchuan Pass is a village in the mountains near the city of Laichow, in this same province. During the former dynasty, a native of Szuchuan Province used to come there regularly to sell his goods, and made a good profit. Therefore finally he settled down there permanently, opened a shop, and in course of time became a very wealthy man. After he died, his sons and grandsons continued this business, and theirs became the leading family in the district. Thus people called that locality Szuchuan Pass, because the leading family came from that province. Thereafter, however, the family fortune declined, their wealth was gradually scattered, and finally they left there. Then people forgot all about them, and called the place Turnip Pass, because the turnips there are large and juicy. Now some years ago, one of Your Honor's predecessors sent me out there on a case and, talking with the old people there, I heard this story about the Szuchuan family. When I returned home, I took a basket of turnips with me and planted them in my garden. They did very well, and I dare say there are none better in this whole district. Now if Your Honor allows me to go home and fetch a few...”

But Judge Dee had not heard his last words. Overjoyed he reflected that Djao Wan-chuan had mistaken Turnip Pass for Turn-up Pass when he heard about Shao Lee-huai's love nest, and that this mistake had been corrected through the bad hearing of the old constable. And he marveled at the subtle way in which the verse in his dream had conveyed the information that the criminal was to be found there.

“You say that you were once in that neighborhood”, Judge Dee said to the old constable, “Now that is excellent, for I must send some men there on a case. I wish you could go with them, to show them the way. Can you make such a long journey?”

“Your Honor”, the old constable said, “I may be old and deaf, but I am still capable of executing your orders. Moreover the place is not too far, we should be able to make it in nine or ten days. Your Honor just tell me when I should go”.

Judge Dee dismissed him with a few kind words, and enjoined him not to tell others about their conversation.

The next day, after the morning session, Judge Dee called Djao Wan-chuan, and told him the good news that Turnip Pass had been located. Djao was amazed, and said:

“Thus one sees how closely woven are the nets of Heaven's justice! Well, since the criminal is there, let me go and get him!”

Judge Dee told him to wait till Ma Joong's return from Huang-hua Village. In the mean time he drew up an official document for the magistrates of the districts they would have to pass on their way out there, stating their business and adding the usual request that if the need should arise, they give them the necessary assistance.

That night Ma Joong came back. He also was overjoyed to hear the news. Judge Dee ordered him to pack his luggage that same night, and set out early the next morning, together with Djao Wan-chuan, Chiao Tai and the old constable. Then he handed him their credentials and money for travelling expenses.

After an uneventful journey, in the afternoon of the seventh day, the four men arrived at the city of Lai-chow, the last stop before they would reach the passes.

They sent the old constable ahead to reserve a room in a hostel. The other three went to the office of the district magistrate to have their credentials stamped. Just as the clerk brought their documents back, the old constable entered the gate of the tribunal and told them he had found a nice room in a cheap hostel. They went there together and informed the manager that they were travelling silk merchants.

When the waiter brought their dinner to the room, Ma Joong asked him about the silk market in the passes. The waiter said that the market was not bad. People there had plenty of money. But he added that he hoped they were not planning to go out there to sell their wares, but would do business in the city. For a very moderate commission, the waiter was willing to introduce them to some people who might be interested in buying. Djao Wan-chuan, however, cut him short and told him that the next morning they were going to Turnip Pass, and that they were not interested in the market in the city.

The waiter gave them a queer look. He said that it was a lonely place, with bad roads. There was a garrison of about six hundred soldiers stationed there, to guard the passes. But doubtless they knew all that.

Ma Joong told him that they were newcomers but the waiter did not seem to believe that. When asked again about a large silk merchant there, he said reluctantly that he had heard a shop Lee Da mentioned. Suddenly the waiter departed without waiting for a tip.

"What", Ma Joong exclaimed, "is wrong with that bastard?"

Djao Wan-chuan looked rather unhappy and said:

"Friends, now I remember that I have been to the place be-

fore, although at that time I did not know that one of the villages
scattered around the passes was called Turnip Pass. Let me tell you
that we shan't have an easy job. The people living there are a
bad lot. In summer, when the grain is standing high in this part
of the province, they lie in ambush along the highroads killing
and robbing all merchants and travellers that happen to pass. So
bad is the reputation of the region that experienced travellers prefer
to make a long detour to avoid passing through there when the
grain is standing high. The garrison is stationed there to prevent
the local people from creating disorder on a large scale rather
than for guarding the passes. All these robbers are banded together in gangs, and Shao Lee-huai must be well in with them.
If we try to arrest him there we will have the whole gang on our
necks".

Ma Joong said laughing:

"Now brother, that is queer talk from you! You don't mean
to say that you are afraid?"

"There you are wrong", Djao Wan-chuan said, "But I know
what I am talking about. I stand up to anyone, but there is a
difference between courage and foolhardiness".

Chiao Tai fully agreed with Djao, and added:

"Let us not forget that we are far from our own district and
that the local authorities won't thank us for stirring up trouble.
You can assume that the district magistrate is content at leaving
that crowd of robbers in the passes well alone, as long as they
don't rebel or refuse to pay their taxes".

Then Djao Wan-chuan said:

"What about the military? We have our credentials and we
could apply through the district magistrate to the garrison commander".

Now the old constable laughed aloud and said:

"You fellows may be strong and good fighters, but in this you
are extremely new. Listen to a old man grown grey in official

service: that garrison commander is either getting a share of the loot or he is completely satisfied with his easy life there. Try to get his help against the gangs, and what will happen? If he has you flogged as trouble-makers and sends you back to Chang-ping in chains, you will be lucky!"

Ma Joong fully agreed with the old constable. They all fell silent and thought hard how this difficulty could be solved. After some time, Djao Wan-chuan struck the table with his fist, and said:

"Friends, I have found it! I have promised the judge that I would get this Shao Lee-huai, and I am going to do it. When we arrive at the passes tomorrow, we will separate as soon as we have located a hostel. Then I will go alone to the Lee Da silkshop and try to locate our man through them. When I have found him, I will tell him some cock and bull story about Manager Loo having cheated me with the silk, and that he must go back with me, in order to get our money out of him and something extra for our trouble. I shall invite him to the hostel where we give him a good dinner and persuade him to leave together with us the next day. And then, as soon as we have left and get near the city, we tell him that he is arrested!"

They all thought that this was an excellent plan and Ma Joong praised Djao's resourcefulness. They had a last round of wine and then went to bed for a good night's rest.

## Seventeenth Chapter

DJAO LEARNS THE WAYS OF THE PEOPLE OF THE PASSES;
HAVING FOUND SHAO, HE IS ENTICED BY A CLEVER LIE.

The next morning they left the hostel early, and towards noon they saw flags fluttering in the wind in the distance. Soon they arrived at the military camp and noted that it was surrounded on all four sides by high walls of packed earth.

Having passed the fort, they found themselves in a lonely mountain landscape. Only here and there were there a few patches of arable land. Rocky surfaces with large boulders predominated. Late in the afternoon they crossed the first pass. Suddenly they came upon a village that had quite a prosperous look. There were shops on both sides of the road and the people that passed were well clad. Before long they saw the signboard of a hostel. The manager seemed not too eager to take strangers, but after some haggling over the price he reluctantly let them have a room.

Ma Joong, Chiao Tai and the greybeard went inside, and Djao Wan-chuan shouldered his two bundles of luggage, and went on alone to find the Lee Da silk shop. After having inquired about the road of a couple of street urchins, he finally came to a large shop, with the two characters Lee Da displayed over the door.

Djao Wan-chuan walked in and asked a young plug-ugly who was standing behind the counter whether this was Lee Da's silkshop.

That fellow immediately started cursing and shouted:

"Can't you read, you fool? Isn't the signboard outside large enough?"

Djao had promised himself that he would do his best to avoid trouble, but this was more than he could stand. He promptly shouted back:

"You bastard, answer a civil question!"

"Would you be looking for trouble?" said the thug vaulting over the counter with amazing swiftness, simultaneously aiming a long blow at Djao's middle.

Djao could not use his hands because he was still carrying his bundles, and a lesser man would have fared badly in this situation. But Djao, being an expert boxer, just lifted his right foot, and placed it accurately in the other's groin. He could not put much force in his kick, but he knew that that would be amply supplied by the impetus of the other's attack. As it was, the ruffian just gasped and doubled up on the floor moaning.

Djao grinned, and said:

"Now you see what a beginner you are in this game, you dogshead! This time I shan't beat you to pulp here, but next time you meet a stranger who asks you a polite question, remember to keep a civil tongue in your mouth!"

While the ruffian was trying to scramble up, four others had emerged from the back of the shop and asked Djao what he meant by bursting in and beating up their friend.

"I only came", Djao said, "to try to locate an old sworn brother of mine named Shao Lee-huai".

The others suddenly became friendly, and said:

"Please come in the backroom, stranger, and have some tea. Don't mind that fellow. He is in a nasty temper today and getting knocked down serves him right".

At that moment a voice called from inside:

"Who is asking for me?"

Djao went in and stood face to face with Shao Lee-huai. Djao greeted him cordially, and Shao took him to the reception room, where they sat down. Then Shao Lee-huai asked him:

"How did you know that I live here and what business has taken you to this part of our province?"

Djao took a few sips of tea, and then answered:

"That is a long story. Suffice it to say that I have been grievously wronged, and that this affair indirectly affects you too. Let me tell you that we shall have to settle it in no uncertain manner. It won't be an easy job, although there is a tidy bit of money in it. But I cannot do it without a couple of stout fellows to help me. Fortunately I remembered that you once told me that you often stayed in this place, so I hastened here to ask for your help".

Shao was quite interested now and wanted to know what had happened.

Thereupon Djao Wan-chuan told him a sad story. When he arrived in Divine Village, he had handed the bales of raw silk of Shao and the late Liu to Manager Loo to sell it for him. Loo had told him he would do his best, and take but a very moderate commission. The very next day he indeed managed to sell the entire lot to a silk merchant from Peking at a good price. But when Djao went to Manager Loo to receive the money, he only reviled him, shouting that he had never got a single bale of silk from Djao. On top of that he had hired a gang of ruffians, who had beaten up Djao badly when he protested. Warden Djiang was absent on a journey to a relative, and since there had been no witnesses, there was nothing Djao could do about it.

Shao Lee-huai got very excited, he swore that Djao could count on him to get even with that crook Loo. After all his own money was involved and he wanted to teach that fellow how to treat decent merchants. They were fully entitled to the money that Manager Loo had received for the silk, and if he happened to have some other sums lying about there, well, after all Djao had a right to comfort money for the beating he had received, and he himself was entitled to a refund of his travelling expenses.

Djao said:

"I knew I could count on you, brother. Now I have already collected three old friends, two tough fellows who used to be in the 'green woods', and one wily old thief. They are waiting in the hostel in the main street. What about accompanying me there.

Have a snack and a drink, and then let us take counsel about how we shall get even with this crook Loo."

"I am at your service", Shao Lee-huai said, "and I shall be honored to be introduced to your friends. We must plan this affair well, for Manager Loo belongs to an old family in Divine Village and the local people there are all on his side. But between the five of us we should be able to manage".

So they walked to the hostel and Djao presented Shao Lee-huai to Ma Joong, Chiao Tai and the greybeard.

Shao called the manager. He told him that these people were old friends of his. The surly manager brightened up visibly and promised to bring a good dinner with plenty of wine. Soon the party was in high spirits, one round of wine followed the other. When the night had well advanced, Djao proposed to Shao Lee-huai that they should leave the village the next morning; they could work out their plans while on the road to Divine Village.

Shao Lee-huai, however, would not hear of that. He said that after all they had come a long way to see him, and he was an important person here who had to act as their host. He proposed that they stay a couple of days, and give him an opportunity to entertain them properly; also to introduce them to a number of old friends of his.

Djao tried to refuse politely, saying that they could not put him to all this trouble. But Shao said that he had also a bit of business to set right, a fellow still owed him a gambling debt, and he wanted to settle that before leaving. At last they agreed that their departure would be deferred one day and that they would set out the day after tomorrow. Then Shao Lee-huai took his leave, promising to come back the next day.

As soon as he had gone, Ma Joong congratulated Djao Wan-chuan in a low voice on the success of his ruse. The stratagem of "enticing the tiger out of his mountains" certainly seemed to have worked well. The only snag was that they could not leave the next

morning.  At any moment a travelling merchant might arrive
in the village who had heard about Judge Dee appearing in Divine
Village, in connection with the murder near Chang-ping.  News
travels fast along the silk roads, and the fight of Ma Joong and
Djao Wan-chuan and their subsequent reconciliation would be the
topic of the day among the local people there.  If Shao Lee-huai
should discover that he had been tricked, and that all four of them
were working for Judge Dee, they would never leave the village
alive.

While Ma Joong, Djao Wan-chuan and Chiao Tai were discussing this risk, the old constable spoke up and said:

"Here again you badly need the advice of an old and experienced police officer. Let me tell you that the danger is even greater
than you think.  Such a well-organized band of robbers as these
scoundrels here in Turnip Pass will certainly have their spies
in the tribunal of Lai-chow. You had your credentials
stamped there, and I am willing to lay a heavy wager that tomorrow a spy will come rushing here from Lai-chow to warn the
people that four officers of the tribunal of Chang-ping are on their
way to arrest the murderer of Six Mile Village. If we are hacked
to pieces here the magistrate of Lai-chow will just report to Chang-
ping that we muddled the affair, and Judge Dee will never solve
his case. Now how about this plan? Let one of us leave before
dawn and run back to Lai-chow as fast as he can. He will report
to the magistrate that we have found the murderer and are returning that afternoon to Lai-chow; he will ask the magistrate to send
a posse of local militia to meet us halfway to help arrest the
criminal."

"What is the advantage of that?", Ma Joong wanted to know.

The old constable pulled at his beard, and said with a smile:

"In the first place, it will give the magistrate a personal
interest in this affair. If a couple of men from the tribunal in
Chang-ping arrest a dangerous criminal in Lai-chow, that does not

interest the local magistrate at all. But if he can report to his superiors that he, as always vigilant in weeding out bad elements in his district, had his constables locate and apprehend a long-sought murderer and duly delivered him in chains to the magistrate in whose district the murder was committed, that will make an excellent impression on the higher authorities, and may accelerate his promotion. You can count on it. He will send out his men to meet us without delay. In the second place, once the local magistrate has committed himself officially in this affair, the bandits here will hesitate to murder us right away, should Shao Lee-huai discover our ruse before we have left; and they won't come after us if they learn through their spies after we have left. For although they won't hesitate to kill a few constables from a far away district, they don't like to stir up trouble with the local authorities. After all, Shao Lee-huai may be their sworn brother, but he still is not a native of this place."

Ma Joong and Chiao Tai shook their heads in admiration and conceded that there was much more in this work than mere courage and a knowledge of boxing. Also Djao Wan-chuan was enthusiastic about the plan and assured them that he would be able to persuade Shao Lee-huai to leave the next day.

They decided that Ma Joong would leave before daybreak, and hurry to Lai-chow. If the others would leave the village with Shao Lee-huai after noon, they would meet with the militia somewhere between the fort and the city.

These matters having been thus decided, they all went to bed for a few hours of sleep.

## Eighteenth Chapter

HALFWAY FROM THE PASSES A CRIMINAL IS ARRESTED;
IN THE TRIBUNAL OF CHANG-PING THE TRIAL IS OPENED.

After breakfast Djao Wan-chuan, Chiao Tai and the greybeard went to the Lee Da silk shop to pay a courtesy call to Shao Lee-huai. Ma Joong had left already an hour before.

Shao Lee-huai received them cordially, and introduced them to the manager of the shop. When all were seated in the reception room after tea and cakes had been served, Shao Lee-huai asked why Ma Joong had not come with them. Djao Wan-chuan answered that he had gone to look up a distant relative who was supposed to be living in the neighborhood; he had said that it might take some time to locate him, and had asked to be excused for not taking part in the courtesy call.

Shao Lee-huai said that a good friend need not apologize. More tea was brought in. He seemed intent on impressing his new friends, and practically had open house in the Lee Da shop. A number of local people kept strolling in. All were introduced to Djao and his companions.

It might have been nice entertainment for them, were it not for the fact that they could not help giving each newcomer an anxious look, to see whether he was perhaps the person bringing the news that would expose them. Moreover the old constable had got into one of his fits of absent mindedness, and they feared that the greybeard would say something that would betray them. Fortunately during such fits he was more deaf than usual and Shao Lee-huai and his friends soon gave up trying to make conversation with him.

Towards noon Shao took them out for a stroll, to give the manager of the Lee Da shop an opportunity to prepare the table in the reception room for a noon meal. They were just walking through the main street, when Djao Wan-chuan was startled by the sight of a tall fellow rounding the corner in the distance, who looked very much like Ma Joong.

When he came near it proved to be perfectly true. To the great consternation of Djao and Chiao Tai, it was Ma Joong himself, with a worried look on his face. Djao managed to conceal his anxiety, and asked cheerfully:

"Well, brother Ma, did you find your relative?"

"No," Ma Joong answered, "I inquired here and there, but it seems that he has left this place." Then, turning to Shao Lee-huai, he added:

"Brother Shao, I apologize for not having called on you this morning. But my excursion proved very useful for both you and me. Outside the pass I met a silk merchant, an old friend of mine, who was travelling with a light horsecart from Chang-ping to the north. He was in a hurry, but he stopped long enough to warn me that he had heard that that crook Manager Loo had traced me to this place, and that he is bringing a suit against you and Djao before the magistrate of Chang-ping, for swindling him. Now I happen to know that the magistrate there, the famous Judge Dee, is a just official and doubtless he will pronounce us innocent, and punish that bastard Loo for bringing in a false accusation. Still, the proverb says: 'If but one word of information against a person gets into court, nine oxen cannot drag it out again.' Not to speak of all the bother and the loss of time. So I rushed back here to tell you this news."

As soon as Shao Lee-huai had heard the word "Chang-ping", his face turned ashen. He said:

"That Judge Dee may be honest or not. But I am not going to let myself become involved in a law suit. After all, your plan is the best. Let us leave here as soon as possible and go to Lai-chow. I have friends there and we can lie in hiding there for a few days, evolving a plan for dealing with that crooked bastard

Loo. As I see it now, it will be best to intimidate him first, so that he officially withdraws his complaint and then kill him before he cooks up more mischief".

Ma Joong pretended to hesitate, but Shao Lee-huai was suddenly in a great hurry, and said:

"You return to the hostel now and pack your things. I shall run back to the shop and explain to the manager. The sooner we leave, the better".

When Shao had left them, Djao Wan-chuan eagerly asked Ma Joong what had happened. Ma Joong said with a smile:

"Luck is with us. We can settle this affair to-day. After I passed the fort, I met a post-carrier on horseback who was on his way to the tribunal of Lai-chow on some urgent business. This man happened to be a former constable of the tribunal of Chang-ping, a most capable and dependable fellow, who two years ago often went with me when our judge sent me out on some case. My meeting with him seemed to me a Heaven-sent opportunity. I explained our predicament to him and he promised to inform the magistrate. Since he is traveling on horseback, he must have reached the tribunal by now, and if all goes well, the militia can be waiting for us halfway on the road there, towards the middle of this afternoon. So I came back here and invented my story on the way. I was certain that Shao would get alarmed and himself propose that we leave here as quickly as possible".

In high spirits they packed their bundles. They had just settled their bill when Shao Lee-huai arrived, all set for the journey. They left the village at a brisk pace, and soon had left the fort behind them.

When they had been afoot for two hours or so along the highroad to Lai-chow, Djao Wan-chuan stood still and said to Shao Lee-huai:

"I think the time has come for some frank talking"

"What is the matter, brother Djao?" Shao asked amazed.

Then Ma Joong closed in on him, and said:

"You left Kiangsu together with a young merchant called Liu. Now, speak up, did not you murder him and another man near Six Mile Village?"

Shao Lee-huai felt as if a tub of cold water had been poured out over his head. He quickly mastered himself however, and turning round, shouted at Djao Wan-chuan:

"You dogshead, so you cheated me! Yes, I killed young Liu. What are you going to do about it?"

He pushed Ma Joong back, in one jump landed on the high bank of the road, and started to scramble through the undergrowth there, in the direction of the forest.

Ma Joong cursed himself for having underestimated Shao's presence of mind. Shao was familiar with that neighborhood, and once in the woods, he would surely make his escape.

Suddenly, however, shouts went up on all sides. Peaks and halberds glittered among the trees. The militia had been lying in ambush there and fell over Shao like a swarm of bees. He tried to grapple with them, but they soon had him securely in chains. Shao cursed horribly and then fell into a sullen silence.

The militia went ahead with Shao Lee-huai in their midst. Ma Joong and his friends brought up the rear.

When they reached the city of Lai-chow night was falling and a group of constables from the local tribunal came with lighted paper lanterns to meet them. A curious crowd thronged round the procession as it wound its way through the streets. The constables shouted:

"Make way, make way! This is a dangerous murderer, arrested on the orders of His Excellency the magistrate of Lai-chow!"

The local people were full of admiration, and shouted: "Long live our magistrate!"

At the tribunal Ma Joong had the necessary documents relating to Shao Lee-huai filled in and sealed, and the magistrate gave them permission to hand Shao over to the warden of the local jail, to be kept there for the night. These things having been settled, Ma Joong and his companions rented a room in the large hostel opposite the tribunal, treated themselves to a good meal, and talked happily till a late hour.

The next morning Shao was duly delivered to them. The only unpleasant occurrence was that the headman of the constables wanted a generous tip from Ma Joong, for the trouble he had taken about the arresting of Shao Lee-huai. Ma Joong was indignant, and wanted to refuse, for after all it was the militia who had done the job. The old constable, however, took him aside and said: "After a couple of years the magistrate here may be transferred to some other post, but that headman of the constables will still be here for many years to come. It is wise to give him something. You may need him later in connection with some other case." Thus Ma Joong gave him some small silver pieces out of their traveling fund and they parted on excellent terms.

On the road back nothing happened. Djao Wan-chuan and Ma Joong repeatedly endeavored to persuade Shao Lee-huai to confess everything to Judge Dee, in order to get his sentence mitigated or deferred. But Shao only cursed them all, and walked on sullenly, Djao holding the ends of the chain that bound his hands behind his back.

On the morning of the seventh day they arrived at Changping and hurried to the tribunal. They first handed Shao over to the warden of the jail, and then went to report to Judge Dee. Although the sun had just risen, the judge was already sitting in his private office, sipping his morning tea. He was very gratified to hear that their expedition had been successful, and soon after ordered the morning session to be opened.

When Shao Lee-huai was brought before the bench by the constables, and his chains had been taken off, Judge Dee asked him:

"What is your name, and what crime have you committed?"

"Your Honor, my surname is Shao and my personal name Lee-huai. I am a native of Kiangsu Province. Since my early youth I have been engaged in the silk business. When recently I heard that a great demand for raw silk existed here in Shantung, I came here to do some business. I was suddenly arrested by the constables of this tribunal, I don't know for what crime. I beg Your Honor to redress my wrong."

Judge Dee said with a cold smile:

"You need not try to fool me, a magistrate, with clever words. Don't you know the old rule that itinerant merchants should help and protect each other on the road? Why did you kill your young colleague Liu near Six Mile Village, and, having stolen his cart with silk, also kill an innocent man who happened to pass by? Tell the truth, and be quick about it!"

Now Shao Lee-huai still hoped that there was no direct proof, and resolved to try the utmost to save himself.

"Your Honor", he said, "I beg your favorable consideration. All this talk about me having killed somebody is a wicked scheme of that man Djao Wan-chuan, who harbors an old grudge against me, and therefore tries to involve me in a murder case. How could I ever think of murdering a travel companion? Everybody knows that in our trade it is a great advantage to have a friend with you when you are on the road. I am being falsely accused, and I pray Your Honor to see that justice is done!"

"You insolent scoundrel", Judge Dee said, "I tell you that Djao Wan-chuan is right here, and I shall confront you with him."

Then he had Djao brought before the bench, and he told again how he had met Shao Lee-huai on the road, how Shao had told him that Liu had died of a sudden illness, and so on.

Shao Lee-huai, however, kept shouting that this was a string of outrageous lies and that he was being falsely accused. Judge Dee gave a sign to the constables. They threw Shao down on his back, placed the screws round his hands and his ankles, and turned them on tight. Soon flesh and bones were crushed and blood stained the floor. But Shao still cried between his groans that he was innocent.

Then Judge Dee ordered two constables to take the thin rattan, and to beat Shao all over his body with full force as he was lying there in the screws.

Shao's body had become hardened by long training in the art of fencing with sticks but he could not stand this torture. The thin rattan cut right into his flesh; soon his screams stopped. He had lost consciousness.

Judge Dee ordered the constables to loosen the screws and throw cold water over him. When Shao had regained his senses, Judge Dee said:

"You dogshead, for a few hundred silver pieces you have murdered two innocent men and involved two innocent outsiders. The death penalty is too light a punishment for these crimes. And now you still aggravate matters by refusing to confess. I have confronted you with the witness Djao Wan-chuan. To-morrow I shall confront you with a second witness and see whether then you still dare to deny your guilt!"

Judge Dee stood up, and with an angry sweep of his long sleeves, he left the dais.

JUDGE DEE CLOSES THE CASE OF SIX MILE VILLAGE;
MR. HUA RUSHES TO THE COURT AND REPORTS A MURDER.

That same day, Judge Dee sent Ma Joong to Six Mile Village,
to tell the hostel keeper Koong Wan-deh, and Warden Pang that
they were wanted for further questioning; he was also to pass
by Mrs. Wang's village, and summon her to appear at the morning session of the tribunal on the following day. But Ma Joong was
on no account to tell them that the murderer had been caught.

The next day, when the session opened, Judge Dee first had
Koong Wan-deh brought before him.

"After you filed your complaint here," Judge Dee said,
"I went to great trouble to unravel this case, and finally I
have located and apprehended the real murderer. It is the merchant Shao, the man who disappeared after the murder. Now
when this man came to your hostel together with the merchant
Liu, you saw him face to face. Give me an exact description of
his appearance."

Koong Wan-deh said in a quavering voice:

"Your Honor, this happened several weeks ago and my
memory is rather vague. But I am certain that he was of middle
height, and seemed about thirty years old. He had a lean
swarthy face. There is one thing, however, that I particularly
remember. When he and Liu were drinking and talking at a
very late hour that night, Shao called me to their room, and asked
whether it was not too late to send a waiter out for another jar
of wine. Saying so he laughed loudly, and as he happened to be
sitting right next to the candle, I noticed that one of his front
teeth was completely black".

Judge Dee asked:

"Is it true that until I told you a few moments ago, you knew nothing about this man Shao having been caught, and that you have not seen him since that night in your hostel?"

Koong Wan-deh having affirmed this, Judge Dee had this fact duly recorded by the clerks. He knew that if Shao proved to have this black tooth, then all possible doubt would be removed. He hastily filled in a slip for the warden of the jail, and told two constables to fetch Shao Lee-huai.

When Shao was kneeling in front of the bench, Judge Dee shouted at him:

"You villain, yesterday you obstinately protested your innocence. Now look up and see who this man is!"

Shao immediately recognized the hostel keeper of Six Mile Village. He knew then that there was no hope and began cursing violently. His black front tooth was there for all to see.

Shao continued cursing Djao Wan-chuan and Koong Wan-deh, and screamed in a blind rage:

"You think you have caught me, but I shall rather die than confess!

Judge Dee banged his fist on the table, and shouted in a thundering voice to the constables to apply the "great torture".

They brought in an iron pan with glowing coals, and thereon laid several feet of thin chain. When these chains had become red-hot, they picked them up with a pair of tongs, and threw them on the floor. Then they stripped off Shao's trousers, and holding him by his arms, made him kneel on the chains.

Shao emitted piercing shrieks of agony. The stench of burnt flesh filled the court hall. Then his screams changed to moans, and he fainted.

The constables dragged him aside. He sank in a heap on the floor. Their headman brought a bowl of vinegar and sprinkled it over the glowing coals. A penetrating smell dispelled the bad odor. Gradually Shao came to his senses again. His face was ashen and his features contorted. Two constables had to support him when he was made to kneel in front of the bench. Judge Dee said:

"If you don't confess, I shall subject you to other tortures. It is now in your own hands."

Shao Lee-huai's spirit had been broken, and at last the full truth was revealed. He said in a low voice:

"I used to pass through this province every year, peddling my silk. I did fairly well until I met a woman who made me spend most of my money on her. After a year I was obliged to borrow, and this spring I found myself heavily in debt. Now this young merchant Liu was a man of the same village as I. His full name was Liu Guang-chi. We had agreed that we should travel together this year. When I saw that he was taking three hundred silver pieces with him, and a pushcart with bales of raw silk to a total value of about seven hundred silver pieces, I conceived the plan to kill him, and take his money and his wares. There would have been enough to pay off my debts, and even sufficient to set up a business in some lonely spot and live in comfort with that woman. Ever after we had set out together, I was on the look out for a suitable opportunity for executing my plan, but other merchants accompanied us. I had to wait till the two of us arrived alone at Six Mile Village. Seeing that Koong's hostel was located in a lonely neighborhood, I persuaded Liu to stay there over night. That night I purposely kept Liu talking and drinking till deep in the night. He was dead drunk when I put him to bed. It was only a few hours later when the last nightwatch sounded. I dragged him up and made him leave the hostel with me, supporting him on my arm. Outside in the morning air he sobered up a bit. I made him push the cart for a while. When we arrived at the market gate dawn was just breaking and there was nobody in sight. I walked up behind him and plunged my knife under his right shoulderblade. Liu fell down with a gasp and then tried to turn round to me.

I kicked him down. When he opened his mouth to scream, I cut his throat. Then I bent over him, and started to loosen his girdle to take his money. But just as I found the silver, I heard the creaking sounds of a pushcart. Looking up I saw a yokel coming towards us, pushing an empty cart. When he came near, he saw the body of Liu lying there and started to say something. I sprang towards him and, gripping his right arm with my left, I stuck my knife between his ribs. He started to scream, so I jerked him round and threw him on his face and then finished him off with a knife thrust in his back. His cart was but a small affair, so I transferred part of Liu's bales to this cart and hastily went away, pushing Liu's cart and dragging the other cart behind me. When I arrived at a safe distance, I threw the small pushcart in a ditch. But although I had thus got rid of the only witness to the murder, I still felt far from safe. So when a couple of hours later I happened to meet Djao Wan-chuan on the road, I told him that Liu had died, and handed the cart with the bales to him. He gave me three hundred pieces of silver as an advance on the price he would get for the silk. Then I hurried on to Lai-chow and from there went to the passes where the woman was waiting for me. This is the whole truth. I crave Your Honor's leniency since I still have my mother to support*."

Judge Dee shook his head, and said:

"Also Liu Guang-chi and the carter Wang had parents to support. I rule that in this particular case this circumstance shall not be considered".

When the clerk had written out the confession, the senior scribe read it out in a loud voice. Shao Lee-huai confirmed that it expressed accurately what he had said, and affixed his thumb-mark to the document. He was led back to the jail to wait for the confirmation of his sentence by the central authorities.

---

* (Translator's note)  For the legal points involved, consult the note to this chapter in Translator's Postscript.

Then Judge Dee had Warden Pang brought before him, and sternly admonished him never again to try to squeeze money out of innocent people by falsely accusing them. The judge ruled that the two severe bamboo beatings he had received previously were sufficient punishment for his offense, and told him that he could go.

Warden Pang knocked his head on the floor several times to show his gratitude for this leniency, for he knew very well that Judge Dee could have meted out to him a much heavier penalty*.

Finally Judge Dee had the widow Wang brought in. To her he said:

"The other day you reported to me that your husband, the carter Wang, had been done to death violently, and asked me to avenge him. I have now found the murderer. He has confessed his crime. As soon as the higher authorities have confirmed his sentence, I shall have him executed, so that your husband's soul can rest in peace."

He added a few kind words to comfort her and told her that, after the execution, a suitable sum of smart money would be paid out to her.

Then Judge Dee left the court hall. In his private office he changed into an informal robe. He had Ma Joong, Chiao Tai, Djao Wan-chuan and the old constable called in, and commended them for their good work on the case. He handed to Djao Wan-chuan one hundred silver pieces as a reward for his voluntary help.

Djao Wan-chuan prostrated himself, knocking his head on the floor several times as his expression of gratitude. He said he would like to return as soon as possible to Divine Village, to look after his various affairs there. Judge Dee gave him an extra sum for travel funds and Djao Wan-chuan took his leave.

When Ma Joong had come back from seeing Djao to the front gate, he asked the judge whether there were any new developments

---

* (Translator's note)   See the notes to this chapter in Translator's Postscript.

in the case of Bee Hsun. Judge Dee told him that as yet Mrs. Djou had made not one single suspicious move, but that Sergeant Hoong and Tao Gan were still keeping a very close watch on that neighborhood. He was just going to add something more, when they suddenly heard the sounds of the gong at the main gate. With a sigh Judge Dee again donned his official robes and ascended the dais, followed by his lieutenants.

In the meantime a large crowd had gathered outside the tribunal. The news that the murderer of Six Mile Village had been caught, and had confessed his crime, had spread like wildfire through the town. All people loudly praised Judge Dee for having brought this complicated case to a conclusion, thus giving peace to the souls of the two victims.

A small group of men and women had wedged their way through the crowd, and were now standing by the door of the court hall. Some were crying, others were shouting that a heinous crime had been committed, and still others were loudly protesting that someone was being falsely accused.

Judge Dee ordered Ma Joong to tell them to stop all the noise immediately, and bring only the complainant before the bench. The others would have to wait at the door.

It appeared that there were two complainants, a middle-aged lady, and a distinguished old gentleman with grey hairs. When these two were kneeling in front of the bench, Judge Dee said:

"Let each of you state his name, and clearly formulate his complaint".

The lady spoke up first, saying:

"This insignificant person's name is Lee. I am the widow of the late Bachelor of Arts Lee Dsai-goong, who used to teach in the School of the Classics, in the Temple of Confucius of this town. After his demise, he left me an only daughter, called Lee-goo. Last year she became eighteen. Through the intermediary of one of our local gentry, she was betrothed to Hua Wen-djun, the son of His Excellency the Senior Graduate Hua Guo-hsiang, the retired prefect. Yesterday had been fixed as the day for the wedding. The bridal procession set out from my house to the mansion of Mr. Hua. Who would have thought that my poor daughter would suddenly die during the very first night that she stayed in the bridegroom's house? As soon as this terrible news reached me this morning, I hurried to the Hua mansion and there found the corpse of my daughter lying on the bridal couch, all covered with blue spots, while blood had been trickling from the 'seven apertures'. These facts showing beyond doubt that someone had done her to death by administering poison to her, I hurried here to report, begging Your Honor to avenge the wrong done to this innocent girl, and to her mother, now left alone in the world, robbed of her last hope and support".

Having thus spoken, she started to cry bitterly. Judge Dee said a few kind words to comfort her, and then thus addressed the old gentleman:

"I presume that you are Mr. Hua Guo-hsiang?"

"I am indeed the Senior Graduate Hua Guo-hsiang", the old gentleman answered.

"How is it possible", Judge Dee said, "that such a terrible thing happened in your house? A man of your experience and learning should know how to keep his house in order. Do you rule your household with such laxity that a criminal can dwell there unmolested?"

"My household", old Mr. Hua said with dignity, "is one where the ancient virtues are honored. My son Wen-djun, although still young, is already preparing himself for the first literary examination. I have had him brought up in respect for the sacred rites and the rules of propriety.

"Yesterday evening, a large number of guests had gathered for the wedding ceremony in the reception hall of my humble abode. When this ceremony had been duly performed, a group of young men accompanied the pair to the bridal chamber, set on 'teasing the newly-weds'*. I joined in the general merriment, and an auspicious atmosphere of joy and happiness prevailed. Among the young men, however, there was one Candidate Hoo Dso-bin, a fellow-student of my son, and one of his best friends. When this Candidate Hoo saw the beauty of my son's bride, he must have become jealous, for he behaved in a most unseemly manner. He teased my son and his bride in an offensive way, making improper remarks, and would not leave them alone for one moment. Since it had become quite late by then, I thought it was time to leave the bridal room, so I invited all the young men to come to my library, and have some rounds of wine there. The young men behaved nicely and accepted my invitation, on condition that the bridegroom empty first three cups of wine in their honor. Only Candidate Hoo obstinately refused to leave the young pair alone, saying that the fun was just beginning. I became angry and scolded him, saying that this was improper behavior. He then flew into a violent rage, he called me an old fogey, and said threateningly that before the night was over, I would be sorry for this. The others thought that this was a joke, and after some final horseplay they all went with me to my library, dragging Candidate Hoo along with them. Who could have thought that this Hoo was in dead earnest, and before leaving the bridal room, motivated by Heaven knows what old grudge, dropped poison in the teapot that was standing by the side of the bridal bed? My son fortunately did not drink that tea, but his bride had one cup before going to bed. When the third nightwatch had been sounded, she complained of a violent ache inside. We all

---

* (Translator's note)  This is an old Chinese wedding-custom, that is still observed to-day. A number of young men—and at present also girls—, friends of the bride and groom, accompany them to the bridal chamber, and there engage for a couple of hours in all sorts of horse-play, trying to make the bride blush, and compelling the groom to drink an unlimited number of toasts.

rushed to the room,and seeing that she was in terrible pain, a doctor was called. Alas, when he arrived, this young girl, beautiful as carved jade and tender as a budding flower, had passed away. This morning, therefore, I, the Senior Graduate Hua Guo-hsiang, kneel before Your Honor's dais, and report that my daughter-in-law has been foully murdered by the Candidate of Literature Hoo Dso-bin, begging Your Honor to see that justice is done".

He then handed Judge Dee his written accusation with both hands. Judge Dee glanced it through, and said:

"Thus both of you accuse Candidate Hoo of having poisoned your daughter. Where is this man Hoo?"

Mr. Hua said:

"Candidate Hoo has also come to Your Honor's tribunal, to file a complaint that he is being falsely accused".

Judge Dee ordered the constables to bring him in. He saw a young man of not unprepossessing mien, clad in the blue robe of a Candidate of Literature. Judge Dee asked him:

"Is your name Hoo Dso-bin?"

The young man said:

"This student is indeed the Candidate Hoo Dso-bin".

Judge Dee then addressed him angrily:

"Are you still bold enough to call yourself a candidate? You have received instruction in the School of the Classics. How is it that you don't know the teachings of our venerable ancient Sages? Don't you know that attaining manhood, marriage, mourning and sacrificing to the ancestors, these four ceremonies are the most important in a man's life? How did you dare to misconduct yourself during a wedding ceremony? And furthermore, since the bridegroom was your fellow-student, you should have treated his bride with special respect. How is it that you, seeing her beauty, became jealous and let this jealousy move you to utter threatening words? You are disgracing that blue robe that you wear. Speak up now, and tell me exactly what happened!"

# Twentieth Chapter

CANDIDATE HOO'S JEST BRINGS CALAMITY OVER HIS HEAD;
JUDGE DEE STARTS AN INQUIRY IN THE HUA MANSION.

Candidate Hoo, prostrating himself in front of the bench, said:
"Your Honor, stay for a while the thunder of your wrath, and allow this person respectfully to explain what happened. My teasing of the newly-weds was nothing but a joke, intended as a contribution to the general jollification. At that time there were at least forty people in the bridal room, all laughing and shouting and engaging in various kinds of horseplay. Hua Guo-hsiang, however, singled me out for a severe scolding. I pretended to be very angry and shouted that he would repent his words before the night was over, just to make fun of him. Why I chose those particular words, I really cannot say. Now as to me having poisoned that poor young lady, Your Honor knows that I am a student of literature. How would I ever dare to commit such a heinous crime? Moreover I still have an old mother, and a wife and children. Would I risk the existence of my entire family by such a rash deed? As to Your Honor reprimanding me for going too far in my jesting, and, while teasing the newly-weds, going beyond the limits of propriety, I humbly accept this just censure. But as to people accusing me of having committed a foul murder, this I cannot but qualify as a grievous wrong. I beg Your Honor's favorable consideration".

While he was speaking, an elderly lady had knelt by his side, and repeatedly knocked her head on the floor, crying all the time. Judge Dee said to her:

"I presume that you are Hoo Dso-bin's mother?"

The old lady affirmed this, adding:

"Your Honor, this boy's father died when he was still a child. I have devoted all my days to educating this only son, and deeply

**Judge Dee's first hearing of the case Lee-Hua *vs*. Hoo.**

Judge Dee is reading Mr. Hua's written accusation. On the left Ma Joong; on the right Sergeant Hoong. Kneeling in front of the bench on the left, Candidate Hoo. Mr. Hua is on the right.

regret that I, being too indulgent, failed to repress this unfortunate habit of his always wanting to be the jester of a company. I implore Your Honor's clemency".

Judge Dee, having heard these various depositions, remained in thought for a while. He reflected that Mrs. Lee and Mr. Hua, seeing their daughter lying there dead on the bridal couch, naturally were beside themselves with anger and grief, and immediately pounced on the first likely suspect. But the young man Hoo had all the marks of an elegant literary student. His explanation sounded plausible and entirely in character. He greatly doubted that young Hoo had committed this crime.

The judge said to Mrs. Lee and Mr. Hua:

"You accuse Hoo Dso-bin, but I am not satisfied with the evidence you adduce. Tomorrow I shall make a personal investigation on the scene of the crime. Both of you may go now, but Hoo Dso-bin is to be kept under detention in the School of the Classics".

Judge Dee then allowed them to take their leave. Hoo's mother was in tears because her son was kept under detention. Judge Dee did not think it necessary to instruct Mr. Hua not to touch anything on the scene of the crime.

Mr. Hua, through his long official career, was indeed thoroughly conversant with the requirements of the law. Before leaving for the tribunal, he had already had the bridal room sealed. Upon returning to his mansion, he gave orders to arrange the large reception room as a temporary tribunal, and had reed mats brought out into the courtyard in front of the hall, for the autopsy. He gave these instructions with tears in his eyes, bemoaning the fate that had brought this calamity to his house in his old age. He only hoped that the constables would not bother the members of his household too much and have some regard for his high official rank.

He tried to comfort his son, but Wen-djun, having seen his

lovely bride die before his eyes after he had held her in his arms for only a few hours, was nearly distracted with grief.

Early the next morning, the warden of that quarter of the city, and a number of constables from the tribunal, arrived at Mr. Hua's mansion. Two constables were posted on guard in front of the bridal couch while others guarded the entrance to that courtyard. They removed the sliding doors of the reception hall, and arranged everything inside for the conduct of the case.

Mr. Hua had charged one of his relatives to place a coffin in the courtyard and lay out the shroud, so that his daughter-in-law could be encoffined directly after the autopsy.

At noon gongs were sounded outside, announcing the arrival of Judge Dee. Mr. Hua hastily donned his official robe and cap, and went with Wen-djun to the front gate to receive the judge.

Judge Dee descended from his palanquin in the front courtyard, and Mr. Hua first took him to his library, to refresh himself. When tea had been brought in, he told his son to greet the judge. Wen-djun knelt down and knocked his head on the floor.

Judge Dee gave Wen-djun a good look and decided that he also was a decent youngster, with the dignified bearing of a candidate of literature. He asked him:

"Did you actually see your wife drink tea before going to bed? And why did you not drink some tea also?"

"After the guests had left our room", Wen-djun said, "my father ordered me personally to thank all of them one by one in the reception hall, as is customary, and personally conduct every guest who was leaving to the front gate. When I had done this, the second nightwatch had already been sounded. I was utterly exhausted. It was only with a great effort that I could perform my last duty of the day, kneeling in front of my father and wishing him a good night.

"When at last I re-entered the bridal room, my wife was sitting on the chair at the foot of the couch. Seeing that I was very tired, she ordered her maid servant to pour out two cups of strong tea. But before I left the reception hall a few moments previous, my throat had felt parched because of all the talking, and I had already had several cups of hot tea. So I told the servant to pour out only one cup from the teapot standing by the side of the couch, and my wife drank hers while I disrobed. Then we went to bed. When the third nightwatch was sounded, and I was just beginning to feel drowsy, my wife started to groan softly. I thought that this was a slight indisposition, but her pains increased and at last became so violent that she could not help crying out loud. I told the maidservant to rouse the household and to have a doctor called. But when the fourth nightwatch was sounded, she had already passed away. When I saw the dark spots that had appeared on her skin, I knew that she must have been poisoned, so I looked in the teapot; the tea had changed into a thick, black substance. Thus I knew that the poison was there".

Judge Dee asked:

"Had Hoo Dso-bin an opportunity to tamper with that teapot during the teasing in the bridal room?"

Father and son looked at each other perplexed, and admitted that they had not noticed whether that teapot was standing there at that time or not. Old Mr. Hua became quite agitated, and said:

"What does this matter? That youngster Hoo had the opportunity to put poison in the teapot. That he had the intention of harming us is proved by his own words. If Your Honor puts the question to him under torture, he will certainly confess".

Judge Dee shook his head, and said:

"This case cannot be decided as simply as that. This is a murder and I am not going to press Hoo Dso-bin further if there is not more evidence. After all, the other guests had the same opportunity as Hoo. The maid servant had the best opportunity of all. I want to question that maid."

Old Mr. Hua, however, protested. He said that Judge Dee should not think that he, a Senior Graduate, who had served with distinction as a prefect in several provinces, would lightly accuse someone of a murder. Furthermore he assumed full responsibility for every single person in his mansion and guaranteed that no one in his household was capable of committing a murder.

Judge Dee felt it awkward to treat this old gentleman who was so much his senior peremptorily. Thus he said:

"The common people model their conduct after that of our leading families. Eminent persons like you are, therefore, in the center of the public eye. Since this case will be followed closely by the population of the entire district you and I must see to it that all the rules are scrupulously observed, lest it be said that the authorities when conducting a criminal case are more lenient to the local gentry than to the common people".

Mr. Hua could not well argue this point and reluctantly had the maid servant called in. When she had prostrated herself in front of the judge, he saw that she was well past middle age.

"Are you a maid of the Lee mansion who accompanied your mistress here, or do you belong to the Hua household?"

"Your Honor's slave," the old maidservant said, "is called Chen. Since my early youth I have received the undeserved favor of Madame Lee, who kept me as her chambermaid. When I had attained womanhood, Madame Lee kindly arranged my marriage with the doorkeeper in the Lee mansion. Recently my husband died, and Madame Lee decided that I would serve her daughter after her marriage to young Mr. Hua."

Now at first Judge Dee had surmised that it might have been the maid servant who had poisoned the bride. He knew that in large mansions secret love-affairs between the young masters and attractive maids sometimes develop, and there were precedents of such a maid servant becoming violently jealous when the young master who had favored her brought home a bride. But this maid did not belong to the Hua mansion at all. Moreover she was well past her prime. He hastily dismissed that theory. He asked her:

"Were you the sole person in charge of preparing tea for the bride, and when did you heat the water?"

"At noon", the maid Chen answered, "I fetched a pitcher of hot water and poured it in the teapot. Several people drank that tea, and when the wedding guests arrived, it was empty. So early in the evening I again went to the kitchen, and filled my pitcher with boiling water from the large pan there. This I poured in the teapot which was in a padded basket to keep it warm and standing on the table beside the bridal couch. Nobody drank from it except the bride just before retiring."

"That means," Judge Dee continued, "that the teapot with the water you fetched the second time stood there all night. Did not you leave the bridal room once or twice to have a look at the gay crowd in the reception hall?"

"I only left the room once", the maid said, "and that was to eat my evening rice, which I ate in the small kitchen adjoining the room. Immediately afterwards I began arranging things in the room for the return of the bride and groom from the ceremony in the reception hall. After that I did not leave the room once, and nobody entered. Finally the bride and groom came back with the crowd of guests, among them that wicked Mr. Hoo, who must have put the poison in the teapot during the general confusion."

## Twentyfirst Chapter

JUDGE DEE DECIDES TO FOREGO AN AUTOPSY ON THE BRIDE;
HE TRIES IN VAIN TO DISCOVER THE SOURCE OF THE POISON.

After the maid servant had been dismissed, Judge Dee said
to Mr. Hua:

"You see that the case against Hoo Dso-bin rests only on suspicion. This investigation has only just begun. I shall now
inspect the scene of the crime."

With Mr. Hua leading the way, they crossed a few courtyards,
and finally arrived at the bridal room. Inside Judge Dee saw the
large bridal couch against the back wall; the bed curtains were
drawn close, and two constables stood on guard in front of it.
By the side of the head of the couch there stood a small table
of carved blackwood, and at the foot a chair of the same material.
On the table Judge Dee saw a large teapot in a padded rattan
basket. Mr. Hua informed him that the two tea cups were unfortunately removed during the excitement following the bride's
death. The teapot itself had not been disturbed.

Judge Dee ordered a constable to bring him a clean teacup,
and told two others to go outside on the street and procure a
stray dog. While they were gone, Judge Dee carefully examined
the room, but he could find nothing of special significance.
He lifted the lid of the teapot and saw that it was half filled
with a thick, black liquid that resembled syrup rather than tea.
Moreover it had a penetrating, musty smell. Judge Dee reflected
that it would be exceedingly difficult to determine what kind of
poison had been mixed with the tea. It might have been arsenic,
but this would not have caused the blue spots on the victim's body.
He poured out a little of the liquid in the clean teacup and noticed
again the musty smell. It was black as ink, but the judge could
discover no particles of alien matter in it.

The two constables brought the dog, a miserable half-starved animal. Judge Dee had a few pieces of meat fetched from the kitchen, and having soaked these in the cup of tea, he threw them on the steps leading down to the small courtyard. The dog swallowed them with amazing quickness, and started sniffing about for more. After a while, however, his hairs stood on end, and he growled angrily. His growls soon changed into drawn-out howling. He ran about in circles a few times, and then the poor beast dropped dead.

Judge Dee was greatly perplexed by the nature of this poison. He ordered the constables to place the dead dog in a box and seal it. It was then to be conveyed to the tribunal as an exhibit.

He entered the bridal room again and opened the curtains. The corpse of the unfortunate young bride was lying on the couch where she had died. Blood had trickled out of her mouth, and dark-blue spots covered her slender body.

Judge Dee drew the curtains and asked for Mrs. Lee. Then he addressed himself as follows to Mr. Hua and Mrs. Lee:

"You represent the families of the bride and the bridegroom. Both your houses are 'permeated by the fragrance of books,' and that this terrible thing happened to people of your standing is a great calamity. I shall not increase your grief by having an autopsy performed, and have the corpse of your poor daughter subjected to exposure and the indignities incident to every post-mortem. It suffices that I have seen the clear evidence of poisoning with my own eyes. The problem of this case is not *how* she was killed, but *who* committed this foul deed. I shall, therefore, now seal the death certificate, stating that she died having drunk poison, administered by an unknown person. The corpse can be forthwith encoffined."

Mrs. Lee tearfully thanked Judge Dee for this kind consideration of their feelings, but old Mr. Hua was very doubtful.

"After all", he said, "according to the regulations an autopsy should be performed on the corpse of a murdered person. Who knows what additional evidence of Hoo's crime may come to light?"

His son, however, sank to his knees before his father, imploring him to spare the body of his poor wife.

Finally Mr. Hua reluctantly agreed, and ordered the servants to start the preparations for dressing the corpse. Judge Dee walked out into the courtyard and stood about for some time, looking absentmindedly at the servants running in and out busily. His official business here was finished, and he should have returned to the tribunal. However, somehow or other, he could not bring himself to leave Mr. Hua's mansion. He had a strong feeling that the key to the mystery was right here, and not outside.

When the corpse had been dressed and brought to the front courtyard to be encoffined there, Judge Dee went back to the bridal room alone. The constables had just placed the teapot and the cup in a leather box. Judge Dee impressed his seal on the slip of paper pasted over the lid. After they had left, Judge Dee closed the door and seated himself on the chair at the foot of the bed.

Everything was quiet now. He could hear only vaguely the distant noise in the front courtyard. Judge Dee reflected that poisoners often use weird means for killing their victim, and wondered what strange mystery this room concealed. The musty smell still hung in the air. Somehow or other it seemed part of the room. Determined to find its origin, the judge looked under the couch, behind the furniture, and walked out into the small kitchen. It was very small, without a fire place, and had only a cold water basin for washing cups and dishes. It had evidently been thoroughly cleaned in preparation for the homecoming of the bride. The walls were newly plastered, and the judge did not notice the musty smell here that hung over the room itself.

Judge Dee shook his head and slowly walked back to the large reception hall. There he said to Mr. Hua:

"You accuse Hoo Dso-bin, but I find that the maid servant Chen had the same opportunity for committing the crime. I shall question Hoo again in the tribunal, but I also want to question again this maid servant. I hope you will permit me to place her under detention".

Mr. Hua did not like this at all, but he knew he could not well refuse. He gave his permission, and when Judge Dee had left, two constables took the maid servant to the tribunal.

Mr. Hua, however, vented his rage on his son, saying:

"That Mrs. Lee allowed the body to be encoffined without an autopsy is only to be expected. Women never understand these things. But you, as the son of a high official, should have known better. Don't you see that that smug judge is only out to make matters easy for himself? Let me tell you that officials are always trying to avoid difficulties; much do they care if somebody has been murdered, if only it does not interfere with their easy lives! I have been an official myself and I know what I am talking about!"

When no news came from the tribunal by the evening of the next day, old Mr. Hua's resentment against Judge Dee increased. He stampeded through the halls and courtyards of his mansion with swinging sleeves, scolding the servants and making himself generally disagreeable. When night had fallen, he swore that the next day he would go to the tribunal himself and urge the judge to question Hoo Dso-bin under torture.

In the mean time Judge Dee had ordered Ma Joong to consult a famous old coroner living retired in the city, and some elder managers of medicine stores. But none of them knew of a poison that produced the symptoms shown on the corpse. Thereafter Judge Dee had sent Ma Joong and Chiao Tai to make discreet inquiries among the people living in the neighborhood of the mansions of Mr. Hua and Mrs. Lee, and had them check the list of the wedding guests. But neither in Mr. Hua's nor in Mrs.

Lee's mansion did there seem to have been any irregularities. The guests who had attended the wedding were all well-known members of the local gentry, none of whom was known to harbor any grudge against either Mr. Hua or Mrs. Lee.

On the third day after his investigation in the Hua mansion, Judge Dee was sitting in his private office, discussing the features of the case with Ma Joong.

"This murder in the Hua mansion", Judge Dee observed, "looks as if it will prove as hard to solve as Bee Hsun's case. One wave has not yet subsided, and another is already rising!"

Just then a clerk entered and handed to Judge Dee a visiting card.

Judge Dee read Mr. Hua's name, and said with a sigh:

"Here is Mr. Hua. Doubtless he has come to urge me to question Hoo Dso-bin again. Bring him to the reception hall."

When Judge Dee had seated himself in the reception hall, he soon saw Mr. Hua ascending the steps, clad in full ceremonial dress, looking very sour.

After the exchange of the usual amenities, Mr. Hua asked:

"To-day is the third day after my daughter-in-law met her death. Would the Father-official deign to inform this ignorant person as to the progress made with this case?"

"You have come at a most opportune time", Judge Dee answered, "I was just going to question the accused Hoo Dso-bin again, and the maid servant of your honorable mansion. If you will please be seated in my private office, you will be able to follow the proceedings from there."

The judge took Mr. Hua to his private office, and had a chair placed for him just behind the screen separating this room from the court hall. Then Judge Dee himself ascended the dais and had Candidate Hoo brought before the bench.

JUDGE DEE FINDS A CLUE TO THE MURDER OF THE BRIDE;
SERGEANT HOONG CONDUCTS A SECRET INVESTIGATION.

Judge Dee addressed him in a stern voice:

"I have investigated the scene of the crime and established
beyond doubt that young Mrs. Hua died of poison. Now you
threatened the Hua family before many witnesses. You had the
opportunity to put the poison in the teapot. Tell the truth!"

Candidate Hoo answered:

"I plead guilty to having used unbecoming language, and
having behaved in an unseemly manner. But I deny most em-
phatically that I have poisoned young Mrs. Hua. And as to my
having had the opportunity to put the poison in the teapot,
I respectfully draw Your Honor's attention to the fact that at
least forty other guests had this same opportunity, not to mention
the servants!"

Thereupon Judge Dee ordered the maid servant Chen brought
before him. To her he said:

"Your master has accused this Hoo Dso-bin of having poisoned
your young mistress, but he persistently professes his innocence.
Now you are an important witness. Tell me again exactly what
happened on that night. Leave out no detail, no matter how insignificant it may seem to you".

"Your Honor's slave," the maid said, "can testify that, until
the bride and bridegroom came back with the group of guests,
nobody entered the bridal room after I had filled the teapot for the
second time. They all were laughing and shouting and making
good-natured jokes, only Mr. Hoo said all kinds of unpleasant
things, and pushed people about. I myself saw him repeatedly
approach the couch and the tea table. Later he threatened His
Excellency the Senior Graduate, and I am convinced that it was

he who put the poison in the teapot".

"Your Honor", Candidate Hoo exclaimed, "this is outrageous slander! I beg you to ask her whether see actually saw me as much as touch that teapot!"

The old maid had to admit that she could not testify to that. Then Judge Dee asked her:

"Now when did you go to the kitchen to eat your evening rice?"

"I don't remember the exact time," she answered, "but I left the room when I heard that the wedding ceremony had started in the main hall. Soon after I came back, I heard the guests laughing in the distance. So then the ceremony must have been over, and the wine must have been served."

Judge Dee shouted at Candidate Hoo:

"So when the guests in the main hall were busy observing the ceremony, and this servant was in the kitchen eating her meal, you sneaked into the bridal room and poisoned the tea! Confess your crime!"

Candidate Hoo knocked his head on the floor, and said:

"I beg Your Honor's favorable consideration. I did not leave the hall once, as can be attested by two of my friends who stood right by my side all the time. After the ceremony I personally drank some toasts with the bridegroom. The first time I entered the bridal room was when we all went there together. This is the complete truth".

Judge Dee remained in thought for a while, slowly caressing his beard. He did not think for a moment that Hoo was guilty. His questioning was merely meant to show old Mr. Hua behind the screen that he did not overlook any possibility. Neither did he think that the old maid had a hand in this affair. He was trying to formulate some more questions when a servant bringing him a cup of tea gave a welcome opportunity for a longer pause.

While he was slowly raising the cup to his lips, Judge Dee

noticed some particles of white dust floating on the surface. He said to the servant:

"How dare you to bring me this dirty tea?"

The servant looked at the cup, and said hastily:

"This is not the fault of this person. I saw to it that the cup was clean, and I personally put the tea leaves in the teapot. It must be that some dust or plaster fell down from the ceiling when the cook was heating the water in the kitchen. Allow your servant quickly to prepare another cup".

On hearing this, Judge Dee was suddenly struck by a new thought. He sternly asked the old maid servant of the Hua mansion:

"Where did you get the hot water to make the tea that night? Are you sure you took it from the pan in the large kitchen?"

She was greatly startled by this sudden question and answered in a faltering voice:

"As your Honor's slave stated before, I used the water that had been boiled in the large pan in the kitchen of the mansion".

Judger Dee gave her a sour look and said to her and to Candidate Hoo:

"Now I know the key to this mysterious case of poisoning. Both of you shall be temporarily detained until tomorrow when I shall have solved this case".

Having thus spoken, Judge Dee left the dais and went back to his private office. Old Mr. Hua, hearing all that had been said through the screen had worked himself up into a great rage, because Judge Dee did not put the screws on Candidate Hoo. Seeing Judge Dee, he said with a sneer:

"I have followed your interrogation with considerable interest. I observe that the methods of judges have changed greatly since my own days. In my time we treated a criminal as a criminal. When he refused to confess, we put the screws on him. You will forgive that I, seeing that your methods fail to produce the slightest result, plan to bring this case before the prefect. We will see whether he shares your views."

He rose to take his leave. Judge Dee, however, detained him, saying:

"The case that was born in your honorable mansion is already perfectly clear to me. I beg you to have patience until tomorrow. Then I shall give myself the honor of calling on you personally for an experiment. If that should fail, I will insist that this case be brought before the higher authorities."

Mr. Hua evidently thought that this was another attempt at procrastination, but he could not well decline the polite proposal. So he said stiffly:

"I shall welcome the honor of receiving your visit", and took his leave.

A young constable in the guard house, seeing Mr. Hua stalk by, said to the headman:

"That old gentleman looks very angry. Why has our judge waited two days before starting the second interrogation?"

"Young man", the headman said condescendingly, "I see that you have still much to learn. Now listen to me. The case of Six Mile Village was just a common street murder. The only time that I saw money change hands in that case was when His Excellency gave a reward of a hundred silver pieces to that fellow Djao Wan-chuan. And did Djao give one copper of that sum to us? After all it was the constables, under my expert supervision, who brought the criminal to confess, while Djao only made a nice trip on the tribunal's expense. The boorish yokel! And take now that case of Bee Hsun, that is just a vulgar domestic brawl. But this case of the Senior Graduate Hua..."

The headman smiled broadly, and, caressing his side whiskers, continued:

"This is a very important case. Don't you know that Mrs. Lee owns most of the large houses in the main street, and have you figured out what she receives every month in rent alone? And old Mr. Hua, well, he was prefect in Kwantung Province, and he managed his affairs exceedingly well; he owns the two largest silver shops in this city, to say nothing of the land he owns outside the East gate. Both he and Mrs. Lee are highly cultivated persons who know how one should behave in a crisis like this. Has not Mr. Hua given us a silver piece for all the trouble we took the other day when the judge made his investigation in his mansion? Did we not have two fine meals there? And has not Mrs. Hoo given the constables guarding her son in the School of the Classics two silverpieces for looking after his food? Moreover has she not given them a certain sum for allowing her to visit him every day? And don't think that that was a small sum just because the guards gave me only a few coppers of it!"

Having said this the headman gave two constables standing there a nasty look, which they pretended to ignore. Then the young constable asked:

"But is it not true that Candidate Hoo is guilty?"

"Of course he is guilty, you stupid person", the headman said, "but our judge knows that such a refined young gentleman will confess as soon as we lay our hands on him. And if we solve such an important case the very next day, will not Mrs. Lee and Mr. Hua think that it was all too easy? No, young man, a case involving our local gentry must be treated with much circumspection. It must be studied from every angle and without undue hurry, so that they see with their own eyes how diligent we are on our jobs. When at long last the case is solved, they will have to give us a reward in proportion to our labors."

While the constables were engaged in this idle talk, Ma Joong went to Judge Dee's private office, and tried to find out from him what new clue he had discovered. But Judge Dee only smiled and repeated that the following day the case would be cleared up. While they were talking, Sergeant Hoong and Tao Gan entered and respectfully greeted the judge. He asked the sergeant:

"You have been gone now for several days. Did your watch in Huang-hua village produce any results?"

"Following Your Honor's instructions", the sergeant said, "we have been staying under cover during the daytime in Warden Ho Kai's house. Every day after dark we have gone out to watch Mrs. Bee's house. We could not, however, discover anything unusual. At last we became impatient. Yesterday Tao Gan and I decided that we would try to have a closer look at things. So when the second night watch had sounded, we climbed on the roof of Mrs. Bee's house and stretched ourselves out on the tiles to hear what the two women were talking about. First Mrs. Djou scolded her mother for quite some time, saying that it was she who had started all the trouble by inviting Your Honor in doctor's disguise to their house. This seems to be Mrs. Djou's favorite theme for their after dinner conversation. Then the dumb daughter suddenly started to make some loud noises. Mrs. Djou shouted at her 'You little brat, what are you startling us for? That is just some rats under the floor. Go to sleep. Your grandmother and I are also going to bed.' This seemed queer to Tao Gan and myself. Why should that girl get so excited just because she heard a rat? Soon afterwards Mrs. Bee and Mrs. Djou apparently went to bed, each in her own room. We stayed where we were. An hour or so later we heard some sounds in Mrs. Djou's room. We glued our ears to the roof but we could not hear clearly. Still we got the definite impression that two people were talking in low voices; one was the voice of Mrs. Djou, the other we could not recognize, but it sounded like a man's voice. I thought this incident important enough to report to Your Honor".

# Twentythird Chapter

JUDGE DEE SENDS HIS VISITING CARD TO DOCTOR TANG;
IN THE HUA MANSION HE REVEALS THE BRIDE'S SECRET.

"This", Judge Dee remarked, "is very curious indeed. Now did
you learn anything by chance about a Mr. Hsu living near there?"

"Warden Ho Kai", the sergeant answered, "has now investigated all the families of the surname Hsu in the village, but
none of them has any connection whatever with the Bee household. That warden, by the way, is really doing well. When
Bee Hsun was murdered, Ho Kai was new to his job. It was
through his inexperience rather than through laziness or stupidity
that he did not notice that something was wrong. Now, having
observed him at his job for several days, I can recommend him
to Your Honor as a diligent and shrewd fellow.

"Although we could not find a Mr. Hsu living in the neighborhood, we checked on the right neighbor of Mrs. Bee as a matter
of routine; for that is the compound adjoining Mrs. Djou's room.
We found that there is but one single dividing wall. It would
seem that Mrs. Bee's house was part of that larger compound
originally. So we thought that there might be a secret passage in
that wall, and that Mrs. Djou and her lover went in and out by
way of that neighboring compound, or perhaps met clandestinely
in a room of that house. We made inquiries, but it turned out
that the inhabitants of that compound are eminently respectable
people. It belongs to a Doctor of Literature, called Tang Deh-
djung. Although he is living in retirement in that small village, it
seems that he is quite famous in the literary world. He hardly ever
goes out, spending day and night among his books in his library.
There are half a dozen or so of the doctor's disciples living there,
all sons of prominent families of this province whom Doctor
Tang instructs in the Classics. Warden Ho Kai has their names

in his register, but there is no one among them of the surname
Hsu. Even so, I would like very much to make an investigation
there. But since Doctor Tang is such a distinguished gentleman,
I did not dare to go there without a good excuse".

Judge Dee thought for a while. Then he smiled and gave
one of his official visiting cards to Sergeant Hoong.

"Take this card with you," he said, "and go with Warden Ho
Kai to Doctor Tang's house. You tell him that the district magistrate desires to see the doctor in the tribunal to consult him regarding an official matter. Tomorrow I also shall proceed to
Huang-hua Village. Then I shall tell you the further details
of my plan".

Early the next morning Judge Dee put on a simple blue robe
and an ordinary small black cap. Taking with him only Ma
Joong, Chiao Tai and two constables, he proceeded to the mansion
of Mr. Hua.

When the house steward was leading them to the reception
hall, Mr. Hua was standing there, clad in his house robe,
supervising the servants putting everything in order for the reception of the judge. Seeing Judge Dee crossing the courtyard, he
wanted to leave hurriedly to change into his official dress. But
Judge Dee retained him, saying:

"Don't go to any trouble on my account. Today I have come
here rather as a friend of your esteemed family than as the magistrate. Please call the person in charge of boiling the water for
the use of the household for me."

Old Mr. Hua did not know what to make of all this. But
he sent his steward to the family kitchen, who soon returned with
a young maid of about eighteen. She hastily prostrated herself in
front of the judge and knocked her head on the floor. Judge Dee
said kindly:

"We are not in the tribunal here, so don't be so formal. Just
stand here and listen to me. Now you remember the day of the

wedding. Did not the maid servant Chen fetch hot water from the kitchen two times?"

When the maid had affirmed this, Judge Dee continued:

"Now tell me exactly what happened in the kitchen. Did you fill the pitcher for her from the large water pan or did she take it herself?"

"The first time Aunt Chen came", the young maid said, "Your Honor's slave herself ladled hot water from the pan into her pitcher. The second time she came I had just gone to the reception hall to help serving the tea and cakes there. When I came back to the kitchen, Aunt Chen was standing on the porch outside the kitchen, with a pitcher of hot water in her hand; she looked sourly at a small waterpan overturned on the floor. It turned out that while I was away the cooks had been so busy preparing the meal for the wedding guests that they had let the fire under the large waterpan go out. Aunt Chen, seeing that there was no hot water, and that it would take a long time to rekindle the fire under the large pan, had taken a small portable stove out to the porch. She lighted it with coal from the large oven and heated a small pan of water. When it boiled, she had filled her pitcher, but then the pan slipped from her hands and overturned on the floor. I asked her if she had scalded her feet. She said not and left the kitchen. That is all I know about this affair."

Judge Dee nodded contentedly and ordered Ma Joong to go to the tribunal quickly and fetch the maid servant Chen; he was also to instruct the headman of the constables to go to the School of the Classics and bring Candidate Hoo from there to the tribunal.

In the mean time Judge Dee sipped several cups of tea, and exasperated old Mr. Hua by talking about other matters, refusing to say one word about the case.

As soon as the old maid Chen was before him Judge Dee took on his role of magistrate again, and shouted angrily at her:

"You stupid old woman, why did you lie to me? Why did

you say that both times you went to fetch water from the kitchen, you took it from the large pan? I have found out now that the second time you heated the water yourself on a small stove outside on the porch. Why did you not report this, although I, the judge, instructed you to omit no detail?"

The old maid, thus harshly addressed, knocked her head on the floor several times in great consternation. She said in a quavering voice:

"I beg Your Honor's pardon. The other day in the tribunal I was so confused by everything that I completely forgot about this occurrence. I pray that Your Honor's slave will be treated leniently".

Judge Dee pounded the table with his fist, and said angrily:

"Your stupidity, woman, has deferred the solution of this case several days. I shall presently give you the punishment that you deserve".

Then Judge Dee said to Mr. Hua:

"We shall now go to the family kitchen".

By now old Mr. Hua was completely at a loss as to what to think about all this. Without a word he rose and preceded Judge Dee through various galleries and courtyards till they reached the large kitchen of the mansion.

Judge Dee looked around. On the right was a large brick oven, where three cooks were busy with their pans and ladles. By its side stood a second brick stove; on top of it a huge iron pan, where the water for the use of the household was boiling. The kitchen opened on a small well yard and a porch with a floor of stamped earth. Judge Dee went out on the porch and looked up. He saw that the roof over the porch was very old. The eaves were covered with cobwebs and one beam especially was blackened by age, and seemed rapidly mouldering away. The whole roof seemed to be so old that it might crash down any day. Judge Dee turned to the maid Chen, and asked her:

"It was out on this porch that you lighted the small stove, was it not?"

When the old maid servant had affirmed this, he continued:

"Now I shall tell you how you shall be punished for delivering false testimony in court. Bring out a portable stove. Put it in exactly the same place as that day of the wedding and boil here water till I tell you to stop. I shall sit here and see to it that this order is carried out properly".

To Mr. Hua he said:

"I beg you to have two chairs placed here".

Old Mr. Hua had now recovered from his astonishment and become very cross. He said:

"You are the judge and I suppose you know what you are doing. But if you think that I am going to take part in this theatrical performance, you are completely wrong. I decline all responsibility for this farce".

He wanted to leave, but Judge Dee said to him with a cold smile:

"All this may seem a farce to you, but I, the magistrate, assure you that this farce will solve the case. So I advise you not to engage in idle talk".

In the mean time the servants had brought two armchairs and placed them side by side on the porch. Judge Dee sat down gravely and offered the other chair to Mr. Hua. The old gentleman was fuming with suppressed rage, but he did not want to make a scene in front of the cooks and the servants who were crowding the kitchen, curious to see what was going to happen. So Mr. Hua sat down by the judge's side.

The old maidservant had placed a portable clay stove on the porch and started fanning the coals to heat the water in the iron pan standing on top. After a while it started to boil and steam curled up to the eaves.

Judge Dee seemed to find this proceeding of absorbing interest.

Leaning back comfortably in his chair, he watched the old maid's every movement, slowly caressing his beard.

After half an hour or so, the water had nearly evaporated. The maid looked bewildered to Judge Dee. He shouted immediately at her:

"Why don't you add more water? And keep on fanning the stove!"

She scurried to the cold water basin in the yard and added water in the pan. Then she squatted down again in front of the stove, and fanned the fire vigorously till the perspiration streamed down her face. Soon the steam was curling up again.

Mr. Hua, who had been fretting in his chair, now thought that this had lasted long enough and abruptly rose from his chair. But Judge Dee laid his hand on his arm, and said:

"Just wait a while, and look! There is the poison that killed your daughter".

He pointed upwards to the roof of the porch. Mr. Hua followed his direction. On the mouldering beam, exactly above the stove, something red shimmered. Judge Dee kept pointing with his finger. Ma Joong, Chiao Tai, the constables, the servants, all came forward and looked intently at the roof.

They saw the shining body of a red adder slowly crawl out of the mouldering spot in the beam; when about two inches had become visible, the adder raised its evil small head, and moved it to and fro, apparently enjoying the warm moisture of the steam. Suddenly it opened its ugly mouth, and a few drops of venom dropped down into the pan with boiling water.

Judge Dee dropped his hand, and said:

"That is the murderer of the bride".

The old maidservant, who had been squatting there looking up at the evil thing above, paralysed with fear, now emitted a piercing cry and the adder hastily withdrew into its hole.

A murmur of astonishment and admiration went up from

the crowd assembled there. Mr. Hua sat motionless in his chair, still looking up at the roof in complete stupefaction.

Judge Dee rose from his chair, and said to Mr. Hua:

"Exactly the same thing occurred on the day that your daughter-in-law died. Fate had decided that her young life should thus be cut short. The water used for making tea in your household is always heated inside the kitchen itself, in the large iron pan. But it so happened on that particular day, that the old maid servant heated the water here outside on the porch. The adder nestling in the mouldering beam was attracted by the hot steam, and its venom dropped in the pan underneath. Fortunately the maid Chen let the pan slip from her hands, and the poisoned water was spilt on the earthen floor; else several other people would have died using it. But this happened after she had filled the pitcher which she took to the bridal room, and poured into the teapot by the side of the couch. From the beginning I noticed that peculiar musty smell in the bridal room, but I could not locate its origin. If the maid servant Chen had told me that she had heated the water here on the porch, I would have solved this case much earlier. Thus nobody is guilty, except that you, as head of this household, bear a heavy responsibility for being so lax in supervising affairs in your mansion as to allow the roof of this porch to fall into such a disgraceful condition of decay".

Old Mr. Hua stood with bowed head while Judge Dee delivered this speech. He could not find one word in answer.

Judge Dee ordered all the servants to clear the kitchen, and told the two constables to fetch a long stake. He ordered the cook to hand Chiao Tai a pair of fire tongs and stand in the yard in front of the cold water basin. When the constables had brought the stake the judge ordered Ma Joong to pull the roof down. It crashed to the floor at the first push, and the adder appeared, trying to crawl to the well. Chiao Tai grasped it by its neck with the fire tongs, while Ma Joong crushed its head with the end of the stake. Judge Dee told the constables to burn it, and to pour the tainted water in the pan into an old pitcher. This he sealed, and ordered the constables to take it to the tribunal, to be destroyed together with the dead dog and the teapot. Then he asked Mr. Hua to guide him back to the reception hall.

Wen-djun and old Mrs. Lee were waiting there. Judge Dee explained to them what had happened and added some appropriate words about the Will of Heaven. Mrs. Lee and Wen-djun were crying softly, while old Mr. Hua tried in vain to comfort them.

Judge Dee advised Mr. Hua to have masses read in the Buddhist temple for the peace of the bride's soul. Then took his leave.

WHAT HAPPENED TO THE OLD DOCTOR OF LITERATURE;
A THIEF IN THE NIGHT MAKES A STRANGE DISCOVERY.

When he returned to the tribunal, Judge Dee told a runner
to go and fetch old Mrs. Hoo, and then had brought Hoo Dso-bin
before the bench.

He reprimanded him sharply in front of his mother, saying
that this occurrence ought to teach him how dangerous it is always
to try to be funny; he exhorted him to apply himself diligently
to his studies of the Classics, so that he would be able to gladden
his mother's old age by passing the literary examinations as the
best candidate. With that he allowed him to go.

Both Candidate Hoo and his mother knocked their heads on
the floor repeatedly to show their gratitude, exclaiming that the
judge had saved Candidate Hoo's life.

Judge Dee dismissed them and retired to his private office to
deal with some documents that had come in. The constables
made preparations for his departure for Huang-hua Village in
the afternoon.

In the meantime Sergeant Hoong had returned to Huang-hua
Village the night before and explained the judge's instructions to
Warden Ho Kai. In the morning they went to Doctor Tang's
house together.

Warden Ho Kai knocked and an old servant came to open
the door. He gave them a surly look and asked what they wanted.

Warden Ho exclaimed:

"Well, if it isn't old Mr. Djoo! Don't you know the man
who eats his rice from the taxes you pay?"

The old servant recognized the warden, and said with a smile:

"Warden Ho, what brings you here? My master is still asleep".

Warden Ho gave the sergeant a wink and both quickly entered

the courtyard. The old servant crossed the second courtyard. The warden and the sergeant followed him until they arrived in front of the library. There the sergeant said to Warden Ho Kai:

"What are you waiting for? Since Doctor Tang is at home, let us have him roused, so that I can deliver my message".

The old servant, knowing from the sergeant's tone that he was a servant of the tribunal, hastened to say:

"Mr. Constable, what do you want to ask my master? Please tell me. I shall go and inform him."

The warden said:

"This gentleman is the sergeant of the tribunal in Chang-ping. He brings the calling card of His Excellency Judge Dee. He has come to invite Doctor Tang to pay a visit to the tribunal for a consultation about an official matter."

The old servant received Judge Dee's visiting card respectfully in two hands and walked round the library. Warden Ho followed him, giving a sign to Sergeant Hoong to remain. Behind the library was a smaller courtyard with three rooms in back of it. He noticed that the room on the extreme left was right next to Mr. Djou's room in the Bee house.

Warden Ho was just thinking that this fitted in exactly with their theory, when the door of the room on left opened and a young man of about 25 appeared. He was tall and slender, and had the dignified bearing of the son of a noble family. His features were regular. One could indeed call him a very handsome youngster. He quickly asked the old servant:

"Who is this man?"

"This is a curious affair," the old servant answered. "Our master, Doctor Tang, hardly ever leaves his house. He spend all his time on his studies and on the instruction of his disciples. Now why should His Excellency, Judge Dee want to see him?"

The mentioning of the name of the judge seemed to startle the young man considerably. He said hurriedly:

"Well, why don't you tell this gentleman that Doctor Tang has renounced all worldly affairs and cannot be bothered with visits to the tribunal?"

Warden Ho Kai thought that if it came to looking for the lover of the beautiful Mrs. Djou, this handsome young fellow, who seemed to live in the room adjoining hers, would exactly fit the role. He said:

"What might be your honorable name, young Sir? Are you living here in this compound? To tell you the truth, His Excellency has heard that Doctor Tang not only is a scholar of wide learning, but also a man of noble character. He therefore wants to consult with him about the organization of some charitable enterprise in the district".

In the mean time the old servant had entered the library, and they heard somebody inside saying:

"You know that yesterday evening I explained the Classics to my disciples till a very late hour. Why do you come as early as this to disturb me?"

After the old servant had said something about Judge Dee and the tribunal, the voice continued:

"Here, take this visiting card of mine and ask the messenger to inform His Excellency respectfully that I am living in complete retirement, devoting myself entirely to my literary studies. I don't wish to have anything to do with social work. If there is something to be organized, there are many among the local gentry in Chang-ping who will be glad to help, and who are much better qualified for such work than I".

The old servant came out again, closing the door carefully behind him and repeated to the warden what Doctor Tang had said.

Sergeant Hoong had heard all this, standing behind the corner of the library. He now came forward, and said to the warden:

"Well, let us return quickly to the tribunal, to report to His Excellency Doctor Tang's answer. Perhaps the judge will visit

Doctor Tang personally and explain matters to him."

The young man entered his room again. The old servant conducted the visitors to the front gate.

As soon as they were outside in the street, Warden Ho Kai said to the sergeant:

"Did you notice that young man there? As soon as I mentioned the name of His Excellency, I saw him change color. Furthermore his room is right next to the Bee house. Why don't you rush back to report to the judge, while I stay here and try to find out that young man's name?"

The sergeant thought that this was a good idea and hastened back to the city.

Judge Dee was most content with what he heard. He thought that affairs in the compound of that learned doctor were highly suspicious. He resolved to go there himself at once, before somebody there became alarmed.

He ascended his palanquin, and hastened to Huang-hua Village, together with his four trusted lieutenants. They arrived as night was falling. Judge Dee took rooms in the same hostel where they had stayed before.

Having refreshed himself, Judge Dee called Ma Joong to his room and gave him the following instructions:

"You accompany the sergeant to Doctor Tang's house and secretly climb on the roof. Try to see what is going on in the library and especially in the room of that young man, whose room adjoins Mrs. Djou's bedroom. After you have gone Chiao Tai and Tao Gan shall go there too and watch the front gates of both houses. Sergeant Hoong shall tell you more on the way".

Ma Joong set out with the sergeant on the dark street. As they walked through the narrow alleys of the village, Sergeant Hoong said:

"Now listen to His Excellency's secret instructions. In the first place, I am to stress to you that this night our judge expects to solve the key problem of this case. The role he wants you to play is not a very pleasant one, but our judge said that it was absolutely necessary for the success of his plan, and . . ."

"Stop beating about the bush", Ma Joong interrupted him, "You and I are loyal servants of His Excellency. He has but to say the word and we obey. Have we not been eating his rice for more than six years?"

"Our judge's idea", the sergeant said, "is that somehow or other we must find the connection between that young man's room, and the adjoining house of Mrs. Bee. Together with Tao Gan, I have been watching both houses from the outside for a number of days. That has proved completely useless. Now the only way to find out whether or not a secret passage exists, is for you to burgle that young man's room. It does not matter if you are discovered afterwards. The judge has taken measures to cope with such event. Probably you shall have to play the role of a captured thief for a while. The judge thought that you would perhaps object to this."

Ma Joong, however, far from being reluctant to do this job, was full of enthusiasm and wanted to go there at once.

But the sergeant pointed out that it was too early. There were still many people walking on the street. So they first went to the house of Warden Ho Kai and talked for a while. When the second nightwatch had sounded, they set out for Doctor Tang's house. Upon arrival, Ma Joong asked the sergeant to watch on the corner, while he took off his jacket and his long robe. Clad only in his under garments, he jumped and just clutched the top of the outer wall. Hoisting himself up, he crawled like a snake on its belly along the wall to the place where it connected with the roof of the doctor's library. Ma Joong crept slowly down to the edge of the roof, and, gripping the protruding eaves, he bent his head over the edge, until he could see through the window.

He saw a large room, well lighted by a number of candles.

Three of the walls were lined with bookshelves. Behind a high writing desk an old gentleman was reading aloud from a book. Five young men were sitting in a semicircle listening intently; these were evidently the doctor's disciples. It all looked very dignified and eminently respectable to Ma Joong.

He left the roof and crawled further along the wall till he reached the buildings at the back of the courtyard. He soon found himself on the wall that separated the young man's room from that of Mrs. Djou. Looking around he was greatly startled at the sight of a dark shape huddled on the roof of Mrs. Bee's house. Suddenly, however, he heard a low whistle. He then knew that that shape was nobody but the sergeant, who had climbed up there in the mean time.

Ma Joong gave him a sign which meant that he should stay where he was. Then he climbed on the roof of the young man's room. Creeping down the sloping roof, he again edged forward, and by craning his head, he could just look inside through a narrow window. He saw a clean room, simply furnished, but in elegant taste, lighted by one candle. Against the west wall there was a large couch. In front of the window was a square table of carved blackwood and two chairs. A young man was sitting at the table, next to the candle. As far as Ma Joong could see, his features answered Sergeant Hoong's description of the young man who had appeared when he and the warden paid their first visit to the doctor's house. He had an open book in front of him, but he was not reading. He just sat there looking straight in front of him, apparently deep in thought. After a while he rose, and, opening the door of his room, looked intently at the lighted windows of the library across the courtyard. Then he closed the door, sat down again, and turned to the couch against the east wall. He looked at that couch for a considerable time, as though he had never seen it before, and then started mumbling something by himself.

Ma Joong saw the door of the library open. A young man came out, went straight to the room which Ma Joong was observing. The student knocked on the door, and called out:

"Mr. Hsu, the master wants to see you".

As soon as he had heard that the young man was called Hsu, Ma Joong said to himself: "So this is indeed our man!" In high spirits he left his precarious position, and crawled back to the wall. Crouching there he saw Hsu come out of his room and cross the courtyard to the library with the other student.

When they had gone in there, Ma Joong jumped from the wall, using the wrestler's trick called "a butterfly alighting on a flower". He landed on the ground noiselessly, and swiftly went to the window of the room in the middle. Looking in, he saw the old servant sitting at a table, sleeping with his head on his folded arms. Ma Joong slowly opened the door and, tiptoeing inside, blew out the candle that was standing on the table.

He opened the door that connected this room with that of the young man Hsu and went inside, quickly closing the door behind him. With one glance he imprinted the location of the pieces of furniture in his mind. Then he blew out the candle. He walked over to the east wall in the pitch darkness and tapped its surface around the couch. But nowhere was there a hollow sound. Then he tried the floor in front, but with the same negative result. He lifted the bed curtains and crept underneath the couch. Tapping the stone floor, he suddenly noticed that one spot produced a different sound. He slowly felt the stone flags and found that four of them seemed slightly raised in comparison to the others. Upon further investigation they definitely produced a hollow sound.

"This", Ma Joong thought, "must be the trapdoor of a secret underground passage. But how does it open?"

He again felt the raised edge very carefully with his finger tips, but could find no groove or hinge. Stretching out both hands, he groped in the dark. Suddenly his right hand touched a piece of rope which dangled behind the couch. Thinking that this rope might be connected with a lever to open the trapdoor, he gave it a pull. Suddenly two stakes of the bedstead came down with a loud crash.

Ma Joong hastily crawled out from under the bed. As he crouched behind the door, he heard people running from the library, shouting at the top of their voices: "Catch the thief. Catch the thief!"

Four students ran across the courtyard to the backrooms but when they saw that the candle in the middle room and in the room on left had been put out, they did not dare to proceed further, fearing that the robbers were lying in ambush in these darkened rooms.

Young Hsu, although apparently more agitated than the others, seemed more angry than afraid. He rushed into the middle room and shook the old servant awake. Then he lighted the candle and quickly went into his own room.

In the mean time Ma Joong had utilized the general confusion for softly opening the door behind which he had been crouching. It opened on the court yard. He swung himself up on the low roof of the gallery and climbed on the roof of Mrs. Bee's house. The people in the courtyard saw his shape outlined against the sky but nobody dared to follow him. Ma Joong slowly crawled over the ridge of Mrs. Bee's house, so that everybody could see him. But as soon as he was covered by the high ridge, he crept back to the dividing wall on his belly, and from there onto the roof of young Hsu's room. The people below thought that he had made his getaway via Mrs. Bee's roof and no one suspected that he was lying on the roof right above them. He remained there, pressing his body flat on the tiles, listening to the conversation.

## Twentyfifth Chapter

A GREAT ADO IS MADE ABOUT ARRESTING A BURGLAR;
THE RUSE SUCCEEDS, AND MA JOONG CATCHES HIS MAN.

Ma Joong heard young Hsu shout at the old servant:

"Are you deaf and dumb, that you don't sound alarm when a burglar enters my room?"

He did not wait for an answer. He set the candle on the table in his room and quickly looked around. The other students had followed him inside and started to look for traces of the robber. Young Hsu turned to them, and impatiently said:

"Well, you see that the burglar only pulled part of my bed down. I see there is nothing missing. What are you waiting for?"

One of the students said:

"You should be glad that the burglar betrayed himself before he could steal anything. There is no reason to be so cross".

Ma Joong crawled back to the roof of Mrs. Bee's house, where Sergeant Hoong waited. They crept along the outer wall again and jumped down in the street. After Ma Joong had put on his outer garments, they went to the house of the warden together. Ma Joong cleaned up a bit and the three of them walked to the hostel.

When they had reported to Judge Dee, he said:

"Excellent work! Now listen to my further instructions".

In a few words he outlined his plan to them and the three went back to the doctor's mansion.

There Ma Joong took off his outer garments and smeared his face with dust. The warden tied Ma's hands behind his back with a strong rope, and Sergeant Hoong took the ends of the rope in his hand. Then the warden gave a thunderous knock on the front door, shouting at the top of his voice:

"Open the door quickly. The thief has been caught!"

The students, who had just been telling the old doctor about the attempted burglary, were overjoyed at hearing this. They rushed across the front courtyard. As soon as they had opened the gate, Warden Ho Kai quickly walked in, followed, by the sergeant, dragging Ma Joong.

Ho Kai immediately started cursing the students in a loud voice.

"Why", he shouted, "didn't you people immediately report that a burglar had been here in this compound? Don't you know that you live in my district? And tomorrow His Excellency himself is coming here to pay a visit to Doctor Tang. Do you know what he will do to me when he hears that there was a burglary which I failed to report?"

The students were frightened by his harsh language, and the threatening attitude of the warden and the sergeant. They ran back to the library and asked Doctor Tang to speak to the authorities. When Warden Ho Kai saw the doctor, he said:

"Luckily we caught this thief as he was trying to run away, Sir. Now I shall have to make a detailed report about what is missing. This ruffian here says he did not steal anything but that is what they always say. When His Excellency comes to see you tomorrow, Sir, I hope that you will kindly tell him that I am diligent about my duties".

Doctor Tang had lanterns brought out in the courtyard and gave Ma Joong a good look. Then he said:

"You insolent ruffian, you look strong and healthy enough. Can you not find some useful work to do, instead of sneaking about in the night, engaging in this disgraceful occupation? At least you did not steal anything here, so I shall not report you to the tribunal. Let this be a lesson to you. Go and reform!"

This was not at all what the warden wanted, so he hurriedly interposed:

"You are very kind-hearted, Sir. But if we let this ruffian go, he will soon try to continue his nefarious trade. We shall keep him under detention till tomorrow and then report to His Excellency the magistrate. Now Sir, please show me exactly where he entered, and how he made his escape, so that I can enter these details into my report". And turning to the sergeant he said:

"Drag that fellow along, so that he can confess on the spot".

As soon as he had said this, a young man came rushing out into the front courtyard. Ma Joong immediately recognized young Mr. Hsu.

"You obstinate yokel", young Hsu said to the warden, "have you not heard that the Doctor told you to let this man go? I know your sort. You only want to curry favor with the magistrate. Don't you know that as long as the Doctor does not file a complaint, the judge can never blame you for not reporting this burglary? Since nothing was stolen, Doctor Tang does not want all this trouble. Here are two silver pieces. Now let this ruffian go and take that constable to the inn to have a nice jar of wine!"

"Now who might you be, young Sir?", the warden asked, "Do you also live here? Are you a pupil of the doctor?"

Before the young man could say anything, one of the other students exclaimed:

"Don't you know that this is Mr. Hsu, the owner of this compound?"

"No indeed", Warden Ho Kai said, "and this is very strange. For this compound is entered in my register as belonging to Doctor Tang. It was never reported that a Mr. Hsu lived here".

"You should look up the records of your predecessor, Warden", old Doctor Tang said. "This compound was the property of the Hsu family for many years. But later old Mr. Hsu went back to his native town in the south. He granted me the use of this compound for my studies on condition that I let his eldest son stay in the back courtyard and instruct him further in the

Classics, in preparation for his second literary examination. Thus your predecessor removed the Hsu family from the register, and entered my name instead".

Warden Ho Kai shook his head, and said:

"It should have been reported, Sir, that one member of the Hsu family had stayed behind here. It is through such negligence that we wardens get into trouble. You know how strict our magistrate is. There is a case pending in the tribunal in which a Mr. Hsu is involved. I shall have to take this young gentleman to the tribunal, Sir, for His Excellency will want to put a few questions to him".

The old doctor became greatly excited, and exclaimed angrily:

"You insolent lout, I order you to leave this house immediately!"

Then Sergeant Hoong who had listened silently to all this, suddenly spoke up:

"You may be a Doctor of Literature but you have been hiding a suspected murderer. His Excellency's orders are to bring both you and this Hsu before him".

He took the rope off Ma Joong and grabbed the doctor by the arm. Ma Joong took young Hsu by the shoulders and marched him off to the front door. Doctor Tang was completely dumbfounded by these unexpected developments and let himself be taken away as if he was walking in a dream. Young Hsu wanted to protest but Ma Joong barked at him to shut up, and off they went to the hostel.

The students hastily locked the front door, and huddled together in the library, agitatedly discussing what steps to take in this emergency.

Judge Dee was in the front courtyard of the hostel, surrounded by the constables carrying lighted paper lanterns inscribed with large characters "The Tribunal of Chang-ping".

As soon as the judge saw them enter with the two prisoners, he ordered Sergeant Hoong to hurry back to Mrs. Bee's house to arrest Mrs. Bee and Mrs. Djou.

When Warden Ho Kai had reported what had happened to the judge he said to Ma Joong and Chiao Tai:

"This young fellow is a criminal. Keep him under close guard in the warden's house. I shall question him in the tribunal tomorrow".

Since Judge Dee was not too sure that Doctor Tang was directly involved in this affair, and because he held such a high literary degree, he did not like to place him under arrest also, without more evidence. So he instructed Tao Gan to take the doctor to a room in the hostel, and see to it that tea was served to him there. But Tao Gan was not to let him out of his eyes.

Then Judge Dee walked to Dr. Tang's house, the constables with the lanterns leading the way.

The constables kicked open the front door and everyone entered.

The students, who were still talking in the doctor's library, suddenly saw that the whole compound was full of constables, who shouted:

"His Excellency the Magistrate has arrived!"

The students saw a tall man in a simple blue robe, a small black cap on his head, presenting altogether a very scholarly appearance. This gentleman quietly entered the library and sat down at the doctor's writing desk. He immediately addressed one of the students, saying peremptorily:

"State your name, and how long you have been here. State your relations with Mr. Hsu and report all you know about him".

The student stammered:

"This student's name is Doo, and I have worked here under Doctor Tang's guidance since last spring. Mr. Hsu's full name is Hsu Deh-tai, he has already passed the first literary examination with honors. He is the favorite disciple of our master, who made him his special assistant. He has a room all to himself across the courtyard there."

Judge Dee nodded his head, and said:

"I have placed him under arrest. Now lead me to his room!"

The student hastily preceded Judge Dee and opened the door of Hsu's room for him. The judge ordered the constables to fetch a number of large candles, and then told them to drag the bedstead away from the wall.

Judge Dee immediately noticed that four stone flags were raised a little above the others, just as Ma Joong had reported. But in the dark Ma Joong had not been able to see the other parts of this clever arrangement. Two thin hempropes were wedged into the grooves of the flags, and ran to two poles at the back of the bedstead. These poles were found to turn on hinges and worked as a lever for lifting the trapdoor. Judge Dee made this contraption work and the four flags opened. It turned out that they were cemented to a wooden square which turned on hidden hinges, attached to a beam under the floor. The open trapdoor revealed a dark cavity underneath.

Judge Dee stooped down, a candle in his hand and saw a flight of steps leading downward. Under the trapdoor he noticed a small bronze bell. Feeling inside, he found that it had a wooden clapper with a thin cord attached to it. One end led down into the cavity; the other end disappeared under the floor of the room. Upon investigating the wall behind the bedstead Judge Dee found that there was a small hole, revealing the end of a cord, with an iron ring. He pulled it gently and immediately the bell made a muffled sound.

Then Judge Dee turned to the headman of the constables, and said:

"It is pitch black inside this secret passage. Who knows what other weird contrivances are hidden down below. You stay here with two constables and guard this room. Tomorrow I shall investigate it further in daylight".

The students, who had been standing about dumbfounded, did

not believe their eyes. Judge Dee said to them:

"This affair has nothing to do with you, so don't be alarmed. I only desire that you let me have your name, age etc., and seal these papers as witnesses to the discovery of this secret passage".

In the meantime the fourth nightwatch had been sounded and Judge Dee thought that it was time to return to the hostel. Just when he was leaving Doctor Tang's house, Chiao Tai arrived and said:

"After I escorted Hsu to the warden's house, I returned to the hostel and had a talk with that old doctor. It seems to me that he speaks the truth when he says that he knows nothing of young Hsu's escapades. He is an inoffensive bookworm who has not the slightest idea about what is going on in this world. Since the night has advanced far, I beg Your Honor to take some rest".

Judge Dee asked:

"Has not Sergeant Hoong returned with Mrs. Bee and Mrs. Djou yet? I trust that they have not made their escape".

He went back to the hostel hastily, followed by the constables.

## Twentysixth Chapter

A BOOKISH GENTLEMAN GETS AN UNPLEASANT SURPRISE;
A SECRET PASSAGE SUPPLIES THE KEY TO THE MYSTERY.

When Judge Dee entered the front courtyard, he heard the sounds of a woman sobbing and cursing. Inside he found Sergeant Hoong with Mrs. Bee and Mrs. Djou.

Mrs. Djou began to revile the judge loudly, but he cut her short, ordering Sergeant Hoong to put them in a small sedan chair and bring them to the house of the warden immediately. They were to be put under lock and key in separate rooms.

Then Judge Dee went to his room for a few hours of sleep.

He rose early and asked Tao Gan to bring Doctor Tang to his room.

When the doctor entered, Judge Dee gave him a searching look. He saw a frail old gentleman with a thin white beard and a ragged moustache. His face was full of wrinkles and his small beady eyes constantly blinked. He had no side whiskers. Altogether the judge thought that Chiao Tai had described him very well.

"This doctor", the other said in a solemn voice, "bears the surname of Tang, and the personal name of Deh-djung. I am still ignorant of the reason why Your Honor had the constables drag me to this hostel and why I have been kept in confinement. I have retired, and renounced all worldly affairs. As regards offending against the laws, well—I would not be as bold to say that I follow in the path of the ancient Sages, yet I dare say that I never engage in any undertaking that is not in strict accordance with the rules of propriety. I beg Your Honor the favor of an explanation".

Judge Dee answered:

"Your scholarship is widely known. I had long been looking

forward to an opportunity of meeting you. Now, as a tutor of a number of young men, you are, as you know, responsible for their morals. Are you quite sure that all of them in this respect are above reproach?"

The old doctor said indignantly:

"All my pupils are without exception the scions of prominent families. During daytime they prepare their lessons; at night they receive my instruction. Their lives are modeled entirely after the time-honored standard for the students of the Classics. How could they ever even think of anything that is not quite proper? I greatly fear that Your Honor has been sadly misinformed".

"Since I assumed my office", Judge Dee said, "I have never taken decisive action on the basis of mere rumours. Your pupils may all be scions of noble families, but do you think that is any guarantee for their morals? I regret that I must inform you that the student Hsu Deh-tai, who has been your pupil for several years, is involved in a murder case".

Doctor Tang was greatly startled by this, and exclaimed:

"Impossible! If there were irrefutable proof you could convince me that one of the others had done some imprudent thing but not young Hsu, my best student! Although I keep studiously aloof from worldly affairs, vague rumours have reached me recently averring that the present magistrate is too rash in his judgement, and shows a regrettable tendency to jump at conclusions. Hearing these wild accusations you brought forward just now, Sir, I am inclined to give credit to those rumours!"

"You, Sir", Judge Dee said impatiently, "are learned in the Classics, but apart from that your ignorance is formidable. As a scholar I bow to your wide learning, but as the magistrate of this district I see no reason why I should spare you. In due time you shall have to bear the consequences of your laxity in supervising the young men entrusted to your care".

He had Tao Gan lead the doctor back to his room.

Then he ordered Chiao Tai to go to the house of Warden Ho Kai and bring Hsu Deh-tai to the hostel.

As Hsu Deh-tai knelt before Judge Dee, the latter, seeing what a handsome young man he was, and how noble his bearing, thought that one need not wonder that Mrs. Djou fell in love with him. He reflected that this young man, blessed with wealth, good looks, a clever brain, and fine education, had had no excuse whatever to engage in the nefarious intrigue that caused the death of an innocent poor shopkeeper. He decided that in this case the law should be applied in its full severity. Having thus reflected, he harshly addressed him:

"I have been searching for you, Hsu Deh-tai, for several weeks. Now at last I have caught you. Tell me the exact truth about your adulterous relations with Mrs. Djou, and how the two of you murdered Bee Hsun! I warn you that I have proof of your guilt, and if you dont confess now I shall not hesitate to question you under severe torture".

Young Hsu was extremely frightened, but he reasoned with himself that after all he belonged to an old and very influential family, and that the judge would never dare to subject him to severe torture. He thought that Judge Dee was just trying to intimidate him. Thus he answered:

"This student is a member of an old, noble house. Both my father and my grandfather were provincial governors, in the service of the Imperial Court. The sons of our house have always been brought up most strictly. How would one of them ever dare to offend against the rules of propriety? Moreover, day and night I am under the supervision of Doctor Tang. My quarters are opposite his library. We have all our meals together. How could I ever engage in the immoral conduct Your Honor accuses me of, even if I had such an evil intent? I beg Your Honor to have all the facts verified again. Then it shall be proved that I am completely innocent".

Judge Dee rose from his chair, and said:

"So you prefer to tell the truth under torture. Well, we shall first take you to have a look at the secret passage in your room, and show you where it leads".

He ordered Chiao Tai and a few constables to take Hsu Deh-tai to the house of Doctor Tang. He sent Sergeant Hoong to the house of Warden Ho Kai, to bring Ma Joong and the two women to the doctor's house also. Having given these orders, Judge Dee left the hostel and set out for the Tang house.

By now the news that there were important developments in the case of Bee Hsun had spread through the entire village, and a crowd of eager spectators had assembled in front of the doctor's gate.

When Judge Dee entered the courtyard he was accosted by Mrs. Bee who wanted to vent her rage on him. But he cut her short, saying:

"You have come just in time. You shall accompany us, and see what disgraceful affair has been going on right under your eyes".

Then the judge walked straight on to Mr. Hsu's room at the back of the compound, followed by Ma Joong and Chiao Tai, who led the two women.

In Hsu's room, Judge Dee had the constables drag him in front of the cavity in the floor, and as he knelt there, asked him:

"Now you pretend to have no interests other than your learned studies. What then is the purpose of the secret passage under your bed?"

Hsu Deh-tai said nothing. The judge gave Ma Joong a sign. Chiao Tai handed him a lighted candle, and Ma Joong let himself down in the cavity. He found himself in a narrow passage, the walls of which were neatly panelled with smooth wooden boards. He stooped down and saw that the floor also was of wooden boards, well polished and without a speck of dust. He went down three steps and ducked under a low archway. He held the candle in front of him, and saw three steps leading upwards, ending in a blank wall. But the ceiling of the passage was of wooden boards which produced a hollow sound. Ma Joong placed the candle on the floor, and began pushing those boards. Suddenly they gave way. Ma Joong pushed the trapdoor up farther and found that he had pushed his head under the bedstead of Mrs. Djou, in the neighboring house. He climbed out, and saw the same arrangement here as in Hsu Deh-tai's room: the trapdoor consisted of four flags, cemented to a wooden frame. When it was closed, one hardly could tell them apart from the other stone flags, but if one worked the levers behind the bed, the trapdoor opened noiselessly and without the slightest effort. Ma Joong, standing over the trapdoor, called out to Chiao Tai, and then walked out of Mrs. Djou's room. He crossed the small courtyard and went out into the street by the frontgate. The crowd of spectators was greatly astonished on seeing Ma Joong emerge from that door, for only a little while ago they had seen him enter Doctor Tang's house, together with the two women. But one clever young fellow immediately understood what had happened, and he exclaimed excitedly:

"The judge has discovered a secret passage!"

Judge Dee was most gratified that everything turned out to be exactly as he had suspected. Turning to Mrs. Bee, who had been standing dumbfounded, her eyes on the trapdoor, the judge said:

"No wonder that your daughter locked herself up every day after noon. This is her secret backdoor, and thus she communicated with her paramour. They had even a secret signal to warn each other when the coast was clear. There stands the lover of your daughter. They murdered your son together".

Mrs. Bee's face had turned ashen. She uttered only one cry and fainted. Judge Dee told two constables to carry her to the doctor's library and give her some strong tea.

Mrs. Djou and Hsu Deh-tai had silently witnessed all these happenings. Their faces were drawn, but in no other way did they betray any emotion. They stared in front of them, as if all these things did not regard them at all.

Judge Dee did not say one word to them. He ordered Ma Joong and Chiao Tai to take them back to the warden's house. There they were to be put in chains, and then conveyed to the tribunal in the city.

Then he also left Doctor Tang's house and went back to the hostel.

A DEPRAVED NOBLEMAN AT LAST CONFESSES TO HIS GUILT;
AN ADULTEROUS WOMAN PERSISTS IN HER INNOCENCE.

Late that afternoon Judge Dee and his retinue arrived at the
tribunal of Chang-ping.

Judge Dee sat down in his private office, and drew up a detailed
report about everything that had happened in Huang-hua Village.
While writing this he reflected how accurate the verse, which he
had seen in his dream, had turned out to be. Now that it had been
discovered that the secret passage was located under Hsu Deh-tai's
bed, one could fully understand the line:

*"One descends the couch, and finds the answer to all past
riddles"*.

When he had completed his report, Judge Dee went on
reading other documents relating to the administration of the
district. He felt happy and peaceful, for he knew that at last also
this complicated case was nearing its final solution.

The next morning he convened the court, and after some reflection decided to have Hsu Deh-tai brought in first. When he was
kneeling in front of the bench, Judge Dee said:

"Yesterday I showed you that I discovered your secret passage leading to the bedroom of Mrs. Djou. You are a man
of depraved character, but after all you are a student of literature,
and should be capable of logical thinking. You will realize that
there is no use in compelling me to question you under torture.
Spare me and yourself unnecessary trouble, and confess to your
illicit relations with Mrs. Djou now, and state in what way Bee
Hsun was murdered. If there is any reason for mitigating your
sentence, I shall not fail to consider it".

"This student", Hsu Deh-tai said, "was completely ignorant
of the existence of that passage. I presume that a former owner

of the house had this passage made as a secret storeroom for his treasures. When my late father, His Excellency the Governor, had retired from official life, he purchased the compound in Huang-hua Village, which then also included the house now occupied by the family Bee. Since my father did not need so much space for his household, he sold the small properties adjoining it and the connecting doors were walled up. Thus this passage remained unnoticed until the present day. However this may be, this student did not know of its existence until yesterday. And as to the allegation that I had relations with that woman who apparently lives in the house on left, this I cannot but qualify as a grievous reflection on my name and the name of my family. I beg Your Honor's favorable consideration!"

Judge Dee smiled coldly, and said:

"For a clever student your reasoning is very poor. If this were really an ancient passage, how do you explain that there was not a speck of dust inside? And what about the trapdoor being worked by levers attached to your bedstead, and the bronze bell which could be sounded by pulling a rope over your bed? Your guilt is clear as daylight and I shall, therefore, now put the question to you again under torture".

The judge then ordered the constables to give Hsu Deh-tai fifty lashes with the thin rattan. They tore Hsu's robes from his back, and soon the rattan swished through the air. Long before the number fifty was reached, blood streamed from Hsu's back, and his screams resounded through the hall. But he gave no sign that he would confess.

Judge Dee ordered the constables to stop. He guessed correctly that young Hsu thought that if he bore with these fifty lashes without confessing, the judge would deem that appearances had been saved, and that he would then leave him alone, in consideration of his influential relations. Judge Dee, however, called out to him in a thunderous voice:

"I shall show you what happens to people who defy the laws of the land! In the tribunal everybody is equal, here there is no regard for rank or position. The great torture shall be applied to you!"

On a sign from the judge, the constables brought in a low wooden cross, that stood on a heavy wooden base. Two constables made Hsu kneel down with his back to this cross and lashed his head tightly to its top by tying a thin cord round his throat. His wrists were put through two holes at the ends of the crossbar, and his hands tied securely to the bar, so that they could not slip through. They passed a thick, round pole between the back of his thighs and his calves, and finally laid a long, heavy wooden beam across his lap. When they had reported that everything was duly fixed, Judge Dee ordered them to proceed.

Then, on either side of the heavy beam, two constables pressed it down, using their full weight. Hsu's knees and wrists were nearly dislocated. One could hear the bones creak. Moreover as his body was pressed down, the cord round his throat tightened and nearly strangled him. When he was nearly suffocated, the headman gave the constables a sign. They immediately relaxed the pressure. Perspiration and blood were streaming from Hsu Deh-tai's body as a result of this fearful torture, but he could only moan, since the cord was compressing his windpipe. When the constables were ready to press the beam down for the third time, the headman reported to the judge that Hsu had lost consciousness.

Judge Dee ordered them to take him down. They revived him by burning vinegar under his nose. It took quite some time before he regained his senses. Four constables were needed to drag him up from the floor, and he could not help crying out loudly when they made him kneel before the bench. His face was contorted. Two constables had to support him.

Judge Dee looked at him intently for some time, and then suddenly said in a kind voice:

"You need not be ashamed for your inability to stand this torture. This hall has witnessed hardened professional criminals confess on that cross. How could you, a refined young gentleman, bear this pain? I am ready to listen to your confession".

On being thus addressed, the reaction set in, and Hsu Deh-tai nodded his head, since he could not speak yet.

Judge Dee told the constables to make him drink several cups of strong tea. A deep silence reigned in the hall. Then the faltering voice of Hsu Deh-tai was heard.

"This student", he began, "now realizes, too late, the extent of his folly. It all began one day, when I happened to go to Bee Hsun's shop to make some purchases. His wife was sitting in a backroom of the shop and she smiled at me behind Bee Hsun's back. I thought she was very beautiful, and next day I went there again, on the pretext of buying something. Bee Hsun was out and we talked together. Then, one day, she told me that that afternoon she would be alone in her house, her mother and daughter having gone to the shop to help Bee Hsun. That was our first rendez-vous and thereafter we met in her house regularly when the others were in the shop.

"After some time, however, she told me that she did not like these chance meetings, where there was always the danger that somebody would unexpectedly come home. She suggested that I bribe a carpenter from some distant place, and have him build a secret passage between our rooms, since it so happened that they were right next to each other, with but one single dividing wall. By this time I loved her passionately, and so I sent for a carpenter from the south, where my family lives. I used the pretext of having some of my antique furniture repaired. It was he who, at night, built the secret passage for us. I gave him a rich reward, and he left without betraying the secret to anybody. Thus we were able to visit each other without any restraint.

"Soon, however, it appeared that she was not satisfied with this situation. She told me that she hated this secrecy about our love, and said that she wanted to be rid of her husband, so that we could be married. I was terribly shocked by these cruel words, and begged her not to do so desperate a thing. She laughed and said it was just a joke. But on the night after the Dragon Boat Festival, she killed Bee Hsun. That night we had not met, and I learned about Bee Hsun's death only the next morning, when I heard the laments next door. Realizing that she must have executed her wicked plan, I saw her as she really was and my love for her disappeared completely. I refused to see her any more, and for several days was tormented by doubts whether to report to the authorities or not. But I am a coward, and did not dare to do so, since this would have meant an exposure of our illicit relations. Thus I resolved to say nothing, and decided to forget this episode as one forgets a bad dream.

"After a week, however, Mrs. Djou insisted on seeing me. 'I have', she said 'killed my husband for your sake, so that you would be able to marry me. Now you don't seem to love me any more, so I shall give myself up to the tribunal. I regret that I shall then have to say that it was you who instigated this crime. If, on the other hand, perchance you still love me, we can quietly wait a year or so and then be happily married as man and wife'. On hearing these words, I knew how true our proverb is that says 'Once one has ascended a tiger, it is difficult to dismount'. Thus I assured her that I still loved her and wanted nothing more than to marry her as soon as a decent interval elapsed. I said that I had refused to see her because I greatly feared that our secret meetings would be noticed, and she be suspected of a crime. She was satisfied, and said with a smile that I need never fear that the murder would be discovered, because nobody could ever find out how she had killed her husband. Later I often asked her how she had done it, but she always just laughed and would never tell me.

Hsu Deh-tai's first meeting with Mrs. Bee, in Bee Hsun's shop. The signboard over the door reads "Shop of Woollen Goods." The sign hanging from the eaves, on the right, represents three strands of wool; this is the traditional sign of dealers in woollen goods.

Since then she insisted that I visit her every other night, and I, my passion for her having changed into disgust, led a miserable life. And later, when Your Honor started the investigation, and when Bee Hsun's corpse was exhumed, I lived in a nightmare. This is the complete truth".

Judge Dee had the senior scribe read aloud his notes of the confession, and Hsu Deh-tai affixed his seal thereto.

The judge slowly reread the document. Then he ordered the constables to bring in Mrs. Djou.

As she was kneeling in front of the bench, Judge Dee briefly summed up the evidence that had been collected against her. Then he pointed to Hsu Deh-tai, who was kneeling by the side of the dais, covered with sweat and blood, and said: "Your lover has just made a full confession, after having been subjected to severe torture. Now that your guilt is thus established beyond all doubt, I advise you to confess, for I assure you that if you don't, I shall not spare you torture even more severe than his".

But Mrs. Djou said in a dull voice:

"You may have extracted a false confession from this Mr. Hsu by torture, but I shall never confess to a crime I have not committed. I don't know anything about secret passages and illicit love affairs. I did not kill my husband. My only desire is to remain a chaste widow for ever after".

Judge Dee gave a sign to the constables. They took off her robes, leaving her only one undergarment, and then stretched her out on the floor. Having brought in the large screws, they made her lie on the heavy boards with her back, and placed her arms and legs in the screws. When they turned them on tight, skin and bone were crushed, and blood stained the floor. She emitted horrible screams, and when the constables went on tightening the screws, she fainted. They loosened the screws, and poured cold water over her until she was revived. Then they again turned on the screws. Her body writhed in vain in the terrible grip, and she shrieked hoarsely, but she gave no sign of wanting to confess.

Hsu Deh-tai could not stand this horrible sight any longer. He called to her in despair:

"I implore you to confess! Why, why did not you listen to me when I begged you not to kill your husband? It is true that our love would have had to remain secret, but you and I would have been spared this terrible fate!"

Mrs. Djou gritted her teeth to suppress her groans, and gasped with difficulty:

"You miserable coward. You abject cur! If I killed my husband, tell them how I did it! Tell them...if you can!"

Then, unable to bear the pain, she lost consciousness again.

# Twentyeighth Chapter

A WEIRD INTERROGATION IS CONDUCTED IN THE JAIL;
A CONFESSION IS OBTAINED, AND THE MYSTERY SOLVED.

Judge Dee ordered the constables to loosen the screws and revive Mrs. Djou. He waited till she had sufficiently recovered to understand what he was about to say. After a while he addressed her in a matter of fact voice:

"As you know, it is stipulated in the Code that a criminal, who still has an old parent to support, may be treated with special leniency. After all Bee Hsun is dead and gone. Nobody can bring him to life again. But your old mother and your small daughter are still alive. Now, when you have confessed, I must, of course, propose the capital punishment for you. But I shall add a recommendation for clemency, in view of the fact that you have an old parent to support, and must bring up your small daughter. Thus there is a good chance that the Metropolitan Court petition the Throne that your sentence be commuted. Now tell me how everything came about, and don't spare this man Hsu, who gave you away as soon as he entered this court".

This clever speech, however, to Judge Dee's disappointment, failed to impress Mrs. Djou. She gave him a disdainful look, and said:

"I shall never confess".

Judge Dee looked at her steadily for a long time, debating with himself what other means he could employ to make this woman confess. He could again apply more severe torture, but he doubted whether this would produce results. Moreover he feared that, her body being already weakened by the previous torture, she might die or loose her mind. He was considerably vexed and finally ordered the constables to take her back to the jail.

He also ordered Hsu Deh-tai back to the jail, but added that no chains should be put upon him, and that the physician of the court should give him some salves and drugs.

Judge Dee left the court and seated himself behind his desk in his private office. Then he had Sergeant Hoong called in.

"I have", the judge said, "worked on this case with you for several weeks. We have done all we could, and now, at the last moment, all our labors seem to come to nothing, just because this woman refuses to confess. You have seen yourself that I have exhausted all the usual means; I employed threats, torture, and persuasion, but all failed. I must confess that I don't know what to do. Let us consult together".

The sergeant said:

"Cannot Your Honor find some clue in the dream? The first part proved accurate in every detail; perhaps the last part can help us to solve this problem".

But Judge Dee slowly shook his head.

"I feel", he said, "that we should not attach too much value to the last part of my dream. At that time I was ready to waken and the inspiration from on High had become blurred, confused by figments of my own brain. The very last part of the dream, where I saw the corpse and the adder, might be construed as an adumbration of the case of the poisoned bride, but I greatly doubt this. No, just as at the time when I was confronted with that case, we must rely on our own wits in solving this last perplexing problem".

Then they talked together for a long time. Judge Dee later also called in Ma Joong, Chiao Tai and Tao Gan.

In the meantime Mrs. Djou lay on the bare boards of the couch in her cell. She was all alone. The matron had left her as soon as she had brought in the bowl with the evening rice.

Her body hurt terribly, and Hsu Deh-tai's betrayal had shocked her more than she had shown in court. "For that man", she reflected, "I have borne the torture inflicted on me at the beginning of this case. For him I have stood up under all questioning and all vexations. And the first time that he appears in court he blurts out everything! Was my 'dream of spring' worth all this?"

Towards night fall the pain in her tortured limbs increased and fever set in. She could not concentrate her thoughts any more, and lay there staring in the dark with burning eyes.

Suddenly she noticed that a cool breeze entered the cell. The musty atmosphere of the jail cleared, and she thought that somebody must have thrown open the doors of her cell. But it was pitch dark and she could discern nothing.

With great difficulty she raised herself on her elbows and looked in the direction of the door. Slowly a bluish light appeared and to her utter horror she saw a large red desk take shape.

She thought in her feverish brain that she had again been dragged to the tribunal in her sleep, and screamed in terror. But then a more horrible sight made her stare in dumb, abject fright.

For in the blue light she discerned the fearful dark shape of the Judge of the Inferno behind the red desk. On his right and left she saw the vague shapes of the Ox-headed and the Horse-headed Demon, their weird animal heads leering at her.

"I have died", she sobbed, "I have died". And suddenly a feeling of utter loneliness assailed her. She only felt a hopeless weariness and futility of all effort.

The Black Judge did not say a word. He just stared at her with his still, wide eyes, and the animal heads by his side goggled.

Then a gruesome greenish shape of an emaciated corpse swathed in a stained shroud floated in front of the desk. It turned round its decayed death mask, the eyes bulging from their sockets. Its fleshless hands raised a document in front of the Black Judge.

"Bee Hsun, Bee Hsun", screamed Mrs. Djou, "don't report your case. You don't know everything. Let me speak, let me speak for myself".

She felt no pain now, only a terrible fatigue, and the strong desire to get everything over and done with. What had her life been, after all?

"Bee Hsun's shop", she said, "hardly brought in enough for one square meal a day. What was there to give me happiness? During the day I slaved and toiled in the household and in the shop. At night I heard the nagging of my mother-in-law. Then Hsu Deh-tai came to our shop one day, handsome, well educated, without a care in the world. I felt a consuming passion for this man, and soon knew that he also was impressed by my beauty. When I heard that he was not married, I resolved that he would marry me, cost what it would. I first made him begin an affair with me, and when I knew that he was passionately in love, I told him to have the secret passage made. When that was successful, I decided that the time had come to kill Bee Hsun. On that night after the Dragon Boat Festival, I made him drink many toasts at dinner. Not accustomed to so much wine, he complained of a stomach ache. Then, in our bedroom, I made him drink still more, to alleviate the pain. At last he sank on the bed in a drunken stupor. I took one of the long, thin needles that we used for stitching the felt soles of our shoes, and drove it into the top of his head with a wooden mallet, until all of its three inches had disappeared completely. Bee Hsun cried only once and then he was dead. Only the head of the needle showed as a tiny speck, impossible to locate if you did not know where to look for it among the thick hair. There was not a single drop of blood, but his eyes had bulged from their sockets. I knew that even an autopsy would not reveal this mortal wound. Afterwards Hsu often asked me how I had killed Bee Hsun, but I never told him.

"Everything seemed safe then. But one day, when I thought that my mother and my daughter had gone out to borrow some money, I called Hsu to my room, giving him the signal by pulling the cord of the bell. But after he had come in by the secret trapdoor, I suddenly saw my daughter standing in the room; she had been sleeping under the covers of the couch in the next room, and had been awakened by our voices. I was afraid that she would say something to my mother, and made her drink a drug that robbed her of the power of speech. After that, I received Hsu when only my mother was out, for I knew that my daughter would never be able to betray me, even if she should understand what it was all about.

"When the magistrate became suspicious, I was called to the tribunal and interrogated for the first time".

Reflecting on her many fights in court with the judge, and her fears during the exhumation, she became more and more weary, and thought whether it was really worth while to relate all this. The blue light grew faint, the red desk faded, and she sank back into the welcome darkness. The last thing she heard was the doors of her cell close with a soft thud.

At this late hour, the tribunal was dark and deserted. Only in the private office of the judge two candles were lighted, and these illuminated him as he slowly removed a gruesome dark mask from his face.

Ma Joong and Chiao Tai extricated their heads with some difficulty from animal heads, made of paper and bamboo, and wiped the perspiration from their foreheads. Tao Gan was hastily scribbling notes on a corner of the clerk's desk, and Sergeant Hoong came in, his hands and hair wet from a washing; he carried a home-made paper mask in his hand.

"So that", Judge Dee said, "was how the murder was committed!"

JUDGE DEE CLOSES THE CASE OF THE STRANGE CORPSE;
AN IMPERIAL CENSOR DRINKS TEA IN THE WATER PAVILION.

Turning to Ma Joong, Judge Dee continued:

"Now that I know for certain that that young girl was made
dumb by a drug, I can dare to administer a very potent medicine,
mentioned in an old book of prescriptions preserved in my family.
When taken by a person who was struck with dumbness because
of natural causes, it may impair his mind; but dumbness caused
by a drug will be immediately cured. Thus I cannot grant you
your well-deserved rest. I desire that you ride on horseback to
Huang-hua Village immediately, and see to it that by tomorrow
morning old Mrs. Bee and her granddaughter are here. This
woman Djou has most remarkable will power and I will not take
the risk of her repudiating her confession in court tomorrow.
As a final effect, I want to confront her with the testimony of her
own daughter".

Ma Joong was so elated by the complete success of their stratagem, that he cheerfully put on his riding jacket and went straight
to the stables to select a horse.

When Tao Gan had written out Mrs. Djou's confession, Judge
Dee read it through again, and with a contented smile put it in his
sleeve. When Tao Gan and Chiao Tai had taken their leave,
Sergeant Hoong stayed on for a while, and offered the judge a
cup of tea.

While the judge was sipping his tea, the sergeant remained in
deep thought. Then he said:

"Your Honor, I think that I now understand the last part of
your dream in the temple. Earlier tonight, when you were explaining to us how we would try to extract a confession from Mrs.
Djou, it did not occur to me. But it now strikes me that

the theatrical performance which you saw in your dream was an accurate forecast of what happened tonight. For did we not just now transform, as it were, the jail into a theatre, each of us playing his appointed role? And as to the woman acrobat and the young man, they must have represented Mrs. Djou and Hsu Deh-tai. And the small girl from the jar, clutching Hsu's sleeve, is Mrs. Djou's daughter, whose testimony will put the final touch to the case tomorrow. Your Honor, you may rest assured that Mrs. Djou won't repudiate her confession tomorrow!"

Judge Dee, however, shook his head in doubt, and said:

"Your explanation may be right, but I am not too sure. I still think that the last part of my dream was very confused and I doubt whether it had any meaning at all. We shall never know".

After some more desultory talk, the sergeant took his leave and Judge Dee retired for a few hours sleep.

The next morning Judge Dee had Mrs. Bee and her granddaughter brought in as soon as the session convened.

He first reprimanded Mrs. Bee for her stubborn attitude all through the conduct of the case; her opposition had considerably retarded the solution. Mrs. Bee started to apologize tearfully, but the judge hastily cut her short, saying:

"I have here a medicine that will cure your grand-daughter's dumbness. But it is a very powerful medicine and will cause the poor girl much distress. Therefore I want your permission before I administer it to her, and I want you to be present while it takes its effect".

Mrs. Bee hastily gave her permission. Judge Dee had already had the medicine prepared, and Sergeant Hoong gave it to the girl, telling her to empty the entire bowl slowly.

After she had drunk it the girl's face contorted in pain, and suddenly she started to vomit. Her small body shook with convulsions and soon she sank to the floor unconscious. Judge Dee told Ma Joong to take her up in his arms and carry her to his private office. He was to make her lie down on the couch there, and as soon as she would wake, he was to give her a cup of strong tea.

After a while Ma Joong reentered the court hall, leading the small girl by her hand. Seeing Mrs. Bee, she rushed to her, and buried her face in Mrs. Bee's gown, crying:

"Grandmother, why are we here? I am afraid!"

Judge Dee rose, and stepped down from the dais. Placing his hand under her chin, he gently turned the girl's face up, and said softly:

"Don't be afraid, little girl. Your grandmother will take you home shortly. But just tell me, do you know Mr. Hsu from next door?"

The small girl nodded and said earnestly:

"Mr. Hsu is a great friend of my mother. He comes to see her nearly every day. But where is my mother?"

Judge Dee nodded to Mrs. Bee, and she quickly took the girl to a far corner of the court hall. Squatting down by her side, she tried to comfort her in a low voice.

The judge resumed his seat behind the bench and filled out a slip for the warden of the jail. Two constables brought Mrs. Djou before the bench.

She had changed greatly overnight. Her face was haggard, and she moved with difficulty. But the small girl immediately recognized her, even in prison garb, and cried out:

"Mother, where have you been all these days?"

Judge Dee hastily gave Mrs. Bee a sign and she took the girl out of the court hall.

The judge spread out a document on the desk, and said to Mrs. Djou:

"I have here before me your full confession. It states how you seduced Hsu Deh-tai; how you murdered Bee Hsun by driving a needle into his head; and how you made your daughter dumb by making her drink a foul drug. This morning I cured your daughter, and she has testified that Hsu Deh-tai frequently visited you at night".

Here Judge Dee paused a moment, looking intently at Mrs. Djou. But she just stared in front of her with unseeing eyes and said nothing. She realized that the vision of last night probably had been a trick of the judge, but she did not really care. She only wished that he would finish quickly.

Judge Dee then ordered the senior scribe to read out aloud the confession as Tao Gan had drafted it. When he had finished, Judge Dee asked Mrs. Djou the formal question:

"Do you agree that this is your true confession?"

A deep silence reigned in the court. Mrs. Djou's head sank still lower. Finally she said but two words:

"I do".

Then the scribe presented the document to her, and she affixed her thumbmark.

Judge Dee then said:

"I pronounce you guilty on three major counts: intentionally delivering false testimony in court, having adulterous relations while your husband was alive, and murdering your husband without provocation. The last crime is the most heinous one. The Code prescribes for this the most severe death penalty known to law, that is execution by the process of 'lingering death'. In forwarding your sentence I shall not fail to record that you still have an old mother to support, but I feel it my duty to warn you that although this fact may procure mitigation of the way of execution, it shall hardly lead to a commutation of the extreme penalty".

Mrs. Djou was led back to the jail, there to await the Imperial pleasure.

Judge Dee then had Hsu Deh-tai brought before him, and said:

"I pronounce you guilty of adultery and conniving in the

murder of your paramour's husband, Bee Hsun. For this crime the Code prescribes death by strangulation. Whether this shall be the regular slow strangulation, or whether it shall be mitigated to quick strangulation in view of the fact that you have a literary grade, I shall leave to the Metropolitan Court to decide".

Hsu Deh-tai seemed dumbfounded on hearing this sentence pronounced. He was led back to jail in a state of complete stupefaction.

Then Doctor Tang was brought before the bench. Judge Dee severely reprimanded him, saying:

"You, a man of wide learning and many years experience, have failed miserably in your duties as a tutor. The crime of adultery took place in your house, and, as it were, under your very eyes. If I were to interpret the provisions of the Code strictly, I could have you severely punished as an accessory*. But in deference to your great achievements in the field of scholarly researches, I shall free you with this public reprimand, enjoining you henceforth to devote all your time to your own literary studies. You are strictly forbidden ever again to engage in the teaching of young students."

Finally Judge Dee had Mrs. Bee recalled, and said to her:

"You failed in your duty of supervising the conduct of your daughter-in-law, and consequently two heinous crimes were committed in your house. In view of the fact, however, that you are by nature an extremely stupid woman, and that you have Bee Hsun's daughter to support, I shall let you go free. Moreover, after Hsu Deh-tai has been executed, I shall allocate a portion of his forfeited property to you, for the education of your granddaughter."

Mrs. Bee prostrated herself in front of the bench, and knocking

---

* (Translator's note) For the legal points involved in these sentences, the reader is referred to the notes to this chapter in the Translator's Postscript.

her head on the floor, shed tears of gratitude.

Judge Dee closed the session and returned to his private office. There he drew up the final report on the case, enclosing the original confessions of Mrs. Djou and Hsu Deh-tai, adding also the prescription for the medicine which had cured Mrs. Djou's daughter. He also added a separate request to the effect that his previous self-accusation concerning of grievously slandering an innocent woman, and having exhumed a corpse without sufficient reason, be rescinded.

\*　　　　\*

\*

Some weeks after this sensational session of the tribunal at Chang-ping, the Governor of Shantung was entertaining a distinguished guest in his palace in the provincial capital.

This was the Imperial Censor Yen Lee-ben, the famous statesman, artist and scholar\*.

That night the Governor had arranged a large official dinner for Censor Yen in the banquet hall of his palace, to which all the high functionaries of the provincial government and the members of the local gentry had been invited. Late in the afternoon he was drinking tea with his guest in a secluded part of the palace garden. They were seated in the Water Pavilion, an elegant small building, in the middle of the curved bridge over the lotus pond.

It had been a hot day, and both enjoyed the cool breeze over the water.

Engaged in leisurely talk, the Governor asked Censor Yen about recent happenings in the capital. The censor sketched the background of some mutations in the Board of Rites, and, slowly fanning himself with a large fan of heron feathers, he added:

"Now that I come to think of it, just before I left the capital there

---

\* (Translator's note) Yen Lee-ben died in A.D. 673, at an advanced age. The Museum of Fine Arts, at Boston, has a painting by him.

was considerable talk in the Board of Punishments about a case of a beautiful young girl who was poisoned on her wedding night. This occurred in a district of your province here, and the local magistrate solved the mystery in three days. The Board was quite impressed by your report and the case was eagerly discussed, even in court circles. At the time I did not inquire into this matter further, but since it occurred in your province, you can probably tell me all about it".

The Governor told the servant to bring a new pot of hot tea, and leisurely sipping from his cup, he said:

"This case was solved by the district magistrate of Chang-ping, an official called Dee Jen-djieh, of Tai-yuan in Shansi Province".

Censor Yen nodded, and said:

"Now you mention his name, I remember that I used to know his late father, the Prefect Dee. The old prefect was highly regarded by the central authorities. The Prefect's father, Dee Jen-djieh's grandfather, was a wise Minister, scrupulously honest, who left some remarkable memorials to the Throne, which are often quoted today. It seems that this magistrate Dee is continuing the great tradition of his family, for I recall that it was said that he had solved a number of other puzzling crimes, aside from the one of the poisoned bride".

"That", the Governor said, "was quite an ingenious solution, and, the topic being a sensational one, I can well imagine that it created some interest in the capital. Yet that magistrate, in the first two years of his terms of office, has solved a number of cases that were at least as puzzling as that of the poisoned bride. All of these you will find in the records of the provincial chancery. And during this present year he has, beside the case of the poisoned bride, already solved two others. The first was a double murder, committed on the highway by some violent ruffian. Although I gather that there were some complications, and although tracing and arresting the criminal seems to have been a burdensome task, yet the solution of the case was, in my opinion, but a matter of routine.

"Personally I am greatly impressed, however, by the magistrate's conduct of the third case, the final report of which I received last week from the prefect, and which I have now forwarded to the capital. This case concerned an adulterous woman who murdered her husband about one year ago in order to be able to marry her paramour. What struck me there was that originally no one had realized that a murder had been committed, and that no complaint had been filed with the tribunal. But this magistrate Dee, having become suspicious on hearing someone's chance remark in the street, set out with astonishing zeal to trace this crime back to its very beginnings, at the risk of getting himself into serious trouble. As a matter of fact, at one time it seemed that he had blundered badly and the prefect reported to me that magistrate Dee had recommended himself for appropriate punishment, having falsely accused and tortured a woman. Knowing his previous record, I did not act on this self-accusation for some time, and kept it on file, hoping that he would be able to set things right. And actually last week the prefect forwarded the report of the solution of the case to me, together with the full confessions of the adulterous woman and her paramour, accompanied by irrefutable proof.

"I appreciate the work on this case far more than the solution of the poisoning of the bride, which after all may have been just a lucky guess. Moreover that case, having occurred in the mansion of a retired prefect, and implying some spicy details about a wedding night, had all the makings of becoming a famous case. The case of the adulterous woman, on the other hand, concerned a poor shopkeeper's family in a small village. The magistrate initiated and solved this case, risking the loss of his rank and position, and estranging the sympathy of the people in his district. He was motivated solely by the desire that justice be done and the death of a miserable, small merchant avenged. This I consider exemplary conduct, worthy of a special citation".

Censor Yen agreed that this was so, and then added:

"After the banquet tonight, you might send the complete Chang-ping file over to me in the library. I find that in my old age I am not sleeping too well, and I have formed the regrettable habit of reading till deep into the night. The library, which you so kindly placed at my disposal during my stay here, does great credit to your elegant taste. I have studied your fine collection of manuscripts, and the view from the northern window, showing the Seven-storied Pagoda against a background of distant mountains, is really enchanting. I have already painted it twice, once with the effect of the early morning haze, and once in an attempt to capture the uncertain atmosphere of twilight. The sight of a lonely sail on a moon-lit lake, the sounds of a temple bell at night...I sometimes wonder whether these things are, after all, not more important than all these complications of official life. Well, tomorrow you shall select the painting which you like best, and I shall inscribe it for you".

The Governor expressed his thanks for this friendly gesture, and then they rose and walked back to the palace to change into ceremonial dress for the banquet.

THREE CRIMINALS SUFFER THE EXTREME PENALTY;
A COURT MESSENGER ARRIVES WITH URGENT ORDERS.

Two weeks later, sooner than Judge Dee had expected, the
prefect forwarded the Imperial ratification of the capital punishments proposed for Shao Lee-huai, Hsu Deh-tai and Mrs. Djou,
with only a few changes made by the Board of Punishments,
on the recommendation of the Metropolitan Court. There was
an additional instruction to the effect that these orders were to
be executed with the least possible delay.

Judge Dee immediately dispatched a message to the garrison
commander of Chang-ping, instructing him to have a detach-
ment of soldiers stand by on the execution ground the next morning. At dawn a military escort was to be ready in front of the
tribunal to convey the three criminals.

Judge Dee himself rose before dawn, and having thrown the
scarlet pelerine over his shoulders, ascended the dais. In the flicker-
ing light of the large candles he called the roll. Somewhat apart
from the constables stood a giant of a man, carrying a naked
sword over his shoulders.

The judge first ordered Shao Lee-huai brought in from the
jail. Shao had been served the customary last meal of wine and
roast and seemed resigned to his fate. As he knelt in front of the
bench, Judge Dee read out his sentence:

"The criminal Shao Lee-huai shall be decapitated, his head
shall be exposed for three days on the city gate, and all his possessions are forfeited".

The constables bound Shao securely with ropes, and inserted
a stake between the rope and his back, bearing a long placard
where his name, his crime and his punishment had been written
in large characters. They took him outside and made him climb

into the open jail cart. A crowd of onlookers had assembled in front of the main gate, the military guard keeping them at a suitable distance with their pikes and halberds.

After this Judge Dee had Hsu Deh-tai brought in. When on entering the dimly lit court hall, he saw the scarlet pelerine of the judge shimmering in the candle-light, the full horror of impending death dawned upon him, and he sank to his knees, crying in abject fright. Judge Dee read:

"The criminal Hsu Deh-tai shall die by strangulation, in such a way that death ensues immediately, but his body shall not be publicly exposed; this mitigation is based on the meritorious services rendered to the State by the said Hsu Deh-tai's father and grandfather. All his possessions are forfeited".

After Hsu Deh-tai had been bound and led away, he also was placed in the open cart, the white placard bearing his name and his crime was above his head for all to see.

Finally Mrs. Djou was brought before the judge. She now seemed an elderly woman. She walked with bent shoulders, never looking up.

Judge Dee read out:

"The criminal Bee, *née* Djou, shall be subjected to the lingering death, in such a way that death ensues after the first cut, this mitigation being based on the fact that she has suffered severe torture during the interrogation. Her possessions shall not be forfeited, in consideration of the fact that she leaves behind an old mother. But her head shall be exposed on the city gate for three days".

Then she also was bound with ropes, and the placard with name, offense and punishment stuck on her back.

As the three criminals stood in the open cart, six soldiers with drawn swords placed themselves behind them, and the other soldiers, shouldering their pikes and halberds, ranged themselves in formation on all four sides of the cart. All the constables and guards of the tribunal took their places, standing in rows of six in front and behind the palanquin of the judge. The procession was headed by ten soldiers on horseback, to clear the way. And directly behind them walked the huge executioner, his sword on his shoulder, flanked by an assistant on either side.

The large gong was sounded three times, and Judge Dee ascended his palanquin. Sergeant Hoong and Ma Joong guided their horses on the right side of the palanquin, and Chiao Tai and Tao Gan rode on left.

Slowly the procession wound its way through the streets of Chang-ping, headed for the western city gate.

Young and old, rich and poor, anyone who could walk had assembled in the street to witness this spectacle. The people cheered loudly as soon as the palanquin of Judge Dee came in sight. But when the cart with the three criminals passed, the younger spectators reviled them, jeering at them at the top of their voices. The elder people in the crowd, however, scolded these youngsters, saying:

"Don't use your tongue to revile them. Use your brains and reflect on the stern retribution meted out to criminals by the laws of our land. Here you see a violent ruffian, a depraved nobleman, and a lascivious woman, all together as equals in the cart of the condemned. Justice has no regard for rank, position or sex. Let this spectacle serve you as a warning, and always remember it, should temptation come your way".

As the procession passed through the West Gate, a crowd of more than a thousand people followed behind. By the time they arrived at the execution ground, the early rays of the sun shone on the helmets of the soldiers, standing there on all four sides of the square.

The garrison commander came forward and welcomed the judge. Together they ascended the temporary dais that had been put up in front of the execution ground during the night, and took their seats behind the bench. The constables and scribes ranged themselves in front of the dais.

The two assistants of the executioner brought Shao Lee-huai to the center of the execution ground, and made him kneel. They removed the placard from his back, and loosened his collar so that his neck was bare. The executioner took off his jacket, revealing his muscular torso. Lifting his sword in both hands, he looked at the judge.

Judge Dee gave the sign, and the head was severed from the body with one terrific blow. An assistant picked the head up by its hairs, and raised it in front of the bench. Judge Dee marked its forehead with his vermilion brush, and it was thrown in a basket standing ready nearby, later to be exposed on the city gate.

In the mean time the other assistant of the executioner had stuck a low wooden cross in the ground, and now Hsu Deh-tai was tied to this cross in a kneeling position, his arms being fastened to the horizontal bar. The executioner threw a noose of thin hempcord over Hsu's head, while the other end encircled the upper part of the stake. He stuck a short wooden stick between the cord and the stake behind Hsu's head, and looked toward the judge.

As soon as Judge Dee had given the sign, the executioner quickly twisted the stick round in both hands, the cord tightened round the criminal's throat, his eyes bulged from their sockets, and his tongue protruded. The executioner stopped turning the stick, and waited. A deep silence reigned over the execution ground. Not a sound was heard among that crowd numbering more than a thousand people. Finally the executioner felt the criminal's heart, and reported to the judge that he was dead.

The assistants took his body from the cross, and laid it in the temporary coffin that a representative sent by Hsu Deh-tai's family had placed there in readiness.

They pulled the cross up, until it was raised to a man's height above the ground. Having stamped the earth close around the middle stake, they nailed a second horizontal crossbar on, one foot above the ground. Then they took off Mrs. Djou's clothes, leaving her only one undergarment. She was tied to the cross, her hands being fastened to the ends of the upper crossbar, and her ankles to the ends of the lower one. The executioner placed himself in front of her, holding a long, thin knife. His two assistants stood by his side, carrying a hatchet and a saw.

As soon as Judge Dee had given the sign, the executioner plunged his knife into her breast with a powerful thrust. She died immediately. Then he proceeded to slice and dismember the body with his assistants, beginning with the hands and the feet. Although the process of the "lingering death" was thus executed on a dead body instead of on the living criminal, it still was a gruesome sight, and many in the crowd of spectators fainted. It took an hour to complete the process. What remained of Mrs. Djou's body was cast in a basket. But the head was marked by the judge, and would be exposed on the city gate for three days, together with a placard stating her crime, as a deterrent example.

Gongs were sounded, the soldiers presented their arms as the judge and the military commander left the execution ground. The judge ascended his palanquin, the commander his military sedan chair. Having entered the city, they first proceeded together to the temple and there prayed and offered incense. In the front courtyard of the temple they took leave of each other, Judge Dee returning to the tribunal, and the commander to his military headquarters.

The gong of the tribunal was sounded three times, and Judge Dee, having taken off the scarlet pelerine in his private office, and having hastily drunk a cup of strong tea, ascended the dais for the noon session. He had previously given orders that Mrs. Bee, the carter's widow Wang, an uncle of the murdered merchant Liu, and the representative of the family of Hsu Deh-tai, were to present themselves at this session.

The judge first had the representative of Hsu Deh-tai's family brought in. He ordered him, on his return to the south, to convey his feelings of sympathy to the elders of the Hsu-clan, and then told him to report the possessions of Hsu Deh-tai.

The representative produced a document, and read:

"One compound in Huang-hua Village, estimated value 3000 silver pieces, furniture and personal assets to a value of 800 pieces, liquid funds 2000 silver pieces. The last item includes the remainder of the quarterly grant Hsu Deh-tai received from his family, last paid out two months ago".

Judge Dee had the comptroller of the tribunal called, and ordered the representative to hand the document to him. The judge told the comptroller to sell Hsu Deh-tai's property, and then dismissed the representative.

Now he ordered the constables to bring in Mrs. Bee, Mrs. Wang, and the uncle of Liu the merchant. When all three were kneeling before the bench, he told the comptroller to report.

This official opened a file, and read out:

"The local silk broker in this city has received a letter from Manager Loo Chang-po in Divine Village, with the information that the silk deposited there by Djao Wan-chuan has been sold for 900 silver pieces. Out of this sum Manager Loo has refunded three hundred to Djao Wan-chuan, this being the sum he had lent to the criminal Shao Lee-huai. Manager Loo, desirous to show his public spirit, has taken a commission of only ten percent of the remainder, instead of the customary twenty, so that the net proceeds of this sale are 540 silver pieces. Manager Loo has authorized the silk broker to pay this sum to the tribunal.

"The district magistrate of Lai-chow has reported through his comptroller that an inventory taken by his constables in Turnip Pass, showed that Shao Lee-huai's possessions there amounted to 200 silver pieces, augmented with 60 which various persons there owed him as gambling debts. From this total of 260 the magistrate of Lai-chow deducted 60 for the costs of collection".

Here there was an interruption, as the headman of the constables started to blurt out highly offensive remarks at the mention of the magistrate of Lai-chow.

"Silence!" shouted Judge Dee in a thunderous voice. Turning to the comptroller, he said: "Proceed!"

"Thus," the comptroller continued, "the net proceeds of the possessions of the criminal Shao Lee-huai amount to the sum of 200 silver pieces. The grand total of the money available to the tribunal is 6540 silver pieces".

Judge Dee said:

"I rule that of this sum, you shall pay 1540 silver pieces to the uncle of the victim Liu present here, for the bales of silk belonging to that merchant, and the cash that Shao Lee-huai took from him. In addition, you shall pay him 1000 silver pieces as smart money.

"Further, you shall pay the sum of 1000 silver pieces to Mrs. Bee, in monthly installments of ten silver pieces, to cover her costs of living in the ensuing years, and to pay for the education of her granddaughter.

"Finally, you shall pay a lump sum of 1000 silver pieces to Mrs. Wang, as smart money.

"The remaining 2000 silver pieces revert to the State and shall be entered in your books as such. In your quarterly report you shall enter these financial arrangements in detail, including a copy of the report from Lai-chow". Looking at the headman of his constables, Judge Dee added:

"No doubt the comptroller of the prefectural office shall study this report from Lai-chow with due care".

Mrs. Bee, Mrs. Wang and the uncle of the merchant Liu prostrated themselves and knocked their heads to the floor several times to show their gratitude.

Judge Dee left the dais, and entered his private office. He

changed into a comfortable informal robe, and, moistening his writing brush, began drafting a report on the execution, to be forwarded to the prefect.

He had not been writing long, when suddenly a panting clerk burst into the room, and said excitedly:

"Your Honor, a Court messenger carrying an Imperial Edict has arrived at the main gate!"

Judge Dee was very astonished at this news, and wondered what was afoot. He hurriedly donned his full ceremonial dress, and at the same time ordered the senior scribe to have the court hall cleared, and to place the special high table with the incense burner, reserved for Imperial Edicts, against the northern wall.

When the judge entered the court hall, the Imperial messenger was already standing there, carrying an oblong box in both hands, which was wrapped up in yellow brocade. This messenger was a tall young courtier, with grave mien, who wore the robes and insignia of a Junior Assistant to the Grand Secretary.

When the judge had greeted him with due ceremony, he guided him in front of the high table, adding new incense in the burner. As fragrant smoke curled upwards, the messenger reverently placed the box on the table, and retreated a few steps. Judge Dee prostrated himself below, and knocked his head on the floor nine times in succession.

Then the judge rose and waited with bowed head while the messenger took off the wrappings and opened the yellow leather box inside. He took from it a scroll mounted on yellow brocade, which he placed in front of the incense burner. The messenger himself added new incense in the burner, and then said solemnly:

"The August Words shall now be read".

Judge Dee took the scroll, and slowly unrolled it, holding it high in both hands, so that the Imperial seal never was below his head.

Judge Dee read aloud in a reverent voice:

Judge Dee reading the Imperial Edict.

# AN EDICT

## The Imperial Seal

Whereas, respectfully following the Illustrious Example of Our August Ancestors, it is Our traditional policy to appoint meretorious officials to those functions where their talents find widest employment, thus enabling them to exhaust their loyalty to Us on high, and to protect and foster Our people below;

Whereas Our Secretary of State, on the recommendation of Our Censor Yen Lee-ben, has brought to Our attention that Our servant Dee, named Jen-djieh, of Tai-yuan, holding the office of district magistrate of Chang-ping in Our province of Shantung, for three years faithfully discharging his duties, has shown exemplary zeal in redressing the wrongs of the oppressed, and meting out just punishment to the wrongdoers, thereby setting Our mind at rest, and giving peace to Our people;

It had been originally Our pleasure to promote the said Dee to the office of prefect of Hsu-djow.

Of late, however, pressing affairs of State leaving Us no rest either day or night, it is Our will that all those of extraordinary talents in Our Empire shall be near Us, so that We may summon them to assist the Throne whenever We so desire;

We now, therefore, on this second day of the fifth moon of the third year of Our Reign, issue this Edict, whereby the said Dee is appointed President of Our Metropolitan Court of Justice.

Tremble and obey!

Drawn up by the Grand Secretary
of State

> Endorsed by the August vermilion
> brush:
> *So be it. Despatch by courier.*

Judge Dee slowly rolled up the Edict and replaced it on the table. Then, turning in the direction of the capital, he again prostrated himself, and knocked his head on the floor nine times in succession to express his gratitude for this Imperial favor.

Having risen, he called Ma Joong and Chiao Tai and ordered them to stand guard in front of the court hall. Nobody was to be allowed inside as long as the Imperial Edict remained there.

The judge invited the messenger to the large reception hall to refresh himself. Seated there the messenger told the judge in a low voice confidential news about a grave crisis that was developing at Court, taking care to express himself concisely and in well-chosen words. For although he was still quite young, he had grown up in circles close to the Throne, and he knew it was wise to make a good impression on an official who was soon to occupy a key position in the capital. Finally he informed Judge Dee that his successor to Chang-ping had already been appointed three days ago, and could be expected to arrive on the following night; the judge was to proceed to the capital as soon as he had handed over the seals of office to his successor.

A servant came in and reported that the horses of the messenger's escort had been changed and that everything was ready for his departure. The messenger said that he regretted leaving so soon, but he still had urgent business in the neighboring district. So Judge Dee conducted him to the hall, where the Imperial Edict was handed back to him with due ceremony. Then the messenger hurriedly took his leave.

Judge Dee waited in his private office, while the entire personnel of his tribunal assembled in the court hall.

As Judge Dee ascended the dais, the crowd of constables, guards, scribes, clerks and runners all knelt down to congratulate the judge, and this time his four faithful lieutenants also knelt down in front of the dais.

Judge Dee bade them all rise, and then said a few appropriate words, thanking them for their service during his term of office. He added that the next morning all would receive a special bonus, in accordance with their rank and position. Then he returned to his private office.

He finished his report on the execution of the criminals, and then had the chief steward called in. He ordered him to have everything prepared in the reception hall early the next morning for the entertainment of the local gentry and the lower functionaries of the district administration, who would assemble there to offer their congratulations. He was also to have a separate courtyard in the compound cleared as temporary quarters for the new magistrate and his retinue. These matters having been settled, he told the servants to bring his dinner to his office.

There was rejoicing all over the tribunal. Sergeant Hoong, Ma Joong, Chiao Tai and Tao Gan talked excitedly about life in the capital and then got busy planning a real feast for that night in the best inn of the city. The constables were happily arguing about the exact amount of the bonus they would receive the next day.

Everyone in the tribunal was happy and excited. But in the street there were heard the wails of the common people assembling in front of the tribunal, bemoaning the fate that took this wise and just magistrate away from them.

Judge Dee, seated behind his desk in his private office, started to put the files in order for his successor.

Looking at the pile of leather document boxes that the senior scribe had brought in from the archives, he ordered the servants to bring new candles. For he knew that this would be another late night.

**THE END**

# TRANSLATOR'S POSTSCRIPT

## I

## The Chinese Text

The original Chinese title of this book is *Wu-tsê-t'ien-szû-ta-ch'i-an**) 武則天四大奇案, "Four great strange cases of Empress Wu's reign."

I have used three texts, viz. (a) a Chinese manuscript copy in 4 volumes, which seems to date from the end of the 19th century, (b) a small sized lithographic edition, in 6 vls., published in 1903 by the Kuang-i Bookstore 廣益書局 in Shanghai, and (c) the most recent reprint in movable type, collated by Mr. Hu Hsieh-yin 胡協寅, and published in 1947 in one foreign vol., also by the Kuang-i Bookstore.

The printed editions (b) and (c) are practically identical. The text of (a), however, is much more compact: it lacks many irrelevant passages contained in (b) and (c), and the contents of some chapters are rearranged in a more logical way. This manuscript is written in indifferent calligraphy, with many unauthorized abbreviated characters. Yet it is singularly free from real mistakes: wrong characters in the names of several historical persons occurring in (b) and (c), are here given in their correct form. It would seem that this novel—as most literary productions of this type—circulated for many years in manuscript form only, and that (a) was edited by a scholar, while (b) and (c) are based upon inferior manuscript copies. I have, therefore, taken (a) as the basic text for my translation.

This book numbers 64 chapters, ch. I-XXX (which hereafter are briefly referred to as Part I) are devoted to the earlier part of Ti Jên-chieh's career, and more especially to three criminal cases solved by him; ch. XXXI-LXIV (hereafter called Part II) describe his career at the Imperial Court. In all texts, these two parts differ widely in style and contents. Part I is written in a fairly compact style, and cleverly composed. The style of Part II, on

---

* In the translation I have transcribed all Chinese names in such a way that they can be easily remembered, omitting the diacritical marks of the Giles system of romanization, which would only confuse the general reader. Judge Ti, for instance, I transcribe "Judge Dee." In this postscript, however, I use the regular system of transcription.

the contrary, is prolix and repetitious, while the plot is clumsy, and the characters of the new persons introduced are badly drawn. Further, while Part I is written with considerable restraint, in Part II there occur various passages which are plain pornography, e.g. where the relations of Empress Wu with the priest Huai-i are described.

If one reads the author's own introductory remarks in Chapter I carefully, it will be found that his summary of the contents of this book recapitulates in a few terse sentences the main happenings described in Part I. The phrase "People who commit murder to be able to live to the end of their days in an odor of sanctity" refers to the young lady in the *Case of the Strange Corpse;* "people who commit crimes in order to amass riches" refers to the murders of Shao Li-huai; "people who get involved in crimes through adulterous relationships" refers to Hsü Tê-t'ai; the phrase "people who meet sudden death by drinking poison not destined for them" refers to *The Case of the Poisoned Bride;* and, finally, the phrase "people who through words spoken in jest lay themselves open to grave suspicion" refers to Hu Tso-pin, in the same criminal case. While thus the contents of Part I are indicated in detail, all the thirty-four chapters of Part II are summed up in but one brief phrase, saying "People who defile the Vernal Palace" 穢亂春宮.

Now in my opinion this last sentence is an interpolation, and the entire Part II a later addition, written by some other author. On the basis of the data available to me at present, I am convinced that Part I was an original novel in itself, entitled *Ti-kung-an* 狄公案, "Criminal Cases solved by Judge Ti." This novel ended in a way which is very typical for Chinese novels, viz. with Yen Li-pên recommending Judge Ti to the Throne for promotion; most Chinese novels dealing with official life end in a veritable orgy of promotions. In my opinion a later scribe of feeble talents added the 34 chapters of Part II, and changed the title, in order to make the book seem more attractive to the general public. For Empress Wu being notorious for her extravagant love-affairs, her name in the title would suggest a book of pornographic character*). Further, the title *"Four*

---

\* I have in my collection a novel entitled *Wu-tsê-t'ien-wai-shih* 武則天外史 "Unofficial Records regarding Empress Wu," 28 chapters in two vls.; the author signs himself with the penname *Pu-ch'i-shêng* 不奇生, and it was published in 1902, in Shanghai. This book is plain pornography, written in vulgar language. The modern bibliographer Sun Kai-ti 孫楷第, in his well known catalogue of Chinese novels *Chung-kuo-*

great strange cases of Empress Wu's reign" is inapposite, inasmuch as Part II does not describe a "case" at all, but simply is a garbled version of some historical happenings.

The present translation, therefore, covers only Part I, which I consider genuine, and which makes a good story in itself.

The hero of this novel is the famous T'ang statesman Ti Jên-chieh (狄仁傑, 630-700); his biography is to be found in ch. 89 of the *Chiu-t'ang-shu* 舊唐書, and ch. 115 of the *Hsin-t'ang-shu* 新唐書. It would be interesting to try to verify in how far the criminal cases related in this novel have any real connection with Ti Jên-chieh. His official biographies mentioned above merely state that as a magistrate he solved a great number of puzzling cases, and freed many innocent people who had been thrown into prison because of false accusations; neither these official biographies, nor local histories and other minor sources which I consulted give any details about these cases solved by Judge Ti. In order to answer this question one would have to make a comparative study of all the famous older detective stories. Here it may suffice to add that for instance the plot of the *Poisoned Bride* and of the *Strange Corpse* are used also in other old Chinese detective novels; cf. below, the notes to chapter XXVIII-XXIX.

Ti Jên-chieh's nine memorials to the Throne are to be found in the *Shih-li-chü-huang-shih-ts'ung-shu* (士禮居黃氏叢書, a collection of reprints collated by the famous Ch'ing scholar Huang P'ei-lieh 黃丕烈 1763-1825), under the title *Liang-kung-chiu-chien* 梁公九諫.

# II
# The Translation

The translation is on the whole a literal one, but since this book is intended for the general reader rather than for the Sinologue, a few exceptions had to be made.

---

*t'ung-su-hsiao-shuo-shu-mu* (中國通俗小說書目, Peiping 1933) lists on page 223 another pornographic novel, with the slightly different title *Tsê-t'ien-wai-shih* 則天外史; he adds that he has not seen the book itself. I would not be astonished if on further investigation in this field it would turn out that this *Tsê-t'ien-wai-shih,* or some other similar older pornographic novel describing Empress Wu's complicated love-life, is the source of Part II of the text discussed here.

In the first place, I aimed at eliminating all proper and place names that were not absolutely necessary to follow the story, in order not to confuse the reader with a mass of unfamiliar names. As an example, I here quote the second half of the first poem, heading Chapter I:

寬猛相平思呂杜。嚴苛尙是惡申韓

In literal translation, this verse would read:

"In balancing severity and leniency, think of Prince Lü and Tu Chou,
"While being strict, yet shun the doctrines of Shên and Han."

Prince Lü was the ancient law maker after whom a chapter in the "Book of History" was named, and Tu Chou was a legislator of the Han Dynasty. The philosophers Shên Pu-hai (died B.C. 337) and Han Fei-tzû (died B.C. 234) advocated a more or less totalitarian doctrine, involving extreme cruelty to the individual. This verse I translated as follows:

"Tempering severity by lenience, as laid down by our law makers,
"And avoiding the extremes advocated by crafty philosophers."

By adopting this principle throughout my translation, and by referring to characters of minor importance by their occupation rather than by their name, I have reduced the total number of names occurring in this novel, which in the original are considerable, to about two dozen.

Here it may be added that I have, quite arbitrarily, changed the family name of the warden of Six-Mile Village from Hu 胡 into P'ang 龐, in order to avoid confusion with Warden Ho 何 of Huang-hua Village. And I have changed the surname of the murdered silk merchant *Hsü* Kuang-ch'i into Liu 劉, to avoid the reader confusing him with the student *Hsü* Tê-t'ai.

Second, I have omitted at the end of each chapter the conventional phrase common to all Chinese novels: "If you want to know what happened next, you will have to read the next chapter," and also, at the beginning of each chapter, the conventional summary of the last alinea of the preceding chapter. As is well known, this tradition originated in the tales of the Chinese public story teller, from which the Chinese novel developed. This same tradition demands that every chapter should, if possible, end at a critical point in the story, in order to encourage the listeners to deposit their copper in the bowl, or to make sure that they would come back to the story teller's street corner on the next night. I have omitted these repetitious statements at the beginning and end of each chapter, but I have retained the original division in chapters, and also the original chapter headings in two lines, common to all Chinese novels.

Third, I have sometimes interpolated an explanatory sentence where the Chinese text takes a knowledge of some peculiar Chinese situation for granted. At the end of Chapter III, for instance, it is related that Judge Ti sets out on a secret tour of investigation, disguised as a physician. Here I added the sentence: "Like all literati, he had a good knowledge of drugs and the arts of healing, etc.," so that the reader would understand that this was quite a natural disguise. An ordinary Western detective would soon betray himself if he tried to pose as a practising physician.

Fourth, I have abbreviated considerably Chapter XXVIII. The original introduces into the jail the entire Infernal Tribunal, the constables acting the part of the minor devils. This is quite interesting to the Chinese reader, who is thoroughly familiar with all these details, while for an uneducated woman like Mrs. Chou they are a horrifying reality. Since, however, a complete rendering of this scene would make a comical impression on the Western reader, I thought it would spoil the effect. Hence this abbreviated rendering, featuring only the Black Judge himself, and his two most important assistants, the Ox-headed and the Horse-headed devil.

Finally, as observed already in my preface to this translation, the 17th or 18th century anonymous author shows a supreme unconcern for historical accuracy. He describes life as he knew it from his own observation, and conveniently forgets that his story plays in the T'ang period, about one thousand years before his time. I let stand many anachronisms, as when, for instance, the judge refers to the Sung scholar Shao Yung, who lived 1011-1077, or when he refers to Peking as the capital of China. Other anachronisms, which might spread further some misconceptions of the general reading public, I have eliminated; I mention, for instance, references to the Chinese queue (which was imposed on the Chinese in the 17th century by the Manchu conquerors, several centuries after Judge Ti's time), and to the blunderbuss being used by the constables of the tribunal.

Other minor alterations are recorded in the notes below. I hope that my sinological colleagues will agree that none of those alterations materially affect a faithful rendering of style and spirit of the Chinese original.

# III
# Literature

For those readers who are specially interested in the Chinese detective novel, and in background material such as ancient Chinese criminal law and judicial procedure, here follows a brief list of the few foreign books that deal with these subjects.

*Ta Tsing Leu Lee,* being the fundamental laws of the Penal Code of China, translated from the Chinese by Sir George Thomas Staunton, London 1810. The passages from the Code given in the notes below are quoted from this translation.

*Notes and Commentaries on Chinese criminal law,* by Ernest Alabaster, London 1899.

*Le droit chinois,* Conception et évolution, institutions législatives et judiciaires, by: Jean Escarra. Peiping 1936. Although this work is mainly concerned with modern Chinese law, there is an excellent historical introduction.

*The Office of District Magistrate* in China, an article by Byron Brenan, in "Journal of the North-China Branch of the Royal Asiatic Society," Vol. XXXII, 1897-1898.

*Village and Townlife in China,* by Y. K. Leong and L. K. Tao, London 1915. Pp. 45 sq. give a good survey of the position and duties of the district magistrate.

*Historic China and other sketches,* by H. A. Giles, London 1882. Part II of this collection of essays by the well known British Sinologue, entitled "Judicial Sketches," is of importance for our present subject. Pp. 125-140, "The Penal Code," gives a good summary of the contents and purport of this code, with interesting comments. Pp. 141-232, "Lan Lu-chow's criminal cases," contains the translation of 12 cases solved by the scholar-official Lan Ting-yüan ( 藍鼎元, literary name Lu-chow 鹿洲, 1680-1733), when he was district magistrate of Ch'ao-yang, in Kuangtung Province. These, however, are real "case histories." Judge Lan gives a faithful account of how he actually dealt with some crimes committed in his district; thus these reports are quite different from "detective stories," they were written for instruction rather than for entertainment.

*Strange Stories from a Chinese Studio,* by H. A. Giles, various editions. This book is a partial translation of the famous *Liao-chai-chih-i* 聊齋誌異, an extensive collection of Chinese short stories, dealing with weird or mysterious happenings. The able translator added copious notes on Chinese manners and customs.

*Lung-t'u-kung-an* 龍圖公案, Novelle Cinesi tolte dal Lung-tu-kung-an e tradotte sull' originale Cinese da Carlo Puini. Piacenza, 1872.

An Italian translation of seven cases solved by the most famous ancient Chinese judge, Pao-kung 包公. His complete name was Pao Ch'êng (包拯, 999-1062), and he held high office during the Sung dynasty. His exploits are mentioned already in such early collections of criminal cases as the *T'ang-yin-pi-shih* 棠陰比事, written in 1211 by the Southern Sung scholar Kuei Wan-yung 桂萬榮. This *T'ang-yin-pi-shih*, I may remark in passing, became very popular in Japan, and served as model for Japanese collections of crime stories as for instance the *Ō-in hi-ji* 櫻陰比事 and the *Tō-in hi-ji* 藤陰比事; the Japanese Sinologue Yamamoto Hokuzan ( 山本北山, 1752-1812) published a carefully edited reprint of the *T'ang-yin-pi-shih*.

The *Lung-t'u-kung-an*, the collection of criminal cases connected with Judge Pao, is largely fiction. Today it is still the most popular Chinese detective novel, and some famous Chinese theatrical pieces are based on episodes borrowed from this collection.

*Some Chinese Detective Stories,* an essay by Vincent Starrett; to be found in his "Bookman's Holiday," published in 1942, Random House, New York. Apart from some minor inaccuracies (a few of which are mentioned below, in my note to Chapter XXIII), this is a good survey of the subject, and, as far as I know, the only one existing in the English language. It must be borne in mind, however, that there are many more ancient Chinese detective novels than are mentioned by Mr. Starrett. The total number must run to well over a hundred. Although it is only in recent years that Chinese and Japanese scholars have started to collect and study Chinese popular novels of the 16th, 17th and 18th century, an amazing number of interesting volumes have already been brought to light. As is well known, old-fashioned Chinese literati considered all novels as inferior literature, and, although they read them with pleasure, they did not keep such books on their shelves. At present, therefore, one must search for such novels in the book stalls of Chinese markets, and in forgotten corners of obscure bookshops.

I think that it might be an interesting experiment if one of our modern writers of detective stories would try his hand at composing an ancient Chinese detective story himself. The "pattern" is given in the novel translated here, while in the books listed above one will find a rich variety of peculiarly Chinese plots. That it is possible to write a fine detective story, which at the same time is acceptable from a scholarly point of view, is proved by Agatha Christie's "Death Comes As the End," the scene of which novel is laid in ancient Egypt.

# IV
## Notes to the Translation

*Chapter III.* The function of the coroner is a very old one in China. There has been preserved an interesting handbook 'for coroners, entitled *Hsi-yüan-lu* 洗寃錄 "Records of the Redressing of Wrongs," which was compiled about A.D. 1250. A French version of this work appeared as early as 1780, in *Mémoires concernant l'histoire, les sciences, les arts etc. des Chinois,* volume IV, pp. 421-440, under the title *Notice du livre chinois Si-yuen.* Later H. A. Giles published an English translation of the enlarged edition of 1843 of this work, under the title "Instructions to Coroners" (in: *China Review,* III, and later in *Proceedings of the Royal Society of Medicine,* vol. XVII, London 1924). Although this old Chinese "handbook" contains some quite fantastic theories, it also shows a good deal of common sense, and gives a number of sound conclusions, based on shrewd observation.

I draw the attention of those interested to a brief Indian treatise on the coroner's work, to be found in a Sanskrit work of the 3d century B.C. This is the famous *Arthasastra,* a voluminous work on the art of government, written by Kautilya. Chapter VII of the Fourth Book, entitled "Examination of Sudden Death," contains an ancient Indian set of "instructions to coroners." Cf. the translation by Dr. R. Shamasastry, 3d edition, Mysore 1929, pp. 245 sq.

*Chapter IV.* The Dragon Boat Festival is held all over China on the fifth day of the fifth moon, in commemoration of a virtuous statesman of the fifth century B.C., who drowned himself in despair because his sovereign would not listen to his wise counsels. The Dragon Boats are long and narrow craft, the prow showing the shape of a dragon's head, and the stern its tail. They are rowed by fifty to one hundred people, the rhythm being indicated by a large gong suspended in the middle of the boat. The winner gets a nominal prize, and all crews are entertained after the race by the wealthier members of the community.

*Chapter VI.* Cf. Chinese Penal Code, Section CCLXXVI: "All persons guilty of digging in, and breaking up another man's burying ground, until at length one of the coffins which had been deposited therein, is laid bare and becomes visible, shall be punished with 100 blows, and perpetual banishment to the distance of 3000 miles. Any person who, after having been guilty as aforesaid, proceeds to open the coffin, and uncover the corpse laid therein, shall be punished with death, by being strangled, after undergoing the usual confinement."

Cf. the judge's speech to the coroner in Chapter VIII, and his warning to the undertaker, in Chapter IX.

*Chapters VII-VIII.* The judge took great risks in arresting the widow and questioning her under torture, without definite proof; if she had proved to be innocent, he would have offended against the law in more than one respect. I quote the following provisions of the Penal Code:

Section CCCCXX. "Female offenders shall not be committed to prison except in capital cases, or cases of adultery. In all other cases, they shall, if married, remain in the charge and custody of their husbands, and if single, in that of their relations or next neighbors, who shall, upon every such occasion, be held responsible for their appearance at the tribunal of justice when required."

Section CCCXXXVI. "When any person is falsely accused of a capital offense, and upon such accusation has been condemned and executed, the false accuser shall be either strangled or beheaded, according to the manner in which the innocent person had been executed, and half his property shall be forfeited. If the execution of the sentence of death against the innocent person has been prevented by a timely discovery of the falsehood of the accusation, the false accuser shall be punished with 100 blows and perpetual banishment to the distance of 3000 miles, and moreover be subjected to extra-service during three years."

Section CCCXCVI. "All officers of government, and their official attendants, who, instigated by private malice or revenge, designedly commit to prison an unaccused and unimplicated individual, shall be punished with 80 blows. All officers of government, and their official attendants, who, instigated by private malice or revenge, designedly examine with judicial severities, any unaccused and unimplicated person, shall, although they should not by so doing actually wound such person, be punished with 80 blows; if guilty of inflicting, by such procedure, any cutting or severe wounds, they shall be punished according to the law against cutting and wounding in an affray in ordinary cases; lastly, if death ensues, the superintending magistrate shall be beheaded. The assessors, and other officers of justice concerned in the transaction, shall, if aware of the illegality of their act, suffer punishment according to the same rule, except in capital cases, upon which they shall be allowed a reduction of one degree in the punishment."

The last paragraph of this section explains the misgivings of the headman of the constables, in Chapter VIII.

*Chapter XIII.* "Divine Village": the Chinese original has *Shuang-t'u-chai* 雙土寨 "Double Earth Village." The judge connects this name with the character for "divination," *kua* 卦, in the verse, which contains two characters *t'u* 土 "earth." I have changed this name to "divine," in order to spare the reader a long explanation of the Chinese art of dissecting characters.

*Chapter XIV.* The art of physiognomy is a special science in China, about which extensive literature exists. It teaches not only how to judge the character of a person by the form of his eyes, eyebrows, ears, mouth etc., but also how to conclude from these data his past life, and his future.

*Chapter XV.* "Turn-up Pass": the Chinese original has *ch'i-t'uan* "green vegetables." The old constable mistakes this for *p'u-ch'i*, which means "chestnuts." Since I could not find in English two words of these meanings which sufficiently resembled each other in sound, I changed them into "Turn-up" and "turnip."

*Interlude.* The three actors play the roles of *tan* "young maiden," *shêng* "young lover," and *mo* "elderly man." The Chinese stage has no side-scenes etc., the spectators are expected to imagine all stage-decoration for themselves. In the original the tunes to which the songs should be sung are indicated.

The festival of viewing the blossoms was formerly an occasion for much license, the strict rules regarding the separation of the sexes being temporarily suspended. The plum-blossom especially has a number of sexual connotations; cf. my book "The Lore of the Chinese Lute" (Tokyo 1940), page 143.

The red candles mentioned in the maiden's song refer to large red candles, lighted during the wedding ceremony.

For a further interpretation of this interlude, see the notes to Chapters XXVII and XXVIII below.

*Chapter XIX.* Cf. Alabaster, op. cit. page 103: "Chinese law regarding the continuance of the succession of a family as infinitely important, in general allows an offender to escape the consequences of his offense—usually in the end by commuting the penalty to a fine—if he is the sole dependence of his family. The leniency extends to most classes of offenses it would seem even to cases of homicide. The leniency does not apparently strictly extend to cases of intentional homicide, and certainly does not to the gravest offenses, such as treason; but as regards the former, it is open to question whether so strong a plea would not prevail in every instance." In this case, however, the judge decides that no leniency shall be extended.

The case of the warden is more complicated. Although he did say that the hostel keeper had committed the double murder, he did so the first time in order to extract money from him, and the second time in order to defend his conduct before the judge. He did not file an accusation against the hostel keeper, and if the latter had not protested, the warden would doubtless have reported the murder to the tribunal as having been committed by an unknown person. It is probably for this reason that the judge lets him off with the 100 blows mentioned in the Code, Section CCCXXXVI (see above), without the perpetual banishment and the three year extra-service; but the judge added a second beating, since the warden had also handed in a wrong report, and had tampered with the corpses.

*Chapter XXIII.* Vincent Starrett, op. cit. page 20, has pointed out the resemblance of this solution to that described in a tale of the Sherlock Holmes cycle, entitled "The Speckled Band." On comparing Mr. Starrett's résumé of the "Case of the Strange Corpse" and of the "Poisoned Bride," with the complete story as given in the present translation, it will be noticed that the former contains some inaccuracies. In the first case, it is not the judge who makes a search under the bed, but one of his lieutenants; and it is not the lover who did the killing, but the widow Chou. In the second case, only the bride dies, and not "a number of persons." These, however, are minor points, which do not affect Mr. Starrett's argument.

*Chapters XXVIII-XXIX.* The nail murder motif occurs in several other ancient Chinese detective stories; I mention, for instance, the *Shih-kung-an* 施公案, "Criminal Cases solved by Judge Shih." This judge was the famous Ch'ing scholar-official Shih Shih-lun (施世倫, 1659-1722); a brief account of his solving a murder similar to that of Pi Hsün is given by Rev. Macgowan, in his book "Chinese Folklore Tales" (London 1910), under the title "The Widow Ho." In the *China Review* of 1881 (volume X, pp. 41-43), G. C. Stent gave an English abstract of another nail murder story, without, however, indicating his original Chinese source. This abstract bears the title "The double nail murders," and gives an interesting variant of the same motif. When the coroner fails to discover any trace of violence on a man's corpse, his own wife suggests to him to look for a nail. When the judge has convicted the murdered man's widow on this evidence, he has also the coroner's wife brought before him, since her knowledge of such a subtle way of committing a murder seems to him suspicious. It then transpires that the coroner is her second husband. The corpse of her first husband is exhumed, and a nail discovered inside the empty skull. Both women are executed.

Hsü Tê-t'ai's sentence may seem to the reader disproportionally severe. Chinese law, however, takes a very grave view of adultery with a married woman, and of being accessory to a murder. Further, strangulation, although in fact more painful than decapitation, in China is considered as the mildest form of the death penalty, since the body of the victim is not mutilated; according to a very ancient Chinese belief, a dead man's soul can only enjoy a happy existence in the Hereafter if his body is buried complete. The regular process of strangulation implies *san-fang-san-chin* 三放三緊 "three times loosening and three times tightening," that is to say that the executioner makes the victim nearly suffocate two times, and really strangles him only the third time that he tightens the noose. Hsü Tê-t'ai's sentence was mitigated by the ruling that death should ensue after the noose had been tightened the first time.

Execution by the process of "lingering death," *ling-ch'ih* 凌遲, is the severest form of the death penalty known to Chinese law. It is the punishment for high treason, parricide, and a wife killing her husband. The executioner kills the victim by gradually slicing and cutting his body to pieces, a horrible process, that is said to last for several hours. For the Chinese, however, the fact that the body is so thoroughly mutilated counts as heavily as the terrible pain inflicted; for thus all the victim's hopes for a life in the Hereafter are destroyed. Instances of this punishment being executed in its full severity seem to have been comparatively rare; usually it is, as in the case of the widow Chou, mitigated in such a way that the victim is first killed, and subsequently cut to pieces.

As regards the guilt of Dr. T'ang and Mrs. Pi, both could have been heavily punished, since Chinese law holds the head of the household responsible for crimes committed by its members, while a tutor stands *in loco parentis*. Neither of them, however, is further prosecuted, because the judge finds that both had been completely ignorant of the crimes committed in their respective houses; moreover, Dr. T'ang had a high literary degree, which in itself is a legal reason for leniency, while Mrs. Pi was an extremely stupid woman.

The above shows clearly how wide a margin the Penal Code leaves to the discretion of the judge.

After the two confessions related in Chapters XXVIII and XXIX, we can understand better the import of the "Interlude." The "maiden" is of course the widow Chou, and the "young man" is her lover Hsü Tê-t'ai. Their conversation shows that Hsü is not as deeply attached to his lady-love as she to him, and that she realizes this in her innermost thoughts; she mentions her troubles with the judge, the "cruel, cruel man at home," but Hsü does not react on these complaints. This eery play, full of *double entendre*, is entirely divorced from the notions of place and time. I think, therefore, that the third actor, the "elderly man," represents Pi Hsün, the murdered husband. This "interlude" is the only passage in the novel where we are given a hint as to his relations to his wife; evidently he loved her very much, it is he who reacts on her complaints, and not Hsü. And are we to assume from his willingness "to go there all three of us" that Pi Hsün when still alive suspected his wife's intrigue with Hsü, but would have condoned it in order to retain her? This question I leave to experts in psycho-analysis to decide.

R.H.v.G.

A CATALOG OF SELECTED
# DOVER BOOKS
IN ALL FIELDS OF INTEREST

# A CATALOG OF SELECTED DOVER
# BOOKS IN ALL FIELDS OF INTEREST

CONCERNING THE SPIRITUAL IN ART, Wassily Kandinsky. Pioneering work by father of abstract art. Thoughts on color theory, nature of art. Analysis of earlier masters. 12 illustrations. 80pp. of text. 5⅜ × 8½. 23411-8 Pa. $3.95

ANIMALS: 1,419 Copyright-Free Illustrations of Mammals, Birds, Fish, Insects, etc., Jim Harter (ed.). Clear wood engravings present, in extremely lifelike poses, over 1,000 species of animals. One of the most extensive pictorial sourcebooks of its kind. Captions. Index. 284pp. 9 × 12. 23766-4 Pa. $12.95

CELTIC ART: The Methods of Construction, George Bain. Simple geometric techniques for making Celtic interlacements, spirals, Kells-type initials, animals, humans, etc. Over 500 illustrations. 160pp. 9 × 12. (USO) 22923-8 Pa. $9.95

AN ATLAS OF ANATOMY FOR ARTISTS, Fritz Schider. Most thorough reference work on art anatomy in the world. Hundreds of illustrations, including selections from works by Vesalius, Leonardo, Goya, Ingres, Michelangelo, others. 593 illustrations. 192pp. 7⅛ × 10¼. 20241-0 Pa. $9.95

CELTIC HAND STROKE-BY-STROKE (Irish Half-Uncial from "The Book of Kells"): An Arthur Baker Calligraphy Manual, Arthur Baker. Complete guide to creating each letter of the alphabet in distinctive Celtic manner. Covers hand position, strokes, pens, inks, paper, more. Illustrated. 48pp. 8¼ × 11.
24336-2 Pa. $3.95

EASY ORIGAMI, John Montroll. Charming collection of 32 projects (hat, cup, pelican, piano, swan, many more) specially designed for the novice origami hobbyist. Clearly illustrated easy-to-follow instructions insure that even beginning papercrafters will achieve successful results. 48pp. 8¼ × 11. 27298-2 Pa. $2.95

THE COMPLETE BOOK OF BIRDHOUSE CONSTRUCTION FOR WOOD-WORKERS, Scott D. Campbell. Detailed instructions, illustrations, tables. Also data on bird habitat and instinct patterns. Bibliography. 3 tables. 63 illustrations in 15 figures. 48pp. 5¼ × 8½. 24407-5 Pa. $1.95

BLOOMINGDALE'S ILLUSTRATED 1886 CATALOG: Fashions, Dry Goods and Housewares, Bloomingdale Brothers. Famed merchants' extremely rare catalog depicting about 1,700 products: clothing, housewares, firearms, dry goods, jewelry, more. Invaluable for dating, identifying vintage items. Also, copyright-free graphics for artists, designers. Co-published with Henry Ford Museum & Green-field Village. 160pp. 8¼ × 11. 25780-0 Pa. $9.95

HISTORIC COSTUME IN PICTURES, Braun & Schneider. Over 1,450 costumed figures in clearly detailed engravings—from dawn of civilization to end of 19th century. Captions. Many folk costumes. 256pp. 8⅜ × 11¾. 23150-X Pa. $11.95

STICKLEY CRAFTSMAN FURNITURE CATALOGS, Gustav Stickley and L. & J. G. Stickley. Beautiful, functional furniture in two authentic catalogs from 1910. 594 illustrations, including 277 photos, show settles, rockers, armchairs, reclining chairs, bookcases, desks, tables. 183pp. 6½ × 9¼. 23838-5 Pa. $9.95

AMERICAN LOCOMOTIVES IN HISTORIC PHOTOGRAPHS: 1858 to 1949, Ron Ziel (ed.). A rare collection of 126 meticulously detailed official photographs, called "builder portraits," of American locomotives that majestically chronicle the rise of steam locomotive power in America. Introduction. Detailed captions. xi + 129pp. 9 × 12. 27393-8 Pa. $12.95

AMERICA'S LIGHTHOUSES: An Illustrated History, Francis Ross Holland, Jr. Delightfully written, profusely illustrated fact-filled survey of over 200 American lighthouses since 1716. History, anecdotes, technological advances, more. 240pp. 8 × 10¾. 25576-X Pa. $11.95

TOWARDS A NEW ARCHITECTURE, Le Corbusier. Pioneering manifesto by founder of "International School." Technical and aesthetic theories, views of industry, economics, relation of form to function, "mass-production split" and much more. Profusely illustrated. 320pp. 6⅛ × 9¼. (USO) 25023-7 Pa. $9.95

HOW THE OTHER HALF LIVES, Jacob Riis. Famous journalistic record, exposing poverty and degradation of New York slums around 1900, by major social reformer. 100 striking and influential photographs. 233pp. 10 × 7⅞.
22012-5 Pa $10.95

FRUIT KEY AND TWIG KEY TO TREES AND SHRUBS, William M. Harlow. One of the handiest and most widely used identification aids. Fruit key covers 120 deciduous and evergreen species; twig key 160 deciduous species. Easily used. Over 300 photographs. 126pp. 5⅜ × 8½. 20511-8 Pa. $3.95

COMMON BIRD SONGS, Dr. Donald J. Borror. Songs of 60 most common U.S. birds: robins, sparrows, cardinals, bluejays, finches, more—arranged in order of increasing complexity. Up to 9 variations of songs of each species.
Cassette and manual 99911-4 $8.95

ORCHIDS AS HOUSE PLANTS, Rebecca Tyson Northen. Grow cattleyas and many other kinds of orchids—in a window, in a case, or under artificial light. 63 illustrations. 148pp. 5⅜ × 8½. 23261-1 Pa. $4.95

MONSTER MAZES, Dave Phillips. Masterful mazes at four levels of difficulty. Avoid deadly perils and evil creatures to find magical treasures. Solutions for all 32 exciting illustrated puzzles. 48pp. 8¼ × 11. 26005-4 Pa. $2.95

MOZART'S DON GIOVANNI (DOVER OPERA LIBRETTO SERIES), Wolfgang Amadeus Mozart. Introduced and translated by Ellen H. Bleiler. Standard Italian libretto, with complete English translation. Convenient and thoroughly portable—an ideal companion for reading along with a recording or the performance itself. Introduction. List of characters. Plot summary. 121pp. 5¼ × 8½.
24944-1 Pa. $2.95

TECHNICAL MANUAL AND DICTIONARY OF CLASSICAL BALLET, Gail Grant. Defines, explains, comments on steps, movements, poses and concepts. 15-page pictorial section. Basic book for student, viewer. 127pp. 5⅜ × 8½.
21843-0 Pa. $4.95

BRASS INSTRUMENTS: Their History and Development, Anthony Baines. Authoritative, updated survey of the evolution of trumpets, trombones, bugles, cornets, French horns, tubas and other brass wind instruments. Over 140 illustrations and 48 music examples. Corrected and updated by author. New preface. Bibliography. 320pp. 5⅜ × 8½. 27574-4 Pa. $9.95

HOLLYWOOD GLAMOR PORTRAITS, John Kobal (ed.). 145 photos from 1926-49. Harlow, Gable, Bogart, Bacall; 94 stars in all. Full background on photographers, technical aspects. 160pp. 8⅜ × 11¼. 23352-9 Pa. $11.95

MAX AND MORITZ, Wilhelm Busch. Great humor classic in both German and English. Also 10 other works: "Cat and Mouse," "Plisch and Plumm," etc. 216pp. 5⅜ × 8½. 20181-3 Pa. $5.95

THE RAVEN AND OTHER FAVORITE POEMS, Edgar Allan Poe. Over 40 of the author's most memorable poems: "The Bells," "Ulalume," "Israfel," "To Helen," "The Conqueror Worm," "Eldorado," "Annabel Lee," many more. Alphabetic lists of titles and first lines. 64pp. 5³⁄₁₆ × 8¼. 26685-0 Pa. $1.00

SEVEN SCIENCE FICTION NOVELS, H. G. Wells. The standard collection of the great novels. Complete, unabridged. First Men in the Moon, Island of Dr. Moreau, War of the Worlds, Food of the Gods, Invisible Man, Time Machine, In the Days of the Comet. Total of 1,015pp. 5⅜ × 8½. (USO) 20264-X Clothbd. $29.95

AMULETS AND SUPERSTITIONS, E. A. Wallis Budge. Comprehensive discourse on origin, powers of amulets in many ancient cultures: Arab, Persian, Babylonian, Assyrian, Egyptian, Gnostic, Hebrew, Phoenician, Syriac, etc. Covers cross, swastika, crucifix, seals, rings, stones, etc. 584pp. 5⅜ × 8½. 23573-4 Pa. $12.95

RUSSIAN STORIES/PYCCKNE PACCKA3bl: A Dual-Language Book, edited by Gleb Struve. Twelve tales by such masters as Chekhov, Tolstoy, Dostoevsky, Pushkin, others. Excellent word-for-word English translations on facing pages, plus teaching and study aids, Russian/English vocabulary, biographical/critical introductions, more. 416pp. 5⅜ × 8½. 26244-8 Pa. $8.95

PHILADELPHIA THEN AND NOW: 60 Sites Photographed in the Past and Present, Kenneth Finkel and Susan Oyama. Rare photographs of City Hall, Logan Square, Independence Hall, Betsy Ross House, other landmarks juxtaposed with contemporary views. Captures changing face of historic city. Introduction. Captions. 128pp. 8¼ × 11. 25790-8 Pa. $9.95

AIA ARCHITECTURAL GUIDE TO NASSAU AND SUFFOLK COUNTIES, LONG ISLAND, The American Institute of Architects, Long Island Chapter, and the Society for the Preservation of Long Island Antiquities. Comprehensive, well-researched and generously illustrated volume brings to life over three centuries of Long Island's great architectural heritage. More than 240 photographs with authoritative, extensively detailed captions. 176pp. 8¼ × 11. 26946-9 Pa. $14.95

NORTH AMERICAN INDIAN LIFE: Customs and Traditions of 23 Tribes, Elsie Clews Parsons (ed.). 27 fictionalized essays by noted anthropologists examine religion, customs, government, additional facets of life among the Winnebago, Crow, Zuni, Eskimo, other tribes. 480pp. 6⅛ × 9¼. 27377-6 Pa. $10.95

FRANK LLOYD WRIGHT'S HOLLYHOCK HOUSE, Donald Hoffmann. Lavishly illustrated, carefully documented study of one of Wright's most controversial residential designs. Over 120 photographs, floor plans, elevations, etc. Detailed perceptive text by noted Wright scholar. Index. 128pp. 9¼ × 10¾.
27133-1 Pa. $11.95

THE MALE AND FEMALE FIGURE IN MOTION: 60 Classic Photographic Sequences, Eadweard Muybridge. 60 true-action photographs of men and women walking, running, climbing, bending, turning, etc., reproduced from rare 19th-century masterpiece. vi + 121pp. 9 × 12. 24745-7 Pa. $10.95

1001 QUESTIONS ANSWERED ABOUT THE SEASHORE, N. J. Berrill and Jacquelyn Berrill. Queries answered about dolphins, sea snails, sponges, starfish, fishes, shore birds, many others. Covers appearance, breeding, growth, feeding, much more. 305pp. 5¼ × 8¼. 23366-9 Pa. $7.95

GUIDE TO OWL WATCHING IN NORTH AMERICA, Donald S. Heintzelman. Superb guide offers complete data and descriptions of 19 species: barn owl, screech owl, snowy owl, many more. Expert coverage of owl-watching equipment, conservation, migrations and invasions, etc. Guide to observing sites. 84 illustrations. xiii + 193pp. 5⅜ × 8½. 27344-X Pa. $8.95

MEDICINAL AND OTHER USES OF NORTH AMERICAN PLANTS: A Historical Survey with Special Reference to the Eastern Indian Tribes, Charlotte Erichsen-Brown. Chronological historical citations document 500 years of usage of plants, trees, shrubs native to eastern Canada, northeastern U.S. Also complete identifying information. 343 illustrations. 544pp. 6½ × 9¼. 25951-X Pa. $12.95

STORYBOOK MAZES, Dave Phillips. 23 stories and mazes on two-page spreads: Wizard of Oz, Treasure Island, Robin Hood, etc. Solutions. 64pp. 8¼ × 11.
23628-5 Pa. $2.95

NEGRO FOLK MUSIC, U.S.A., Harold Courlander. Noted folklorist's scholarly yet readable analysis of rich and varied musical tradition. Includes authentic versions of over 40 folk songs. Valuable bibliography and discography. xi + 324pp. 5⅜ × 8½. 27350-4 Pa. $7.95

MOVIE-STAR PORTRAITS OF THE FORTIES, John Kobal (ed.). 163 glamor, studio photos of 106 stars of the 1940s: Rita Hayworth, Ava Gardner, Marlon Brando, Clark Gable, many more. 176pp. 8⅜ × 11¼. 23546-7 Pa. $11.95

BENCHLEY LOST AND FOUND, Robert Benchley. Finest humor from early 30s, about pet peeves, child psychologists, post office and others. Mostly unavailable elsewhere. 73 illustrations by Peter Arno and others. 183pp. 5⅜ × 8½.
22410-4 Pa. $5.95

YEKL and THE IMPORTED BRIDEGROOM AND OTHER STORIES OF YIDDISH NEW YORK, Abraham Cahan. Film Hester Street based on Yekl (1896). Novel, other stories among first about Jewish immigrants on N.Y.'s East Side. 240pp. 5⅜ × 8½. 22427-9 Pa. $6.95

SELECTED POEMS, Walt Whitman. Generous sampling from *Leaves of Grass*. Twenty-four poems include "I Hear America Singing," "Song of the Open Road," "I Sing the Body Electric," "When Lilacs Last in the Dooryard Bloom'd," "O Captain! My Captain!"—all reprinted from an authoritative edition. Lists of titles and first lines. 128pp. 5³⁄₁₆ × 8¼. 26878-0 Pa. $1.00

THE BEST TALES OF HOFFMANN, E. T. A. Hoffmann. 10 of Hoffmann's most important stories: "Nutcracker and the King of Mice," "The Golden Flowerpot," etc. 458pp. 5⅜ × 8½. 21793-0 Pa. $8.95

FROM FETISH TO GOD IN ANCIENT EGYPT, E. A. Wallis Budge. Rich detailed survey of Egyptian conception of "God" and gods, magic, cult of animals, Osiris, more. Also, superb English translations of hymns and legends. 240 illustrations. 545pp. 5⅜ × 8½. 25803-3 Pa. $11.95

FRENCH STORIES/CONTES FRANÇAIS: A Dual-Language Book, Wallace Fowlie. Ten stories by French masters, Voltaire to Camus: "Micromegas" by Voltaire; "The Atheist's Mass" by Balzac; "Minuet" by de Maupassant; "The Guest" by Camus, six more. Excellent English translations on facing pages. Also French-English vocabulary list, exercises, more. 352pp. 5⅜ × 8½. 26443-2 Pa. $8.95

CHICAGO AT THE TURN OF THE CENTURY IN PHOTOGRAPHS: 122 Historic Views from the Collections of the Chicago Historical Society, Larry A. Viskochil. Rare large-format prints offer detailed views of City Hall, State Street, the Loop, Hull House, Union Station, many other landmarks, circa 1904–1913. Introduction. Captions. Maps. 144pp. 9⅜ × 12¼. 24656-6 Pa. $12.95

OLD BROOKLYN IN EARLY PHOTOGRAPHS, 1865–1929, William Lee Younger. Luna Park, Gravesend race track, construction of Grand Army Plaza, moving of Hotel Brighton, etc. 157 previously unpublished photographs. 165pp. 8⅞ × 11¾. 23587-4 Pa. $13.95

THE MYTHS OF THE NORTH AMERICAN INDIANS, Lewis Spence. Rich anthology of the myths and legends of the Algonquins, Iroquois, Pawnees and Sioux, prefaced by an extensive historical and ethnological commentary. 36 illustrations. 480pp. 5⅜ × 8½. 25967-6 Pa. $8.95

AN ENCYCLOPEDIA OF BATTLES: Accounts of Over 1,560 Battles from 1479 B.C. to the Present, David Eggenberger. Essential details of every major battle in recorded history from the first battle of Megiddo in 1479 B.C. to Grenada in 1984. List of Battle Maps. New Appendix covering the years 1967–1984. Index. 99 illustrations. 544pp. 6½ × 9¼. 24913-1 Pa. $14.95

SAILING ALONE AROUND THE WORLD, Captain Joshua Slocum. First man to sail around the world, alone, in small boat. One of great feats of seamanship told in delightful manner. 67 illustrations. 294pp. 5⅜ × 8½. 20326-3 Pa. $5.95

ANARCHISM AND OTHER ESSAYS, Emma Goldman. Powerful, penetrating, prophetic essays on direct action, role of minorities, prison reform, puritan hypocrisy, violence, etc. 271pp. 5⅜ × 8½. 22484-8 Pa. $5.95

MYTHS OF THE HINDUS AND BUDDHISTS, Ananda K. Coomaraswamy and Sister Nivedita. Great stories of the epics; deeds of Krishna, Shiva, taken from puranas, Vedas, folk tales; etc. 32 illustrations. 400pp. 5⅜ × 8½. 21759-0 Pa. $9.95

BEYOND PSYCHOLOGY, Otto Rank. Fear of death, desire of immortality, nature of sexuality, social organization, creativity, according to Rankian system. 291pp. 5⅜ × 8½. 20485-5 Pa. $8.95

A THEOLOGICO-POLITICAL TREATISE, Benedict Spinoza. Also contains unfinished Political Treatise. Great classic on religious liberty, theory of government on common consent. R. Elwes translation. Total of 421pp. 5⅜ × 8½. 20249-6 Pa. $8.95

MY BONDAGE AND MY FREEDOM, Frederick Douglass. Born a slave, Douglass became outspoken force in antislavery movement. The best of Douglass' autobiographies. Graphic description of slave life. 464pp. 5⅜ × 8½. 22457-0 Pa. $8.95

FOLLOWING THE EQUATOR: A Journey Around the World, Mark Twain. Fascinating humorous account of 1897 voyage to Hawaii, Australia, India, New Zealand, etc. Ironic, bemused reports on peoples, customs, climate, flora and fauna, politics, much more. 197 illustrations. 720pp. 5⅜ × 8½. 26113-1 Pa. $15.95

THE PEOPLE CALLED SHAKERS, Edward D. Andrews. Definitive study of Shakers: origins, beliefs, practices, dances, social organization, furniture and crafts, etc. 33 illustrations. 351pp. 5⅜ × 8½. 21081-2 Pa. $8.95

THE MYTHS OF GREECE AND ROME, H. A. Guerber. A classic of mythology, generously illustrated, long prized for its simple, graphic, accurate retelling of the principal myths of Greece and Rome, and for its commentary on their origins and significance. With 64 illustrations by Michelangelo, Raphael, Titian, Rubens, Canova, Bernini and others. 480pp. 5⅜ × 8½. 27584-1 Pa. $9.95

PSYCHOLOGY OF MUSIC, Carl E. Seashore. Classic work discusses music as a medium from psychological viewpoint. Clear treatment of physical acoustics, auditory apparatus, sound perception, development of musical skills, nature of musical feeling, host of other topics. 88 figures. 408pp. 5⅜ × 8½. 21851-1 Pa. $9.95

THE PHILOSOPHY OF HISTORY, Georg W. Hegel. Great classic of Western thought develops concept that history is not chance but rational process, the evolution of freedom. 457pp. 5⅜ × 8½. 20112-0 Pa. $9.95

THE BOOK OF TEA, Kakuzo Okakura. Minor classic of the Orient: entertaining, charming explanation, interpretation of traditional Japanese culture in terms of tea ceremony. 94pp. 5⅜ × 8½. 20070-1 Pa. $3.95

LIFE IN ANCIENT EGYPT, Adolf Erman. Fullest, most thorough, detailed older account with much not in more recent books, domestic life, religion, magic, medicine, commerce, much more. Many illustrations reproduce tomb paintings, carvings, hieroglyphs, etc. 597pp. 5⅜ × 8½. 22632-8 Pa. $10.95

SUNDIALS, Their Theory and Construction, Albert Waugh. Far and away the best, most thorough coverage of ideas, mathematics concerned, types, construction, adjusting anywhere. Simple, nontechnical treatment allows even children to build several of these dials. Over 100 illustrations. 230pp. 5⅜ × 8½. 22947-5 Pa. $7.95

DYNAMICS OF FLUIDS IN POROUS MEDIA, Jacob Bear. For advanced students of ground water hydrology, soil mechanics and physics, drainage and irrigation engineering, and more. 335 illustrations. Exercises, with answers. 784pp. 6⅛ × 9¼. 65675-6 Pa. $19.95

SONGS OF EXPERIENCE: Facsimile Reproduction with 26 Plates in Full Color, William Blake. 26 full-color plates from a rare 1826 edition. Includes "The Tyger," "London," "Holy Thursday," and other poems. Printed text of poems. 48pp. 5¼ × 7. 24636-1 Pa. $4.95

OLD-TIME VIGNETTES IN FULL COLOR, Carol Belanger Grafton (ed.). Over 390 charming, often sentimental illustrations, selected from archives of Victorian graphics—pretty women posing, children playing, food, flowers, kittens and puppies, smiling cherubs, birds and butterflies, much more. All copyright-free. 48pp. 9¼ × 12¼. 27269-9 Pa. $5.95

PERSPECTIVE FOR ARTISTS, Rex Vicat Cole. Depth, perspective of sky and sea, shadows, much more, not usually covered. 391 diagrams, 81 reproductions of drawings and paintings. 279pp. 5⅜ × 8½. 22487-2 Pa. $6.95

DRAWING THE LIVING FIGURE, Joseph Sheppard. Innovative approach to artistic anatomy focuses on specifics of surface anatomy, rather than muscles and bones. Over 170 drawings of live models in front, back and side views, and in widely varying poses. Accompanying diagrams. 177 illustrations. Introduction. Index. 144pp. 8⅜ × 11¼. 26723-7 Pa. $8.95

GOTHIC AND OLD ENGLISH ALPHABETS: 100 Complete Fonts, Dan X. Solo. Add power, elegance to posters, signs, other graphics with 100 stunning copyright-free alphabets: Blackstone, Dolbey, Germania, 97 more—including many lower-case, numerals, punctuation marks. 104pp. 8⅛ × 11. 24695-7 Pa. $8.95

HOW TO DO BEADWORK, Mary White. Fundamental book on craft from simple projects to five-bead chains and woven works. 106 illustrations. 142pp. 5⅜ × 8. 20697-1 Pa. $4.95

THE BOOK OF WOOD CARVING, Charles Marshall Sayers. Finest book for beginners discusses fundamentals and offers 34 designs. "Absolutely first rate . . . well thought out and well executed."—E. J. Tangerman. 118pp. 7¾ × 10⅝. 23654-4 Pa. $5.95

ILLUSTRATED CATALOG OF CIVIL WAR MILITARY GOODS: Union Army Weapons, Insignia, Uniform Accessories, and Other Equipment, Schuyler, Hartley, and Graham. Rare, profusely illustrated 1846 catalog includes Union Army uniform and dress regulations, arms and ammunition, coats, insignia, flags, swords, rifles, etc. 226 illustrations. 160pp. 9 × 12. 24939-5 Pa. $10.95

WOMEN'S FASHIONS OF THE EARLY 1900s: An Unabridged Republication of "New York Fashions, 1909," National Cloak & Suit Co. Rare catalog of mail-order fashions documents women's and children's clothing styles shortly after the turn of the century. Captions offer full descriptions, prices. Invaluable resource for fashion, costume historians. Approximately 725 illustrations. 128pp. 8⅜ × 11¼. 27276-1 Pa. $11.95

THE 1912 AND 1915 GUSTAV STICKLEY FURNITURE CATALOGS, Gustav Stickley. With over 200 detailed illustrations and descriptions, these two catalogs are essential reading and reference materials and identification guides for Stickley furniture. Captions cite materials, dimensions and prices. 112pp. 6½ × 9¼. 26676-1 Pa. $9.95

EARLY AMERICAN LOCOMOTIVES, John H. White, Jr. Finest locomotive engravings from early 19th century: historical (1804–74), main-line (after 1870), special, foreign, etc. 147 plates. 142pp. 11⅜ × 8¼. 22772-3 Pa. $10.95

THE TALL SHIPS OF TODAY IN PHOTOGRAPHS, Frank O. Braynard. Lavishly illustrated tribute to nearly 100 majestic contemporary sailing vessels: Amerigo Vespucci, Clearwater, Constitution, Eagle, Mayflower, Sea Cloud, Victory, many more. Authoritative captions provide statistics, background on each ship. 190 black-and-white photographs and illustrations. Introduction. 128pp. 8⅞ × 11¾. 27163-3 Pa. $13.95

EARLY NINETEENTH-CENTURY CRAFTS AND TRADES, Peter Stockham (ed.). Extremely rare 1807 volume describes to youngsters the crafts and trades of the day: brickmaker, weaver, dressmaker, bookbinder, ropemaker, saddler, many more. Quaint prose, charming illustrations for each craft. 20 black-and-white line illustrations. 192pp. 4⅜ × 6. 27293-1 Pa. $4.95

VICTORIAN FASHIONS AND COSTUMES FROM HARPER'S BAZAR, 1867–1898, Stella Blum (ed.). Day costumes, evening wear, sports clothes, shoes, hats, other accessories in over 1,000 detailed engravings. 320pp. 9⅜ × 12¼. 22990-4 Pa. $13.95

GUSTAV STICKLEY, THE CRAFTSMAN, Mary Ann Smith. Superb study surveys broad scope of Stickley's achievement, especially in architecture. Design philosophy, rise and fall of the Craftsman empire, descriptions and floor plans for many Craftsman houses, more. 86 black-and-white halftones. 31 line illustrations. Introduction. 208pp. 6½ × 9¼. 27210-9 Pa. $9.95

THE LONG ISLAND RAIL ROAD IN EARLY PHOTOGRAPHS, Ron Ziel. Over 220 rare photos, informative text document origin (1844) and development of rail service on Long Island. Vintage views of early trains, locomotives, stations, passengers, crews, much more. Captions. 8⅞ × 11¾. 26301-0 Pa. $13.95

THE BOOK OF OLD SHIPS: From Egyptian Galleys to Clipper Ships, Henry B. Culver. Superb, authoritative history of sailing vessels, with 80 magnificent line illustrations. Galley, bark, caravel, longship, whaler, many more. Detailed, informative text on each vessel by noted naval historian. Introduction. 256pp. 5⅜ × 8½. 27332-6 Pa. $6.95

TEN BOOKS ON ARCHITECTURE, Vitruvius. The most important book ever written on architecture. Early Roman aesthetics, technology, classical orders, site selection, all other aspects. Morgan translation. 331pp. 5⅜ × 8½. 20645-9 Pa. $8.95

THE HUMAN FIGURE IN MOTION, Eadweard Muybridge. More than 4,500 stopped-action photos, in action series, showing undraped men, women, children jumping, lying down, throwing, sitting, wrestling, carrying, etc. 390pp. 7⅞ × 10⅝. 20204-6 Clothbd. $24.95

TREES OF THE EASTERN AND CENTRAL UNITED STATES AND CANADA, William M. Harlow. Best one-volume guide to 140 trees. Full descriptions, woodlore, range, etc. Over 600 illustrations. Handy size. 288pp. 4½ × 6⅜. 20395-6 Pa. $5.95

SONGS OF WESTERN BIRDS, Dr. Donald J. Borror. Complete song and call repertoire of 60 western species, including flycatchers, juncoes, cactus wrens, many more—includes fully illustrated booklet. Cassette and manual 99913-0 $8.95

GROWING AND USING HERBS AND SPICES, Milo Miloradovich. Versatile handbook provides all the information needed for cultivation and use of all the herbs and spices available in North America. 4 illustrations. Index. Glossary. 236pp. 5⅜ × 8½. 25058-X Pa. $6.95

BIG BOOK OF MAZES AND LABYRINTHS, Walter Shepherd. 50 mazes and labyrinths in all—classical, solid, ripple, and more—in one great volume. Perfect inexpensive puzzler for clever youngsters. Full solutions. 112pp. 8⅛ × 11. 22951-3 Pa. $4.95

PIANO TUNING, J. Cree Fischer. Clearest, best book for beginner, amateur. Simple repairs, raising dropped notes, tuning by easy method of flattened fifths. No previous skills needed. 4 illustrations. 201pp. 5⅜ × 8½.    23267-0 Pa. $5.95

A SOURCE BOOK IN THEATRICAL HISTORY, A. M. Nagler. Contemporary observers on acting, directing, make-up, costuming, stage props, machinery, scene design, from Ancient Greece to Chekhov. 611pp. 5⅜ × 8½.    20515-0 Pa. $11.95

THE COMPLETE NONSENSE OF EDWARD LEAR, Edward Lear. All nonsense limericks, zany alphabets, Owl and Pussycat, songs, nonsense botany, etc., illustrated by Lear. Total of 320pp. 5⅜ × 8½. (USO)    20167-8 Pa. $6.95

VICTORIAN PARLOUR POETRY: An Annotated Anthology, Michael R. Turner. 117 gems by Longfellow, Tennyson, Browning, many lesser-known poets. "The Village Blacksmith," "Curfew Must Not Ring Tonight," "Only a Baby Small," dozens more, often difficult to find elsewhere. Index of poets, titles, first lines. xxiii + 325pp. 5⅜ × 8¼.    27044-0 Pa. $8.95

DUBLINERS, James Joyce. Fifteen stories offer vivid, tightly focused observations of the lives of Dublin's poorer classes. At least one, "The Dead," is considered a masterpiece. Reprinted complete and unabridged from standard edition. 160pp. 5³⁄₁₆ × 8¼.    26870-5 Pa. $1.00

THE HAUNTED MONASTERY and THE CHINESE MAZE MURDERS, Robert van Gulik. Two full novels by van Gulik, set in 7th-century China, continue adventures of Judge Dee and his companions. An evil Taoist monastery, seemingly supernatural events; overgrown topiary maze hides strange crimes. 27 illustrations. 328pp. 5⅜ × 8½.    23502-5 Pa. $7.95

THE BOOK OF THE SACRED MAGIC OF ABRAMELIN THE MAGE, translated by S. MacGregor Mathers. Medieval manuscript of ceremonial magic. Basic document in Aleister Crowley, Golden Dawn groups. 268pp. 5⅜ × 8½.    23211-5 Pa. $8.95

NEW RUSSIAN-ENGLISH AND ENGLISH-RUSSIAN DICTIONARY, M. A. O'Brien. This is a remarkably handy Russian dictionary, containing a surprising amount of information, including over 70,000 entries. 366pp. 4½ × 6⅛.    20208-9 Pa. $9.95

HISTORIC HOMES OF THE AMERICAN PRESIDENTS, Second, Revised Edition, Irvin Haas. A traveler's guide to American Presidential homes, most open to the public, depicting and describing homes occupied by every American President from George Washington to George Bush. With visiting hours, admission charges, travel routes. 175 photographs. Index. 160pp. 8¼ × 11.    26751-2 Pa. $10.95

NEW YORK IN THE FORTIES, Andreas Feininger. 162 brilliant photographs by the well-known photographer, formerly with *Life* magazine. Commuters, shoppers, Times Square at night, much else from city at its peak. Captions by John von Hartz. 181pp. 9¼ × 10¾.    23585-8 Pa. $12.95

INDIAN SIGN LANGUAGE, William Tomkins. Over 525 signs developed by Sioux and other tribes. Written instructions and diagrams. Also 290 pictographs. 111pp. 6⅛ × 9¼.    22029-X Pa. $3.50

ANATOMY: A Complete Guide for Artists, Joseph Sheppard. A master of figure drawing shows artists how to render human anatomy convincingly. Over 460 illustrations. 224pp. 8⅜ × 11¼. 27279-6 Pa. $10.95

MEDIEVAL CALLIGRAPHY: Its History and Technique, Marc Drogin. Spirited history, comprehensive instruction manual covers 13 styles (ca. 4th century thru 15th). Excellent photographs; directions for duplicating medieval techniques with modern tools. 224pp. 8⅜ × 11¼. 26142-5 Pa. $11.95

DRIED FLOWERS: How to Prepare Them, Sarah Whitlock and Martha Rankin. Complete instructions on how to use silica gel, meal and borax, perlite aggregate, sand and borax, glycerine and water to create attractive permanent flower arrangements. 12 illustrations. 32pp. 5⅜ × 8½. 21802-3 Pa. $1.00

EASY-TO-MAKE BIRD FEEDERS FOR WOODWORKERS, Scott D. Campbell. Detailed, simple-to-use guide for designing, constructing, caring for and using feeders. Text, illustrations for 12 classic and contemporary designs. 96pp. 5⅜ × 8½. 25847-5 Pa. $2.95

OLD-TIME CRAFTS AND TRADES, Peter Stockham. An 1807 book created to teach children about crafts and trades open to them as future careers. It describes in detailed, nontechnical terms 24 different occupations, among them coachmaker, gardener, hairdresser, lacemaker, shoemaker, wheelwright, copper-plate printer, milliner, trunkmaker, merchant and brewer. Finely detailed engravings illustrate each occupation. 192pp. 4⅝ × 6. 27398-9 Pa. $4.95

THE HISTORY OF UNDERCLOTHES, C. Willett Cunnington and Phyllis Cunnington. Fascinating, well-documented survey covering six centuries of English undergarments, enhanced with over 100 illustrations: 12th-century laced-up bodice, footed long drawers (1795), 19th-century bustles, 19th-century corsets for men, Victorian "bust improvers," much more. 272pp. 5⅝ × 8¼. 27124-2 Pa. $9.95

ARTS AND CRAFTS FURNITURE: The Complete Brooks Catalog of 1912, Brooks Manufacturing Co. Photos and detailed descriptions of more than 150 now very collectible furniture designs from the Arts and Crafts movement depict davenports, settees, buffets, desks, tables, chairs, bedsteads, dressers and more, all built of solid, quarter-sawed oak. Invaluable for students and enthusiasts of antiques, Americana and the decorative arts. 80pp. 6½ × 9¼. 27471-3 Pa. $7.95

HOW WE INVENTED THE AIRPLANE: An Illustrated History, Orville Wright. Fascinating firsthand account covers early experiments, construction of planes and motors, first flights, much more. Introduction and commentary by Fred C. Kelly. 76 photographs. 96pp. 8¼ × 11. 25662-6 Pa. $8.95

THE ARTS OF THE SAILOR: Knotting, Splicing and Ropework, Hervey Garrett Smith. Indispensable shipboard reference covers tools, basic knots and useful hitches; handsewing and canvas work, more. Over 100 illustrations. Delightful reading for sea lovers. 256pp. 5⅜ × 8½. 26440-8 Pa. $7.95

FRANK LLOYD WRIGHT'S FALLINGWATER: The House and Its History, Second, Revised Edition, Donald Hoffmann. A total revision—both in text and illustrations—of the standard document on Fallingwater, the boldest, most personal architectural statement of Wright's mature years, updated with valuable new material from the recently opened Frank Lloyd Wright Archives. "Fascinating"—*The New York Times*. 116 illustrations. 128pp. 9¼ × 10¾. 27430-6 Pa. $10.95

PHOTOGRAPHIC SKETCHBOOK OF THE CIVIL WAR, Alexander Gardner. 100 photos taken on field during the Civil War. Famous shots of Manassas, Harper's Ferry, Lincoln, Richmond, slave pens, etc. 244pp. 10⅝ × 8¼.
22731-6 Pa. $9.95

FIVE ACRES AND INDEPENDENCE, Maurice G. Kains. Great back-to-the-land classic explains basics of self-sufficient farming. The one book to get. 95 illustrations. 397pp. 5⅜ × 8½. 20974-1 Pa. $7.95

SONGS OF EASTERN BIRDS, Dr. Donald J. Borror. Songs and calls of 60 species most common to eastern U.S.: warblers, woodpeckers, flycatchers, thrushes, larks, many more in high-quality recording. Cassette and manual 99912-2 $8.95

A MODERN HERBAL, Margaret Grieve. Much the fullest, most exact, most useful compilation of herbal material. Gigantic alphabetical encyclopedia, from aconite to zedoary, gives botanical information, medical properties, folklore, economic uses, much else. Indispensable to serious reader. 161 illustrations. 888pp. 6½ × 9¼. 2-vol. set. (USO) Vol. I: 22798-7 Pa. $9.95
Vol. II: 22799-5 Pa. $9.95

HIDDEN TREASURE MAZE BOOK, Dave Phillips. Solve 34 challenging mazes accompanied by heroic tales of adventure. Evil dragons, people-eating plants, bloodthirsty giants, many more dangerous adversaries lurk at every twist and turn. 34 mazes, stories, solutions. 48pp. 8¼ × 11. 24566-7 Pa. $2.95

LETTERS OF W. A. MOZART, Wolfgang A. Mozart. Remarkable letters show bawdy wit, humor, imagination, musical insights, contemporary musical world; includes some letters from Leopold Mozart. 276pp. 5⅜ × 8½. 22859-2 Pa. $7.95

BASIC PRINCIPLES OF CLASSICAL BALLET, Agrippina Vaganova. Great Russian theoretician, teacher explains methods for teaching classical ballet. 118 illustrations. 175pp. 5⅜ × 8½. 22036-2 Pa. $4.95

THE JUMPING FROG, Mark Twain. Revenge edition. The original story of The Celebrated Jumping Frog of Calaveras County, a hapless French translation, and Twain's hilarious "retranslation" from the French. 12 illustrations. 66pp. 5⅜ × 8½.
22686-7 Pa. $3.95

BEST REMEMBERED POEMS, Martin Gardner (ed.). The 126 poems in this superb collection of 19th- and 20th-century British and American verse range from Shelley's "To a Skylark" to the impassioned "Renascence" of Edna St. Vincent Millay and to Edward Lear's whimsical "The Owl and the Pussycat." 224pp. 5⅜ × 8½.
27165-X Pa. $4.95

COMPLETE SONNETS, William Shakespeare. Over 150 exquisite poems deal with love, friendship, the tyranny of time, beauty's evanescence, death and other themes in language of remarkable power, precision and beauty. Glossary of archaic terms. 80pp. 5³⁄₁₆ × 8¼. 26686-9 Pa. $1.00

BODIES IN A BOOKSHOP, R. T. Campbell. Challenging mystery of blackmail and murder with ingenious plot and superbly drawn characters. In the best tradition of British suspense fiction. 192pp. 5⅜ × 8½. 24720-1 Pa. $5.95

THE WIT AND HUMOR OF OSCAR WILDE, Alvin Redman (ed.). More than 1,000 ripostes, paradoxes, wisecracks: Work is the curse of the drinking classes; I can resist everything except temptation; etc. 258pp. 5⅜ × 8½. **20602-5 Pa. $5.95**

SHAKESPEARE LEXICON AND QUOTATION DICTIONARY, Alexander Schmidt. Full definitions, locations, shades of meaning in every word in plays and poems. More than 50,000 exact quotations. 1,485pp. 6½ × 9¼. 2-vol. set.
**Vol. I: 22726-X Pa. $16.95**
**Vol. 2: 22727-8 Pa. $15.95**

SELECTED POEMS, Emily Dickinson. Over 100 best-known, best-loved poems by one of America's foremost poets, reprinted from authoritative early editions. No comparable edition at this price. Index of first lines. 64pp. 5$\frac{3}{16}$ × 8¼.
**26466-1 Pa. $1.00**

CELEBRATED CASES OF JUDGE DEE (DEE GOONG AN), translated by Robert van Gulik. Authentic 18th-century Chinese detective novel; Dee and associates solve three interlocked cases. Led to van Gulik's own stories with same characters. Extensive introduction. 9 illustrations. 237pp. 5⅜ × 8½.
**23337-5 Pa. $6.95**

THE MALLEUS MALEFICARUM OF KRAMER AND SPRENGER, translated by Montague Summers. Full text of most important witchhunter's "bible," used by both Catholics and Protestants. 278pp. 6⅝ × 10. **22802-9 Pa. $11.95**

SPANISH STORIES/CUENTOS ESPAÑOLES: A Dual-Language Book, Angel Flores (ed.). Unique format offers 13 great stories in Spanish by Cervantes, Borges, others. Faithful English translations on facing pages. 352pp. 5⅜ × 8½.
**25399-6 Pa. $8.95**

THE CHICAGO WORLD'S FAIR OF 1893: A Photographic Record, Stanley Appelbaum (ed.). 128 rare photos show 200 buildings, Beaux-Arts architecture, Midway, original Ferris Wheel, Edison's kinetoscope, more. Architectural emphasis; full text. 116pp. 8¼ × 11. **23990-X Pa. $9.95**

OLD QUEENS, N.Y., IN EARLY PHOTOGRAPHS, Vincent F. Seyfried and William Asadorian. Over 160 rare photographs of Maspeth, Jamaica, Jackson Heights, and other areas. Vintage views of DeWitt Clinton mansion, 1939 World's Fair and more. Captions. 192pp. 8⅞ × 11. **26358-4 Pa. $12.95**

CAPTURED BY THE INDIANS: 15 Firsthand Accounts, 1750–1870, Frederick Drimmer. Astounding true historical accounts of grisly torture, bloody conflicts, relentless pursuits, miraculous escapes and more, by people who lived to tell the tale. 384pp. 5⅜ × 8½. **24901-8 Pa. $8.95**

THE WORLD'S GREAT SPEECHES, Lewis Copeland and Lawrence W. Lamm (eds.). Vast collection of 278 speeches of Greeks to 1970. Powerful and effective models; unique look at history. 842pp. 5⅜ × 8½. **20468-5 Pa. $14.95**

THE BOOK OF THE SWORD, Sir Richard F. Burton. Great Victorian scholar/adventurer's eloquent, erudite history of the "queen of weapons"—from prehistory to early Roman Empire. Evolution and development of early swords, variations (sabre, broadsword, cutlass, scimitar, etc.), much more. 336pp. 6⅛ × 9¼. **25434-8 Pa. $8.95**

AUTOBIOGRAPHY: The Story of My Experiments with Truth, Mohandas K. Gandhi. Boyhood, legal studies, purification, the growth of the Satyagraha (nonviolent protest) movement. Critical, inspiring work of the man responsible for the freedom of India. 480pp. 5⅜ × 8½. (USO) 24593-4 Pa. $8.95

CELTIC MYTHS AND LEGENDS, T. W. Rolleston. Masterful retelling of Irish and Welsh stories and tales. Cuchulain, King Arthur, Deirdre, the Grail, many more. First paperback edition. 58 full-page illustrations. 512pp. 5⅜ × 8½.
26507-2 Pa. $9.95

THE PRINCIPLES OF PSYCHOLOGY, William James. Famous long course complete, unabridged. Stream of thought, time perception, memory, experimental methods; great work decades ahead of its time. 94 figures. 1,391pp. 5⅜ × 8½. 2-vol. set.
Vol. I: 20381-6 Pa. $12.95
Vol. II: 20382-4 Pa. $12.95

THE WORLD AS WILL AND REPRESENTATION, Arthur Schopenhauer. Definitive English translation of Schopenhauer's life work, correcting more than 1,000 errors, omissions in earlier translations. Translated by E. F. J. Payne. Total of 1,269pp. 5⅜ × 8½. 2-vol. set. Vol. 1: 21761-2 Pa. $11.95
Vol. 2: 21762-0 Pa. $11.95

MAGIC AND MYSTERY IN TIBET, Madame Alexandra David-Neel. Experiences among lamas, magicians, sages, sorcerers, Bonpa wizards. A true psychic discovery. 32 illustrations. 321pp. 5⅜ × 8½. (USO) 22682-4 Pa. $8.95

THE EGYPTIAN BOOK OF THE DEAD, E. A. Wallis Budge. Complete reproduction of Ani's papyrus, finest ever found. Full hieroglyphic text, interlinear transliteration, word-for-word translation, smooth translation. 533pp. 6½ × 9¼.
21866-X Pa. $9.95

MATHEMATICS FOR THE NONMATHEMATICIAN, Morris Kline. Detailed, college-level treatment of mathematics in cultural and historical context, with numerous exercises. Recommended Reading Lists. Tables. Numerous figures. 641pp. 5⅜ × 8½. 24823-2 Pa. $11.95

THEORY OF WING SECTIONS: Including a Summary of Airfoil Data, Ira H. Abbott and A. E. von Doenhoff. Concise compilation of subsonic aerodynamic characteristics of NACA wing sections, plus description of theory. 350pp. of tables. 693pp. 5⅜ × 8½. 60586-8 Pa. $14.95

THE RIME OF THE ANCIENT MARINER, Gustave Doré, S. T. Coleridge. Doré's finest work; 34 plates capture moods, subtleties of poem. Flawless full-size reproductions printed on facing pages with authoritative text of poem. "Beautiful. Simply beautiful."—*Publisher's Weekly*. 77pp. 9¼ × 12. 22305-1 Pa. $6.95

NORTH AMERICAN INDIAN DESIGNS FOR ARTISTS AND CRAFTSPEOPLE, Eva Wilson. Over 360 authentic copyright-free designs adapted from Navajo blankets, Hopi pottery, Sioux buffalo hides, more. Geometrics, symbolic figures, plant and animal motifs, etc. 128pp. 8⅜ × 11. (EUK) 25341-4 Pa. $7.95

SCULPTURE: Principles and Practice, Louis Slobodkin. Step-by-step approach to clay, plaster, metals, stone; classical and modern. 253 drawings, photos. 255pp. 8⅛ × 11. 22960-2 Pa. $10.95

THE INFLUENCE OF SEA POWER UPON HISTORY, 1660–1783, A. T. Mahan. Influential classic of naval history and tactics still used as text in war colleges. First paperback edition. 4 maps. 24 battle plans. 640pp. 5⅜ × 8½.
25509-3 Pa. $12.95

THE STORY OF THE TITANIC AS TOLD BY ITS SURVIVORS, Jack Winocour (ed.). What it was really like. Panic, despair, shocking inefficiency, and a little heroism. More thrilling than any fictional account. 26 illustrations. 320pp. 5⅜ × 8½.
20610-6 Pa. $8.95

FAIRY AND FOLK TALES OF THE IRISH PEASANTRY, William Butler Yeats (ed.). Treasury of 64 tales from the twilight world of Celtic myth and legend: "The Soul Cages," "The Kildare Pooka," "King O'Toole and his Goose," many more. Introduction and Notes by W. B. Yeats. 352pp. 5⅜ × 8½. 26941-8 Pa. $8.95

BUDDHIST MAHAYANA TEXTS, E. B. Cowell and Others (eds.). Superb, accurate translations of basic documents in Mahayana Buddhism, highly important in history of religions. The Buddha-karita of Asvaghosha, Larger Sukhavativyuha, more. 448pp. 5⅜ × 8½. 25552-2 Pa. $9.95

ONE TWO THREE . . . INFINITY: Facts and Speculations of Science, George Gamow. Great physicist's fascinating, readable overview of contemporary science: number theory, relativity, fourth dimension, entropy, genes, atomic structure, much more. 128 illustrations. Index. 352pp. 5⅜ × 8½. 25664-2 Pa. $8.95

ENGINEERING IN HISTORY, Richard Shelton Kirby, et al. Broad, nontechnical survey of history's major technological advances: birth of Greek science, industrial revolution, electricity and applied science, 20th-century automation, much more. 181 illustrations. ". . . excellent . . ."—Isis. Bibliography. vii + 530pp. 5⅜ × 8¼.
26412-2 Pa. $14.95

*Prices subject to change without notice.*

Available at your book dealer or write for free catalog to Dept. GI, Dover Publications, Inc., 31 East 2nd St., Mineola, N.Y. 11501. Dover publishes more than 500 books each year on science, elementary and advanced mathematics, biology, music, art, literary history, social sciences and other areas.